ALSO BY
JAY CROWNOVER

RETREAT

Cover design by:
Hang Le
www.byhangle.com

Photographed by and Copyright owned by:
Wander Aguiar Photography
www.wanderbookclub.com

Editing by:
Elaine York, Allusion Graphics, LLC/Publishing & Book Formatting
www.allusiongraphics.com

Proofreading & Copyediting by:
C.J. Pinard
www.cjpinard.com

Interior Design & Formatting by:
Christine Borgford, Type A Formatting
www.typeAformatting.com

THE
GETAWAY
SERIES

RETREAT

NEW YORK TIMES BESTSELLING AUTHOR
JAY CROWNOVER

Dedicated to anyone and everyone who has told me they would read a grocery list if I wrote it.

Let's put that to the test, shall we!

Are you scratching your head in befuddlement and asking yourself where in the hell this book came from? Are you reading and then rereading the blurb trying to figure out what it's all about? Well, have no fear, my friends, in my very typically upfront and blunt way, I'm going to tell you everything you need to know moving forward.

First of all, if you clicked this book just because my name is on it, thank you. Thank you for trusting me. Thank you for believing in me. And thank you for having faith in my words. If you clicked because you liked the cover, the blurb intrigued you, or simply for the hell of it . . . ain't nothing wrong with any of those reasons in my book. I will tell you this isn't a copy and paste of anything I've written before, so if you're expecting tattoo artists, heavy metal singers, or car thieves you are going to be bummed out. It's also set up like an old-school, romantic suspense. That doesn't mean there isn't plenty of the main couple getting on and getting on each other's nerves . . . it just means there is also a very definitive bad guy who shows up and makes life miserable for everyone involved. This book is also a single POV, the story unfolding as we follow our little lion through the most important week of her life. I have reasons for writing it that way that I'll get into here in a hot minute.

Where did *Retreat* come from?

Well, that's both easy and complicated. At the end of 2015 and early on into 2016, I found myself dealing with some pretty persistent and crippling pain resulting from a messed-up tooth extraction. It ended up infected and I needed surgery, which also got infected and so on and so forth. IT WAS MISERABLE. I was miserable. I was also doped up on any number of pain meds for around four months. I couldn't concentrate, I definitely couldn't write. I was worthless. That forced downtime meant I spent a lot of time in front of the TV with Netflix.

I found myself binge watching all the seasons of *Longmire* and got sucked into Ashton Kutcher's show *The Ranch*. I watched the *Hateful Eight*, *Jane's Got a Gun*, and all kinds of other western-based movies and TV shows.

I know you're thinking . . . why? I thought you only watched *Die Hard* and *Bob's Burgers*, Jay . . . but alas . . . I actually grew up in a small mountain town littered with cowboys and ranchers. The boys I went high school with had gun racks in their pickup trucks and wore Wranglers, not Dickies. As a teenager, my boy bestie worked on the ranch next to my grandma's property up in the hills. I would spend the weekends waiting for him to get home from either stock shows or the rodeo, or to come in from riding the property and beg him to take me for rides. (I never quite got the hang of horseback riding . . . but I can do-si-do with the best of them.)

I think because I was so sick, and in so much pain, I digressed back to my childhood when my mom took care of me and I didn't have anything to do other than bug Jesse for rides on his horse. I got really nostalgic . . . a little reminiscent, and decided I wanted to write a book that was familiar to me in a different way than ink is. I wanted to step back into a place that no longer fit me, but still hangs in the back of my closet as a reminder of what was.

I decided I wanted to write a book based in the mountains, on a ranch that was run by guys who are not quite cowboys.

Come on now . . . you didn't think I'd go full ten-gallon hat, boots, and spurs on you, did you? You should know me better than that by now!

I wanted to write my kind of guys but put them in a western

setting and see how they fared. They fared pretty fucking great if you ask me! But you'll have to read on and meet the Warner brothers to see if you agree with me or not.

As for why this book is told only from our heroine's perspective . . . that's because it's her story, her journey, her week where everything went so wrong even though she was trying so hard to do everything exactly right. Since I was hurting physically, I think that manifested itself into telling the story of a woman who was hurting the same way I was emotionally. There was no room for the hero's voice in my head because I was too deeply wrapped up in purging all the nasty stuff that was happening inside of me out into our heroine's tale. I can't write a character if I don't hear them speak; Cy was silent but Leo had plenty to say.

She's probably going to rub you the wrong way at first . . . but give her time to get it together. Betrayal burns deep and it takes a long time for those embers to die down.

So, anyway . . . that's the long and short of where this book came from. It's completely different from anything else I've ever written . . . but it is startlingly similar to all the books I most love to read. You won't be able to compare this to any of my words that came before it so I hope you give it a chance based on what it is and not what you think it might (or should) be.

As always, thank you for being here . . . and thank you for letting me be here. ☺

Happy reading!
xoxo
Jay

CHAPTER 1

Not Quite a Cowboy

"THEY DON'T EVEN LOOK LIKE real cowboys." I muttered the words under my breath low enough so that only my best friend could hear them. She turned her head in my direction and gave me a look that told me she had had enough of my whining and endless snarky commentary. We'd gotten up early to fly out of San Francisco and had landed in Billings, Montana, only to then hop on a teeny-tiny charter flight that brought us out to Sheridan, Wyoming. It had been a day filled with travel, and my sarcasm and snark were at an all-time high. Partly because I really had no interest in being here, but mostly because, for the last few months, I'd been a miserable human being to be around and I couldn't seem to rein in my bad attitude, even when I really wanted to. She was getting tired of it, and frankly, I couldn't blame her.

"Just because they don't have on cowboy hats and leather chaps doesn't mean they aren't cowboys; you have no idea what a real cowboy even is. When have you ever been on a ranch before or traveled any farther east than Las Vegas? The closest you've been to any kind of cowboy was when we went to see Garth Brooks a couple of years ago. You promised to keep an open mind, and so far you are sucking at it."

I sighed and shifted away from Emrys. Her dramatically shaped eyes could see right through me and I didn't need a guilt trip from her when I already felt like crap. I turned my attention back to the three men standing before us and begrudgingly admitted to myself that two of them could pass as the sexified, carefully marketed country music version of what a cowboy should be. They could easily give Luke Bryan a run for his money with the way they were packed into their tight jeans. They were both more than passably attractive from what I could see under the brims of their matching camo baseball hats, the ranch's logo stitched on the front. When they introduced themselves, I found out that they also had what I would consider authentic cowboy names, Sutton and Lane. I wasn't sure which one was which because I was completely distracted by the third member of the not-so-welcoming committee. He was the one I was specifically talking about when I made the 'not a cowboy' comment. He looked as out of place on this working ranch in the middle-of-nowhere Wyoming as I felt. He was also watching me just as closely as I was watching him. His name was Cyrus . . . which was maybe a cowboy name but to me sounded more like the ruler of some ancient kingdom. In fact, he would fit in way better in Sparta than he did here on the range. The thought made me snicker, which got me an elbow in the side from Em, even though I kept the wayward thought to myself.

The man, who most definitely didn't look like a cowboy, didn't have any kind of hat on so there was no mistaking the fact that his narrowed eyes were locked on me. His lack of headwear also revealed that he had his dark hair buzzed in a trendy undercut and styled back in a way that required product and know how. Two things I would never associate with an actual cowboy. It also showed that he had the faintest hint of silver at his temples above his perfectly even sideburns. Even with the dusting of gray,

I still only put him at somewhere in his early- to mid-thirties. The silver in his hair should make him look prematurely aged, but it didn't. He looked tough and distinguished, and if he was dressed in something other than lovingly worn Levi's and a faded Jack Daniel's T-shirt, he would give the executives and CEOs who I did business with a run for their money in the silently intimidating department. Not that I could imagine any of the men I worked with looking as good as this one did. He did something special for that cotton T-shirt that stretched tightly across his broad chest. And the way he impatiently shifted his weight from one heavy-looking black boot to the other pulled denim tight around places I should be embarrassed to be looking. I wanted to ask him why he had boots on that belonged on a Harley rather than in the stirrup of a saddle, but I didn't want another sharp poke from Em, so I kept my musings to myself.

No, the man named Cyrus didn't fit what I had thought would be waiting for me when I agreed to this crazy plan of Emrys's, and if he hadn't walked out to greet us with the other two men when the passenger van we had taken from the miniscule airport dropped us off, I would have automatically assumed he was part of the tour group and not one of the guides. He didn't look like what I expected someone who was intimately familiar with the outdoors or the inhospitable and uninhabited terrain of the Wyoming landscape to look like. His rough appearance and unwavering gaze made me question again why I had let Emrys talk me into this vacation that sounded more like punishment than any kind of fun I was familiar with. I was even more hesitant to venture off into the wooded mountains than I had been before, as my stare-down with the man dragged on and on to the point that I knew looking away would mean some kind of defeat. I wasn't sure what the battle I was engaged in was about, but I was a sore loser at the best of times, and considering

I was at the lowest point I'd ever been, I knew there was no way I could be the first one to break eye contact. I loved my best friend, but at the moment I could happily strangle her for deciding we needed this girl's only trip that would force us both to unplug and regroup over the next week.

"You ladies are the last of the group to arrive. We'll get you settled in and then everyone can meet in the main house for dinner so we can all go over what to expect for the next week." It was the guy in the middle who spoke. He was the shortest of the three and he was the only one who seemed capable of smiling. The man with all the muscles and the scowl kept watching me, while the last guy looked bored and annoyed. His expression indicated that he felt like he was being put out having to play welcome wagon for a couple of city girls. Considering this little jaunt was costing both Em and me an arm and a leg, the least these not-quite-cowboys could do was roll out the welcome mat and pretend that they were thrilled to do so. We were paying for an unforgettable experience, and so far they had delivered, but not in a good way.

I stiffened my spine and narrowed my eyes. Unfortunately, my intimidation factor was nil considering I was dressed in comfy leggings and an oversized Henley that I stole from my ex. My outfit was great for traveling in, but not so great for trying to look like a badass who wouldn't stand for the blatant indifference coming from a third of the trio who was supposed to be responsible for my health and wellbeing for the next seven days. I also wasn't going to keep quiet over the overt hostility radiating off the one I couldn't look away from. I was one of those women who was always a little unkempt and disheveled, so I had to work at appearing put together and polished. It was a constant battle every single morning as I got ready for work. I could pull off cute with minimal effort, but it took some time and some serious skill with both my clothes and my makeup to push me into the chic and professional sphere. Considering I had woken up at the ass crack of dawn, my wardrobe, hair, and war paint were nonexistent. With my unruly, wavy, strawberry blonde hair pulled back in a sloppy ponytail, I was keenly aware that I looked more like Raggedy Ann than a highly successful market analyst who was also a street-savvy and independent woman. Or at least I had been, until I fell for the wrong guy and he proved otherwise.

The single pleasant member of the trio smiled again and inclined his head toward the bags sitting at our feet. When Em had booked the trip they had been very clear that this was an outdoor adventure. We would be venturing deep into the mountains on horseback and we were to leave any kind of technology and civilization behind us. There had been strict instructions on what we needed to pack, and as a result, the bag at my feet was stuffed full and contained mostly new and untried mountain appropriate attire. It was all stuff that would end up shoved in the back of my closet and then, years later, donated to Goodwill because I had very little use for any of it in my day-to-day life back in the Bay Area.

"Sutton and I will take your bags and show you where you're bunking for the night. You ladies have about an hour before dinner, so you can relax and get freshened up." Getting freshened up sounded delightful. Maybe if I put on some blush and drew my eyebrows in, I could get Mr. Personality—with the death stare—to take me seriously when I told him that his behavior was unacceptable.

The bored guy must have been Sutton because he took a step forward and bent to pick up Emrys's bag. I thought I heard her sigh when he bent over but it could have been the air shifting and moving around me. The man, who looked like he didn't belong anywhere near a place that was often referred to as the

'Cowboy State', took a few steps closer to me. I had no choice but to tilt my head back and look at him. I sucked in a breath as I was struck by the sharpest, clearest, most flawless pair of gray eyes I had ever seen in my life. They were the color of smoke and silver. His eyes cut through me like the honed blade of a knife as they raked over me, from my messy hair to the toes that had curled up in startled response where they were encased in a pair of super-comfy Uggs. Again, my choice in footwear had been great for traveling in, but not so great for leaving the most impactful first impression.

Cy's voice when he spoke was deep and raspy. It sounded slightly broken and jagged, like maybe he didn't use it a lot and when he did, it took a minute for the words to find their way out. It was the kind of voice that belonged to a real cowboy "This isn't a spa or some kind of all-inclusive retreat where your every want and need is catered to, Ms. Connor. This is the wild, wild west, and if you don't listen to the boys and pay attention to what they are telling you, then things can go bad faster than you can blink." There was a warning there, but all I could think of were nights around the warm campfire and even warmer nights in the bedroom. He had a voice that made me think about rough sex and talented hands that I wouldn't want to say no to. "Sutton and Lane are good at dealing with girls from the city who want to come out and play cowgirl, but I would advise against looking at them like they aren't fit to carry your bags or like they somehow aren't meeting your high standards." Cy had a great voice, but goddamn, did his personality leave a lot to be desired.

So, smiley was Lane and grumpy was Sutton. Emrys had read the brochure aloud to me no less than twenty times when she was trying to convince me that we needed this vacation and that I really, really needed to get away. So I knew from the literature that the men who owned the ranch and ran the excursions were all brothers. From his protective stance, the attractive silver in his hair, and by the way he was trying to put me in my place for some perceived slight, it wasn't hard to guess he was the big brother . . . emphasis on *big*. I was totally normal sized, hovering a tiny bit over five-six, but this guy towered over me and he has zero problem with his intimidation factor. He didn't raise his voice, he didn't loom or posture. He simply stood in front of me and his words, with their rasp and growl, made me shiver in both fear and awareness.

"I am aware this isn't a spa or a retreat, Mr. . . ." I blushed and trailed off as I realized I'd been too busy evaluating him and his ability to keep me alive over the next week rather than paying attention to the introductions.

"Warner, but I'm Cy to most folks."

I cleared my throat and begrudgingly stuck out a hand for him to shake. "Okay, Cy, I wasn't looking at any of you in any way. I was just wondering about the qualifications you have to take a large group of inexperienced people into the wilderness. I think that's a pretty fair concern to have. We seem to have simply gotten off on the wrong foot." That happened a lot with my lack of filter and overt honesty. I had a hard time keeping my foot out of my mouth and here I was chewing on my shoe, again.

"I'm Leora, but most of my friends call me Leo." My hand was left extended between the two of us for an uncomfortable amount of time until I let it fall as he continued to stare at me. I felt Emrys shift next to me and I became acutely aware that this little standoff was no longer happening between just him and me. His brothers were also standing a few feet away, watching our tense interaction with curious expressions. I'd promised my best friend that I would go into this with an open mind. I assured her that I would embrace the change of scenery and do my best to enjoy myself. Lately, I'd been a super-shitty friend, so I owed it to Emrys to keep my promise, even if this man, who was not quite a cowboy, seemed determined to prove me right in my thinking that coming here was nothing but a mistake.

"Sutton and Lane will keep you alive because that's their job. They'll also make sure your trip is worth every single penny you spent because our reputation is everything in this competitive market, and, lucky for you, they actually enjoy what they do. Their qualifications are outlined in all of our literature and clearly displayed on our website. Just because they may or may not look like your version of qualified wilderness guides doesn't make them any less skilled or competent." Boom! He took blunt and in-your-face to a whole other level. Part of me respected that, as much as it made my hackles rise and spine snap straight in irritation. I wondered if this was what it felt like to be on the other side of my brutal honesty when I forget to pull my punches and play nice.

I took a step back and opened my mouth to retort that *he,* not either of his admittedly attractive siblings, was the one I thought appeared to look under-qualified to guide us into the woods and through the mountains. Emrys put her hand on my forearm and intervened before my inherent Irish temperament really flared to life. I was ready to go toe to toe with this big, unpleasant man. In about a second flat, I was going to demand my money back and berate him for his rudeness and tactlessness. As always, when I was fired up and ready to go off halfcocked, Em waded in and threw water on the fire that was getting ready to ignite.

"Forgive my friend, Mr. Warner. She's a born and raised city girl and I think she's just feeling a tad bit intimidated by all the fresh air and peace and quiet. I assure you that we are both extremely grateful for your time and we're so excited to be here. We're both looking forward to seeing what your wonderful state has to offer." Her elbow dug into my side and I turned my head to give her a dirty look. "Isn't that right, Leo?"

I rolled my eyes at my mostly flawless best friend and wondered how she could look so refreshed and unrumpled after a day full of traveling. Where I was pretty average all around, Emrys Santos was anything but. She was tall, standing close to six feet without the aid of high heels. Her shiny, sable-colored hair hung flat and perfect along her back, like it had never heard of humidity or static electricity. Her dark eyes, which were currently pleading with me to behave, had a slight slant to them that only added to her overall exotic, undeniable beauty. She was almost perfect, except for the fact that she was interfering, determined to get her own way, and could guilt trip like no one's business.

She knew I was having a hard time with my most recent breakup. On top of that, I was having issues at work, the one thing in my life that had always been stable and in control. But she pushed, prodded, and pleaded until I had agreed to spend this week with her in the great outdoors, even though roughing it was absolutely not my thing. Part of me wanted to tell her she had to deal with the fact I was here but less than thrilled about it, but a bigger part of me knew she was just trying to help, and doing her best to wrestle me back on track. So I corralled my rebellious temper and bit my tongue, giving her a stiff nod of agreement. Cy's iridescent eyes sparked with humor and I swore he knew I was fighting to behave.

I bit out through my teeth and through a smile that was so fake it actually hurt my face, "Like I said, I think we just got off on the wrong foot."

The only response I got was a grunt as his attention turned to the other two men, who were purposely ignoring the heated interaction between me and their older brother. In fact, they both had moved a few steps away like they knew their older sibling's anger was hot enough to burn anything that got close enough for it to touch. Gruffly, he barked out, "Go ahead and get them situated, I'll head up to the house and make sure Brynn knows everyone is here."

Just like that, we were dismissed as he turned on the heel of his very much not a cowboy boot and stalked off in the direction of a huge, sprawling home made entirely out of logs. The main house was more of a rustic mountain mansion but I figured pointing that out wouldn't win me favors, and I was already in the red around these parts, even though I'd been on the ranch for less than an hour.

Lane, the brother who had no trouble flashing his teeth in a charming smile, hefted my bag up and gave me that adorable grin that I was starting to associate with him. "Don't worry too much about Cy. His bark is way worse than his bite and you won't see much of him after tonight. He doesn't come on the trail unless he has to."

For some reason, the idea of Cy's bite had a full body shiver quaking through me. I followed behind Lane, his brother, and Emrys as they started toward a row of what looked like cabins that were a few hundred yards away from the gigantic main house.

"I can't imagine you have much repeat business if he speaks to all of your guests that way when they first get here."

There was a deep chuckle from him that made me want to smile in return. This brother was clearly the easiest going of the three. I decided I liked him the best.

"It was the 'not real cowboys' crack. Cy gets touchy about people from the city coming here with preconceived notions about what the west is like, and about what it takes to survive out there in the mountains. We get a lot of weekend warriors who think they can take the wilderness on, and they end up being a pain in the ass for the entire ride. He's protective over the land and our lifestyle, so it's hard for him to let outsiders in, even if that's how we make our living. Not all cowboys wear ten-gallon hats and have Sam Elliott mustaches. Cy has never dressed the part, even when we were younger. Trust me, you are far from the first person to book an excursion with us and end up underwhelmed when we didn't show up dressed like a character out of the *Hateful Eight*."

I sighed and shot him a look out of the corner of my eye. "I don't know how you even heard that." I was so sure I whispered it low enough so that only Emrys could hear me.

"You're used to city noise and the sounds that come from being in such a crowded place covering up what you don't want people to hear. In the great wide open, there isn't anything to hide behind and all sound carries. You get used to saying what you mean out here and you learn real quick that words are permanent. You can try and take them back but they always linger."

"I'll keep that in mind." I tilted my head to the side and asked him, "If you and Sutton are the ones who guide the trips, what does Mr. Personality do . . . other than intimidate and berate the paying guests?" I wasn't sure why I was curious about the most unpleasant of the brothers. But I had a lot of questions and it was all I could do to keep from blurting them out all at once.

Another laugh, and this time I did smile back at him. Up close and without the shadow from his hat hiding his face, I could see he was more than passably attractive like I first thought. Lane was much younger and his eyes were much more blue than gray. He had a similar jawline and the cut of his cheekbones matched his older brother, but this guy was handsome in a more approachable, accessible way. Lane Warner also had a dimple in one cheek when he grinned, which made him downright adorable in my book. I didn't know if real cowboys had dimples, but I decided they all should if it was going to make them look as good as this one did. Lane had the kind of easy good looks that would appeal to any and every woman under the sun, while his older brother had the kind of brooding intensity and harshly hewn good looks that appealed to women who wanted something special, something unforgettable and impossible to overlook.

"Mr. Personality . . . Cy would lose his shit if he knew that's what you were calling him. He usually avoids the guests for that very reason. He always shows up when guests arrive and he hangs around to make sure everyone is paying attention when we go over the rules and regulations for the week, but after that, he goes back to running the ranch and all the other businesses he's got his hands in. Sutton and I do the grunt work but Cy is the brains behind the operation. He took over the ranch a few years ago when things got tough with my old man, health-wise. The guided tours and adventure vacations were his idea. When he was in college, all his buddies used to want to come home with him when they were on break so they could ride and camp out in the woods. Cy took something as simple as his college buddies hanging out and having a good time and turned it into a business plan. Since you paid to be here, you know how profitable the venture has been for us. He saved the ranch and gave my dad an easy last couple of years so our old man didn't have to worry about us his last few years."

It was more information than I asked for, but it was valuable insight into the man who had both annoyed me and intrigued me from the get-go. The younger man spoke with obvious pride when he talked about his older sibling, which made me smile at him; however, my smile died when we reached the cabin and the grumpy brother—who looked less like the one I was fascinated with—shoved open the door and dropped Emrys's bag with a loud 'thud' on the floor. Sutton tipped his chin at her and then swept past us until he was at the bottom of the steps. He was tall and broad like his older brother but his eyes were green, nowhere near blue or gray. The downturn of his mouth and the furrow between his eyes made him appear sulky and moody, rather than brooding and intense like his older sibling. He was still an outrageously attractive young man, one that I noticed Emrys couldn't seem to quit staring at. Considering I was in my own mental funk and had an unshakable cloud of piss-poor attitude hovering over my head, I had no time or interest in his sour disposition or the cause behind it. Lane put my bag down far more gently, gave me a rueful grin, then he touched the tip of his fingers to the brim of his ball cap.

"Working with family is never boring, that's for sure. You ladies are going to have a great trip. Just leave it to me."

The brothers disappeared as Emrys swung the door shut and turned on me with a swish of perfect hair and the narrowing of her captivating, dark eyes.

"You are too much, you know that, right?" She was pissed and I couldn't find fault with her feeling that way.

"I'm sorry, okay? I really didn't think anyone but you could hear me or that me pointing out the obvious would be considered fighting words."

She tapped her foot, which was encased in a far more appropriate leather riding boot, and huffed out an annoyed breath.

"I know you didn't think anyone could hear you, but that isn't the point. The point is, you think everyone is pretending to be something they aren't after all that crap Chris pulled on you. You're making everyone suffer for it."

Chris was the ex-boyfriend I was so sure I was going to spend forever with. He was the ex-boyfriend I had blissfully planned a future with and dreamily envisioned having children with. He was the ex-boyfriend I let in when I kept everyone else out because I thought he was perfect, and, more importantly, I thought we were absolutely perfect together. It was so easy to be together, effortless, uncomplicated. He was the ex-boyfriend who was everything I ever wanted, and he was the ex-boyfriend who had lied about everything.

He lied about what he did for a living. He lied about his past and his future. He lied to me about who he was and who I was to him. He lied, and he lied, and he lied some more, and when I called him out on his endless untruths, he made me feel like I asked for the dishonesty. He told me I made it easy for him to lie because I never asked him for the truth. He told me that I ignored all the obvious signs that I was being duped. This galled because I had turned a blind eye when things didn't exactly add up because it was easier for me than digging in and risking more than I already had.

I'd broken up with Chris over three months ago. I was still licking my wounds because I couldn't believe that I had been so stupid to fall for someone so fake, so phony. The end of the relationship was responsible for my current level of self-loathing and for my general misanthropy. His lies and my gullibility left me spinning and feeling like I could no longer trust my judgment or my decision-making skills. I was always so careful, so cautious, but Chris had broken through my defenses and now I felt foolish and scorned. As a result, I built my walls back up and made them so high and impenetrable, not even my best friend could climb over them.

The only person in my life who wasn't my family, who I trusted without question, was the woman standing across from me. I hated that I had let her down repeatedly over the last few months. During my relationship, I had ignored her time and time again when she warned me that things with Chris didn't add up. She told me over and over I should have seen where he lived, met his friends, been introduced to his family, considering we had dat-ed for over six months. I let her down after the breakup, when I retreated into myself while I licked my wounds. I pretended that the last half of a year hadn't completely destroyed my self-es-teem. I wasn't the girl who ever went out on a limb, and the one time I did, the branch snapped underneath me. Emrys deserved a better friend, because even when I'd been caught up in my own bullshit issues, she had never wavered.

I reached out my hands and put them on her shoulders. I had to look up at her to meet her eyes, but I did so sincerely. "We are going to have a great week together. I promise, no distrac-tions. I will put a sock in it when it comes to the guys being not quite cowboys. I'll lighten up and enjoy all this disgustingly clean, unpolluted air and unspoiled serenity. I'll even try and smooth things over with Mr. Personality if it will make you happy, okay?"

She shook her head but a reluctant grin pulled at her mouth, a mouth that didn't need lipstick or liner to make it look like a perfectly painted on Cupid's bow. If she wasn't my very best friend in the entire world, and I didn't know how big her heart was and how endlessly giving and kind she was, it would be easy to dislike her for how seemingly easy she made being flawless seem. Luckily, we met long before Chris had turned me into a suspicious asshole who questioned everyone and everything. It would have been the greatest loss in my entire life to have missed out on the friendship Emrys and I had just because she was so intimidatingly faultless.

"I want you to reset and recharge, Leo. I want you to re-member that you are the smartest, most capable woman I know. What happened with Chris isn't what defines you. You got taken for a ride by a charming guy with a pretty face. There are conse-quences to that, but it isn't the end of the world. You aren't the first woman that has happened to. You won't be the last. I want you to move on, get back to being the woman who has always been my best friend." She sounded so sad, so frustrated, that it made my belly twist into a tight knot. She shook her head a little bit and gave me a look that made my heart twist painfully in my chest. "Because this woman," she motioned to me, and I looked down and winced when I saw that she noticed the shirt I was wearing. I should have burned it when I told him I never wanted to see him again. "I'm not a huge fan of her."

I wasn't a huge fan either, but wasn't entirely sure how to make her go away. In fact, I was starting to wonder if she was who I was destined to be from now on. That thought was so depressing, I insisted, "I am moving on." I let my hands fall from her shoulders as I bent to pick up my bag and move it to one of the tiny twin beds that was set in a charming rustic frame. They had gone all out making the accommodations very ranch-like and I hated to admit that it was really cute and very charming. They did a good job researching what would appeal to their clients, and since that was how I made my living, learning and analyzing what people would spend their money on, I always appreciated it when a business had taken the extra steps to understand their client and their market.

I heard Emrys sigh from behind me. "You would never have discounted those guys as real cowboys before Chris. You would have been too distracted by how amazing their asses look in those jeans to worry about if they were cowboy enough or not." Sadly, she had a point.

A strangled laugh escaped my lips and I turned to look at her over my shoulder. "Their asses did look pretty phenomenal in those jeans." Cy's especially when he had marched away after dressing me down with his long-legged and confident stride. He was a man who moved with purpose and determination. He moved like nothing would distract him or deter him from the path he was on, like whatever he had to do was far more important than anything else happening. I always envisioned a real cowboy would move like that, minus the slightly bow-legged stance that my overactive imagination often added for dramatic effect.

Emrys laughed and some of the weight I'd been carrying around in my heart lately lightened a bit.

"Just play nice with everyone for the next week, Leo. That's all I'm asking."

"I can do that." She wasn't asking for much, and as long as big brother Warner stayed away from me, I should be able to comply with no problem. I was here to invest some quality time in our friendship and to give my battered heart and sense of self some much needed space. My ability to trust and my faith in my own judgment had been eviscerated. Maybe the quiet and disconnect from everything that was familiar would work at healing all the things Chris and his lies had left torn and tattered.

I was going to do my best to trust these not quite cowboys to not only guide us through the mountains and the wilderness but hope that along the way, they somehow managed to guide me back to who I was before I was broken.

CHAPTER 2

Not Quite the Typical Dinner Conversation

SINCE MY SHOWDOWN WITH MR. Personality had eaten into the allotted hour that we'd been given before making our appearance at dinner, I offered Emrys the tiny, perfectly rustic but still modern bathroom instead of claiming it for myself. I figured I'd already tanked any kind of good impression I was going to make for the day, so there was really no point in trying to spruce myself up and pretend to be someone who was more pleasant and put together than I actually was. Plus, I was determined to pull my head out of my ass where my best friend was concerned, and give her the memorable, bonding experience that she obviously wanted from this trip. There weren't many people in the world I would attempt to adjust my attitude for. Emrys just happened to be at the top of that list, and truth be told, I was tired of being miserable and of making others who cared about me miserable, as well.

At first, when the truth about Chris and our sham of a relationship came out, I was heartbroken and devastated. It didn't take long for those emotions to bleed into embarrassment and anger. That embarrassment meant I did my best to keep to myself. I wanted to lick my wounds in private, which had me doing everything I could think of to keep my bossy best friend away.

I blew her off. I ditched our regular weeknight get-togethers. I ignored her calls and left her hanging. I even ditched several of the previous business engagements we'd agreed to go to together, leaving her to fend off horny businessmen all on her own. I missed her birthday and purposely started a knock-down-drag-out fight with her when she called me on my bullshit. I didn't want anyone close enough to see the way I was hurting, especially not the person who knew me better than anyone else. Luckily for me, Em was as stubborn as she was demanding. I pushed her away as hard as I could but she never went anywhere. She scaled those mile-high walls and did her best to drag me back to the land of the living. I owed her the best week I could possibly give her.

Emrys disappeared into the bathroom and I took the time alone in the room to change into jeans and a fitted plaid shirt. I pulled my tangled hair out of the ponytail it was more than likely going to live in for the next week and rubbed my fingers over my scalp as it tingled in relief. I smirked when I caught sight of myself in the big mirror that hung on the back of the closet door. Once I added the new Justin Roper boots I had bought specifically for this trip, I would look more like what I always envisioned a traditional ranch hand looked like. Going with that, I plaited my hair into twin braids that ran down either side of my head in a style I hadn't worn it in since I was a little girl. My hair had just enough red in it that when I was younger I was afraid of the Pippi Longstocking jokes but because it curled wildly and in every which way, what I got instead was Little Orphan Annie. The jibes hurt, mostly because of the reasons behind the name calling. It was well known that my grandparents were raising me because my mother didn't want me and my father was never in the picture. Knowing that you weren't wanted by the person who brought you into the world was a tough pill to swallow. Luckily, my grandmother and grandfather had gone out of their way to make sure I grew up knowing they more than loved me and would give me everything they could to make up for my mother's neglect. I'd never wanted for anything in my life, except for the ever-elusive answers as to how my mother could decide she didn't love me when I wasn't even old enough to give her a reason not to.

I'd asked the question to both my grandparents and to the woman who had given me life. No one had a response that offered any kind of relief. There was no answer. There was no reason. To her, I was simply unwanted, an inconvenience. She already had her life planned out and I was never supposed to be a part of it. I was problematic, and to her that made me unlovable and that was enough for her to give me up and walk away from me forever.

Emrys told me it was my good fortune she left me behind. My grandparents put me in the best schools, in every kind of extracurricular activity that struck my fancy, took me to see the world, taught me about different cultures, and instilled an appreciation for hard work and self-reliance. They raised me to be independent, to think for myself, but the fact that the reason I had all those opportunities at my fingertips was because I was abandoned always niggled at the back of my mind. It drove me to be as close to perfection in all things as I could get. I knew there wasn't anything wrong with me, that the problem lay within the woman who couldn't be a mother. Still, the questions remained, and with them the fear that maybe, just maybe, there was something about me that people found hard to love. It made me defensive and prickly around people, especially people who tried to get close.

Annoyed at the morose thoughts, I plucked the ranch brochure that Em had been toting around like some kind of vacation bible for the last few weeks out of the top of her bag and thumbed through it.

There were pictures of the mountains and the beautiful terrain. A flawless mountain lake fed by a pristine river and, of course, there was a requisite fisherman in waders in the image with a smile the size of Montana on his face. There were pictures of attractively dressed tourists on gorgeous horses loaded down with gear, all of them laughing and clearly having a grand old time. There were pictures of the adorable cabins and the stables, full of horses. There was a picture of Sutton sitting on a horse. I tapped it with a finger because he had on a black Stetson and a jean jacket with shearling at the collar. He was leaning on the saddle horn and because he seemed incapable of smiling, he looked every bit the rugged and trail-ready cowboy. There was also a picture of Lane. The brother who did smile. In the picture, he was doing just that as he sat in front of a blazing campfire with a guitar in his hands. He also had on a cowboy hat, only his was straw and his shirt was similar to the trendy flannel one I had just changed into. In the brochure, they were full-on cowboy; in person, not so much.

I snorted and flipped the thing over. I couldn't stop the breath that I sucked in when I saw the picture on the back. There were a few images of the main house and the huge wooden dining table that looked like it was straight out of the show *Vikings*. There was a picture of a gorgeous, redheaded woman laughing with her head thrown back as she kneaded dough on a flour-covered counter. But, it was the picture of Cyrus Warner in his office, sitting behind a massive desk, leaning back in a leather wingback chair, with his arms crossed over his broad chest, and an intense look on his face, that sucked the air right out of my lungs. It wasn't like any office I had ever seen before. There was a gigantic longhorn skull hanging on the wall above his head. It looked like the lighting fixture was made from an old stagecoach wheel. Not to mention the adjacent chairs were covered in a cowhide pattern that I was willing to bet was actually from a cow. It was unmistakably western and unquestionably an office that belonged on a ranch. It was also unequivocally masculine and powerful, exactly like that man who commanded the space. Even in print he was impressive, but still nowhere close to being considered a cowboy. Unlike his brothers, he was dressed much like he had been today, black T-shirt, slickly styled hair with the glint of silver on the sides. He didn't look like a cowboy or a businessman. He didn't look like anything I could label or compartmentalize, which made a shiver of challenge and curiosity shoot up my spine.

"You're finally interested in how we're spending our time this week?" Emrys exited the bathroom with her long hair wrapped up in a towel and a billow of steam following. She was dressed similarly to how I was, though that was how she had arrived as well. Unlike me, Em was well acquainted with the great outdoors. "I'm glad. I really think we'll have a lot of fun if you give it a chance."

I sighed and tossed the brochure next to me on the bed. "You did see where it said you need to be a proficient rider, right? I haven't been on a horse since I was a teenager."

One of the extracurricular activities I'd wanted to try when I was younger was horseback riding. My grandpa had grown up around horses in Texas, well before he'd moved to Northern California. He's been elated when I showed an interest in something that we could do together. He signed me up for riding lessons at a local equestrian center faster than I could say 'giddy up'. I stuck with the lessons for a whole summer. I got pretty good with the big animals and really started to love riding. I liked the way being in total control of such a massive and powerful animal made me feel. Or at least I did until I got thrown when a skittish mount, that didn't want to take a jump, tossed me like I weighed nothing. I broke my wrist in two places and decided I'd had enough of horseback riding. It was too unpredictable and I didn't have as much control as I fooled myself into thinking I did. Story of my life it seemed. I bailed and never went near a horse again. I hated to fail, and when I did, I didn't risk a repeat of the experience.

"Proficient doesn't mean professional. You know how to put on a saddle, and a bridle, and you can ride for several hours a day without falling off. That was all the waiver we signed required." She took her hair out of the towel, the dark waves cascading down around her shoulders like black silk. "I haven't been on a horse in years. Not since I dated that Spanish polo player in college."

We exchanged a look and both let out a dreamy sigh. The polo player had been hot, but then again, every man Em dated was hot. My best friend didn't do average. It was one of the traits I most admired about her. She refused to settle for anything.

"Your hair looks cute like that." She reached out and pulled on the end of one of the pigtails as I got up from the bed. "Very Elly May Clampett."

I swatted her hand away as my stomach growled, letting me know the cereal bar and the Pepsi I'd guzzled hadn't been enough sustenance for the day.

"I think Elly May was a hillbilly, not a cowgirl. Let's head up to that house, I'm starving."

She pointed to her still soaking wet hair and lifted an eyebrow. "I need to dry this mop first, but you can head up without me."

I knew that her hair would take a minimum of a half an hour to get even remotely dry, since she had so damn much of it. I was going to tell her that I would just wait for her when my stomach made another angry sound that was loud enough that even she heard it. She lifted both her eyebrows at me as I slapped a hand over the offending noise and felt heat work its way into my face.

"Okay. I'll head up and see if they have something I can shove in my face before my body starts to devour itself. I'll let them know you're running a little late."

She nodded and moved to the sink, where she watched me in the reflection as I made my way over to my new boots and shoved my feet into them. They were unlike anything that usually graced my feet, but I had to admit the little fringe at the base of the laces was super cute. I put my hands on my hips as she surveyed me in the glass with a grin.

"You're adorable, Leo. Thank you for trying, it really does me a lot." There was a lightness in her tone, which had been missing ever since I had pulled the turtle move by ducking my head in my shell of misery. I ignored the rest of the world while I tried to pull together the edges of the wounds that cut far deeper than anyone realized.

I huffed out a breath and made my way to the door. "Wish me luck. I hope I don't get eaten by a bear or attacked by a mountain lion on the way to that log mansion."

She laughed and gave me a look in the mirror. "If you scream, I bet good money more than one of those boys in the tight Wranglers will come running to your rescue. It might be worth it just to try it out. Who doesn't want to be saved by a sexy as hell cowboy?"

I snorted as I pulled open the door. "Well, I'm still not convinced those guys are cowboys, so the chances are I'd have to save myself." Something I was so sure I could do before Chris had rattled the very foundation of my belief in myself. Now, I wasn't so sure I was up to the task of keeping myself safe and protecting those places that were too tender and soft. "I'll see you in a few."

Em gave me a little wave over her shoulder. I winced at how loud the door sounded when it shut behind me, how clearly I could hear the tap of the heels from my boots on the wooden landing that led to the ground. It was so quiet, so soundless and still. I could hear my heart beating and each breath I took. I could hear the way my clothes moved against my skin and the way the light breeze moved through my hair as I made my way to the brightly illuminated main house. I was acutely aware now how easily any sound would travel without buildings and swarms of people to block it. My voice would carry all the way to the mountaintops when I spoke, so it was no wonder Cy and his brothers had heard my snarky comments from earlier.

Say what you mean . . . Lane's words floated through my head as I got closer and closer to the striking and imposing house. There was a wide porch which circled the entire front of the house, with several wooden chairs covered in what looked like horse blankets spread across the space. There were antique-looking lanterns burning with a soft glow, and someone had taken the time to scorch the brand that was associated with the property on each of the pickets of the wooden railings. The setting was straight out of an old western movie but nice enough and welcoming enough to appeal to a wide range of visitors. Whoever was in charge of the setting and staging of this ranch had put in painstaking time to get things just right, with no detail missed. The line between working ranch and vacation property had been traversed perfectly, and I was having a hard time seeing any of the men I'd met so far being responsible for that kind of knowing touch. It was something the CEOs I worked with every day spent millions of dollars trying to cultivate. Knowing how to appeal to a consumer and what would get them to part with their hard-earned money was the ultimate tool in a professional's bag of tricks. It seemed like someone here had wielded it with a deft hand.

I was running my hand over the smoothly milled wood of the railing on the steps that led up to the wood and iron front door. I was appreciating the way the wood felt, so warm under my hand. I was used to steel handrails that were sticky with Lord only knew what. It was like everything in this place had life to it, had some kind of soul that was absent from the institutionalized and severe buildings that crowded San Francisco's skyline. I loved the city I called home, loved the quirky uniqueness of the rolling hills and dips, the varied history that came from living in a place founded by gold miners and dreamers, but it was nothing like this.

I took a deep breath and was getting ready to walk up the front steps when the front door was suddenly flung open and I came face to face with the aggravatingly attractive not quite a cowboy. I couldn't remember ever being around a bigger man or one who was so effortlessly impactful. It was like his presence and charisma obliterated every other thing that was going on around me. For some reason, everything seemed to slow down and sharpen directly on him when he was present. The same thing had happened when I looked at his picture on the brochure. It made me uneasy. I didn't like that he didn't have to do anything to have every single thing inside of me, and lots of the outside parts of me, reacting to him like he was the most dynamic thing in the universe. It was startling and made my internal warning bells, which were all polished and ready to be put to use after the disaster that was Chris, jingle jangle loud and clear.

"I was just coming to make sure you and your friend didn't get lost along the way. There are a lot of dangerous things waiting to put their teeth into pretty woman when the sun goes down around here." I liked the rasp in his voice a little too much but I didn't care for the seductive warning in his tone at all. I tilted back my head to look up at him as he made his way to the top step so he could loom over me.

"I'm fine. I'm perfectly capable of taking care of myself. I know when to run." Or at least I used to know. Everything inside of me was telling me to hightail it away from this man as fast as I could. Remembering that I was supposed to be burying the hatchet, I forced a smile and cocked my head to the side in what I hoped was an engaging and friendly gesture. "Thank you for thinking of us and our well-being. That's very hospitable of you." I bit back the sharp, 'finally' that was hovering on the end of my tongue.

A smirk that lifted one corner of his mouth crossed his face. It made my breath catch and my knees go weak. The man shouldn't be allowed to look that good when his personality was so unpleasant. It wasn't fair. He rubbed me the wrong way, but against my will I kind of enjoyed the fact he was rubbing me at all. I liked the friction and the way it made my blood warm.

"Just making sure nothing happens to the pretty girls from the city. That would be bad for business." He lifted a dark eyebrow at me and the smirk turned into a full-fledged grin. "It's always the ones who think they can take care of themselves that end up needing the most help along the way. Come inside and get settled. I'll head down and grab your friend so she doesn't have to walk up here by herself in the dark."

I was reeling from the fact that he had called me pretty more than once. I would typically discount it as nonsense. I was his client and our rocky interactions thus far probably made him nervous that I was going to tear him and his business apart on TripAdvisor and any other travel site that brought him customers. However, he didn't strike me as the type to waste words and Lane had already told me the Warner boys only said things they meant because words had weight when everyone could hear what you were saying. The compliment did something to my insides that I was too nervous to examine. I didn't have room for butterflies. All that space was supposed to be filled up with rock solid resolve so that I never ended up in a situation like I'd been in with Chris again. Regardless, I felt a flutter and it made me panic so I did what I always did when I was challenged and tested . . . I tried to run.

I took another step up onto the porch and opened my mouth to tell him I was starving but the sound ended on a gasp as I was almost knocked backwards as Sutton came flying around his brother at breakneck speed. He grunted as we both wobbled unsteadily, and he wrapped his hard hands around my upper arms to keep me upright. Like I was a piece of furniture he had accidently tripped over, he forcibly moved me to the side and looked over his shoulder at his older brother who was now glowering at him in obvious warning.

Sutton swore under his breath and looked away from his brother. "Daye just called me. I have to go pick her up."

My attention snapped between the two of them as Cy angrily bit out, "You can't keep running every time Alexa drops the ball, Sutton. You have responsibilities here."

I flinched for Sutton—and yelped a little because the hands he still had wrapped around my arms tightened enough that he was hurting me.

"I have responsibilities there, too, Cy. One that isn't going to go away for at least another thirteen years. Daye is my goddamn daughter and it isn't her fault her mother is a fucking lunatic. She needs me and I'm going. It won't kill you to get off your ass and do some work that isn't stapled together." The hard hands released me, and suddenly he was behind me, which put me, once again, face to face with a decidedly furious Cyrus Warner. His gaze skipped over me, making sure I stayed on my feet, and then it went over my head to where I could clearly hear his brother stomping down the steps behind me.

"I told you not to let any woman lead you around by your dick. One would think you and Lane would have learned from my mistakes." I gulped audibly, even though he wasn't talking to me, it felt like a warning. One that was directed right at me.

Sutton took his hat off and smacked it against his leg while he shoved his other hand through his hair. It was a pretty bronze color and not at all as dark as the man looming in front of me. "I'm not living your life, Cy, and I'm not living Dad's. I'll make my own mistakes, and so will Lane. We aren't all cut from the same cloth, no matter how badly you want us to be. Now I've got to go get my kid. She's scared and crying because her mom is a worthless drunk who passed out in front of her for the second time this week. She's hungry, alone, and she needs her dad. You can head out with Lane in the morning. When I have Daye back here and settled in with Brynn, I'll ride out and relieve you. It's only a couple of days."

There was a tense stare-down that happened over the top of my head. It lasted until I saw Cy's broad chest move with a deep sigh. He didn't sound any happier when he relented. "Fine. If you need help, call me."

There was a grunt from the younger man and then Sutton was gone, leaving me on the receiving end of that formidable glower.

"Sorry about that. That's a conversation we should have saved for another time. Sutton can be a hothead and forgets family business doesn't have any place in our actual business. Are you okay? He bumped into you pretty hard when he went flying out of here."

I wasn't expecting that kind of concern from him, so it

threw me for a minute and I absently lifted my hand to one of my biceps that was without a doubt going to have a bruise on it in the morning. I was fair skinned, so it didn't take much to leave a mark. "It's fine. He was obviously upset." I was trying to play nice just like I told Em I would, but my response seemed to make the imposing man before me even angrier.

He swore under his breath and pushed off the door so that he was standing directly in front of me. "He's bleeding from self-inflicted wounds. He put a baby in the wrong girl and he's been paying for that mistake for five years. That doesn't give him the right to be careless with our guests. You could have been really injured if he hadn't had quick enough reflexes to keep you from falling."

I flinched at the total lack of sympathy in his tone and cocked my head to the side as I considered him. "So your niece is only five and she's alone with her mother, who is passed out, which means she is probably terrified and undoubtedly upset."

He simply stared at me while I stated the horrifying facts I had stumbled into.

"And you're upset with your brother for going to get her out of that situation? What kind of cold-hearted monster would leave a child in those kind of conditions?"

His amazing eyes blazed down at me and a muscle ticked hard and fast in his cheek as his teeth clenched together. I didn't know the entire history of what was going on, but this single moment, this split second, did not paint this man I was intrigued by in a very flattering light. He wasn't a cowboy, and I wasn't sure what kind of businessman he was, but one thing was abundantly clear . . . he was an asshole. An unfeeling, cold, callous, and cruel asshole. How could any man disapprove of any action that was done in the best interest of a child . . . especially a child he shared blood with?

I wanted to get away from him and from the strange magnetic pull I seemed to have around him. I didn't like him, and I really didn't like the way he made me feel. Like everything inside of me was boiling hot and freezing cold at the same time. My foundation was already rocked and unsteady. I didn't need this big, brooding man and his unreadable persona doing any more damage to it.

I went to step around him and into the house when one of his hands landed on my arm, much lighter than his brother's touch had been. The contact made me feel like I had touched a live wire. Tingles popped and buzzed up my arm and had me whipping my head around to stare at him. He was looking at my arm where his hand rested and I prayed he couldn't feel the way that simple touch had my blood raging like lava through every single vein.

"I love my brother and I love my niece. What I don't love is the manipulative woman who uses both of them to play games. I'm not mad that Sutton is going after his kid, I'm mad that it's something he has to do in the first place. Custody for Daye has been an ongoing issue since Sutton's ex got knocked up. I would say the real cold-blooded monster in this situation is the woman who willingly brought a child into the world that she had zero intention of caring for. Daye was a pawn, nothing more and nothing less. It pisses me off that Sutton has no choice but to play the games because he loves his kid and he's a good dad. I want my brothers to make better choices than the men in our family who chose before them. Lucky in love the Warners have never been."

I blinked, and then blinked again, because I was all too familiar with the kind of monster he had just described. I had one of my own hidden not so deeply in my closet. I blew out a breath and plastered a smile on my face to divert any of those old feelings of inadequacy back into the dark where they belonged.

"Well, this wasn't at all what I was expecting, but I have to admit that this vacation has been anything but boring so far. I'm actually starving, so if there's food, let me at it." It was a blatant attempt to change the subject and I was praying that he would take the soft lob and run with it. He didn't strike me as the type who wanted some stranger in his family business. His youngest brother had mentioned that Cy considered those of us taking advantage of his property and his wilderness to be just that, outsiders. I didn't belong in his world and I sure as hell didn't belong in his personal business any more than I wanted him in mine.

I hadn't seen Chris coming when he worked his way into my life, but there was no missing Cyrus.

Suddenly he took a step back. The gleam that shown out of his glittering gray gaze dulled slightly and he dipped his chin down in a slight acknowledgement that I had given him an out and he was going to take it. This was business . . . nothing more. "Go on in. I'll introduce you to the rest of your group and to Brynn when I get back with your girl. There's eight of you riding out with us in the morning and you'll be spending the week pretty much in each other's pockets, so it's best if you make an attempt to get along with everyone."

I bristled a little at his reminder of our first encounter and haughtily went to flip my hair over my shoulder, only to be reminded that it was in pigtails and that it was impossible to look haughty when you were trying to look like a proper cowgirl—or really, when you were me because cute and haughty didn't really mesh.

I wouldn't ever go as far as to say that I typically got along great with other people because that would be a lie. I had a hard time trusting people, and an even more difficult time opening up, so my social circle was relatively small. It was no secret that strangers often found my blunt manner and general disinterest in niceties off-putting. I was not one of the popular kids and had never striven to be one. However, when you spent your days studying people, their spending habits, their preferences, and their triggers, it was inevitable that you figured out what made most humans tick. So I could fake being outgoing and adventurous for a week and maybe, just maybe, some of that faking it would end up being real.

Now that I knew Cy was going to be going with us on our trip for a few days, at least, I was suddenly much more excited about spending a week in a tent in the mountains of Wyoming. He was a man I couldn't figure out, a puzzle that everything inside of me was dying to solve. I wanted to see what the complete picture of Cyrus Warner looked like. Maybe I was so desperate to see the whole image because the last riddle I tried to solve had come with a whole lot of missing pieces. It was terrifying when you couldn't trust your own judgment about what was real and what was fabricated to feel like it was real.

Chris had ruined my trust and my confidence.

And somewhere deep down, I had a feeling that if I let him get close enough, Cyrus Warner would have the power to obliterate all that was left of me.

All I could do was cross my fingers and hope I was fast enough to outrun that kind of devastation.

CHAPTER 3

Not the Usual Suspects

I F I HAD BEEN FORCED to guess what kind of people would book a trip into the Wyoming wilderness for a week, I would have picked middle-aged businessmen who always wanted to live the fantasy that they were John Wayne or Clint Eastwood. I would have picked disenchanted hipsters, those who were bored by everything in metropolitan cities and decided to venture out to get in touch with Mother Nature. I would have pegged women like me and Emrys financially secure and maybe a little lost and definitely overworked, who were looking for something to shake up the status quo. I, however, would not have picked the obviously affluent and well-to-do family that hailed from the Upper East Side who was currently seated across from me at the long wooden dining table. The mom fiddled with the diamond tennis bracelet on her wrist while the plastic smile on her face never faltered. The dad kept glancing discreetly at his cellphone while the teenaged son refused to look away from the handheld video game that beeped incessantly in his hands. I, begrudgingly, wondered what kind of cell plan they had because my phone was a brick with zero bars in this dead zone while they seemed to have no trouble interacting with the outside world. It was like fate was trying to force me to unplug and stop thinking about every single thing that I'd gotten wrong. The teenaged girl in their group was a few years older than the boy, and from the minute Cy entered the room with Em in tow, she hadn't taken her wide-eyed gaze off of him. I couldn't blame her; he was impossible to ignore. I wanted to nudge her mother and clear my throat at the inappropriateness of such a blatantly sexual appraisal when Cy was so much older than the girl.

I also never would have pegged the two other men who would make up our caravan as choosing this place as their first choice escape from reality. Two men who barely spoke to one another, who watched the rest of us at the table with suspicious eyes, and who offered up very little information about themselves when introductions were made. My initial thought was they were a very unhappy couple using this trip and its remote destination as a way to rekindle their romance. But their body language and the stiff way they interacted with one another, as well as with the rest of us, made it seem like they could barely stand to be in the same room as each other, so the likelihood of them being a couple in love seemed slim. Since they didn't appear to be friends either, I couldn't really figure out any other reason for two men to be traveling alone together into the woods. It was odd. I think they could tell I thought it was strange because the younger of the two men, the one who was probably around my age, kept giving me a harsh look from underneath furrowed eyebrows. I simply stared back at him until Emrys placed herself next to me with a flourish and a sigh. Once she was seated at the table, all attention shifted to her. Even the gamer boy lost interest in his device so he could make moon eyes my too-pretty-for-her-own-good best friend.

The vibe around the table was tense and uncertain. I forgot all about grabbing a snack before dinner as I evaluated and assessed, and in turn, weighed and judged. It felt like it was some kind of audition, not just a bunch of strangers meeting for an adventure of a lifetime. Cy's introductions were brief and to the point. He offered up everyone's name, the two silent men being Grady and Webb, and the family of four being Marcus, who was the disinterested father, Meghan, who was the distressed mother, and Evan and Ethan, the kids who both seemed like they wanted to be anywhere else. He also mentioned where we were all from before he took a seat at the head of the table and seemed happy to shut us all out so he could be alone with his obviously pensive thoughts. No one offered up any more info than what was given so it made the moments that passed incredibly awkward. I shot Emrys a look that she pointedly ignored. Lane was the only one at the table who seemed able to keep up a steady stream of conversation, but that was a lot to ask of one person when the other nine were clearly caught up in their own noise and issues. Eventually, he heaved a deep sigh, rolled his eyes at his older brother, and excused himself to help the elusive Brynn, the woman the brothers kept mentioning, in the kitchen. I hadn't met the woman yet, but I was ready to tackle hug her and smother her in love, if the food she was bringing to me tasted as good as it smelled coming out of the kitchen.

"So, what do you do for a living, Ms. Santos?" That came from the Manhattan dad who was either a workaholic or totally had a girlfriend on the side. His phone pinged every five minutes and he was taking great pains to make sure neither his wife nor his children could see the screen every time he replied. The idea of him stepping out on his family made my skin crawl. When all the lies Chris told came to light I realized I'd spent our entire relationship being the clueless other woman. No one liked a cheater but when you were stupid enough to get your heart broken by one it made you even more judgmental and critical of the way others treated the people they were supposed to love. I decided on the spot I didn't like the dad, and there was no way in hell I would ever trust him.

Emrys smiled in her disarming and easy way and I had to stifle a giggle as it made almost every single one of the men at the table shift in their seats. The two non-talkers were definitely not a couple if they were affected Emrys. She was potent and my most favorite thing about her was that she was very aware of her power and the exponential impact she had on people. It was nice that she had decided early on to use her influence for good instead of evil.

"I work in Human Resources." She waved a hand in front of her and laughed lightly. "I push paper around all day, pretty much. There's a form for every other form. It's endless."

She did a lot more than that but she would never expound on her own accomplishments and as she glanced at me out of the corner of her eye, I knew she wasn't interested in trying to impress the overly interested father of two.

"That sounds interesting. I'm in real estate. New York is one of the most competitive markets in the world. I have to be on top of my game all day, every day." I fought back the urge to roll my eyes as the mom cleared her throat nervously and shifted her fidgety hands from the diamonds on her wrists to the one on her ring finger.

"Yes, Marcus works very hard, which is why we all needed this vacation. It's going to be so nice to spend time together . . . as a family." Her last words were a tad brittle and the teen girl jerked her head to the side with a glare, like she had been nudged where no one could see. I watched as she clearly decided to refrain from saying something smart to her mother, and instead narrowed her eyes at her father who was once again tapping away on his cell. The girl shook her head and switched her attention back to the big man at the head of the table with a wistful sigh.

It was ridiculously reminiscent of something out of a bad sitcom and this family was straight out of central casting. This vacation was turning out to be one surprise after another. I was becoming more and more invested in seeing how it all played out. This kind of drama and impending tragedy was exactly what I needed to distract me from my own recent failings.

I swallowed a laugh and shifted my gaze to Cy when his deep voice suddenly broke through the tension surrounding the table. He was looking right at me, and if I wasn't mistaken, there was a challenge stamped on his face. "What about you, Sunshine? What do you do?" It should have been an innocent enough question, but like every other interaction I'd had with this man in such a short time, it felt loaded and full of subtext I wasn't sure I fully comprehended. It seemed like he wasn't simply asking me what I did for a living or how I supported myself, but more like he was asking what I did as a human being. Like he was questioning my worth and value as a woman. The unexpected nickname threw me. It implied the kind of intimacy and connection I was doing my very best to avoid. It was also ridiculous. I was the least easygoing and carefree person on the planet. I was a storm cloud that ruined picnics, not something full of warmth and light.

"I told you that you can call me Leo, and I'm a market research analyst."

"I've never met a girl named Leo before." That came from the gamer boy and I couldn't help but smile at his totally baffled look.

"It's not very common. My grandpa used to call me his little lion when I was a little girl. It kind of stuck."

Emrys lifted her eyebrows and cocked her head in my direction. "She's also the queen of the concrete jungle and has a roar you can hear from miles and miles away."

Her explanation made almost everyone in the room chuckle,

including Lane, who must have overheard them as he came back into the room from the kitchen. Once he was done laughing he declared dinner would be served in just a few more minutes. Apparently, the biscuits had burned and we were waiting on a second batch. He shifted his attention back to me and decided he wasn't done with the conversation about my name. "It's the hair. It's the same color as a lion's mane. I can totally see why he called you that."

I let out a huff and lifted a self-conscious hand to the curly tresses trapped in the pigtails on either side of my head. Clearly the nickname was fitting for a lot of reasons, though lately, my roar had faded into more of a whimper.

I found my gaze locked on Cy as he tilted his head to the side and considered me for a long and silent minute. "So, you spend your days figuring out how to get people to part with their money, getting them to spend it on stuff they really don't need?"

I felt my spine stiffen and my fingers involuntarily curled into a fist on the top of my thigh under the table, where I hoped no one could see. I schooled my features into an even mask and nodded in what I hoped was a polite and neutral way. I had heard that my job was manipulative, that it was invasive and calculating, from a wide variety of people. For some reason, I really didn't want to hear that from him. I wanted to appear successful, secure, confident . . . even if I wasn't feeling any of those things at the moment—especially in front of him, and more importantly, about my current job security.

My response was cool and as unemotional as I could make it. "I do. I study market trends, spending habits, price points, and consumer behavior. The way people shop, why they choose one product over another . . . it is a science." I motioned to the meticulously decorated dining room we were in and scrunched up my nose as the smell of fried chicken got stronger. "Humans are programmed to respond to our senses. When a company or a business knows how to appeal to as many of those senses as possible, they will inevitably come out ahead of the competition. For example, if you could put how heavenly that fried chicken smells on your website, you guys wouldn't have any kind of competition when it comes to booking guests. Their stomachs would book the trip for them."

"Well, aren't you just the sweetest thing? I love to hear nice things being said about my food." A gentle voice, laced with humor and warmth, had me turning my head and my mouth falling open a little bit in surprise as a woman, who was every bit as lovely and as exotically beautiful as Emrys, came waltzing around the end of the table with a large serving tray in her hands. She didn't look like a Brynn. Her name should be something lyrical and exotic that was impossible to pronounce and spell. She didn't look like a woman who should be toiling away in a kitchen on a secluded ranch in the middle of nowhere.

Nope . . . she looked like a woman who should be on the cover of a Victoria's Secret catalog or attached to the arm of a NFL player while making the rounds in the tabloids.

"It smells amazing and authentic. People are willing to pay a lot of money for authentic." The words sounded stiff as they worked around my shock at how pretty and welcoming she was.

She laughed and it was airy and tinkling. She seemed so happy and easygoing as she hustled tray after tray of food onto the massive table. Her smile was effortless, and she chatted with all the stonily silent guests like it was no big thing. Her attitude was bubbly and infectious even when she was gifted with awkwardness and silence in return. I found myself wanting to smile just because she was smiling and I still wanted to tackle hug her because after the first bite of the buttery, flaky biscuit and crispy hot chicken, I knew I would never taste anything better in my life.

Emrys was talking to Lane about playing guitar since he was pictured with one on the brochure. He launched into a story about learning to play so he could pick up chicks, which made her laugh and toss her head back. The two silent men were picking at their plates like they didn't realize they had just been handed food from the gods, their eyes silently assessing everyone else around the table in an unnervingly intense way. The family of four was making awkward small talk as the daughter continued to gaze lovingly toward the head of the table. No one seemed to be paying any kind of attention to me or Brynn as she quietly told me, "Well, I always feel obligated to make sure all of our guests eat really well the first night, because after you saddle up, it's only rations and whatever you catch on the trail for a week. I consider this your send-off feast, or your last meal, depending on how well you fare in the wilderness."

I wasn't sure if she was joking about the food for the rest of the trip or not because her dark eyes danced with merriment. I found myself studying her with open curiosity. Her long, red hair was the color of copper and fire, far richer and deeper than my own strawberry blonde locks. Her eyes were dark and mysterious, with a slight angle to them that hinted at a heritage that wasn't run-of-the-mill. She was obviously at home around the big table, and when she took a seat next to Cy toward the head of the table, I almost choked on my chicken leg when she reached out, putting a hand on his thick forearm. She muttered something to him in a voice low enough so only he could hear. He leaned a little bit toward the stunning woman and replied to whatever she had asked him. I felt my breath whoosh out of my lungs in a gust loud enough that it had Em turning her head to look at me in question.

He was different with her.

There wasn't a hint of the intimidation that he wielded so

effortlessly when he faced off with me. There was no glowering and growling, no stalking and scowling. All he had for her was a half grin and gently gruff words that sounded like thunder rumbling over the hills. The twist of his lips made his hard face impossibly handsome, and had the besotted teenager at the table audibly sighing in appreciation while I stifled my own jolt of reaction.

Of course, a man like him wouldn't be out here, miles and miles away from everything, without a woman who looked like she did at his side. That had a sharp pang shooting through me, even though it absolutely and completely made no sense. The two of them together made so much sense and it bugged me that the perfection of them together bothered me.

We were all happily awaiting the promised dessert after dinner when the overly amorous father of two switched his attention from texting his 'customers' and blatantly trying to impress Emrys, to the other two men, who had yet to join any kind of conversation. The way they watched us all without engaging was off putting, but since I typically had no patience for small talk and banal conversation, I decided I was in no place to question their odd behavior.

"Did you guys leave the wives at home for the weekend?" If they had been a couple, the way he asked the question would have been confrontational and insulting. The older of the two men narrowed his eyes and curled his hand around the water glass in front of him.

"We aren't married." His tone was brisk and clearly irritated. He didn't want to have a conversation about himself and it was obvious, even if the clueless dad didn't pick up on the mile-wide hint.

"Really? So, you two just took a week off of work to tromp around the woods together and play cowboy?" The implication that he found that disturbing and uncomfortable was clear. As if the guy, who I was positive had a side chick, had any room to pass judgment on anyone while his wife was worrying herself sick about his rudeness and the blatant break in her family unit.

The younger of the two men schooled his face into an impassive mask but there was a hard glint in his gaze when he replied, "We're here on a training exercise for work. Grady here was working with a different partner for a long time and it's been a rough adjustment since the restructure. Our boss thought this would be a good way for us to get on the same page. I would never say no to a week fishing on the boss's dime but my partner isn't big on the outdoors." The older man grunted in apparent agreement.

"What kind of business are you gentlemen in?" It was supposed to be a friendly enough question, but I don't think anyone seated at the table could miss that the dad was clearly looking for an in—or a new client—but neither of the men sounded like they came from the East Coast or particularly looked like they were interested in owning property in the Big Apple.

"We're in sales." The older gentleman muttered at the exact same time the other man stated, "Finance. We're in finance."

They exchanged a heated look and the older man cleared his throat. "We're in sales and finance management, which is also pushing a lot of paper around just like Ms. Santos mentioned earlier. Nothing too exciting but it makes life easier when you're working with someone you can trust and rely on." He cut the younger man at his side a hard look and went all in to change the subject. "So, what kinds of things do we need to be on the lookout for while we're on the trail for the next few days? Like Webb said, I'm not exactly a great outdoorsman and I Googled a wide range of things that could eat us or maim us throughout the excursion, so I do have my reservations."

Lane chuckled and Cy lifted a quizzical eyebrow and stated, "It's the wilderness so we will undoubtedly encounter local wildlife. There are elk and a variety of deer but they typically smell and hear the horses so they steer clear. There are bears and an occasional big cat but we ride out armed and take care to make sure all the campsites we set up are as safe for you and our animals as possible. There are birds, fish, plus more wild game than you can shake a stick at, but that's why you're here. To get close to it all, to be part of the wild in a way you won't be back at home. People have existed with the wildlife in these parts since Wyoming was settled. It's part of what makes this land so special."

"What about other people?" That question came from the younger of the two men and seemed more pointed than it should. There was nothing and no one out here, even though the town of Sheridan was an adorable and touristy location. The commute back to 'civilization' was an hour away from the ranch and the likelihood of running into another person out of the blue seemed impossible. That had both the teenagers at the table scowling when they realized exactly how isolated they were going to be for the next few days. If I was saddled with the kind of parents they had, I would be longing for kids my own age and the Internet as a distraction, as well.

Lane was the one who fielded that particular question. He did it with a grin and a rueful shake of his head. "No one around for miles and miles. Most of the trail we follow is on our land with some of it crossing through the national forest. Occasionally, we'll run across a rafting trip on the river or another guided trip at one of the two established campgrounds we use so you can catch a shower, but those times are few and far between. Occasionally, a lost hunter stumbles across our path. They generally hurry along because we make too much noise for them to shoot at anything. We always carry a satellite phone so if there's an emergency, we can get in touch with Brynn back here at the ranch, but it's just us and the horses once we ride out tomorrow."

"So, if something goes wrong, if someone gets hurt, what's your standard operating procedure in that scenario?" That question was posed from the younger man, and if I didn't know any better I could have sworn there was a hint of confrontation in his tone.

Cy must have heard it too because his big body stiffened and he sat up straighter in his chair as he replied, "We've had a few minor injuries since we started doing the guided tours. We're dealing with horses, unpredictable weather, and people from the city who aren't always forthcoming about their actual skill level. We've had a few folks get too close to the campfire and one got a pretty nasty gash from a fish hook, but so far, the biggest injury we've encountered is a broken leg when one of the horses got spooked and threw a rider."

Cy's jaw went hard and his gray eyes turned flinty with his own kind of accusation. "It was the rider's error and could have been prevented if he had been honest from the get-go about how inexperienced he was. He wasn't on a gentle mount and he paid the price for it . . . which is why we make everyone sign liability waivers."

The other two men exchanged a look and the younger one slumped back down in his seat, some of his bluster gone in the face of Cy's unwavering confidence. "I've heard stories about people getting lost out here for days, just disappearing."

Lane shook his head and that grin that never seemed to waver stayed firmly on his handsome face. "Not on our watch."

There was an exchange of looks across the table like neither of the men really believed the reassurances given. However, the besotted teenager picked that lull in the conversation to change the subject, and when she did, it put me and Em on the hot seat so I couldn't wonder what was really going on with the two men across the table anymore.

"So, what about you guys? Are you here because you love to fish, too?" There was sarcasm in her tone and a challenge in her gaze that must have come from the fact I couldn't stop watching her crush or the way he was with the beautiful redhead at his side. She was a perceptive little thing, which meant there was no way she missed her mother's anxiety or her father's shady behavior.

Emrys tapped her fingers on the side of her glass and offered the young woman a friendly smile. "I actually really do love to fish and I've even been known to hunt a bird or two. My dad always wanted boys but was stuck with three girls. He took us out and did all the things he would have done if we had been sons instead of daughters. I begged Leo to come with me because I thought it would be fun to see if I still could hold my own with the boys. We both have pretty busy jobs back in the city so this seemed like the perfect girl's trip, even if it is as un-girly as you can get."

The teen lifted her eyebrows and cocked her head to the side. "You don't really look like you know how to fish and hunt."

Emrys wiggled her own eyebrows up and down. "Looks can be deceiving,"

"I think it's awesome." Her brother chimed in with a voice full of admiration and prepubescent approval. Their dad wasn't the only one who had succumbed to my friend's effortless charm and affability.

"What about you? Do you fish and hunt?" The question was lobbed at me with more than friendly curiosity, and despite myself, I found that I liked the girl's grit and moxie. I wasn't sure why she viewed me and not the other redhead at the table as a threat to her budding crush on the big, menacing man who seemed oblivious, but I admired her fight. It reminded me that I needed to find where mine had been buried under my own doubt and uncertainty.

"Nope. I used to love to ride horses when I was younger but I haven't done that or been camping and fishing since I was a little girl. I like my memory foam mattress and I'm in a happily committed relationship with the Chinese restaurant at the end of the block down from my apartment. I'll be clueless and helpless all week long but I'm excited to see the mountains and to spend some quality time with my bestie." I offered the girl a lopsided grin that she didn't return but my assurance that I was no Pioneer Woman, about to wow the men in charge of our well-being with my skills, seemed to put her at ease and some of the tension around her mouth loosened.

"You sure you aren't running away from anything in the city, using all the fresh air and nature to escape something that went sour?" That rumbling question came from Cy and it was so unexpected it made me jump a little bit in my seat. He seemed so focused on the woman at his side, I sort of thought he forgot the rest of us were at the table still.

I tilted my chin in a defiant manner. "What would I be running from?" He couldn't know about the lies and the self-doubt or the tight wire I was walking at work. There was no way he could read me so well after such a short amount of time. At least I hoped he couldn't. I didn't like the idea of being that transparent to anyone. There was nowhere to hide if he was able to see right through me.

"I don't know what you left behind but I do know this is a long way to come when you don't really want to be here." He had a point.

But as I opened my mouth to argue that he didn't know me

well enough to know if I wanted to be here or not I suddenly realized I really *did* want to be here. The more minutes that passed, the more I *did* want to see how this crazy vacation that hadn't even really started yet was going to play out. Nothing had caught my attention or held my curiosity like this man had. The distraction from everything that had been pulling me down lately was a nice reprieve. Butting heads with Cy made me feel like my old self, and I missed her.

I slid a look to Emrys and then back to him. The other redhead at his side was switching her dark gaze between the two of us, like we were opponents in a tennis match. She seemed fascinated by our banter and it made me cringe because I shouldn't like the zing of life that verbally sparring with the darkly complicated man gave me. I was supposed to be smart enough to run from that zing.

"The idea of spending a week here is growing on me. I'm not a big fan of change so it takes me a minute to settle in, especially when it's something I wasn't expecting." I lifted an eyebrow at him and gave him a smile that showed a lot of teeth.

It was Brynn who asked with wide eyes and a hushed voice, "What were you expecting?" Almost like she was scared of the answer I was going to give.

Luckily, Lane was the one who gave a good-natured reply. "She wanted real cowboys and was disappointed when she got Cy instead. He's never wanted to be a cowboy but he didn't get much of a choice in the matter."

I wasn't disappointed . . . I was stunned and off my game because I couldn't believe how viscerally and violently I had reacted to the man who wasn't quite the cowboy I'd been anticipating. I'd been oblivious to so much lately, it was a shock to be so fully engrossed in another human being. I wasn't prepared for someone to be as blunt and honest with their feelings like he had been.

I was too accustomed to people trying to placate and patronize. Even though he was rude and insulting, Cy's in-your-face manner was oddly refreshing and weirdly satisfying to be around.

He said what he meant. There weren't any lies or deceptions because they would carry.

The stunning redhead made a distressed sound in her throat and rose from her place next to the man in question. She looked down at him, then over at me, and her lips quirked like she suddenly had a secret she was dying to tell someone.

"Oh, dear . . . well, I guess when you ride out tomorrow you can see for yourself that a cowboy hat and a big belt buckle isn't what makes a real cowboy." She wiggled her eyebrows at me as she started to clear the plates off the table. "Though you should see him in a Stetson. I told him he needs to put that picture on the front of the brochure. We would be booked year round with single women trying to lasso their very own rancher."

I blinked at her in confusion. She didn't sound jealous or bothered by the fact that other women would indeed show up to chase the attractive, brooding man around if they knew he was hiding up here in no man's land. I couldn't figure it out. I couldn't figure them out.

I met his unflinching and probing gaze with one of my own. "It's going to be an interesting week to say the least." I gave him a saccharin smile and turned to look at Brynn, who was still watching us with eagle-eyed attention. "And who knows, maybe if we get lucky, he'll do us all a favor and bust out the cowboy hat."

Cy snorted, Lane laughed, Emrys sighed, and the two men grumbled under their breath. The family from the coast started peppering Cy and Lane with questions about what to expect with the kids for the next few days, all while ignoring me for the most part while the dad continued to none too subtly hit on Em.

I had a distinct feeling that "interesting" wasn't even close to covering how the week was going to go, but I had to admit that I really couldn't wait to experience it all. That, and I owed Emrys an apology.

I was happy she had harassed me into coming on this trip. I couldn't say for certain that going toe to toe with Cy every minute we were together was going to be fun, but I did know that all the places inside of me that felt ravaged and torn weren't as raw as they had been. They still ached, but all around, that hurt was a heat, a flickering flame of anticipation and awareness that seemed to be cauterizing those wounds.

I knew that if I could hold my own with a man like Cyrus Warner, if I could escape this week with my sanity and heart intact, then it would prove to my battered sense of self that what happened with Chris was just a fluke.

It would show that I'd been taken in by a professional con-man, one who knew exactly what to say. It would verify that my walls were still strong and my fortress was still impenetrable, and that no matter what Cy thought, I was perfectly capable of taking care of myself.

I didn't need his help or his approval.

CHAPTER 4

Not Quite the Ass Crack of Dawn

EMRYS TRIED TO WAKE ME up before the sun was fully in the sky to do yoga on the tiny front porch. I didn't even get up to do yoga with her back home so I had no idea what she was thinking. I tossed a pillow at her and growled a lot of ugly words, pulling the covers back over my head. She laughed at me and told me I was going to regret not stretching out after the first few hours in a saddle. I'd spent most of the evening tossing and turning, my restless mind a messy tangle of thoughts that made sleep elusive, so a sore ass would go right along with my grouchy mood.

I spent the night fretting over the upcoming week and over how I was going to function with all the solitude and none of the regular hurry and hustle that filled my days. It was easy to hide my bad attitude and wounded ego when I was busy with work and could make reasonable excuses to avoid my everyday life, but I had none of that here. That meant the journey I was on, planning to take back to my old self, would be on full display. The thought of Cy bearing witness to the shattered parts of me fusing back together made we want to curl up in a ball and die. The fact that I was lost, had wandered off course somewhere along the way and was a failure, I didn't want to share with anyone.

It all made for a long night. I swore I had just dozed off when Emrys shook me awake and tried to get me to greet the day with her. Once she left the room, making sure to make as much noise on her way out as she possibly could, sleep was once again impossible to find. I threw the quilted covers off with a litany of swear words and stumbled my way into the shower. I made sure it was hot and I took my time to enjoy every steamy second of it because Lane had informed us last night when we went over the itinerary for the week that we would only be stopping twice at public campgrounds during the next seven days for a shower. He also pointed out that the water was often frigid and sometimes didn't work. We were all going to have to get comfortable with cowboy showers, which consisted of slathering on deodorant and using wet wipes to battle our B.O. It sounded awful, but part of my brain recognized that it would be much easier to stay away from Cy and his brooding intensity if he smelled like the backside of a horse all week. The downside was I would also smell that way.

After every inch of me was scrubbed and shiny pink, I sluggishly crawled into my new western wear and wrestled my unruly hair into the braid that it was going to have to live in for the remainder of the week. By the time I was done, Emrys was back inside the tiny cabin looking totally energized and ready to tackle the day. She had some fresh fruit and a stack of big, fluffy pancakes on the table. I walked over to the plate and took a bite out of one without saying a word. They were so good that I moaned out loud and almost picked one up with my hands to better achieve my goal of shoving the syrupy treat into my face.

She laughed at me as she started rummaging through her bag so she could pull out her gear for the day. "Lane brought those down from the house for breakfast. He said everyone else was already up there and they already ate. We have an hour before we have to meet at the stables. They need us to bring our stuff over so they can pack the mules and so that we can meet our mounts for the week."

I wrinkled up my nose and worked on devouring another pancake. "The sun isn't even up yet. It's not like I slept in."

Em pulled off her yoga pants and wiggled her way into a dark pair of skinny jeans that made her long legs look even longer. "Things start moving early around here. Lane mentioned that he'd been up for a couple hours taking care of chores that needed to get done before we left. Obviously Brynn had been up earlier than that if she had breakfast ready for everyone. I haven't seen the boss man yet, but he doesn't strike me as the type who takes it easy while everyone else is working."

"It's inhumane to be up before the sun is all the way in the sky." I practically growled at her when she made her way over to the table to snag a banana from the pile she brought in.

"Watching a new day start is pretty special. I never get to do that back home. I'm always too distracted by what happened the day before and thinking what's waiting for me going forward. They sky seems so big out here with nothing blocking it, it's like watching the world hit reset and start over." A soft smile played around her mouth as she lifted an eyebrow at me. "Everything that happened before doesn't matter."

Her message was clear. I could use some resetting of my own, and now was the perfect time to retune everything that had gotten so out of whack because of the blind way I'd allowed myself to fall for a charming con artist . . . a spoken-for con artist.

I polished off the rest of the pancakes with a satisfied sigh and tapped my fingers on the table as Em also pulled her long hair into a complicated-looking braid at the back of her head. With her tall, leather boots and her perfectly polished look, I thought she looked more like she should be getting ready to ride a thoroughbred in an Olympic jumping competition rather than hitting the trail in the backcountry. She definitely didn't look like any kind of cowgirl I had ever seen, not even the glossy, manufactured kind that sang sad country songs and sold make-up on TV. Emrys was always going to be her own brand of perfection. I think I gravitated toward her because I was always trying to make the right choices, do the right things to avoid screwing up and getting hurt. I was careful in everything I did and letting someone in with so few flaws seemed like an easy enough decision to make. I was fortunate her goodness ran all the way through the very core of who she was.

When she was ready to go, we hoisted our weekend bags, which were packed with only the essentials outlined for us, onto our shoulders and made our way across the property to the long, rustic-looking stables. It was a good ten-minute walk, and by the time we arrived, the rest of the group was already there standing inside of a massive corral, petting and talking to a rainbow variety of different horses. Lane and Cy were wandering between the people and the already suited-up animals, muttering softly to both. The seemingly docile steeds tolerated being fawned over and appraised by a bunch of people who were duly impressed by their size and stature. All the horses were gorgeous and obviously well cared for. The smells and sounds immediately took me back to a time where I was slightly more willing to be brave and adventurous.

Lane made his way over to us and took each of our bags in a hand. I felt my lips twitch because today he had on a cowboy hat and his boots looked like they had spent years locked in a pair of stirrups. There it was; he was finally the embodiment of the cowboy I had been expecting all along. And as superficial as it might have been, the fact he looked so thoroughly the part put some of my anxiety about getting back on a horse and riding into the unknown to rest.

Cy was dressed much like he had been yesterday, faded jeans, and boots that looked like they belonged on a motorcycle, not a horse. He had on another black T-shirt, but today it was hidden underneath a heavy flannel shirt that was buttoned half-way up his chest. His face was covered in a sprinkle of salt and pepper stubble that made me wonder if I was totally off in thinking he was only in his early thirties. He didn't look like he was old enough to have so much silver in his facial hair, not that it detracted from his appeal or blatant masculinity, in any way. In fact, if it was possible, the scruff made him look even more rugged and roughly handsome. I wanted to laugh when I noticed he had product in his hair, even though daybreak was still pink in the sky. I still didn't think one single thing about him appeared cowboy-like. He looked good, there was no question about it, but he didn't look like a man who knew his way around a horse or around a treacherous backcountry trail. There was simply something too urbane about him for me to ever buy Cyrus Warner as a born and bred country boy.

"I'll get this stuff packed for you. Em, we picked the buckskin quarter horse for you." His lips twitched and his eyebrows danced upward under the hat when he looked at me and pointed to the only other horse that didn't have a human clamoring all over it. "Cy picked out the speckled Appaloosa for you, Leo."

The horse was stunning, all black with white and silver spots across his face and hind quarters. His mane was shiny midnight except by his ears, where it was sterling silver. I didn't miss the fact that the beautiful beast was oddly reminiscent of the man who decided we were a perfect match for the week. I walked over to the animal and extended my fingers so the soft end of his nose could brush against them. I gave Lane a questioning look and tilted my head to the side as the big animal nuzzled into me.

"Do I want to know why your brother picked this horse out for me? I mean, he doesn't even go on these trips usually, so how would he know which horse is right for a particular rider?" I was being argumentative for no reason and I knew it. It wasn't like I had a choice in the matter.

Lane pushed the brim of his hat back with the tip of his finger and gave me a pointed look. "You think you know, but you don't. Cy knows more about the horses and livestock on this property than either Sutton or I could ever dream of." He inclined his head toward the horse that was nudging my hand impatiently with his nose looking for a treat I didn't have. "In fact, Boss here was one of the first horses Cy bought and trained specifically for trail riding. They go way back. When we were growing up, it was my dad who had Cy on the range and tending to the ranch day in and day out. My brother sits in an office now but that's because someone has to and neither me nor Sutton have the patience for it. I hate paperwork and Sutton has other things occupying his time. No one ever wanted to be in charge when Dad got sick, but Cy stepped up because that's what he's always done. If he thinks you and Boss here are a good fit for the trail, then you guys will be a match made in heaven. Do you ever trust anyone or take anything at face value, Leo?"

His question stung and I realized Cy wasn't the only Warner who was alarmingly perceptive. I shrugged and smiled as the horse puffed out a breath of air against my hand. "I took someone at face value once. It didn't work out so well for me." I was never going to let it be that easy to get to my secret, soft center again.

Lane made a noise low in his throat and took a step away from where I was silently berating myself for being such a coward when I was younger. Sometimes it really sucked to run away from the things that scared you and could hurt you. I would much rather be the type of woman who stood her ground and faced that fear head on. But so far, history had proven I was much more likely to beat a hasty retreat when threatened.

"Everyone mount up. We're gonna circle the corral for a few minutes to make sure everyone can ride in a group and to make sure everyone can handle basic control of their horse." Cy's voice seemed even raspier and rougher early in the morning and he didn't appear to be amused by the crushing teenager, who was whining and grumbling that her stirrups weren't the right length. Begrudgingly, he fiddled with the buckles and leather until she declared things a perfect fit. Someone needed to tell her that there was subtlety in the art of flirting, that when you tried to bash the object of your affection over the head with your feelings, it missed the point and only left the other person with nothing more than a splitting headache. Again, I was annoyed that the girl's mother seemed oblivious to her child's inappropriate advances toward a much older man. I knew that if it continued, I was going to have to break my promise that I would play nice with others and lay down some hard truths at the girl's expensively booted feet. Honestly, I wouldn't be able to stop myself. Someone had to save the poor girl from herself, and maybe I wanted to save Cy from having to be the bad guy as well. Something told me he was comfortable in that role. Even if it wasn't one he necessarily wanted to play.

Left alone with Boss, I muttered nonsense words to him and checked the cinch on the saddle and the fit of the bridle. They were habits long unused but my hands skimmed over his soft, silver and black body like the big animal was an old friend. The gestures and the memories that came back from before I was afraid and from when I was more willing to take risks made me smile. It was nice to remember a time when I didn't feel broken down and betrayed. I sighed and stiffened involuntarily when a pair of black boots—that were most definitely not cowboy boots—stopped on the other side of the horse. Cy's big hand landed on the horse's head between his twitching ears and the animal let out a nicker of greeting. The beast recognized the man and so did my stupid, out of control libido.

My breath hitched a little.

My skin felt like it tightened all across my body.

His rough palm grazed the back of my hand making my skin pebble in response as my spine tightened. It was like my subconscious was readying for battle or for bed.

My nipples pulled tight under the layers of clothing I wore, and places I thought would never tingle again more than tingled when my gaze locked with his storm-colored one over the polished leather of the saddle. Those tingling places pulsed deep and hard. They also fluttered in a way that no man had ever made them flutter before, and that made me blush. I felt heat work up my neck and into my cheeks. I pulled my eyes away from his unwavering and far too penetrating ones.

"He's a beautiful horse." My voice sounded like it did when I woke up in the morning next to someone I'd spent the night naked and wrapped around. Cy had that same effect on me, without any of the practiced moves or easy words other men used to arouse and seduce. If nothing more than his deep voice and steely eyes could make my body respond so fully and so effortlessly, I didn't even want to imagine what the man could do if he actually put his mind toward being charming and getting a heated response.

"Boss is a good mount. He's rock steady, won't spook, and should give you an easy ride. He's stubborn, though, so you need to stay on top of him. He wants to go his own way and he doesn't like to stay in line with the other horses." He sounded like he was proud of that fact.

I couldn't hold back a little snort of amusement that had his dark eyebrows lifting up. It sounded like the big Appaloosa didn't just have similar coloring to the man across from me. It sounded like they had similar temperament, as well. "I'll keep that in mind. I'm good at staying on top of things that are a handful." I made it clear I also wasn't referring to just the horse. Because I said it loud enough that anyone and everyone could hear it, I hoped he knew I meant it.

Cy narrowed his eyes at me and patted the horse on the side of his neck. "Hop up and I'll fix your stirrups, too. They probably need to be adjusted."

It was my turn to lift my eyebrows. "I can get them myself. Like I mentioned last night, I used to ride. I know my way around a horse and the tack fairly well."

His eyes narrowed even more and he stepped back so he could cross his arms over his flannel-covered chest. I tried not to ogle the way the motion pulled the checkered material tightly across thick biceps and his broad chest. Cy was a visual treat for sure, but the look on his face as we stared at each other over the back of the horse was anything but sweet and friendly.

"You might know your way around a horse but you and your friend were also the last to show up. You're holding the entire production up by arguing with me, which means everyone is waiting on you, Sunshine. Get that cute ass in the saddle and let me help you with your fucking stirrups."

Instead of thinking about the fact I really liked that he thought my ass was cute, I put a hand on the saddle horn, and one on the center of the saddle, and hoisted a leg into the stirrup hanging in front of me. I took a deep breath, told myself I could literally get back on the horse, and hefted myself up into the curve of the saddle. Boss whinnied and moved sideways toward Cy, which had my heart rate speeding up and a flashback of panic roaring to life inside of me. I grabbed for the reins and put a shaking hand on the horse's glossy mane while whispering "Whoa, boy," as softly and as calmly as I could.

My nervousness was quickly replaced by a different kind of nerve jangling, breath- stealing awareness as Cy's hand curled around my calf. He bent his head down and fiddled with the straps and buckles that would adjust the length of the stirrup. I had boots and jeans on but I felt the imprint of every single one of his fingers where they pressed into my leg. Once he that the fit right, he guided my foot where it belonged on the side of the horse but not before those fingers tightened and then brushed their way all the way up the curve of my leg to the back of my knee. I gasped and shot him a wide-eyed look that made him smirk up at me knowingly. The horse snorted and shifted his big body under me. I was sure he could feel the heat and tension that was pinging and bouncing between his rider and the man who had trained him.

I watched him carefully as he made his way to the other side to repeat the process, and this time when he curled his fingers around my leg, I asked, "Don't you have your hands full with another redhead? Do you collect us and play with whichever one isn't boring you at the moment?" When I was scared and uncertain, I could be vicious. I had a lot of weapons at my disposal but my razor-sharp tongue was often the one I leaned on the most. I was lashing out because I wanted him to be as unsettled and off center as he made me. I thought throwing the woman he was so gentle with, the one who he showed such easy affection to, would be a good diversion. It wasn't. The man saw right through me like I was made of glass.

My foot was shoved in the stirrup and he stepped back with a scowl. "What nonsense are you going on about now, woman?"

I met him scowl for scowl and tilted my head in the direction of the beautiful wooden home that housed the even more beautiful woman from the night before. "Brynn. She's gorgeous and she can make a mean stack of pancakes. Do you think she would approve of you telling me I have a cute ass and all the fondling you seem so inclined towards in the morning?" I felt my mouth tighten and my chin lift defiantly. "I'm not interested in being a convenient distraction while you're stuck with us until your brother shows up. Whatever games you're playing to keep yourself amused, stop it right now."

His lips twitched, and when he opened his mouth I was positive he was going to tell me I had the wrong idea about everything, that Brynn was their cousin or half-sister or something else entirely that would explain the light and gentle way he was with her. What I got was a sexy half-grin that made those fluttering places inside me start to throb.

His voice was pitched low enough that I was the only one who could hear his gravelly growl. "Oh, you're one hell of a distraction, Leo, and there isn't a goddamn thing about it that is even slightly convenient. I don't play . . . games or anything else. I'm all business, just ask my brothers." He tapped the horse I was perched on with his palm. Boss started to move just like the other horses everyone else was mounted on were doing. "Remember to keep a firm hold on him. He'll be good to you but you need to show him who's boss."

I cut him a look over my shoulder as the horse started a slow trot around the corral. He was grinning at me. The flash of his teeth against that dark scruff across his jaw made him look like the bad guy who had eliminated the hero and knew he was going to get away with every wicked thing he could think of. There was knowing in that smile. There was taunting and provocation in it. There was satisfaction and intent in that smile, and it made my skin pebble up in reaction, and had desire running thick and free through my veins.

He was right. There was absolutely nothing convenient about any of this, but that didn't stop me from watching him as he moved to a very pretty white and gray horse. He swung himself up in the saddle like he had been doing so since the day he was born. Even mounted on the horse and handling the animal like it was second nature, he still didn't look like any kind of cowboy I had ever imagined . . . he looked so much better.

CHAPTER 5

Not Quite Easy Rider

GETTING BACK ON THE HORSE was harder on my body than I realized it was going to be.

Even back when I rode pretty much every day after school, I had never spent more than a couple of hours in a saddle and that was in a perfectly maintained corral, in an arena that was made for the animals to practice jumping and cutting around barrels. I'd never ridden a trail or been on one of the big animals as they traversed uneven terrain, fighting to find their footing, as the ground shifted from open range to hilly backcountry.

The brothers' vast property was impressive and seemed endless when we started our journey just as the sun was fully taking its place over the mountains in the distance. Fenced in fields of green that housed bored-looking cattle and adorable little creeks and ponds made up the first part of our morning ride, which I quickly figured out was the easy part of the trip. By early afternoon, the ride shifted to a narrow trail that cut through a dense thicket of trees and started to sharply incline. Boss was sure of foot and reluctantly stayed in line where we lumbered along between Emrys and the Upper East Side mother. He pulled against my hold on the reins whenever he had to step over something on the trail or whenever the horse in front of us sped up. He did not like to follow and I couldn't say I blamed him. I was sick of staring at the unflappable woman in front of me, with her perfect posture and her lack of any kind of discomfort. She should strive to have as much control of her marriage and her husband as she did over her horse. I was sweaty from the midday sun and already knew I was going to be aching and saddle sore as soon as I got down from Boss's back. I was also irritated that Meghan had let her too young daughter maneuver her way up to the front of the line so that she was riding right behind Cy and the pack mules he was guiding with a steady hand. The girl hadn't stopped peppering him with questions since we took off.

The teen's voice was high and clear, so I had no problem hearing her over the thump of the horses' feet and the occasional snort and whinnies they let out. Cy's gruff voice was too low and rumbled too deep for me to hear his responses, which drove me nuts because the determined young woman had no qualms about asking him if he had a girlfriend. I wanted to know the answer to that particular question as well. The man didn't wear a wedding ring and shared his home with a knockout woman who seemed very nice and could really, really cook. If he was playing house with a woman like the beautiful Brynn, there was no way in hell he should be even mildly attracted to someone like me. Regardless of how cute my ass was.

To distract myself from the conversation happening ahead of me, I turned my attention back to the girl's mother and decided it wouldn't hurt anything to give her a little push in the direction of caring that her kid was chasing after a man who was old enough to be her father.

"You seem pretty comfortable on that horse. You must ride a lot." The woman turned and looked at me over her shoulder and immediately her mouth pulled into a frown as she looked past me. I turned to look over my own shoulder and rolled my eyes when I noticed that the woman's husband had worked his way up so that he was riding right next to Em, even though the trail was way too narrow to be riding side by side. Emrys had on dark sunglasses, so I couldn't catch her eye but her mouth was twisted into a tight line and her shoulders were stiff. I could tell she was annoyed by the attention and the man's lack of concern for his or her safety, since he didn't seem to have the best control over the horse he rode.

Meghan snapped her attention back to me, and I watched as whatever lingering hope she had that this trip would bring her and her family closer together fall from her face. It was what defeat looked like and it made my heart hurt for her.

"I actually grew up in a place very similar to the ranch the brothers run. My dad was a cattleman and my mother ran a small shop in the town we lived in up in Montana." A wry grin twisted her mouth and she looked from me back to her husband. "I hated all of it. I hated the horses and the cows. I hated that my high school only had a hundred kids, at most. I couldn't wait to leave. I graduated and headed to New York and never looked back. I wanted to live a better, more glamorous life than I could have back home. I met Marcus in college and he made that happen for me."

Boss made a noise underneath me and I reached down to pat the side of his neck. I could have sworn he leaned in to my touch and that made me smile softly, even though the animal couldn't see me.

"Your kids seem pretty comfortable around horses, as well. You must have made sure they were in touch with a little bit of where you came from." She was an easy read. She wanted more but when she got it she realized it wasn't ever going to be enough to fill up that empty place inside of her. She was the kind of consumer my clients would kill for. Easily swayed with tons of disposable income lying around. She shopped for the small thrill it gave her because nothing else in her life satisfied her.

She shook her perfectly coiffed head and let out a sigh. "No. Marcus insisted the kids go to an exclusive boarding school in Massachusetts. They learned to ride there. He wasn't pleased when I made him take time off this summer for this trip." Again, her gaze slid to where her husband was trying, very unsuccessfully, to impress and amaze my best friend.

"If you don't get to see your kids much, I'm surprised you aren't keeping them closer. Don't you want as much time with them as possible before they go back to school?" I mean my mother wouldn't want that but I figured most normal mothers would. As an adult, one with a new appreciation for the people who had always loved me and had been there for me even when I wasn't the easiest person to be around, I wanted to take back all of the time I had wasted chasing after love I would never get. I wanted to invest more in the relationships that mattered. I'd spent a lot of time watching where I stepped and I could see now how that dance had kept me just outside of reach of the people who wanted to hold me close.

The woman gave me a startled look over her shoulder and turned her attention toward the front of the line. Her daughter was still rambling on to Cy and her son was sitting sullen and unenthused on a pretty, tan Tennessee Walker in front of Lane.

I cleared my throat a little, inclining my chin toward the ardent teenager. "She should be bonding with you and her brother, not chasing after him. He's too old for her, and honestly, he doesn't seem like the type who will be careful with those kinds of tender feelings. She's going to end up hurt and embarrassed. This trip is going to be nothing more than a bad memory for her if that happens."

The woman narrowed her eyes at me and once again looked

over me toward her husband. Her mouth tightened and her already stiff shoulders got even more rigid and taut. "Evan wanted to spend the summer in Saint Thomas with some of her friends and Ethan wanted to go to a baseball camp in the Poconos. Neither one of them are thrilled to be here. Evan has been acting out more and more lately. They are both growing up so fast and I feel like I'm missing their entire lives."

I shifted in the saddle and bit back a groan as the back of my thighs burned. My ass was going to be a thousand shades of purple and blue by the time I climbed off this horse and there wasn't a single place to get a massage within a thousand-mile radius.

"You know the reason she's focused on a guy old enough to be her dad is because of what is going on with her own father, right? You might think the tension between the two of you and the way his eyes wander is harmless, but it isn't. Kids know when one or both of their parents aren't happy, and if you only see your kids occasionally, then all they know when they see their family together is that tension. It bleeds onto them. Kids are far more perceptive than people give them credit for." I always knew my mom didn't want me, no matter how many times my grandparents tried to convince me that she simply wasn't ready for me. I might've bought into that bullshit if the woman had bothered to give any inclination that she was interested in how I was doing once I was old enough not to need her anymore. She didn't care and she never had. Meghan cared, but about the wrong person. She needed to stop trying to salvage a marriage that clearly meant more to her than it did to her husband. There was still time for her to put all her focus on her kids before they were old enough to make their way in the world without her.

She made a noise in her throat and turned back around in her saddle. She clicked her tongue and pulled her horse up next to Lane, who was ahead of her. After a few words, Lane dropped back and the woman moved her ride up until she was between her kids. I heard the daughter snap something at her but the barrage of questions being aimed at Cy's back stopped. He cranked his head around and pinned me with a look that made my belly warm and my heart thud heavily.

I turned to look at Lane as he slowed down until we were side by side on the narrow trail. Boss made a noise and danced to the side a little bit as Lane's horse got close to his side. Old fear prickled at my skin as my hands tightened on the reins and my knees locked tighter on the animal's muscular sides.

"If this horse throws me off and I end up with a broken neck because you're riding so close, I'm going to sue the shit out of you, Warner." My voice was a little shaky.

"Boss won't throw you. He might take off down the side of the mountain like a bat out of hell, but he won't buck you off. All you gotta do is hold on tight and you'll be all right." That smile that never seemed to dull or falter flashed across his handsome face. "And you can't sue. You signed the liability waiver."

I swore at him under my breath and pointed behind me. Making sure to keep my voice extra low so that it wouldn't carry through the silence around, I told him, "Stop bugging me and go save Emrys from the creep. She could use a rescue."

Lane shot a glance in the direction I was pointing, letting out a sigh that moved his broad chest up and down. "That's going to be a problem."

"Maybe the wife will nip it in the bud." I didn't think she had it in her, but there was no telling what all this fresh air and solitude could do to a person. It was hard to see anything other than the mess the husband was making of his family and their vacation when it was just the eight of us and the forest surrounding us. There were no packed schedules, hurried meetings, showings across town, personal assistants, and nights at the gym for him to hide behind. His sleazy behavior was on full display under the pressing sunshine, beneath the call of the birds, and the chatter of the squirrels in the trees.

"Maybe. She doesn't seem overly concerned that her kid is all but asking my brother to put a baby in her. Cy isn't very patient and this is exactly why he never wants to come on the trail. He isn't a people person." Lane's voice wasn't as quiet as mine so I was sure everyone in front of and behind us heard his sharply worded statement.

I laughed nervously, embarrassed for Evan but admittedly amused by the younger Warner's astute observation. Cy whipped his head around again. This time those slate-colored eyes narrowed when he noticed how close his little brother was to me. I smiled back at him and tried to make my expression look as innocent as possible. The wide eyes and grin faded quickly when the trail took a sharp turn that led us downhill, which had Boss picking up speed and my backside thumping even more solidly against the leather beneath it.

Lane laughed at my groan. "You need to move with the horse. Stand up higher in the stirrups and grip him with your knees. It'll save the wear and tear on that cute ass."

I scowled at him but took his advice and moved in the saddle so that my stance mirrored his own. "Did you hear Cy tell me that this morning?"

"Nope. But I'm not surprised he mentioned it. You do have a nice ass and he's always had a thing for redheads." His brow furrowed, like he was remembering a particular redhead from the past he wasn't very fond of. "He tends to speak his mind even when it's better that he doesn't."

"He likes redheads, like Brynn?" I asked the question because I wanted to know and because I was too scared to ask the brother who should be answering it. Not that I thought Cy would give me a straight answer. He seemed to enjoy yanking my chain in order to get me riled up. He also wouldn't love the fact that his younger brother seemed perfectly inclined to share personal details with me, and had been since that first meeting when he told me there was more to his older brother and his bad attitude than meets the eye.

Lane ran his hand over his jaw and lifted one of his shoulders in a shrug. When he spoke, his voice didn't have any of the easy charm and happy-go-lucky affability in it that I had come to expect from him during our short acquaintance. In fact, there was a thread of something sharp and pointy in his tone that reminded me a lot of the way I sounded when I had found out that not only was Chris not who he seemed to be, but who I was when I was with him was also a lie. Those pointy things were painful, raw, and opened places for hurt to pour out from.

"Brynn is family. We love her and she loves us. She's beautiful and just happens to be a redhead, but she isn't Cy's. She isn't any of ours." There was something there that made me think the youngest Warner brother would change that if he could. He looked at me with shrewd perception and masculine knowing shining out of his gunmetal-colored eyes. "I don't talk about my brothers' private lives but Cy is stubborn and he is always his own worst enemy. He wouldn't say anything about Brynn even while he's looking at you like you're the first drop of rain to hit after years of a drought."

I frowned at that smartly worded revelation and pulled my gaze away from his. "I'm not interested in giving up whatever it is your brother might want from me." Even though I selfishly wanted to know everything there was to know about the enigmatic man who fascinated me.

Lane laughed under his breath and reached up to settle his hat more fully on his head. This time he made sure his voice was soft, practically whispering as he muttered under his breath, "You're a smart woman, Leo. You know what he wants and you know that he's not going to stop until he gets it. Gotta admit, it's gonna tickle me pink watching you try and outmaneuver him for the next few days. Cy's really good at getting his way."

My eyebrows dipped down to a point over the bridge of my nose. It was hard to admit the truth out loud, which was part of the reason I had been so sullen and miserable lately, but I liked Lane and I liked the open and relaxed way he had about him. Before I could stop them, the words that had been haunting me for the last few months tumbled out, sounding just as sharp and pointy as his had a moment ago. "I recently got out of a relationship with a man who was also really good at getting his own way." I gulped and fought back the surge of foul-tasting regret and choking recrimination that worked its way up my throat. "Getting his way meant that he fucked me and then went home to a wife and his kids in the suburbs that I knew nothing about. It went on for six months. I didn't want to date him when he first showed interest me. I didn't want to care about him, but he out maneuvered me and all I got when I finally figured out I was being played was enough embarrassment to drown in and so much guilt that it nearly suffocated me."

"Ouch." Lane's quietly murmured word and the sympathy clear on his face had my heart pressing tightly against the barbed wire I had wrapped around it. "That sucks, but sometimes the heart just chooses wrong. All you can do is wait for it to figure that out and hope it picks better the next time around."

I gave him a look that spoke volumes about what I thought about that. "You can absolutely choose who you care about. If you're smart about it." Which I intended to be from here on out. I would let my brain lead and my irresponsible, reckless heart could take a backseat. The poor thing had been kicked around so much there was no wonder it wasn't functioning the way it was supposed to.

He shook his head at me and started to pull his horse back so that he was no longer next to me. "You're wrong, Leo. Love isn't logical or reasonable. Our hearts make no sense."

I watched him with narrow eyes as he dropped back and forced the dismissive dad to do the same thing and leave Emrys's side. She gave the youngest Warner a relieved smile and nudged her horse so that she was closer to me, as Lane forced the middle-aged philanderer back in line so he was riding in front of the two other men who hadn't said a word to any of us or to each other all morning long.

"Thank you, Commander Cockblock. For the last half an hour I've been envisioning kicking him off his horse. If I had to listen to his catalogue of his investments any longer, I was going to throw myself off the side of the mountain." She sounded disgruntled and properly disgusted. "I can't believe he was hitting on me right in front of his wife and kids. The man has no shame."

I nodded in agreement. "And no class."

She muttered a dirty word under her breath as I swatted at a mosquito that landed on the side of my neck. The hotter it got, the more the bugs decided I was a feast and I hadn't had enough time this morning to slather myself in bug spray. I was going to have to add a coat to all my visible skin when we finally stopped for lunch at midday. The brochure said we would picnic in a scenic valley that the trail led through, surrounded by wildflowers and that was often used as a resting place for much of the region's wildlife. I didn't care about wildflowers or wildlife, but I did want a chance to stretch out my sore muscles and the opportunity to eat some more of Brynn's amazing food. Lunch today was the last meal that we were supposed to get without working for it. Aside from granola for breakfast and beef jerky in the case of emergency, we were really supposed to fend for ourselves for the duration of our time on the trail. It made me wish I had paid closer attention when I agreed to fly to Wyoming. I had only smuggled a jar of peanut butter into my bag just in case. I'd never caught a fish in my life and I got snippy and short tempered . . . well, snippier and even quicker to blow a fuse than normal when I was hungry.

"The wannabe Donald Trump isn't the only one throwing out some game. I saw the way Cy grabbed your leg this morning. You two are throwing off enough sparks that I'm slightly worried you're going to ignite a forest fire around us." I shushed her and looked around with wide eyes hoping no one else was paying that much attention to us. Luckily Cy was talking to Meghan and the kids and Lane had the dad engaged in a low hum of conversation. The two oddly silent men hung at the way back of the pack, and every time I'd caught sight of them throughout the day, they'd had their heads bent together like they were engaged in serious conversation.

Sighing, I let my words exit on the same breath, keeping them as quiet as I could. "Gotta have fuel to start a fire and for it to burn. I'm all tapped out, Em. I don't have anything left to go up in flames, not even a tiny bit of kindling left inside of me. I was burned once and it won't happen again."

She made a noise low in her throat that had her horse prancing a little closer to the edge of the trail than I was comfortable with. I watched, with a stalled breath, until she pulled the animal back in line and only exhaled once she seemed to have total control again.

"You're not only ridiculous but you're also oblivious. There was no spark with Chris. There was no fire and definitely no heat. He spoon fed you his perfectly crafted persona, knowing you wouldn't fall for someone that lit you up and pushed all your buttons. He knew you wouldn't jump into bed and let anyone in your life that consumed you and forced you to put them first. You're full of things that are dry and brittle and you have been since you were old enough to figure out that your mom didn't want you. The right guy isn't going to just make you burn, he's going to scorch all that useless shit inside of you, turning it into nothing but ash, once and for all."

My shoulders stiffened and I pulled my gaze away from her. "You think an ill-fated vacation fling with a guy, who I know nothing about and who definitely isn't an actual cowboy, will fix everything that's wrong with me, fix everything that has been wrong with me from the start?" I couldn't keep my incredulousness or how absurd that idea sounded to me out of my tone.

"Nothing is wrong with you, Leo. Nothing has ever been wrong with you, but I've known you a very long time and I know how reluctant you are to take any kind of risk. You like things predictable and staid. That isn't any way to live, because no matter how hard you try you can't control everything. Look at the situation with Chris. You let him in because he was all the unassuming and simple things you told yourself you wanted. Maybe the sexy, not quite a cowboy is exactly the kind of outrageous and unexpected experience you need so you can see not all risks will end up with you getting hurt. Then maybe you'll realize that even if you do get injured, sometimes the experience on the way to the pain was worth suffering through. I see you on that horse, Leo; we both know you shouldn't have given riding up just because you got thrown one time. You're a natural."

The discomfort that came from sitting in the saddle too long definitely didn't take away from the fact I really did enjoy being mounted back up. I knew my granddad would be so proud of me for eventually conquering my fear. A pang of regret stabbed into me that I was too late to show him that I could overcome the fear that always held me back. He had passed away a few years ago after a valiant fight with a heart that just wouldn't work right anymore. He'd passed peacefully in his sleep. After my grandmother got their affairs in order, she had surprised both me and my mother by packing up her entire house in Nor Cal and moving it all to a swanky retirement community in Florida. I never thought of my grandparents as elderly or old, but with granddad gone, she insisted the house and its upkeep was too much. She'd outright laughed in my face when I offered to move back to help her out so she didn't have move all the way across the country from me. She told me it was her job to raise me well enough that I could live out in the world on my own, and she wasn't interested in going backwards or reversing roles where it was my turn to take care of her. She told me she fully intended to have a life on her own terms and that meant being around people her own age and out of the middle of the constant tug of war between me and my mother. She loved us both (I liked to think she loved me more) and that was much easier for her to do with some space between all of us.

I'd promised to visit as often as I could. So far, I'd been to see her twice. The last time was after I broke things off with Chris and knew I needed to get out of the city so I didn't do something I'd regret, like show up at his house in the 'burbs, pulling the curtain off his double life and breaking his family apart in the process. It might have made me feel better, but I knew what it was like to be a child with a parent who was nothing more than a stranger. I didn't want to be responsible for putting Chris's kids in that situation. So far, my mother had yet to get on a plane and I don't think my grandmother was at all surprised. I know I wasn't.

Lost in thought, I was glad Boss was paying attention to the horse in front of me as he pulled his head back and came to a halt. I didn't even notice that the trail had dumped us into the center of a postcard. The mountains rose in the background, tall and majestic, as a riot of colorful flowers blanketed the ground under a sky that seemed bluer than any blue I had ever seen before in my life. There was a brook that was actually babbling, and like the brothers had purposely set the scene so that their guests wouldn't be disappointed, a doe lifted her head from the water where she was drinking as we all came to a stop. I could have sworn she looked right at me before she startled and leapt over the water, disappearing back into the trees. I didn't think places like this actually existed outside of landscape calendars at mall kiosks and screen savers on the computer.

Lane pulled out of his place in the lineup and rode up next to Cy. The brothers exchanged some words and Lane took the leads attached to the mules and grabbed the bridle on Cy's horse as he started toward the water.

Cy put his hands on his hips and told us, "You can all hop off the horses. Take them over to Lane. He'll take care of them while you all eat lunch. Remember, it's the last prepared meal, so what you catch here in the brook or later on tonight by the river is what's going to be for dinner."

"Can you help me down?" Evan's voice had a practiced whine to it and I couldn't help an eye roll as I worked myself out of the saddle.

I didn't hear Cy's response. My yelp of surprise as blood rushed to cramped muscles and hit sore places I didn't know could hurt so badly, drowned out everything. My knees almost buckled and I almost hit the ground but hard hands caught me around the waist and pulled me back into an even harder chest. He smelled like sunshine and man, without even a hint of horse or sticky bug spray. He felt solid and real behind me, like someone built to bear his fair share of burdens and never break under the weight of the responsibility.

"I have Tiger Balm in one of the packs. I'll dig it out for you, but it stinks like hell and it's greasy as fuck. You won't be able to wash it off until we hit the camp the day after next, but it will help with your muscles being saddle sore."

I put a hand over his where it rested against the soft curve of my belly and couldn't ignore that where he touched me did indeed get warm, then hot, then something hotter than hot. Through my clothes, his touch burned and smoldered against my skin. He was made of fire and Emrys was right, I was made up of things that wanted to go up in flames whenever he got close to me.

I sucked in a breath through my teeth and tried to straighten up. It involved a lot of grumbling and swearing, but eventually, my knees stopped shaking and my glutes quit screaming at me. Cy held me up throughout the ordeal while Emrys watched with a smirk and the crushing teenager watched with murder in her eyes. I kept waiting for a snide remark or something mean to come out of Cy's mouth. After all, I had started off questioning his authenticity. It was clear he could sit on his big steed all day without an ounce of discomfort, whereas I was a hot mess and barely able to stand. He didn't say a word, just waited until I was back in control of my jelly-like limbs and held me up.

I turned around in his hold so we were face to face and told myself not to lean in to him. He might be all kinds of fire and flame but I wasn't going to let myself melt. I put a hand in the center of his rock hard chest and pushed a little so that he got the hint and took a step backwards, letting me go as he went.

"I've got it. Thanks."

He dipped his chin down and then leaned closer to me so that his lips were almost touching my ear. His breath was warm but it made me shiver as he told me, "If you need help getting the ointment on the hard to reach places, let me know."

I shivered at the suggestion and at the image his words brought to mind. I cleared my throat so I could get a response out. "I think I'll be able to reach."

"Good, because you handle it yourself or you ask me, but you do not ask my little brother. He flashes that smile of his and women fall at his feet, but he is not for you and you are not for him."

I stiffened and planted my hands on my hips, fully prepared to tell him he could take a long ride down a short trail, that he didn't get to decide who was for me or who I was for because he didn't know a damn thing about me. All my righteous feminist indignation prickled and riled up, ready to flay him in half with barbed words. However, what came out of my mouth was, "At least Lane knows how to smile, even if he uses it to make women fall."

Cy's raven-colored brows shot upward and his very unsmiling mouth twitched at the corners. "I can smile."

I huffed, "When?"

He bent close again and my whole body wanted to press into his. "I smile when something makes me happy."

"What makes you happy?" I couldn't picture him as the jovial, cheery type to save my life, but I really was curious about what would make that stony expression he always wore turn into something more approachable. A smile from him would mean heartbreak and devastation. I wouldn't just melt, I would dissolve into nothing more than particles that were made up of desire and need for this man and this man alone.

"Behave and you'll find out soon enough. Go take care of Boss so he can keep on taking care of you."

He walked over to Em and all I could think was that whatever it was that made a man like him smile was bound to be nothing but trouble for the woman he was smiling at.

CHAPTER 6

Not So Alone

MRYS WASN'T LYING ABOUT KNOWING how to fish, which was a good thing, because I didn't have the patience that it took to bait the hook, cast, and recast for hours upon hours in order to secure dinner. I was bored out of my mind after the first fifteen minutes. But she declared that if she was going to feed both of us then it was going to be my job to clean the catch. I almost threw up when I watched her do the first fish. However, when my reaction made not only the kids, but also the Warner brothers, and the two silent men laugh at me, I sucked it up and managed to power through the next few slimy, fishy executions without making a mess of it. Em told me that she was proud of me and oddly enough, I was proud of myself as well because that was the kind of thing I would typically walk away from. I hated not knowing what I was doing and I was paranoid about doing things wrong.

Ethan, who complained the entire time that he would rather be playing Xbox, also managed to pull in quite a haul. It didn't go unnoticed by any of the adults in our group that it was Lane who congratulated him and told him job well done rather than his father.

With enough provisions secured for dinner, Cy declared it was time to get back on the horses and ride to the riverside clearing where we were bunking down for the night and setting up camp. Once there, I begrudgingly took the small glass jar of ointment he offered me and found a secluded spot where I could work my jeans down around my hips so I could work the potent salve into my skin. He didn't lie. It smelled to high heaven and it made my skin slippery and slick under the denim. Emrys wrinkled her nose at me when I made my way back to the horses. Boss made a noise that I swore was one of disgust when I went to climb up onto his back. You could smell me coming from a mile away. The situation wasn't going to be helped at all when the smoke from the campfire that night and the bug spray I slathered all over myself was added to the mix.

After taking care of the animals and making dinner, that was followed by a surprise dessert of campfire s'mores that Lane seemed to pull out of nowhere. I was so tired I could barely see straight. Em and I went to crawl into the tiny pop-up tent that we were to share for the week, even though everyone else was still up and gathered around the campfire chit chatting, everyone except for Cy. The big man had wandered off about the time Lane busted out the surprise sweets and hadn't come back to camp by the time I was ready to call it a night. I was pretty sure his disappearing act was prompted by the fact Evan was stuck to his side like a blood-sucking tick. It was his way of spurning her advances without being outright rude. Lane was right, his older brother really wasn't much of a people person.

"You stink." Emrys's sleepy voice rolled over me as I groaned and tried to shift on the barely-there mat that was supposed to cushion my backside from the unforgiving ground I was stretched out on.

I did stink. But the balm had helped relax the sore muscles

in my legs, and the only way I was going to be able to ride the following day was if I kept smearing it all over myself.

"I know, but you were the one who wanted an adventure in the great outdoors. This is what I smell like when I don't get to shower every day."

She laughed lightly and shifted next to me. "I haven't showered either and I don't smell as bad as you."

I laughed until I was gasping and turned my head to look at her. She had her eyes closed and somehow still managed to look as fresh and as perfect as she had when we rode out that morning. "That's because you aren't human. You're some kind of flawless extraterrestrial that makes the rest of us mere mortals look like dog chow in comparison."

She laughed again and turned her head to look at me so that we were staring at each other. Her dark eyes softened a little as she grinned at me. "I'm really glad you came with me, Leo."

I returned her grin and sighed as I stretched out, making my joints pop and my muscles scream in protest. "Even though you have to smell me all night?"

"Even then. You're a good friend, and I've missed you." Her voice got quiet and the affection in it pushed some of those bricks in my newly fortified wall out of place. She always managed to find her way in. She let out a whispery sigh and then her hand curled around mine in the dark. "Do you remember the guy with the Harley from freshman year who was screwing my roommate? The one I walked in on because they were fucking in *my* bed because it was closer than hers?"

I did remember that. She'd been devastated and almost flunked her first year of college because she was heartbroken and never wanted to go back to her dorm room, which led to her crashing with me more nights than not and solidifying our friendship for the years that followed.

"Or what about the artist from Australia, when I was twenty-one? Do you remember him, with his man bun and constantly bare feet? He wanted to get married so he could stay in the country and when I turned him down, he stole my credit card information and disappeared. It took two years to get my credit fixed and almost that long to get all the paint he spilled on my hardwood floors stripped off so I could re-stain them."

I squeezed her hand and nodded into the darkness. "I remember. Most of the time he smelled worse than I do right now."

That made both of us laugh and I could feel her looking at me from her side of the tent. "You told me to stay away from both those guys, Leo, and a few others along the way. You never pretended to like them and you have always told me that I deserved better. I didn't listen to you. Not because I didn't trust you, but because there are some things we have to go through in order to know what better actually is. Chris gave you a hard lesson to learn, and you've always avoided those, so it hit you even harder than it would most. Now you know you deserve more than a man who will allow you work around him. You need a man who is impossible to move and takes up as much space as he possibly can in your life."

Immediately, Cy came to mind. He wasn't the kind of man you could ignore or overlook. There was no working around him, only facing him head-on, hoping he bent enough to let you get by. There was also running right up against all of that solid strength and unbendable power and hoping it didn't cause you to shatter when you hit it.

"Maybe we should listen to each other a little more carefully moving forward, Em. We could save each other a lot of heartache and wasted time." I let go of her hand, rolled over on my side, stacking my hands under my cheek, and closing my eyes. I wasn't very comfortable but I knew I would sleep like a rock as soon as she quit talking.

She shifted and her voice was full of suggestive humor when she muttered, "Well, if you're going to start listening to me now, then that means you need to take Mr. Broody and Badass for a ride while you have the opportunity."

I responded with a groan and tried to keep the image of what riding Cyrus Warner would actually be like out of my head. It was a futile effort. As sleep claimed me, it was the vision of a naked Cy, stretched out under me as I worked myself over his rock-hard body with a wanton abandon that I'd never had in my real sex life. It was his graphite-colored gaze, cloudy with passion, as he hovered over me that I was dreaming about when a loud *bang* and the sound of the rest of the camp scrambling to life woke me a few hours later. I shook Em's shoulder and clamored over her still sleeping form as I lurched for the opening of the tent to see what was going on.

The horses were nickering at each other, stamping their feet in annoyance as another loud bang echoed through the valley we were camped in. I pushed my completely unruly hair that had long since escaped the braid I foolishly thought would tame it, out of my face and looked around with wide eyes. Both Lane and Cy were stalking around the camp with flashlights bobbing, their faces set in flinty lines. The brothers were clearly aggravated as they attempted to search out the source of the noise in the darkness. The two men who didn't say much were also out of their tents looking at the thick woods that surrounded us. In fact, they were both fully dressed and didn't look like they had bothered to bed down for the night at all. The younger of the men even had a flashlight similar to the one Cy held in his hand. As he swept the trees with beam, he muttered, "That was gunfire."

"It could have been." Cy was frowning and didn't stop to say anything more as he made his way over to where the horses were clearly uneasy and unsettled from the loud noise.

The older man, the one called Grady, shook his head and crossed his arms over his chest as he gave Lane a hard look. "There was no maybe about it. That was gunfire. I served eight years overseas for this country and have been in the worst hell holes you can imagine. I know what gunfire sounds like and I know that shot was a lot closer than you probably want us to think it was. These mountains and this backcountry aren't quite as isolated as you made it seem."

Lane bristled, clearly not appreciating his brother's integrity and veracity being called into question. It was the first time I saw a little bit of his older brother in him, as his spine snapped straight and his usually smiling mouth pulled tight. He didn't do intimidating quite as well as Cy, but he was big enough and rough enough around the edges that the menace in both his face and body language was hard to miss.

"Isolated doesn't mean the same thing as deserted. Like I mentioned, some of this area is a national forest, so we can't control who uses it. That includes people who might be poaching game illegally off season, which they would be doing in the dark. It could also be vacationers camping close by who don't know we run tours through here and are blowing off steam by firing into the sky. Guns are commonplace in Wyoming. Just because you heard a shot doesn't necessarily mean there needs to be a cause for concern. There are a lot of possibilities, and whatever the situation may be, the safety of the guests in our care is always the number one priority." Lane gave his little speech firmly and confidently. It made me believe he really would give up everything to keep all of us safe. Lane looked more cowboy than his brothers, but it was his dedication and his stalwartness that really pushed him over the edge into being everything I ever wanted a cowboy to be in real life. He was the kind of man woman wrote romance novels about and built fantasies around.

Cy made his way back to where we were all huddled, sparing a quick glance at my bare legs since I hadn't bothered to pull my jeans on when I crawled out of the tent. He stopped by his brother's side and let his gaze wander around the tense circle we had all gathered in. "Probably just kids screwing around. This is the first day on the trail and we're still really close to the river. A lot of locals use it for weekend getaways in high season. Everyone, go back to bed and I'll walk a mile down river and a mile up river and see what I can find."

I let out a strangled little sound of alarm, and without thinking about what I was doing, reached out a hand and set it on his arm. The muscle felt like heated stone under my fingertips and I almost groaned when his skin shifted and flexed enticingly under the tips of my fingers. There was something about the sheer strength of him, the overwhelming command he exuded that was intoxicatingly attractive. Touching him wasn't smart or good for my resolve. Unfortunately, I wanted to put my hands all over him and I wanted to do it when he was far more naked than he was right now. I wanted to learn his entire, massive body through every sense I had and imprint it on my memory, so that I could forever keep those riotous and rebellious sensations only he seemed able to spark.

"You can't go traipsing through the woods and along the river in pitch-black darkness. What if a bear comes along, or what if you do stumble on some kids and spook them? If they are trigger happy, they might be twitchy enough to put one in you. And what if it *is* poachers? The last thing they're going to want is some guy poking his nose into what they're doing. It sounds dangerous. I'm not a fan of that plan at all."

His eyes landed to where I was holding onto him, and instead of moving my fingers from where they rested, I curled them in tighter so I was clutching him like he was my tether to the very earth under my feet. As if without him to ground me, I would fly off into nothing.

"You smell to high hell, woman." I balked at the rudeness and the blunt honesty in the face of my unwanted concern for his wellbeing. I also released my hold on him like the skin I was holding onto had suddenly grown thorns and barbs. I took a step back and crossed my arms over my chest.

"Fine. Go get eaten by a mountain lion or shot by some weekend warrior. See if I care. I'm going back to bed." I wanted to huff and puff with a flounce so it was obvious I was irritated with him, but none of the men were even paying attention to me.

Grady, the newly revealed former military man, was trying to convince Cy to take him with him as he explored the area around the river. Cy didn't seem overly enthused about the idea but he eventually acquiesced.

Lane was busy questioning Webb about why neither of them had been in their tents when the first shot fired off. He told him he watched them come down from the woods behind where we had set up camp.

I was figuring out the more that I watched the two silent, suspicious men that Webb was a better liar than Grady. Without pause or hint of embarrassment, he told Lane that he was looking for a spot to use the bathroom and he asked Grady to come with him as a lookout. Lane calmly explained that he and Cy had already gone over the safest and preferred places to take care of business while we were on the trail, and wandering into the woods wasn't one of those options. Webb simply shrugged and said flatly, "We're supposed to be working on our teamwork skills. Helping another man shit in the woods seems like a damn good team building exercise if you ask me." He walked away without further explanation, leaving Lane to turn to me with a questioning look on his face.

I shrugged my shoulders and pursed my lips into a tight grimace. "I haven't been the best at picking out the truth from fiction lately, but I would bet my yearly bonus that neither one of those guys is who they say they are."

"Something ain't right." Lane's voice was hard and sharp.

"There is something going on there we are not a part of for sure." I was fully aware that some of the puzzle pieces to this big picture were still in the box and not dumped out on the table waiting to be sorted through.

"Hard to hide anything that isn't real out here. Lies and make-believe can get you killed real quick in the backcountry." Lane sounded tired and there was a thread of worry in his tone. I nodded and moved to the entrance of the tent where Emrys had her head poking out and was watching me with sleepy eyes.

I stopped when he said my name. "And, Leo . . ." I turned to look at him over my shoulder and noticed his trademark grin locked firmly back in place on his ruggedly good-looking face. "You really do stink. Tell Em if she wants to bunk with me in my tent, I have room."

Considering he was so big on saying what he meant and standing behind his words, I had no doubts that he would welcome my best friend with open arms. However, that would mean he would be putting his sullen and surly older brother out and I wasn't about to offer up the limited space in my tent to him if Em took his place. Especially not when I could smell myself and the fumes made my nose twitch. Initially, I thought the offensive odor would be a good way to keep Cy and my rebellious fascination with him at bay. The truth of the matter is, I was far less keen on the idea of keeping the man at bay than I should be. I wanted him close and I didn't want anything about me to put him off from getting closer than close. Emrys was just going to have to tough it out until we got to the camp showers that were promised.

I maneuvered past Em and threw myself down on the sleeping bag as she asked me, "What was that all about? Was that fireworks?"

"Not fireworks. It was a gunshot. Cy took off to see if he could find out where it was coming from."

I heard rustling as she maneuvered her way back into her sleeping bag. There was a long pause before she muttered, "Not quite as alone out here as I thought we were going to be."

"No, we're definitely not alone." And for the first time in my life I was okay with that. The truth was it took a lot of energy and effort to keep everyone out. Surrounded by these strangers, all of us scrambling to find our footing in an unfamiliar place, I was finding I liked how easy it was to let the right people in.

CHAPTER 7

Not So Squeaky Clean

THE NEXT DAY, THERE WAS no mistaking the tension radiating off the brothers and the barely concealed suspicion they had toward the two other men on the ride. Just like the day before, the older man and the younger man stayed mostly silent, unless they spoke to each other. Even the normally oblivious mom and dad seemed to pick up on the thick undercurrents working throughout the rest of the group. Meghan wrangled her mouthy offspring and made them ride between her and her husband, who I noticed smelled almost as badly as I did. He must not have been accustomed to being in the saddle all day either but waited until Em and I turned in for the night before he did something about it. The man was ridiculous and I made sure that I put myself between him and my friend so that she didn't have to waste another day fending off his oily advances.

Cy didn't say a word about his trek into the dark, so I assumed his search didn't turn up anything either harmless or dangerous. I found myself off guard at how ridiculously happy I was that he had returned to the camp uninjured. Even though I was exhausted, I hadn't been able to sleep until I heard booted footsteps and his deep voice growling at Lane when he got back last night. I didn't want to spend too much time thinking about my reaction or what it might mean, so instead I spent the rest of the day reminiscing with Em and enjoying the ride, now that my backside was slightly more accustomed to the jarring bounce.

The second day's agenda included a nature hike and rock climbing that both the kids seemed ecstatic about. I didn't mind the hike but heights weren't my favorite. I was nervous about doing something I'd never done before, something I'd never even thought about doing. I'd promised Em I would embrace the experience, so instead of grumbling about dangling in the air from a rope like I typically would, I worried myself sick about taking on something new. I was cataloging everything that could go wrong and mentally planning my funeral. I forced a smile I knew she didn't buy for a single second but there was relief on her face that I wasn't trying to drag her down into my ocean of fear and hesitation.

When it came time to strap into the harness I balked when Cy moved toward me with the contraption. I told him I wanted Lane to be the one who strapped me in. I couldn't formulate an explanation, one that didn't admit to him that I didn't want him within touching, or rather smelling distance while I was gross and stinky.

He gave me a dark look. "Who do you think taught Lane and Sutton how to do any of this shit?" I opened my mouth to try and make peace but he wasn't done proving that he really was Mr. Personality and a man not afraid to speak his mind. "You're annoying and mouthy, but I'm not going to let anything happen to you, Sunshine."

I opened and closed my mouth like a beached fish while I tried to figure out how to respond to his rude assessment of my character. I crossed my arms over my heaving breasts and stamped my foot on the ground, counting backwards from ten as I worked at keeping my temper and sharp tongue in check.

This man riled me up and lit my fuse faster than anyone else ever had. "I am not annoying; you're just impatient and far too accustomed to people doing whatever you say."

He bent a little closer to me and I automatically leaned away so that he wouldn't get a good whiff of the minty, chemical smell that was my current scent.

"People do what I say because I know what I'm doing, which means I'm the man in charge more often than not. Now get your ass in the harness and up the rocks, Leo."

Deciding that arguing with him in front of everyone else was only going to waste time and ultimately end in embarrassment, I begrudgingly moved closer to him and rested a hand on his shoulder as he crouched down in front of me and helped me step into the sturdy canvas rig. His shoulders felt as hard and as sturdy as the rock face I was about to try to tackle. Everything about him seemed like it was made to be indestructible and unyielding. I gasped when he situated the straps between my legs so that they were secure between my legs and around my hips. There was no teasing touch like there had been when he helped me on the horse, but having him that close to the center of me, to the part of me that wanted more than sweaty, sexy dreams, was unnerving. All it took was a puff of air from between his pursed lips as he adjusted buckles and straps to fit me for my entire body to light up and tingle. I wanted to feel the rough scrape of his dark scruff across my legs and between them. I wanted to see if any part of him could be soft or if he was hard all the way through. I wanted him to put his mouth where my body was silently begging for him. My fingers curled into the sinewy strength that was practically holding me up as I leaned on him. His slate-colored gaze shot up to mine like he knew exactly what was going through my mind.

He shot to his feet and gave the straps one last tug that had me slamming into the immovable wall of his chest. My hands flattened against the hard muscle and my fingers curled into my palms as I felt the way his heart was racing. "In case you're wondering, I happen to like annoying and mouthy. When a woman doesn't have anything to say that means there's trouble brewing, and you find yourself blindsided when she finally does tell you what's bothering her. By then, it's too late to fix things. Now go have the good time you're paying a fortune for and maybe when you don't smell like the inside of a medicine cabinet, I'll forget my better judgment and make this a vacation you remember forever." He plopped a helmet on my head and tightened the strap under my slackened jaw before turning to face the rocks.

I yelped, not only from the shock of his words, but from the soft tug that followed them as he pulled on the end of one of my pigtails. I blinked up at him in question as I grabbed the safety rope and turned to look up at the vertical rock face in front of me. It was a gentle gesture, something soft, like he knew I was a nervous wreck and could use the soothing. I didn't want to do this. But the fact that I didn't want to it because I was scared was exactly why I put a booted foot on the first foothold that Cy pointed out and hauled myself up. There literally was nowhere for me to run. All I could do was face my fear. This entire trip had been me being forced to do just that.

It took me a long time to reach the pinnacle. Way longer than it took the kids and Em. It took longer than it probably should have because when I was only halfway up, Lane offered to take the rest of the group down to the river to go fishing. Everyone left except Em, who stayed to cheer me on. I slipped a few times as I worked my way up, and each time I almost called down for Cy to come and get me or to help me down by releasing the rope, but I didn't. I bit back the terror and slowly but surely found the next place for my hands and feet to go. Slow and steady I pulled myself back up and found the next foothold.

What felt like hours later, I reached the top and I almost cried. From the way Em was shrieking and dancing around below me, I was pretty sure she may have shed a tear. And even up as high as I was, I could see the white slash of a grin cut across Cy's face. It wasn't quite a smile but it was close and it did something sweet and hot to my heart to know that me conquering this hurdle, no matter how small it may have been, made him not quite happy, but something close to that.

From the top, I let out a victorious whoop and threw my arms out. I was embracing this new side of myself and I owed Emrys more than I could ever repay for introducing me to this whole other side of the woman I was. This was the woman I needed to be in order to get over my own insecurities. It took climbing a rock and venturing into the unknown for me to figure that out. Lane was right, the city made it way too easy to ignore some of the quieter things in life that I really should be focusing on. The country life and all of its serenity allowed me to hear a lot of unsaid things that were tumbling around in my own head, words that were shouting to be heard, words that I'd chosen to ignore for too long. I was figuring out that I could survive this upheaval in my life and I was doing it one challenge—one hurdle—at a time.

"Hey, Leo, come on back down. We need to saddle up and head to the campsite for the night. There's a shower waiting for you." I looked down at Cy and gave him a nod as he walked me through the easiest way to rappel back down without scraping my knees and palms all to hell. Before I descended, I took one last long look at the awe-inspiring landscape. Miles of trees and rivers painting the mountains green and blue. It was unspoiled and pure as far as the eye could see. At least it was until my gaze caught on a weird void in the tree line way up the river. It looked like a meteor had dropped from the sky and left a huge empty spot in the thick and lush foliage. I thought it was strange and I meant to ask Cy what it was, but as soon as my boots hit the ground I was engulfed in a hug that made me forget. It was a hug that almost made up for all the hugs I missed from my mom growing up, for all the hugs that were nothing more than lies that came from Chris. And it was from the one person I wasn't expecting to ever hug.

Cyrus Warner hugged hard. His arms were tight. His body was massive and warm where it engulfed mine. The way he squeezed me was anything but gentle. His voice was low and raspy in my ear as he told me, "You were scared and you did it anyway. Proud of you." His arms tightened a fraction, then he let me go so that Em's arms could replace his as she wrapped me up in a much softer embrace.

I was right about Em's crying for me. She had shiny eyes but her smile was bright and I could see both pride and relief mixed with equal fervor in her dark gaze. "I'm so fucking proud of you, Leo."

I moved back so I could pull the helmet off and shake out my hair. "I'm pretty proud of me, too." But there was no denying that having Cy's approval, and now Em's, made me feel like I had tackled something bigger than a mountain.

She laughed and let me use her to brace myself as I worked the harness off my legs. "Just think how many more amazing experiences we're going to have by the end of the week. There won't be anything we can't handle by the time we get back home."

Little did we know then how those experiences would ultimately shape the rest of our lives. Those experiences would change the women we were and the way we loved. There was no running from any of that either.

THE REST OF THE DAY passed with less excitement and with no unexpected wakeup calls in the middle of the night. Day three brought another long ride, but also a little reprieve from the saddle when we got to go canoeing on a beautiful mountain lake. It was so crystal clear and unendingly blue that I could see all the way to the bottom to watch the occasional fish swim by. The water was as cold as the snow runoff that fed it, and I was tempted to jump in and scrub the smell of three days of riding, sweat, sunscreen, and bug spray off, even though we had a shower waiting later that night. I held off though because Em was actually starting to wilt. She was no longer as fresh as a daisy either, so I was feeling less self-conscious about my transformation into the Pioneer Woman.

The lazy day on the lake was followed by a ride into an actual campsite that was maintained by the Wyoming Parks department, which meant there was a real grill, actual campsites, and minimal facilities for us to use for the evening. They weren't five-star accommodations by any stretch of the imagination, but to me the camp looked like The Ritz-Carlton and I almost kissed Lane when he told me we were having chili for dinner instead of fish. I liked fresh fish, and there was something very primal and cool about catching and eating your own dinner, but after two days of nothing but trout, PB&J, and granola, I was ready for something different. I would have preferred Brynn's pancakes, but since they weren't an option, canned chili and campfire cornbread would do.

I wanted to push everyone else out of the way and dive into the rusted and slightly scary looking showers, but I figured I would take the longest, since I was the one who smelled the worst, and because my hair had really turned into the wild and untamed lion's mane Lane accused me of having. I offered to help the younger Warner brother with dinner while everyone else was shuffling around getting settled and cleaned up. Cy pulled his typical disappearing act and when I questioned Lane about it, he laughed and told me it was better to let Cy handle the horses than try and force him to interact with humans. Both brothers were still on edge after the midnight gunshots, but Lane effortlessly slipped back into his happy-go-lucky persona, while Cy seemed hypervigilant and overly aware of every noise and sound that we didn't make on the trail. So far, we hadn't encountered anyone else or been surprised by anything unexpected. While the silence made me breathe easier when we bunked down for the night, the absence of anyone or anything else appeared to make the two men who didn't bother to engage with the rest of us angry. Their expressions were hard. Their conversations with each other clipped and silted. One or the other was always wandering off away from the rest of the group and when they returned it was with heavy footsteps and lots of mumbled dirty words. They continually brushed off the warning that Cy and Lane gave about sticking together and didn't seem at all interested in any of the required camping activities. It was as if they were expecting something else, and were searching for something they couldn't find. Though what they could possibly be looking for out here in the middle of nowhere baffled me.

When everyone settled down to eat, looking refreshed and slightly back to their normal, non-trail riding selves, I asked Em to save me dinner and took myself, my small toiletry bag, and a change of clothes clutched in my eager hands to the shower. The whole time I walked to the tin and wood building, I told myself this wasn't Camp Crystal Lake and there wasn't any chance that a chainsaw-wielding Jason was going to jump out from behind a tree and slaughter me. It was creepy—or maybe that was my mind making more of this scenario than it should. When I opened the door, I quickly learned that it was also a his and hers facility. It took a minute for my eyes to adjust in the dim light, but when they did, they landed on the most stunning thing I had ever seen in my life. A very naked and very wet Cyrus Warner. There was no mistaking that massive, hard-cut body, or the midnight hair shot through with shiny silver. Water sluiced over unending plains of muscle and tanned skin making him look like some ancient sea god . . . or like a real life fantasy, even if he wasn't quite a cowboy. He was built for women to worship and for other men to be impressed by. I swore there wasn't a finer ass on the planet than the one I couldn't seem to look away from, even as the muscles flexed and tensed as he turned to look over his shoulder at me.

He had one hand braced on the wall in front of him and he lifted his raven-colored eyebrows as that not quite a smile pulled at his mouth again. His scruff was quickly shifting to more of an actual beard and I kind of loved how overtly masculine everything about him was. There was no missing his virility or his in-your-face masculinity. I never thought I was the kind of girl who went weak in the knees for big muscles and a bossy demeanor. Turns out my libido thought very differently. I took another shaky step forward when he told me, "I'm doing what I was getting ready to do before you walked in, but now I don't need to use my imagination since you're standing right there." I faltered to a stop at his words and licked my lips as his hand leisurely slipped up and down his erection. I'd never seen a man touch himself in such an intimate manner before and I'd definitely never had one tell me I was the inspiration he was using to get off with. It felt private and secretive in a good way. It felt like a moment that was mine and his. I never really thought of myself as masturbation material but Cy was proving me wrong and he was proving it while turning me into a blazing pillar of arousal and need.

"Are you imagining me because you like redheads and I just happen to be a redhead?" I was breathing shallow and deep, want and desire laced in my tone as I got even closer to him. I was close enough now that I could see the way his ab muscles tensed, the way the slit on the head of his rigid cock glimmered with aroused moisture. I groaned aloud when he stroked the flat of his thumb over that taunting drop and swirled it around the tapered head. He let out a grunt and our eyes locked as his broad chest rose and fell with his quickened breathing.

"I don't like all redheads, Leo. Don't let my brother fill your head with nonsense when he's spilling my secrets. The redheads I do like, I tend to more than like." His hand moved faster and faster as he head fell back with a groan. His eyes drifted shut and his other hand curled into a fist at his side, the other in front of him rocking back and forth at a leisurely pace at his waist. My mind immediately went to all the dirty and sexy things that pose and that particular motion could mean. I knew what I wanted it to mean, so all I could do was gawk and try to remember to breathe. I forgot about the stuff in my hands as I lifted one to my thundering heart, the other to my throat, where I was pretty sure his name was trapped there on a strangled sigh.

He twisted at the waist and I couldn't hold back a painfully aroused and shocked groan. He stopped before I got the full-frontal image but he was turned enough that I could see the heavy muscles in his chest and the light dusting of dark hair that covered his pecs. The man had more than a six pack working and that V at his hips wasn't just cut in on the side of his abs, it was chiseled there because he looked like he was crafted and designed by a Renaissance sculptor. The entire female population would descend on Wyoming in droves if they knew men like this were hidden away out here in the middle of nowhere.

"'Bout time you made your way over here. You need a

shower twice as much as the rest of them." He pushed his big hands through his wet hair and slicked the dark strands away from his face. I wanted to lick every single droplet of water off him, especially the ones that were sliding down the column of his strong throat. I watched his jaw clench and a twitch start in his cheek as I continued to stare at him numbly. I felt like I was seeing for the first time what a man, a real, true, and honest to God man should look like. I was mesmerized by the strong lines of his back, the strong bulk of his thighs, and the chiseled line of his jaw as he watched me watch him.

"I helped Lane with dinner since I knew I was going to be a while, so I thought I would go last." My voice was high and breathy to my own ears and when I looked down at my hands, they were shaking. I wanted to touch him so bad.

"Oh, so she can be charming and pleasant when she wants to be." He turned back around and suddenly the water turned off. "Bring me that towel over there and I'll get out of your way so you can do us all a favor and wash the stink off."

I didn't move for a long minute because I was stuck on the fact he called me charming, just like he'd told me I was pretty and that I had a nice ass. I wasn't used to someone being that upfront with me and I wasn't used to those kinds of compliments. I was jerked out of my lust-filled stupor when he suddenly turned all the way around and I was introduced to ALL of Cyrus Warner in his magnificent and erect glory. My jaw unhinged and my breath wheezed out of my lungs. I knew I should look away but I couldn't. Like everything else about him, his cock was impressive in size and seemed more solid and real than any I had seen before it. I'd also never really considered that part of the male anatomy particularly appealing. I mean, I liked what they could do with it and the purpose that it served, but I had no desire to stare at a penis for any length of time, until Cy's. I couldn't stop staring at it and I definitely thought that part of him was as attractive as the rest of him. I wanted to put my hands on it. I wanted to put my mouth on it. I wanted him to put his hands on it while I watched.

I stuck my tongue out and slicked it across my lower lip while I continued to admire him, like he was some priceless work of art hung in the Louvre. My feet still wouldn't move from where they seemed to be planted to the ground beneath them.

"Leo, bring me the towel or get over here and put that tongue to better use." His already deep voice dropped even lower and rasped even rougher as he answered my silent plea and dropped one of his hands to the rigid shaft that was pointing straight up at his corrugated stomach muscles. I sighed softly as he slid his grip slowly up and down.

Pleasure looked rough on him. It made the veins on the side of his neck stick out and flushed his face a dark shade of red. His thigh muscles bulged and his torso went tight and taut. There was power in every line of his big body and desire leeched out of every part of him. His breathing was harsh, loud, and erratic against the tin walls. I swore I was on the verge of my own orgasm simply by watching him chase his own. His cock slipped easily in out of his grip as his forearm jacked up and down. There was a breathless moment, a stillness when his eyes popped back open and met mine. He didn't say my name but it was on his lips anyway as the thick and creamy threads of his release jetted out and smeared across his thick knuckles and hit the rusted wall in front of him.

I wanted him to come on me that way, mark me up and claim me in a way that was as wild and as untamed as the area we were in. I wanted to tell him he could come on my ass, on my tits, on my stomach . . . anywhere he wanted to, as long as he was the one making me his. I'd never let anyone do anything remotely close to that in bed before. In fact, I was typically the girl on top kind of lover so I could get mine and go home, but this man had me wanting all kinds of things that I had never wanted before.

He turned to crank the water up so he could wash away the evidence of his little . . . well, not so little . . . show, and when his back was to me I finally made it all the way to him so that I could hand him the towel. When he turned back to me our eyes met, his blazing, mine full of more questions than I'd had before.

"What does that mean, you more than like most of the red-heads you like?" He took the towel and rubbed it over his hair first, then across his chest. It wasn't until he got to his waist and had it wrapped around his hips that he answered me.

"My mom was a redhead. She broke my dad's heart a hundred times and left my brothers and me every chance she got because this life was not for her. We always let her come back. I loved her anyway, because she's my mom and because my dad worshiped her. My ex-wife is a redhead. I met her in college and it was love at first sight. She only broke my heart once, but it was enough that I never intend to repeat the experience." I felt my eyes go wide at his curt description of the most important women in his life. I was also struggling with the fact that a woman had had him and was brave enough to let him go. I wondered if the woman woke up every morning kicking her own ass for not being able to make it work with a man like Cy.

"Brynn is a redhead and I love her like a sister, but she's broken my little brother's heart more than once and she doesn't even know it. Redheads are easy to love but are hard to keep ahold of, which is why you went from distracting to dangerous as soon as you opened that smart-ass mouth of yours, Sunshine. I don't have the time or the patience to deal with the kind destruction you are capable of."

I reared back and almost slipped in the pool of water he had left underneath him. He reached out to grab me. When he had me in his grip, he pulled me to his bare chest. My hands landed on the hard muscle and curled into the smattering of hair there.

"I'm not here to destroy anything. I'm trying to rebuild something." And I was making pretty good headway. And it was partly due to the way he fired me up after I'd allowed myself to be frozen in my own self-blame and regret. Like Em said, he made me burn and I was made up of stuff that was dying for him to blaze his way through it.

"Women like you don't have to try and destroy things, Leo. You just do, because men like me aren't strong enough to stay away and we end up wanting things the other isn't capable of giving."

Those were probably the most honest words anyone had ever spoken to me. They were so sweet in a twisted and tragic kind of way. It was better to be wanted knowing it wasn't going to be perfect or thoughtfully planned. I'd been wanted because I made it so easy to and that hadn't worked out at all. I much preferred being desired because I was a challenge, and as much of a risk as I thought he was. I didn't want a manufactured, faultless man. I wanted this one. One who was real, flawed, and so far out of my comfort zone I couldn't even see safety and security anymore. I still wanted to run but now it was toward him and the way he made me feel.

I kissed him because he could be sweet, even if he hadn't meant to be.

The first touch of my lips to his ignited my blood and made my head swim. I could feel the strength in his big body and the coiled tension that locked in all of his muscles as I pressed against him.

I kissed him because he was in front of me, almost naked, still wet, and outrageously sexy.

That sexiness went up a million notches when he took a step into my space and walked me backwards into the tin wall behind me. I heard it rattle but couldn't think beyond that because one of his hands wrapped around my jaw and forced my mouth open as the other tangled in my hair. I couldn't move. There was nowhere to go . . . and I'd never been happier to be trapped in my entire life. I could feel his wakening erection pressed against my stomach and it made me groan. He took the opportunity to slip his tongue between my parted lips.

I kissed him back with slippery tongue and nibbling teeth because I'd just watched him get off while thinking about me and I wanted the next time it happened to be *because* of me. I wanted to own his pleasure and his desire. I wanted to come with him and feel what it was like to have all that power and passion unleashed on me and inside me.

I curled my hands around his sides and let myself get lost in the moment. I'd never been as aware of the parts of me that made me distinctly female as I was with Cy pressing into them. I could feel the rasp of my aroused nipples against my shirt. I could feel my inner thighs quiver and my center clench hard and fast. I was dizzy and I was wet between my legs. He must have been able to feel the effect he was having on me because he shoved one of his legs between mine and leaned more fully into my chest. My pointed nipples rasped against his damp chest hair and my hips moved of their own volition against the rock-hard thigh that was pressed into my softest spot. I wanted to be wanton and wild. I wanted to rub myself against him until the throb between my legs went away. My heart couldn't beat without knocking into his and every breath I took tasted like him.

I kissed him with every ounce of longing and passion I had because he let me and didn't run away. I'd never had the thing I was scared of chase after me. I'd never had the challenge I was working my way through refuse to let me quit, even when it might be the best option.

I kissed him because I wanted to know what kissing him was like and because I was fairly certain no one else would ever kiss me the way he did.

His scruff was abrasive against my face, his hand was hard where it was around my jaw, but his thumb was a gentle caress against my cheek as he tilted his mouth over mine in every direction. His lips were light but insistent as they brushed across mine and his tongue was tender and soft as it slicked across mine teasingly. His softness was contrasted by all parts of him that were hard and I liked all of it; if the truth be told, I wanted more of it.

I was trailing my other hand over the contours of his defined pecs, fully intending to work my way to the inadequate knot holding the towel at his waist when he pulled back, curled his hand lightly around my throat so that he could feel my pulse racing, and lightly set me away from him with a frown. I liked how my mouth made his shiny and red. I liked the heat in his cheeks and the fire in his eyes. I liked the way his pulse kicked at his neck and the way his dick jerked in obvious annoyance at the now chilly space between our bodies.

He pushed his hands through his hair and gave his head a shake. "Lane's going to come looking for me or your girl is going to come looking for you. This is bad timing and without a doubt a really bad idea for both of us. I'm gonna go and let you get cleaned up while I still have enough blood above the belt to make good decisions."

He made his way over to a rickety looking ledge that held his clothes after stopping to pick up the stuff I dropped and placing it there as well. I turned my back to him as he dropped the towel and started to get dressed. I pulled my own clothes off and reached for the water, shrieking in surprise when I felt how cold it was. If I had known I was going to be bathing in ice water, I would have jumped in the lake earlier when I was thinking about it and rinsed the stink off then.

I took the frigid spray right in the face and shivered as it ran over my scalp and through my hair. I jumped when Cy's rumbling voice reached me over the sound of the water.

"I could definitely more than like you, Leo, and there is no question, I more than like what you look like without your clothes on."

I let my gaze roll over him and noticed he was looking down at his cock, the thick flesh lifting and elongating more and more as we both took note of his reaction to me. He was standing in the same spot I had been in earlier with his boots in his hand and the expression he had on his face was similar to the one I had worn while I watched him only harsher and more intense. When his gaze shifted to me I swore I could feel the impact of it like a physical touch. I was aware that I would never be asked to walk in a Victoria Secret's fashion show but I'd never had a problem with the way I looked. The expression on Cy's face as his eyes drifted over every curve, every dip, every dimple and mark that mapped out a life lived in this skin, made me feel like something extraordinary. His look, the way his entire face tightened in hungry, appreciative lines made me feel like something more, made me feel like I deserved to be worshiped and maybe even loved. If that was how he looked at his girl, then I never wanted to be anything else.

I lifted a shoulder and let it fall. "I guess if we're going tit for tat that means I also get to think about you thinking about me while I take my turn . . . relaxing." I grinned at him because the way he made me feel and the things he made me want to do to myself were anything but calm and restful. "You can stick around and watch—or come back over here and help—because that would only be fair."

His eyes sparked with threads of molten silver as he swore low and long under his breath.

I wasn't the type of woman who would typically take control of her own pleasure in front a man. I was too rigid, too worried about what the other person might be thinking. But today was the day I climbed a mountain and kissed a man who was all wrong for me so I had bold and brazen running through my blood in a way it never had before. I wasn't typically open enough to share what I liked, and I wasn't ever transparent about what I was feeling but in this moment with him, when it felt like we were the only two people in the entire world, I wanted to give him everything. With Cy, there was no fear and I didn't have to guess what he was thinking. Every emotion and every ounce of desire and encouragement was stamped clearly across his darkly handsome face. He was going to call my bluff and we would both just have to suffer the consequences.

Eyes locked on his I trailed a single hand down between the valley of my breasts. The icy water had made my skin pebble up and my nipples tighter than they were when I had kissed him. I caught one of the velvety peaks between my fingers and gave it a little tug before rolling my thumb around the softness to soothe the delicious ache. I let out a little groan of pleasure, eyes going to half-mast as I heard him swear again.

Tossing my head back I shifted my legs so they were open just enough to tease him with all the wet and wanting he had awoken inside of me. I curled my other hand under the curve of my breast and let it skate over the ridges of my ribs and across the soft plane of my stomach. It wasn't the cold water that made me shiver. It was the way Cy growled my name. It sounded like both a promise and a warning.

I circled the indent of my belly button with my index finger and sighed when I let my fingers skip lower. It was a shock to my overheated senses when my chilly touch met liquid heat. My folds were slippery and almost too sensitive to touch. My clit was throbbing and begging for any kind of attention. When my touch brushed across the aching little point of pleasure, my entire body jolted and I couldn't stop the low moan that ripped out of my chest. I was caught up in a hurricane of sensation, the contrast of hot and cold making my head spin and my body already primed and ready to let go from watching Cy work himself over. All it was going to take was a few flicks of the wrist, a twist of my fingers, and maybe another sharp tug on my nipple to get me off. I was certain there had never been a time in my life when I'd been this aroused and it had everything to do with the man watching me like he would die if he had to look away.

His chest was rising and falling like he couldn't get enough air. His eyes were so sharp I could feel them cutting into my skin. His face had a hot flush to it and his mouth was parted just enough that I could see the straight line of his teeth sinking into the inside of his lip.

This wasn't fun for him like it had been for me. This was torture.

I let my eyes drift closed and whispered, "I'm soooo close. It never happens this fast for me." My voice was breathy and I barely recognized my own words. I wasn't a woman who ever sounded that aroused, but because of Cy I was.

I slid my thumb around my clit and gasped as the contact set off an entire fireworks display of sensation under my skin.

"Holy fuck." The words sounded like they were ripped out of the man watching me. I heard twin thuds as the boots he was holding hit the floor. As soon as I managed to get my heavy lids open all I saw was man.

I yelped as his hand once again circled around my neck as he pushed me back into the wall. The trickle of water coming from the shower could barely get between us; that's how close he was to me. He didn't seem to mind that he was getting just as wet as I was.

His mouth hit mine with punishing force. Biting and bruising. His fingers tightened around my throat but his thumb skated up and down the long line of my neck chasing the chills he caused. His knee pushed mine farther apart and his free hand covered mine. I couldn't breathe. I could think. I couldn't even move.

All I could do was feel.

And what I felt was enough to flip my entire existence upside down.

He pressed my fingers harder onto my clit and used his to start an intoxicating circular motion. Once I was so wound up and shaking from head to toe, he pulled his lips from mine and moved them to my cheek. It was the sweetest kiss I'd ever received and it almost made me fall over when it was combined with the sudden invasion of his fingers inside my fluttering opening.

My back bowed. My eyes rolled back in my head. My lungs stopped working and I was pretty sure my knees turned to water. The only thing keeping me upright was his hold on my throat and the way he had me pinned with his unwavering stare.

It didn't take much. He pumped his rough fingers into the slippery desire that was waiting for him and hooked one like he knew exactly how to get to spot the would set me off. Pleasure rushed out of me, surprising in its intensity. I'd never had an orgasm that left me feeling like I couldn't function anymore. Never felt satisfaction so potent and strong.

I put my hands on Cy's wet shoulders and blinked up at him like I was an owl. I felt like he turned me inside out and I wasn't sure if I should thank him or swear at him. I didn't get the chance to do either because as soon as he saw I wasn't going to wilt into a useless pile of woman at his feet he released me like my skin was made of burning ember.

"Like I said, I'm not strong enough to stay away." His words were clipped and almost angry. None of the passionate heat and approval that had been shining out of them when he had his hands on me could be found, just frustration and simmering fury.

He turned away, running a hand over his wet shirt and the damp fly of his jeans. I wasn't sure if that was from me or the crappy shower but I honestly kind of wanted it to be from me. The door closed with a little click behind him and I turned back to the shower.

I should be hurt at his rude dismissal, but I wasn't. I didn't have to guess what he meant by his parting words because he meant exactly what he said. It was the wrong place and the wrong time, and we were most definitely the wrong two people, but he wanted me and he couldn't stay away. Cyrus Warner had just as many control issues as I did, which was why we both liked to test the other's limits and neither one of us liked to fail.

If this was what failing felt like, I couldn't wait to do it again. When I thought I was making good decisions, I ended up with a busted heart and shattered self-esteem. Bad decisions already had proven to be way more fun.

One thing was for sure, he had already made good on his word to make this a vacation I would never forget.

CHAPTER 8

Not So Fancy Meeting You Here

"HOW LONG WERE YOU MARRIED?" I asked the question to Cy's back after a couple hours of pervading silence.

I wasn't sure why I thought the fact that we had seen each other in all our glory, and shared kisses that were defining and delicious, meant that he would put Mr. Personality to rest and be a little bit more approachable. He had started out the morning ride as grumpy and withdrawn as he always was. I wasn't sure how I ended up in line behind him for the ride today but since I was so close, I could feel his silence like a cloak settled around my shoulders. I had no clue what he was ruminating on, but whatever it was didn't seem to be very pleasant. In hindsight, my question probably wasn't the best opportunity to turn that dark disposition in a different direction.

His head whipped around so he could look at me and I winced at the scowl stamped across his rough features. "Why do you want to know?"

I wanted to know because he'd had his tongue in my mouth and his hands all over my body. I wanted to know because he always spoke the truth but his eyes kept secrets. I wanted to know because I wanted to know him the way he seemed to already know me.

I frowned back at him. "I have a hard time picturing any-one wanting to let you go, even though you have being grumpy down to an art from." I was surprised by my own honesty—and he seemed to be, as well. His features lightened a fraction and some of the storm that was always raging in his eyes cleared right before it darkened to the point they were almost black. He was no longer thunderous, he'd passed that and moved onto some-thing darker and infinitely scarier. I didn't think he would answer, and when he did I wasn't prepared for his honesty to gut me, or for the way it made my heart ache for him. His story made my own seem silly and insignificant by comparison and I suddenly I knew the bruises on my heart were nothing compared to the scars sashed on his.

"She didn't want to let me go and I didn't want her to let me go. We loved each other and she was my everything. But I was stuck here. She didn't want to stay in Wyoming. She loved me but hated my life and the responsibilities that came with it. She wanted me but not the responsibilities and obligations that came with me. I would have given up anything and everything to make her happy, but she wanted me to give up the one thing I couldn't." There was no bitterness in his tone just sad accep-tance of the fact that sometimes love wasn't enough to keep two people together no matter how much they truly cared for one another.

It sounded like the worst rock and the hardest place ever to be caught between. When it was a fight between love and loyalty there never really ended up being a winner.

"Didn't she know who you were and where you came from before she agreed to spend the rest of her life with you?" Cy didn't strike me as the bait and switch type. I couldn't exactly nail down what he was, not a cowboy and not a suit for sure, but *who* he was as a man had been crystal clear from the very start. A man who took care of his family and protected those who mattered to him.

Cy turned around so he was once again facing the trail up ahead of us. His deep voice easily carried to me as he snorted and then replied, "I told you I met her in college. I went away for school. They were the only four years I spent away from the ranch and away from my family. I came back during breaks with friends, but that wasn't the same as working a breeding season or getting the herd ready for auction. It wasn't the same as all of us busting our asses together to make it through the winter." I saw him shift in the saddle and watched as he ran a hand over his meticulously styled hair. "I never wanted to stay in Wyoming. When I was growing up, I resented the hell out of the isolation and the hard work. All I wanted to do was get laid and have a good time like every other teenager in America.I never got the opportunity and it pissed me off. I was always a solid student and scored high on all my college placement tests. I wrote a sob story entrance essay about my mom leaving us when we were young and how hard our life on the ranch had been, which got me into Boston University. I jumped at the chance to get as far away from home as I could. I felt guilty as hell, leaving Dad alone with Lane and Sutton, but I had to take a shot and see what the rest of the world was like. I was looking for the greener grass and had a shit attitude about it."

"Boston is beautiful." It was one of my favorite big cities on the East Coast but no matter how hard I tried, I couldn't picture him wandering the narrow streets and blending into the urban sprawl, not even a younger, more naïve version of him.

"It is beautiful, and so was Selah. I stopped in my tracks when I first saw her. I met her freshman year and wasted no time claiming her heart and her time as mine. She was a sweet girl from the middle of nowhere Colorado, so we connected instantly. Neither one of us ever thought we were going back to small town living and spent many nights together planning a grand, adventurous life together. We were engaged by junior year and I marched her down the aisle not even a month after graduation. We were young and stupid in love . . . stupid being the key word."

He glanced at me over his shoulder and I saw his mouth was pulled in a line so tight it looked like his entire face might shatter from the tension in it. "My dad brought the boys to the wedding and I noticed he didn't look so great. I didn't come home much during school, partly on purpose because I think I knew if I left the city, the chances of me making it back were slim to none. I liked the city, but it was never home and there was no greener grass to be found. My favorite part of Boston was Selah. I was arrogant enough to believe that we would be happy wherever we were, as long as we were together."

My heart tripped over itself at his words. "That doesn't sound arrogant. It sounds romantic and sweet." I knew I could desire him and turn into a quivering mass of greedy want and need for him. I was amazed that I could actually like him and admire him as well. His tough outer shell hid a lot of really delicious and decadent things on the inside. It made me wonder if we had more in common than I originally thought.

Cy made a noise low in his throat which had Boss jerking his head at the sound. I reached down to run my fingers through my steed's midnight mane and to settle us both.

"I was idiotic and short-sighted. I should have known what was waiting for me, considering I watched my mother flit in and out of my life whenever she decided life in Wyoming was too stale and too hard. Dad was sick, had been sick for a couple of years, and didn't want me to know. I wanted to experience life away from the ranch and he knew the instant I found out how sick he was, how dire the situation back home was, I would head back no questions asked. That's exactly what I did. Only I came back with a wife who had no desire to be there." He put a hand to the back of his neck and rubbed like it would release the chains of tension that were linked there.

"Selah did her best. At first, she tried to help out and find her place, but she was never happy, and the sicker dad got, the deeper I dug in so she knew there was going to be no persuading me to leave. My brothers were getting older but they still needed someone to take care of them. By that time, Brynn lived with us as well and needed someone to look out for her. There were too many people relying on me, but the one who mattered the most, I was helpless to do anything for."

I wanted to give him a hug because it sounded like an impossible situation to be caught in. Love was often about sacrifice; I knew this because my grandparents had given up a lot when they took me in, but they never complained about it and always made sure I had had every opportunity to succeed.

"She was here for a year, and each day I could see a little bit more of her happiness die. Her spirit was suffocating and the sweet girl I loved was turning into someone I didn't recognize." He shook his head and his voice dropped lower. "I thought it would all turn around when she found out she was pregnant."

I gasped a little because he hadn't mentioned having kids. My breath caught at the image of him holding a dark haired little girl with gray eyes, atop a horse that had the same black and silver coloring as her dad. I had no idea where the picture came from but it made my heart race and my palms sweaty.

Cy's shoulders turned to stone in front of me and his horse obviously sensed the change in his rider's mood because it pulled to the side and jerked its head hard in the bridle. "Dad was down to his final hours but business was doing better with me at the helm. I thought starting a family would settle her in and make her see this was as good a place as any to raise our kids. We were surrounded by family and our baby would have a legacy that they grew up preserving, just like I did. Being away made me appreciate everything I'd worked for, and the fact that I had helped build it with my own hands gave me a sense of pride that I didn't have in the city. She finally seemed hopeful and reluctantly okay with us building our lives here."

He went quiet for a minute and when he finally did speak again, his voice sounded like it was being dragged from someplace inside of him that was filled with all those sharp and pointy things I'd been running from when I found him. "It was the middle of winter when something went wrong. She started having cramps and before any of us knew what was happening, she was bleeding and in more pain than I knew any human could feel. The closest town to the ranch is an hour away. In winter, that's easily two hours or more. By the time I got her to the hospital, she lost the baby and almost lost her life." He cleared his throat and shook his head as if he was trying to dislodge the painful memory. "She never came back to the ranch. She refused. She blamed this place for taking both her husband and her baby away from her. She begged me to go with her when she was finally well enough to travel, but I couldn't do it. I had my dad and my brothers. I had the ranch and things that were always going to be my responsibility. She broke my heart but in all honesty, I broke hers even more. She left and I stayed and that's how it ended. It was a mirror of how things ended between my mom and dad."

It took me a second to find my voice, and when I did it was strained and thin with compassion. "That's sad. I'm so incredibly sorry for both of you." It also explained why he might not be a cowboy on the outside but was one hundred percent cowboy in the inside. His life was what sad country songs were written about. It sounded tragic and heartbreaking. Most people split up because they fell out of love or simply couldn't remember what they loved about the person in the first place. It seemed entirely unfair that Cy and his ex loved and cared enough but that still wasn't enough to get to happily ever after.

"Don't be. Selah is remarried to a chiropractor and lives outside of Boston in Salem. She has three kids and sends me a Christmas card every year. She offered to fly back when my dad finally passed, but I couldn't handle seeing her on top of putting him to rest and the drama my mom tried to create once he was gone. Selah was always a good woman, she just wasn't the woman for me."

"You weren't for her." I tossed his words from the other day back at him and was rewarded with a half grin. Gah, it made me feel warm all over and had those tingles in private places pulsing happily to a tune that only he seemed to know how to sing. I lifted my eyebrows, not because he was still on friendly terms with a woman who mattered so much to him, but because of what he said about his mom. "Your mom caused a scene when your dad passed away? That sounds like something my mother would do."

He shot me a look over his shoulder and our eyes locked. "Dad divorced her when he found out he was sick, not because he stopped loving her, but because he didn't want her to try and sell the ranch out from underneath us once he was gone. She stopped coming around, but by that time he had remarried so there was no way for her to really manipulate him and play games with him anymore. She took the opportunity to make her feelings known at his funeral about being cut out and left without so much as a dime from him, until I dragged her ass out of the church and told her I never wanted her to step foot back in Wyoming. I must have made my point because she has a five-year-old granddaughter she's never attempted to meet."

"Do you still see your stepmom?" I liked the idea that his dad had managed to experience a few moments of happiness before passing away. He sounded like a good man, a strong man. He sounded a lot like my own grandfather and there was no doubt he had imparted all those qualities on the man before me who he had raised in his own image.

He gave a chuckle that had no traces of humor or amusement in it. "I see her almost every day. You've met her." His dark eyebrows shot up and a muscle twitched in his jaw. "Brynn grew up in a trailer park not too far away from our ranch. She and Lane are the same age and were in the same class at school. Her home life wasn't the best, partly because of her being a quarter Native, but mostly because her dad likes to drink. My brother has always had a soft heart. He brought her home with him time and time again, and each time she was in worse shape than the last. Dad offered to take her in on a permanent basis but her old man wouldn't hear of it. Every time she was here he would show up drunk, pissed off, and drag her back home. Local police couldn't do much about it because the trailer park was between state land and Native land so they were always trying to pass the buck."

My mind was spinning and couldn't seem to land on a place where serene and pretty Brynn was married to man more than twice her age and terminally ill.

"After years of trying to protect her and keep her safe, dad had had enough. The only way to get her away from her family and the abuse permanently was to tie her to a different family. I was in Boston, Sutton was all tangled up with Daye's mom, and Lane was too young to get married. Since he's so fond of telling you all about me I don't have any problem telling you he would have put a ring on her finger in a heartbeat. Brynn was barely eighteen and dad married her to set her free, but a lot of folks didn't see it that way. They accused him of taking advantage of her and her of just wanting to get her hooks in a fairly well off, but not long for this life man. It wasn't easy for either of them, especially since Lane has always had a thing for her but it was the best, most effective option. She's always been family and she did a good job taking care of everything until I could get back home where I belonged."

I blew out a long breath and shifted on the saddle. "That's one hell of a story."

He grunted in front of me. "It's not my favorite one to tell. What about you? You ever make it down the aisle?"

I choked on a laugh and shook my head even though he wasn't looking at me. His attention was focused back on the trail ahead.

"No. Not even close. I've only had one serious relationship in my entire adult life and it turned out not to be as serious as I thought." That got me a curious look but the mules started to act up and he had to shift his attention away from me just as quickly as I got it. "In fact, it was all a joke." That was on me.

"You're skittish and unsure, but there is no doubt that you have good lines and will make for one hell of a ride. What the hell is wrong with the men where you come from?" He tossed out the very Wyoming compliment without looking at me.

I gaped at his back and couldn't hold back an actual laugh of disbelief. "Did you just compare me to a horse?"

He shot me a smirk as he shifted the reins in his hand to the saddle horn in front of him so he could work on the ropes attached to the mules. The other animals obviously wanted to stop and it was taking everything Cy had to keep them going.

"You wanted a cowboy, cowboys know about two things: good women and good horses. Just so happens that both have similar traits."

I huffed, torn between being flattered and insulted. "Well,

thanks . . . I think. And there's nothing wrong with the men where I'm from. Most of them want someone who is willing to put them first and is open to sharing their life with them. I'm not that girl. I'm too focused on my own life and my own issues to take on anyone else's, and honestly, I'm not very nice most of the time."

He let out a low whistle. "Control freak."

I snorted at him and muttered, "Takes one to know one."

"So, what's the deal with the guy who turned out not to be so serious?" He had been so open and transparent with me when talking about his marriage, I figured I owed him the same.

"He tricked me by being so agreeable and unassuming. He was attractive, but not head turning. Warm rather than hot. He was smart and witty, but not obnoxious about it. I thought he was perfect, and for once there was someone in my life I enjoyed spending time with for more than a few hours besides Em. He never cared that I didn't want him to stay over. Never got upset when I canceled plans because of work. He never made any kind of demands on me. He never questioned me. He never bothered me. He never challenged me or tested me. He fit himself seamlessly into my life and because of that, I was sure we were meant to be. I thought he got me." No one knew that I was perpetually on the defense against everyone because I had an uncontrollable fear of being left, thanks to my crappy mother. I never let anyone get close because I didn't trust them to stay if they had the choice to be with me or to leave.

"I ignored the fact that it shouldn't be that easy. I totally blew off Em when she pointed out it was weird that Chris always came to my house and never invited me over to his. He met her but never offered to introduce me to his friends, and he never cared that we always stayed in, never really going out anywhere in public together. I figured he was going out of his way to make it work the way I wanted it to because he was so into me. Turned out, I was custom made to be the perfect side piece. He had a wife and kids at home in the burbs."

Cy's dark head whipped around and I was taken aback by the angry snarl on his face. He was livid, not at me, but for me. It made me shiver and like him even more than I was already starting to. "How did you find out he was married?"

I made a strangled noise that was almost a laugh. At some point during this trip, I'd managed to find more than heartbreak and disappointment in the situation. It was all so outlandish and ridiculous I couldn't help but find the humor in parts of the pain. "His wife hired the firm I work at for a consultation to do some market research on a new vegan makeup line her company is getting ready to launch. When I went to her office for the first meeting, there were pictures of her and Chris and their kids all over her desk. It was a major contract that stood to make my company a lot of money. I couldn't say anything to her because I was afraid she would drop the contract and fire my firm. I would have lost my job and there's no way I would be able to find another one without solid references. It was a nightmare, but I got through the meeting and called Chris on his bullshit the second I got the chance."

I snorted at the memory of his blasé reaction. "He was surprised I cared that he was married. He told me that he figured I knew after the first few months because I was always so eager and agreeable when he had to go. He figured I knew he had a wife at home and that I was making his life easier by not being clingy or needy. I thought he was being considerate of my feelings, but what he was actually doing was taking advantage of all the things that are inherently wrong with me."

I pointed at myself and made a face. "I was so excited to have someone who seemed to really understand me. I was blinded by his acceptance of what I wanted out of a relationship. I never checked his Facebook or Googled him. I never checked into his work or his background. When I did, it was obvious he was married, and when we started the work for his wife, it was clear I was far from his first affair. She still has no idea, but Chris has fucked his way through half the women on her staff." I sighed. "I like my job. I'm good at it and I don't want to start over somewhere else." Not only that, but the idea of getting fired for a lapse of judgment in my personal life made me want to throw up.

"Sounds to me like the guy gets off on manipulating strong women. His wife owns a company that can afford you, you've got your own shit going on and aren't interested in anyone messing that up, so this guy finds women who are doing just fine without him and makes it his mission to fuck with them. That's what he gets off on, that's what gets him hard. I bet he has a small dick." Cy's voice had a furious shake making it sound like an earthquake ready to take everything down around him. I was seriously getting turned on by the fact that he was so annoyed on my behalf.

Finally, a real laugh, light and free, made its way out of where it had been trapped inside me. Cy made it sound like I really had been a target rather than a desperate and foolish woman. And I had to admit, I liked the reasons he laid out for Chris going after me in the first place. I really hoped he saw me as a woman who had her act together, rather than the one who was scrambling to find her footing.

I leered at him and lifted my eyebrows up as I looked pointedly at his belt buckle. "It wasn't anything to write home about. I've seen bigger and better." His deserved more than a letter home, it deserved a whole novel of descriptive words and flowery admiration. I would even go so far as to say it deserved a medal and an award of honor.

He lifted his eyebrows in return and a cocky grin tugged at the corner of his mouth. I felt a flush work into my cheeks as we both were clearly recalling exactly how much bigger and better he was.

Pulling myself back to reality, I sheepishly admitted, "The worst part was how awful I was to everyone after it all happened. I blew Emrys off. I let my grandmother, who raised me, move across the country without a proper goodbye. I let my coworkers handle the brunt of the work for the cosmetic contract, even though I was the one in charge of the research. I had a hard time looking Chris's wife in the eye knowing what he was doing behind her back. I wanted to tell her, but I wanted to keep my job more and that makes me a shitty person and a horrible woman. We're supposed to look out for one another because the *man* never will."

I made him chuckle. "When is your contract with the wife's company up? Can't you break the news to her then?"

I groaned and let out a frustrated harrumph. "The contract will be up in three more months. I could tell her then but I'm still afraid of it getting back to my boss and what that would mean for me long term."

"That's a tough spot to be in." There was such sympathy in his voice showing yet another way all his hardness was tempered by hidden bits of something more. I wanted to press my body into the parts of him that were firm and stiff, while burying my fingers into all the things that were pliable and velvety. He was a giant sensory overload and I wanted to let every single one of my senses gorge on him. I wanted to run my tongue across the rough and smooth parts of his skin, while inhaling the fresh and sharp scent that was all his. Man and wilderness, with a hint of wild and west thrown in to make it all the more masculine and authentic. I was dying to hear him say my name, low and deep.

The sound rumbling across naked skin and echoing forever into the vast solitude surrounding us.

"Well, this entire trip has been about forcing myself to take risks and do things I wouldn't normally do. Maybe when I get back, some of this newfound bravery will hitch a ride back to the Bay Area with me."

I waited for him to respond with something snarky, or maybe something sweet since he was showing me that side of himself when I least expected it, but the mules chose that moment to come to a complete stop, which yanked Cy's horse to a grinding halt. The swiftness of the stop sent Boss skirting nervously to the side, and had the domino effect of making the entire line behind us stutter and skip to an awkward pause.

"What's the holdup?" Lane's voice carried up the line, and before Cy or I could answer him, the sound of something motorized and very out of place in the quiet came from up head at the bend in the trail.

The mules brayed nervously as the unmistakable whir of an engine roared from somewhere up ahead. Cy's horse jerked its head as he fought the big animal to purposely move him in front of me instead of off to the side of the trail into the trees, where he obviously wanted to retreat.

"Sounds like a dirt bike," Cy hollered the response back to Lane, sounding calm but I could see the way his spine went arrow straight and the way his broad shoulders stiffened and squared like he was preparing himself for a battle.

"All the way out here?" The question came from one of the two suspicious men and I winced when I saw the look Cy shot over his shoulder at his brother. This wasn't something they were expecting or typically encountered and he didn't like it. Neither did the horses. They were all making noises and I could hear their hooves shifting and pawing at the ground.

Boss pranced wildly to the side as the noise grew louder and louder. Cy ordered us all to move to the side of the trail in as much of a line as we could make with the anxious animals fighting us. He said that he figured whoever was on the motorcycles would see us and hopefully, ride right on by our nervous line or stop when they saw the commotion they were causing. He was hoping they would agree to turn the bikes off so the horses weren't spooked any further. He mumbled so low that only I could hear that if the riders were from around these parts they would know trail code and abide so that the animals were safe.

That obviously wasn't the case. The camouflage painted machines roared and raced their way through the trees and down the narrow path like they owned the mountains. They careened way too close to the scared animals, like they were trying to purposely drive them into a panic. They succeeded because debris flew everywhere, and I knew if it was pinging against my skin and stinging, then it had to be hitting the unprotected horses. The men on the dirt bikes were garbed in camo and had their heads covered in menacing black helmets that didn't show any part of their faces. The engines revved and the wheels bit into the ground as they thundered by, kicking up earth and chaos, as they raced past with little concern for the horses or for those of us trapped on top of the skittish animals. Their intrusion was going to end badly. We could see it coming from a mile away.

I heard Cy swear and Lane yell something at the men as they sped by, but then everything was lost in a whoosh and a blur as Boss suddenly bolted. I could feel the big animal's fear as his body leapt through the air, desperately seeking an escape from the motorized growl that had disrupted our quiet afternoon. I called the horse's name and struggled with reins as I dug the heels of my boots into his sides. He was in such a panic and so terrified that he ripped through the woods, not caring that branches and tree limbs ripped at both of us. His sides were heaving and I could hear him breathing like he was running the Kentucky Derby, with me clinging helplessly to his back. I was wide awake yet caught in a nightmare from my past.

I contemplated jumping out of the saddle, but there wasn't a spot clear enough of timber and rocks to make a safe landing. I would end up with a broken neck if I risked it, so my only option was to hold on for dear life and pray that Boss tired out before I lost my grip.

All I could think as we careened wild and out of control, was that I had royally failed at showing the horse and the man who put me on him who was boss and that I really didn't want to die trying to experience life flavored with a little bit of risk and chance. I didn't want getting back on the horse to be the choice that ended it all.

CHAPTER 9

No Bed of Roses

I HAD NO IDEA HOW long the horse plowed through the unforgiving forest, but it felt like an endless loop of time where I struggled with no success to get control back. Terror clawed up my throat and fear raked its sharp edges down my spine. I screamed so long and loud that my voice cracked and I was pretty sure at some point I closed my eyes and prayed. My stomach hurt from all the knots it was tied in. The only thing that kept me holding on was the fact that Boss didn't seem interested in throwing me off of his back. He was, however, determined to get as far away from what had spooked him as quickly as possible. Just like Cy had told me when I first climbed on. Boss was dodging and weaving his way through trees and leaping over rocks and brush at a dazzling pace.

He was hell bound for safety and he was taking me with him, whether I wanted to go or not. All I could do was hold on for dear life and ineffectively swat at the branches and pine needles that were ripping at my skin. At one point, a stick smacked me sharply across the cheek and I let out a little scream because the skin split under the assault and I could feel blood trickling down my face and dripping off of my chin. I was too scared to let go of the wild animal to swipe at the crimson proof of my predicament, so all I could do was swear in frustration.

Suddenly, as if my unspoken pleas were heard and some divine force decided it wasn't quite time for me to be done learning all kinds of lessons about life and love, Boss broke out of the tree line and stampeded his way into a clearing that seemed completely out of place in the lush and dense woods. The wide-open space looked like the kind of tilled field that was found on a farm. As alien as it was in this forested terrain, it was a Godsend because the soft soil under the horse's hooves startled him enough that his furious bolt slowed enough and I could safely throw myself off of his back to the ground. I hit with a jarring thud, and of course found a rock to land on. The wind was sucked forcibly out of my lungs and the sky blurred into an abstract blue swirl as tears of pain flooded my eyes.

I wheezed and groaned my way to my knees, head bent down as I tried to catch my breath, as my wrist screamed in pain as it let me know it had taken the brunt of the rock's damage. I was sure with Boss now free of his burden he would continue on his rampage through the woods, but a velvety nose pushed against the top of my head making my hair move as he huffed out a breath. I think he was making sure I was all right as I struggled to get my feet back under me and my fright under control.

I lifted the back of my hand to my cheek and ineffectively rubbed at the blood that was trickling there. I reached up and patted the muzzle that was persistently pushing me and tried to mutter reassuringly that I was okay to the horse. I wanted him to know everything was fine. I wanted to tell him that I knew all about acting instinctively and foolishly when something scared you. I didn't blame him for doing exactly what I did in the same situations. I even dragged people along for the ride with me as I raced away from whatever it was that spooked me, leaving them to suffer the damage.

"It's okay." I said it over and over again as I worked my way to my feet. My shoulder wasn't the only part of my body protesting the move as one side of my hip throbbed and my head started to pound in a rapid beat. I ran my hand down Boss's neck and gave him a quick once over to make sure he hadn't hurt himself ripping through the flora and fauna like a bat out of hell. I cooed over his scraped fetlock and worried over an ugly looking gash that was slashed across his cannon. Last time a horse had injured me I'd refused to so much as look at another one for years and years. This time, I was more worried about the damage the animal had done to himself than I was the bumps and bruises I knew I would bounce back from.

"Poor baby. Those guys really worked you up, didn't they?" Boss titled his head in my direction and I rubbed my uninjured cheek against his. "They were jerks and they sure as hell didn't belong out here."

He huffed out of his nose and then nickered loudly and tossed his head in warning. I stiffened next to him as I heard the sound of branches breaking and the pounding of heavy hooves as another horse and rider broke into the unexpected clearing. I knew I shouldn't be surprised that Cy came after me, but I was. I was also touched and slightly overwhelmed by the look of concern on his face. I knew he had to be worried about his horse and how my wild ride would affect his business, but I also knew, without a doubt, that some of his anxiety and fret was for me, as well.

He swung out of his saddle before his horse came to a full stop. His arms were around me and pulling me to his chest before I could get out any words to tell him that both Boss and I were banged up, but fine. His hands were tangled in my hair before I could get my breath back from the force of being yanked around by hard hands and his voracious mouth was all over mine before I could register that his heart was racing and that there seemed to be a fine tremor working its way through his entire body. The hands in my hair were desperate and shaking. The lips against mine were demanding and brutal.

He kissed me to reassure himself I was in one piece and unharmed.

He kissed me because he was worried about me.

He kissed me because that was the easiest way for a man like him to communicate his way through all the complicated emotions and feelings that surged and pulsed between the two of us.

He kissed me because I let him and wouldn't let him stop, even when he tried to pull away.

I wrapped my good arm around his neck, lifted myself up on the tips of my now worn-in boots, and sealed my lips to his as I inhaled the affirmation that I was okay and had a whole lot left to experience before my time on this planet was done.

I twisted my tongue with his and let my teeth graze across that damp curve of his lower lip. I could taste the tang of his fear there and it was sweet because it was fear for me. He breathed life and passion into me as I absorbed it all and tried to give back reassurance and comfort. I never wanted anyone to leave me but I'd never really let anyone show up for me when I needed them either. I was always pushing away but as his mouth punished and praised mine, there was no way I wasn't pulling Cy closer. I sighed against his lowly muttered "thank fuck" as he pulled away and rested his forehead against mine.

One of his hands escaped the disorderly mess my hair was in and slowly skimmed over my torn cheek and across my jaw. His touch was feather light and barely there, but I felt it like a ton of bricks. When all his hardness faded to soft, it was enough to make me explode. His gentleness was a spark that made the things that were hot and heavy smolder deep inside of me. His hand curled around the side of my neck and his thumb swept back and forth over my pulse, like he was counting the times my heart beat and making sure it was enough.

"Scared the shit out of me when Boss broke free. That nervous bastard has you about five miles away from where you're supposed to be. He looks like a badass but inside he's a big ol' baby. I thought I was going to find you wrapped around a tree or on the ground with your head split open. I should've known you could take care of yourself." His words whispered across my lips and the vibration of them made me slip my tongue out so I could try and catch the sweetness of them before they faded away.

"I didn't do anything other than hold on." My voice was as shaky as his hands were, but I sounded turned on, not afraid, and that fact had me feeling oddly proud of myself.

Cy pulled back and the hand at my throat slid down the center of my chest. The buttons on my shirt popped and snapped out of his way as his palm settled over where my heart was racing and silently pleading for more of his touch. His hands weren't soft or smooth. The fact that he worked with them for a living was evident against my skin, but the roughness made my breath catch and my knees quiver. The look in his eyes as he watched me while he tried to touch my heart through the delicate cage it was trapped in had my nipples pulling into hard peaks and desire tugging at that now damp and achy place between my legs. All the man had to do was look at me with those cloud colored eyes and I ended up wet with want and weak-kneed with neediness.

"Sometimes that's all you have to do to make the best out of a bad situation. You hold on when letting go is so much easier." His words rumbled out of his chest and I felt them work their way through me.

I wanted to hold on—to him and to this woman I was while I was out here with him—but now wasn't the time or the place.

In fact, I was still confused about where exactly we were in the seemingly endless woods.

"Why is this clearing here? I saw it from the top of the rocks when we were climbing the other day and I thought it was weird, and now that I'm in the middle of it, I know it's extra weird. It doesn't belong here."

Cy moved away from me and bent down to look at the wound on Boss's front and hind legs. He ran soothing hands along the animal's sides, his gentle handling of the animal made my heart squeeze. I liked him when he was gruff and unapproachable. I more than liked him when he was kind and thoughtful.

"If I was a betting man, I would put good money on this field and the guys on the motorcycles being connected." He straightened back up and put his hands on his hips. "I would also bet that they were the ones behind the gunshot the other night. This part of the trail is pretty remote as we go up into the high country. Only our tour and hunters ever really come up this way. I think we're standing in someone's grow spot." He sounded grim and the expression on his face matched his tone.

"Grow spot?" We were in Wyoming, not Columbia or Mexico. "You mean a drug field?"

He nodded and collected Boss's reins in one hand and his horse's in another. "Pot is big business a state over and a couple to the west of us. Marijuana growers have made their way into the mountains to grow product so they can ship it to the states where it's been legalized. I haven't seen it here, but some ranchers I do business with out of Montana had several acres of weed growing on their property without them knowing about it. They were clueless until the DEA came knocking on their door with warrants. It looks like it's a problem that found its way here, and we are unfortunately right in the thick of the operation."

"Why would they grow the pot here if it's legal to grow in

other places?" I was still confused about what was going on and what it meant for us, since we were still out in the middle of nowhere with several days to go until we got back to civilization.

"When the government gets involved that means fees and regulations. Typically, people who deal in narcotics don't like to be told what to do and they don't like to give Uncle Sam a cut of their profits. They grow the drugs in places that are hard to get to, heavily forested, and rarely visited by other people. They can sell the drugs for top dollar to the dispensaries and not worry about paying taxes and being regulated. This isn't good. We are way too close to comfort to this operation and they are letting us know it. We need to get back and get everyone on a different trail. I'm going to move us all down so that we're following the river. It's more populated, so whoever has this operation out here is more likely to avoid areas with more people. I also need to see if I can catch Sutton before he heads out this way. I need let him know to alert the authorities. I don't want him riding up here on his own with all this stuff happening." His gaze drifted over me and his mouth dipped into a frown. "Are you feeling up to riding out of here? I can't put you back on Boss until we get some salve on those cuts and get him bandaged up, but we can both hop up on Edgar."

I lifted my arm and sucked in a pained gasp as my wrist protested, sending blinding pain shooting up to my elbow and beyond. Focusing on something else so I didn't throw up from the pain, I wheezed, "You named your horse Edgar?"

He grimaced. "He was a wedding present from my dad when I moved back home. He was supposed to go to Selah. She loved Edgar Allen Poe."

I walked over to him and put a hand on his arm. The muscle tensed under my fingers and his eyes shifted from stormy to graphite. "And you were supposed to love each other with a love that was more than love." The line was from Annabel Lee, which was my favorite Poe poem. Somehow, even though it had only been days and minutes, time I spent with Cy felt more important than any that came before it.

"Didn't quite work out that way." The words were gruff and so was the man who muttered them low and deep. I could feel his regret and his remorse. It made me understand the difference between losing someone you really loved and losing someone you merely thought you loved. My heart hurt but it was already starting to bounce back from Chris's mishandling of it. When Cy spoke about his past and what he had left there, it was evident his ex-wife had taken a big chunk of his heart with her when she left.

I squeezed the arm I was holding onto and asked, "Does it ever?" I mean, my grandparents had that kind of love but that was the only example I could think of.

We stared at each other for a long, silent moment, his eyes searching mine with unreadable intensity. Eventually, he reached out the hand with the leather reins wrapped around it and brushed the back of his knuckles across my cheek. They came away stained rusty red and I remembered I was still bleeding and banged up. Now wasn't the time to allow myself to turn all mushy and sentimental about things that were never meant to be. It also made no sense to let myself fall for a man who wasn't for me . . . but my heart was ignoring my head in a major way.

He tilted his head toward the saddle and told me to hop up. "Sometimes we get more than we asked for because we've settled for less for so long. When you pay your dues, you're bound to be rewarded, eventually."

With my wrist burning and my head back to pounding, I needed his help to get up onto his horse. His help involved a hand across my ass and a push, but it got the job done and it took my mind off the fact that I was back on a horse so soon after my terrifying ride through the woods. Balking and refusing to ride again didn't even cross my mind, which was a revelation. It made me feel brave and proud of myself. My mission to locate that self-confidence and sense of who I was felt like it was well on its way to being complete.

Cy maneuvered Boss closer so that he could heft himself up behind me in the saddle. No matter how far forward I scooted on the saddle, his bulk and his heat took up all the available space, so I didn't argue when he wrapped a heavy arm around my waist and tugged me to rest against his chest. It felt like a hug that was more than a hug and I liked that even his comfort was a mix of all his hardness and his softness. The man was an intoxicating mix of both and I was getting hooked on him at an alarming speed.

We rode quietly for a few minutes, the pace slow but steady to allow for Boss's injured legs. I could see the broken branches and turned over earth where we had barreled our way through the forest. It was a clear as day trail that any shady character growing drugs in a remote location could follow right back to the rest of the group. I was nervous about stumbling onto something we obviously weren't supposed to find, but I knew that Cy would do whatever it took to keep me and the rest of the riders safe. He wasn't a cowboy, but he was a good man, a man who took responsibility for those in his care seriously. He was a man who would stand between any kind of threat and those who needed his protection.

"How do you know your dues have been paid?" I asked the question so quietly that I wasn't sure he heard me.

His arm tightened around my middle as I laced my fingers through his where he held me, keeping my other wrist held tightly to my chest to protect it from the jarring steps the horse took.

"You just know. Suddenly, there's something or someone in front of you that you know you've earned."

"What if they're only in front of you for a split second? Is it really a reward if you don't have the time to fully appreciate it?" I rubbed my thumb over his wrist and felt his pulse kick under the caress.

"Of course it is, because even if you only get the pleasure of enjoying what you've been given for a second, or a minute, or a day, you still get to experience it. That experience will stay with you forever and that's the reward. No one can take those memories away from you. No one can strip you of the moments you've had. Even if the trophy is gone, you still won it and that victory lasts forever."

My head hurt and so did my heart. The ache in my chest was vastly different from the one that lived there after Chris's machinations and manipulation. This pain was dull and deep. It was one that took up all the available space and let me know when I left this place and this man, there was a good chance I was going to be leaving a part of myself behind with him.

"Honestly, I've never felt like much of a prize. I mentioned that my mother was also kind of a mess but that doesn't even really touch it. She got knocked up by accident and my grandparents had to beg her to keep me. She dumped me on them the second I took a breath. She was always around when I was growing up, but she was never in my life, which made the fact she didn't want anything to do with me even more obvious. My grandparents worked themselves to death making sure I had a wonderful, happy, and secure childhood. They loved me harder than most of the other kids' actual parents did. For some reason none of it ever blocked out the fact I wasn't wanted. My mother's rejection made me defensive and distrustful. I never let anyone get very close. Honestly, the only person who refused to respect my boundaries and KEEP OUT signs was Em." I laughed a little. "I think she pushed so hard because I was so desperate not to be her friend. She was sick of being used by other girls because she was, and is, so pretty and well liked. Everyone wanted to bask in her glow and I was all about hiding in the shadows."

He rubbed his chin on the top of my head which made some of my curly hair cling to his scruff.

"Maybe she's just smart. Everything that is precious and valuable is usually kept behind glass. It takes someone unafraid of the shards and the edges to break through that so that they can get to the treasure inside. Your friend doesn't seem like she's scared of much. She has wild in her eyes and adventure in her soul. Even with all the crazy stuff happening on this ride, she's having the time of her life. She isn't scared of a little bit of work and I can almost guarantee she knew that the cuts and scrapes of your friendship would be worth it, if she broke through your shield to get at you." Mr. Personality had given way to Mr. Philosopher and his words were doing things to my insides that were never going to be undone.

"For a guy who everyone says isn't very good with people, you have a way of handling them and understanding them that is pretty remarkable."

I couldn't keep the praise out of my tone but he made me want to hit him when he replied with a dry, "Just women, remember? I know women and horses."

I wished I could turn around and glare at him but didn't want to risk setting us of balance so I settled for a snappy, "Do you pretend to be such a jerk most of the time so your brothers don't bug you about being more hands-on with the guests?"

He made a noise low in his throat that was halfway between a laugh and a grunt. "I don't have the time or the patience for most of the people who want to come out here and play cowboy. I'm too busy looking after my family and my land to take the time to be invested in anyone who is only going to be in my life for a few days. I'm happy to take their money and show them a good time, but I don't care about who they are or where they're from. Occasionally, a pretty girl from the city finds her way into my bed before she makes her way back home and we both have a pleasant memory of her visit here. Who she is doesn't matter to me, only what she's willing to offer." I stiffened at that particular admission but like everything else about him, his honesty was real and unfiltered. "Who you are matters to me, Leo. I want to know why you're the one who is on my mind all the time." His head moved and his lips were suddenly by my ears. "You pissed me off and turned me on the second you opened your mouth. I knew in that second, that for whatever reason, you were here for me. We only get this moment, Sunshine, just one, so it needs to matter to you as much as it matters to me."

I turned my head the fraction of an inch I needed to put my lips on his. It was just the press of lips lightly together but it was a kiss that spoke volumes. I wanted him and I wanted as many moments as we could cram into the short amount of time we had left together.

"It matters and you matter, Cy." And every moment that we had, regardless of what it was made of or what was inside of it, mattered. He made me mad, he made me happy. He turned me on and he put me out with his hot and cold attitude, but with him I felt more than I ever had before because I wasn't running from those feelings. I couldn't control them, or my reaction to him, and that terrified and excited me equally. Inside, my head was threatening my heart with all kinds of ugly, painful warnings. However, my tender and newly enlightened heart decided not to listen. Lane was right, there was no place for logic in love.

CHAPTER 10

Not So Fast

WHEN WE GOT BACK TO the trail, where everyone was anxiously waiting our return, it was anything but welcoming. Emrys immediately was buzzing all around me and wasted no time in attacking my torn face with the limited supplies the brothers had packed away in a tiny first aid kit. She was apologizing profusely for making me come on this knowing how nervous I was to get back on a horse after my past experience with them. I told her, no less than a hundred times, that I was fine on both the inside and the out, but she was caught in a guilt vortex. Nothing I said to her and no amount of reassurance that I threw at her seemed to be getting through. I let her fuss over me while Cy took care of Boss and spoke to Lane in low, serious tones.

Marcus and Meghan were making pointed complaints about the trip not being the tranquil, relaxing commune with nature they had been expecting, and Evan was glaring at me like I was personally responsible for all the things that were going wrong in her life. I even overheard her murmuring to her brother that I had purposely let my horse run out of control, so I would have an excuse to spend alone time with Cy and that he would be forced to share his saddle with me. To his credit, Ethan rolled his eyes and told her to get a life but that didn't stop the nasty looks the girl was tossing my way or the misplaced jealousy that was radiating off of her.

Lane told everyone the plan to ride a few miles through the woods to take us back down by the river for everyone's safety. Without mentioning what we had stumbled on deep in the woods, he told everyone that the gunshot from a couple nights before coupled with motorbikes today, made this trail too unpredictable and the group's safety needed to be first priority. He promised the rest of the ride would be quickly back to nature and the unspoiled majesty of the Wyoming wilderness. He sold the kids on the idea of being down by the river by dangling a trip on inner tubes through the light rapids one of the days. The adults were a harder sell.

Marcus was making noise about a refund because of the change in plans, but I was pretty sure he was just talking to hear himself speak. Meghan had long since grown tired of his peacocking and pretension. She may have started this trip trying to hold her frayed family together but something told me once they got back to the city she would be cutting loose the dead weight. She told her husband to be quiet and assured Lane that whatever they needed to do in order to safely enjoy the rest of the trip, they would gladly do. She also thanked him for having the best interest of her kids in mind while giving her husband a look that said maybe he should try that sometime.

Webb and Grady also grumbled about changing trails. They both seemed to be overly interested in where the men on the dirt bikes had come from and where they had gone. They asked both Cy and Lane a ton of questions that the brothers either refused to answer or couldn't answer. Grady even suggested that someone go after the men on the bikes to hold them accountable for spooking the horses and putting me in danger. He even looked at me for support when he spouted off the crazy idea.

Cy laid down a 'no' that left zero room for argument. I could tell he was worried and impatient at having to deal with everyone else's concerns. He missed Sutton when he called to the ranch on the satellite phone. Brynn told them that the middle Warner brother was already on his way to us without any kind of warning about the danger he could be facing. Both Cy and Lane were even more on edge after Brynn relayed that information and it was clear they wanted us to get packed up and relocated to a new spot as quickly as possible. The only good news was that Brynn agreed to call the local rangers and let them know what was going on. Cy gave her our rough coordinates and told her that she needed to warn whoever came to investigate that the people who had disrupted our trip were armed, assuming the guys on the bikes were the same ones shooting in the middle of the night, and they should be considered dangerous. Even over the crackling and static-filled line, the concern in Brynn's voice was evident as she told Cy to take care of himself and Lane.

When it was time to saddle up and make our way down to the river, Evan graciously offered her horse with fake, wide-eyed innocence. Boss was still moving much slower than he had been and favoring his back leg. I took her up on the offer even though I knew she was going to try and put herself on Cy's horse when I displaced her. Luckily, before the teen could make a scene or put him in the position of having an awkward conversation with her about why that was totally inappropriate, her mother ordered the girl to share her brother's mount. It was obvious neither sibling was thrilled with the prospect, but I wanted to give Meghan a high five for finally doing her job. I wasn't the only one who found a piece of myself that was lost by coming out here and doing things I normally wouldn't do.

For some reason, I really wanted Meghan to take her life

back. I wanted it for her and her kids. I really, really wanted the oblivious and ostentatious dad to get a dose of karmic retribution. I still couldn't figure out a way to tell Chris's wife what he was up to without it blowing back on me, but after watching this woman suffer all week at the careless hands of a man who was supposed to love her, I was feeling more and more compelled to come clean with her. Ignorance wasn't bliss.

I needed help onto the horse because my wrist had swollen and turned into a scary shade of purplish black. It burned so badly that I was hardly able to breathe through it and moving my arm was practically impossible. Lane made his way over to give me a boost; however, he was rudely shoved out of the way by his big brother when Cy noticed his sibling's hands at my waist. I needed more than a hand on my ass to get me in the saddle this time around and there was no hiding the grimace and gasp of pain that whooshed out when I leaned forward to reach for the reins.

Cy gave me a concerned look from under his brows. "You gonna make it?"

It took a minute for me to get my breath back so I could form words. When I did, they were weak and shaky. "I'll make it. I don't really have much of a choice."

He nodded grimly. "When Sutton finds us I'll have him and Lane finish out the ride and I'll take you back to the ranch so you can get that wrist looked at. It might be broken. Emrys can catch up with you after the ride. It should only be a day's difference if we push hard."

I didn't love that idea and I knew Em would hate it. She was already hovering over me like a mother hen. If she knew I was in enough pain to need a doctor, there was no way she was going to let me take off alone with Cy. I figured that was a bridge I would cross when I had to, right now I needed to concentrate on staying in the saddle and not passing out every time I got jolted and jostled in the saddle.

"I'll be all right." And I would be because I finally understood that when you got kicked around, hurt, even abandoned, it was possible to bounce back from it, you just had to be willing to try. Hell, Cy was living with half a heart and he was still more of a man and a better person than most people who were whole. I would heal and I would live to fight and fuck another day. It was empowering knowledge and it finally shut the door on all the doubt and uncertainty that had been pushing its way over all the confidence and conviction inside of me.

"That's my girl." He patted my thigh and gave it a squeeze.

The ride to the river was a tooth grinding, stomach clenching, white knuckled trip. I almost threw up twice and my vision kept blurring in and out to the point that Cy took the reins from me and guided the horse I was on because I couldn't hold on anymore and barely managed to stay in the saddle. Emrys was asking me if I was okay every five minutes and I was still getting dirty looks and annoyed scowls from Evan. It was miserable and I was a mess. My brain was shouting at me to give up, to let the pain take over and surrender to the all-encompassing feelings of uselessness and hopelessness swirling under the surface.

By the time we got to a place that was flat and far enough away from the riverbank that we wouldn't get flooded out if it decided to rain, I was nothing more than a live wire of agony and torment. The slightest movement had tears pricking my eyes and my breath whooshing out in sucking gasps and groans. I couldn't get off the horse without help, which meant I literally fell into Cy's waiting arms. He caught me without complaint but the harsh expression on his face as he looked at me let me know my suffering was pretty evident on my face.

"You were white as a ghost when we started out and now

you're gray with a little green thrown in to keep things interesting." I couldn't stay upright any longer. I collapsed into him, my forehead hitting the center of his chest as his arms wrapped around me to keep me somewhat vertical.

"That was rough." The words were garbled together and didn't make much sense. I felt like I needed a hundred naps and one million Tylenol.

"It was, but you made it." He twisted his head and told Lane, who was also watching me like I might keel over at any minute, "I'm gonna take her back. She's barely holding it together and her wrist might be broken."

Lane's frown cut even deeper into his good looking face. "You sure that's safe? If something happens to you on the way back she's gonna be all on her own with a busted wing."

The thought of getting back on a lumbering, trotting horse made me groan out loud and I held up my good hand in protest. "I'm not getting back in a saddle. It isn't broken. I might have a hairline fracture, at most. It's sprained and swollen but I'll live. The bouncing around on the back of a horse isn't helping things at all and that's what feels like it might kill me." And I didn't want to think about what would happen to me if I ended up alone in the woods.

"The only thing we can do is rig a sling together for her if she doesn't want to ride back to the ranch. I'll check it out more closely once I have her away from prying eyes." He gave me a lopsided grin that didn't quite reach his eyes. "I know a secret spot I can take you to that will help with the sore muscles and take some of the stiffness out of that wrist. It's not much of a fix but it's the best I can do in a pinch."

Emrys and Evan were both watching us with narrowed eyes. Emrys's were full of curiosity and question. She was worried about me, but she didn't want to get in the way of whatever it was that had Cy's arms wrapped so tightly around me. Evan was silently wishing horrible things upon me with every glare and glower she shot my way, but I was in way too much pain to worry about her innocent crush getting obliterated. She would survive and be stronger for it. I wish someone had taken the time to teach me that young hearts could heal so quickly before I built a fortress around mine.

I returned the weak smile he was giving me. "A secret spot? How can it be secret if you know about it?"

He blinked in surprise and lifted an eyebrow at me. "She's still mouthy. That's a good sign." He turned to walk away but not before throwing over his shoulder, "I know all kinds of things no one else knows, Leo."

That was the truth. He knew how to push and pull me at the same time. He was the only person who made me want to chase full speed after heartbreak. He was the only one who saw through all my standard defenses and barreled his way past them like they weren't even there. He knew I was prickly and pointy, but more than that, he knew the reasons why and my thorns didn't seem to bother him in the slightest.

Grady and Webb had wandered off to start setting up camp. As usual, they were having an intent conversation between themselves and didn't seem at all interested in what was going on with the rest of the group. Frankly, I was surprised they were still with us. The pretense that they were here on some kind of business trip seemed long abandoned. They had ulterior motives for being out here in the woods with the rest of us and their focus on who else might be lurking on the remote and hard-to-reach trails was so obvious there was no ignoring it. I couldn't worry about that either because Cy turned me around, plastered my back to his front and started marching me toward the river and away from camp. He was still holding me up and each step he took, he bore most of my weight as I tripped and lagged in front of him. I was nothing more than a Leo-sized marionette and all my strings were wrapped around Cy's fingers.

"You want me to come after you if you're gone for more than an hour?" Lane's voice shifted from serious to salacious and a knowing light glinted in his denim eyes. The smile on his face made me blush.

"Give me a little longer than that. We're going to have to alternate being on lookout tonight, so we can keep an eye out for Sutton." And for whoever else might be lurking in the woods, but he didn't say that part out loud. "Get everyone fed and settled in. We'll be back in a bit."

Cy started marching me in the opposite direction we'd started out in. Lane started laughing and shouted at me, "Remember that there's nothing to block sound out here, Leo. If you're a screamer the entire camp is going to know it."

I blushed even hotter and tried to turn my head so I could tell him to fuck off, but Cy wouldn't let me. He was on a mission and nothing was going to deter him from it. When my legs quit working because the pain from my shoulder sucked all of my remaining energy and stamina, he simply picked me up and carried me like I was a baby, cradled against his chest for the last ten minutes of the trek to the hidden hot springs.

There was a bend in the river and an outcropping of rocks that looked too steep to climb. Cy walked us around the back of the formation and I was shocked to see a bubbling pool of water that was about the size of an apartment swimming pool behind the boulders. Someone had walled the water in with stone so that it was a natural hot tub hidden away in the middle of nowhere.

"This place is insane." I exhaled the words out in awe. It was surrounded by nothing but wide open sky and craggy rocks. It was like something out of a movie or a glossy 'Come to

Wyoming' travel brochure.

"Wyoming is covered with thermal vents. There are all kinds of spots along the river folks have blocked off to make natural soaking pools. This one is hidden because it's behind the rocks. Dad used to bring us out here in the middle of winter." He stepped away from me and turned me around to face him.

"Why in winter?" I asked the question as he rubbed his hand over his face like his patience was at the breaking point.

"He always told us we wouldn't appreciate it fully in the summertime. Ranch work is always hard and grueling on your body, but that goes into overdrive in winter. You aren't just battling stubborn livestock and unforgiving landscape, you're also trying to fight Mother Nature, and that bitch is undefeated around here." He tilted his head toward the water. "It's hot, but I think it will help some of those bumps and bruises."

I looked at the water and then back to him. I could feel heat rising in my neck and my cheeks getting warm. My reaction made his eyes spark with silver threads of arousal.

"Great. But I don't think I can get in there by myself." If I did get in, there was no way I was getting myself back out.

"I'll help you in." His deep voice was dripping with velvet and promise.

I flushed under his unwavering scrutiny. "We didn't bring anything to change into."

That almost smile lifted the edges of his mouth and I knew if he ever managed to get all the way there, I was going to hand my heart over to him with no questions asked. His half a smile already owned me, his entire smile was bound to consume me.

"We're going in the water, our clothes aren't."

Well, when you put it like that . . .

I moved to start unbuttoning my shirt and almost ended up on my knees in front of him as searing agony shot through me when I tried to move my bad wrist to grab the buttons. Through watery eyes and a tight throat, I told him, "I don't think I can get undressed either. This is going to be incredibly awkward."

He took a step toward me, then another. We were almost touching chest to chest and we were sharing breaths and heart-beats. He lifted his hands to the front of my shirt and was aching-ly gentle as he slid one button after the other free. "Don't worry, Leo, I've got you and I'll take care of you the best I can."

He did have me. More of me than I'd ever let anyone have before. He had my attention and my time. He had my interest and my investment. He had my heart and my mind at war over him. One demanding that I leave him and the devastation that he would be responsible for in the dust, the other clamoring at me to open up, to embrace the memories we were bound to make together. We might not get forever together, but we could cram a lot into the moments we did get. They could be more import-ant than any of the other ones I'd had with anyone else. He got me because I gave myself to him and I was about to give him so much more.

It wasn't like anything was on display that he hadn't seen already. He took my shirt off so carefully I almost didn't feel the fabric leave until the mountain air hit my skin. I shivered as he rubbed the back of his knuckles along the edge of my boring cotton bra and tingled like only he could make me do when his other hand snaked around my back to release the hook.

My instinct was to reach up and cover myself as the bra fell away, but I couldn't move my arms and the hungry look that cut into his face when I was exposed before him kept me still. I'd never had a man look at me like I was anything special before. Cy looked at me like I was *everything* special and that had my body warming and twitching with desire. I was used to being average and acceptable. Being more and magnificent was heady enough to make me drunk on swirling lust and longing.

"You've seen me naked, Cy. What's the holdup?" My voice quivered as his palm skimmed across my lower ribcage and played teasingly below the top of my jeans. He flicked open my belt buckle and smirked at me.

"I haven't been given many gifts in my life, so when I do get one I like to take my time getting the wrapping off of it." His eyes glinted with sexy intent and humor. He wasn't going to be rushed and I might die waiting for him to get to the good stuff.

"Our time is limited. You might want to keep that in mind." I didn't want to remind him that this was destined to end. That we were on borrowed time, working with stolen seconds. I felt there was a clock counting down, hanging over our heads, ticking away with every blink and every word uttered.

"I'm not going to worry about the time we don't have. I'm going to focus making the time that we do have count." He had my belt undone and my pants open before I could think of something fitting to say about his poignant declaration.

I put the hand of my uninjured arm on his shoulder as he crouched down in front of me and began to work on getting my boots off of my feet. The new position had his face directly in line with the part of me that had never been shy about getting all kinds of wet and ready when he was in the vicinity. I was on the verge of falling over again, only this time it had nothing to do with pain.

"I don't know that I'm up for any strenuous activities at the moment, Cy. I'm not exactly in tip-top form." I hated admitting it but I didn't want to end up in the dirt on my ass, naked and sprawled out like an uncoordinated centerfold in front of him. My newly repaired ego couldn't take a hit like that so soon. My wrist hurt when I moved it but the rest of me was all onboard for letting him do whatever the hell he wanted.

He rocked back a little bit so that he was sitting on his heels. Those eyes the color of an angry heaven swirled with passion and promise as he gazed up at me. His heavy hands landed on either side of my hips and slowly, oh so slowly, he started to peel away the dirty and tattered jeans down my legs. Once I was mostly naked he leaned forward so that his soft lips and scratchy face marked each jutting hipbone. His nose dragged a tantalizing trail along the top of my underwear and his breath lapped hotly against the cotton that was barely covering my aching clit and clenching center.

"Do you trust me, Leo?" It was a silly question. I hardly knew him, even if I felt like I understood him inside and out.

I shifted my grip off of his shoulder and let my fingers drift through his thick hair. It was slippery against my fingers—not in an unpleasant way—from whatever he used to keep it styled. I liked the idea that when I was done with him he was going to be ruffled and sexed up. I wanted to leave those marks on him.

"I trust what I know about you, Cy, which isn't very much." The last word ended up strangled and strained as his thumbs slipped inside the leg band of my panties and started rubbing in circles toward my damp folds and aching core. There was no hiding how much I wanted him or how effective his touch was at turning me on.

"You trust what I've given you, and you trust what I tell you. I'm telling you I've got you, Leo. I'm not going to let you fall or hurt you."

Trust was huge for me. I didn't give it lightly and I didn't have a lot of it to spare. With him looking up at me, eyes bleeding promises and possibility, there was no way I could deny him anything . . . no way I could deny myself.

CHAPTER 11

No Going Back

I NEVER LET ANYONE THIS close, physically or emotionally.
There was no going back from this. I could feel it and him
all the way through me. There was life before Cyrus Warner
and life after. The two didn't even slightly compare and neither did any amount of pleasure I had experienced before this
big, brooding mystery of a man. Every touch between us was
a memory in the making and every word as he eased me in the
water was a vow I knew he intended to keep.

He promised pleasure and passion.

He promised gratification.

He promised obliteration.

He promised adoration.

He promised a distraction from the pain that was still making my hand tingle and my fingers throb.

I was ready to take him up on all of it because the warm water had worked wonders and I knew our time was limited. The
ache in my wrist was bad, but so was the ache between my legs.
One I had the opportunity to take care of as soon as I got back to
the ranch. I had no idea if I would get another shot to soothe the
other one with the man who was responsible for it.

I gasped his name and pitched forward in shock and

surrender as one of the hands clasping my ass slid between my legs and disappeared into the torrent of desire he had encouraged. I knew what he would find when his fingers slipped inside of me. Grasping muscles, silky moisture, a greedy channel that wanted more because with Cy there didn't seem to be enough.

I put my good hand on the rigid plane of his shoulder and almost exploded across his tongue as his pitch-black lashes lifted revealing eyes that were furious and thunderous with longing. It was a storm I wanted to come . . . on me or in me. I didn't really care. His mouth was wet and red from working me over, and while he still wasn't smiling, his usual smirk had much less of an edge to it. I wasn't sure if he was happy or not, but whatever was happening between the two of us at this very moment had definitely given him a reason to forget that he only had half a heart. He wasn't missing anything at the moment because he was focused entirely on me and on all the ways he was making my body give him the reactions that he wanted. Who knew that letting go could feel so fucking good?

I lifted my hand so I could trace his chiseled jaw and almost went under the water when I felt his mouth move over mine, his tongue pushing between my lips and moving in time with his pumping and plunging fingers. The dual stimulation was too much to process and my body gave up trying. I was in his hands, and I was going to let him guide me somewhere I had never been before. I was used to giving orders and making sure what needed to get taken care of got done. With Cy, no direction was needed as he skillfully stroked and sucked, sending pleasure skating up and down my spine. The more I leaned on him, pressed in to him, the faster his fingers curled and tapped against some hidden hot spot inside of me I never knew existed.

"What are you doing to me?" The words whispered out, surprised and questioning as I felt the crest of release uncoiling low in my belly and burning at the base of my spine. I had one hand in his hair, holding him. In fact, I felt the tip of his rigid shaft as close to my open and exposed center as it could get. He rocked himself between my slippery, silky folds as we both gasped from the contact.

I was exhilarated and so, so close to coming undone all over his questing tongue and plundering fingers. I couldn't feel my wrist anymore. Everything was a blur of blinding pleasure and decadent desire.

His warm breath danced across my lips. "I'm making sure you know that you matter, Leo. Time might be limited, but all the different ways I want to make you whisper and then scream my name feel infinite now that I have the taste of you on my tongue and the feel of you on my fingers."

It wasn't his fingers curving into my backside and disappearing to trip over places no man had ever dared try and touch before that set me off. It wasn't the bite of his deep kiss or the talented twist of his tongue. It wasn't the fingers touching, tapping, torturing all the sweet and starving places inside of me that seemed like they had been waiting for him to fill them up forever. It wasn't the press of his leg between mine or the careful way he held my injured wrist against his chest, making sure it didn't move that pulled my orgasm out of hiding and made me sob his name.

It was his deep voice and the rumble of his words against my skin when he told me, "You are so much more than I expected you to be."

To have this extraordinary man, with all his history and heartbreak, tell me that I was something special, it tore me apart. I was buried under an avalanche of passion and praise. I shattered on waves of approval and bliss. I drifted away on an orgasm so intense that twisted me up and turned my idea of what sex and satisfaction should be on its head.

He caught me as I fell against him and told me that he wanted to suck my nipples to see if they tasted like candy because they were so pink and pretty. He growled that he wanted to bend me over and take me from the back so he could lose his hands in my crazy hair.

I nervously cleared my throat and untangled my hand from his hair so I could trace the arch of his eyebrow and sharp ridge of his cheek. I liked touching all his soft places.

"I've always liked a man with a plan, Cyrus." I sighed as he whispered in my ear, that if we had enough time, he would show me how fun it could be if I let him take me in that place I never let anyone near before his gentle caresses went exploring there today. That sparked pulses of curiosity and interest inside a soaked center that was already begging for more of his attention. I wasn't that daring, but for him I might be. His thumb rubbed circles on the back of my knee, as I shivered and shook my way down from the pinnacle of pleasure and back to reality. When I could think straight I realized he had me sprawled naked across his lap where I was straddling a very hard erection.

He grabbed my chin in one of his hands and tilted my face up. His lips twitched and it was my heart that tugged in response instead of my greedy core. My body liked his mouth and his hands, my heart was all about the things that made him drop his stony, impenetrable shield. "When you're not in pain, I'm going to fuck you with my face while you suck my cock. Then I'm going to have you ride me so hard that neither one of us will be able to walk straight for a week."

That was the best promise he's made yet.

I brushed my lips across the side of his neck and traced the vein that was throbbing there with the tip of my tongue. I felt his breathing hitch and the hardness underneath my ass pressed insistently into me, letting me know this moment was far from over.

"Promises, promises." I breathed the words into his ear and used the tip of my tongue to trace the shell. He tasted like mountains and man. The way his entire body shuddered at the light touch was almost enough to make me forget about my banged-up wrist.

Considering I knew what kind of exciting equipment he was working with, I couldn't stop myself from rolling my hips against the delicious length that was solid as steel and velvety soft against my opening. I rolled my hips, unknowingly searching for some kind of fulfillment. The seductive rocking motion had the abs I was pressed against pulling tight and shoulders I was held against locked hard and straight. I rubbed the end of my nose along the bristly edge of his jaw and touched my lips to the corner of his mouth.

"I'm safe, if you're safe, just in case you were wondering." The tip of his cock was teasing my entrance, giving me just enough of a taste that I was dying for more. At my words, he shifted his weight just enough that the swollen head tapped against my equally eager clit. Declaring to him that I was ready and willing to see where this thing between us was going without *anything* between us was without a doubt the most daring and risky thing I had ever done.

His rough fingers tightened again around my neck and I had to concentrate really hard on keeping my breathing slow and steady as his cock jerked excitedly against my ass. I was so irritated I couldn't move my other arm the way I wanted to. I really wanted to get my hands on that throbbing, thick flesh. It was even warmer than the water swirling around us.

"I'm definitely not safe when I'm with you, Leo, but I'm safe when it comes to sex and I would never put you at any undue risk. You know that, right?" His hold on my neck loosened and his hand skimmed back down over my chest and disappeared under the water. I sucked in my stomach as his fingers played over the soft skin, then dipped lower as he shifted behind me. His stiff cock behind me moved until it pressed and rubbed between the valley back there. Then it was lower, sliding between my legs that I willingly spread open to give him access. His tip pressed in far enough that my body had to yield to his invasion. We both made a noise, mine strangled, his hungry.

"I wouldn't be here if I thought you had any intention of hurting me, Cy. I'm here because you promised to make everything feel better." That was a tall order but so far he seemed up to the task.

He grunted and then he was easing his cock inside my eager folds, while his fingers dipped into my warmth from the front so that they could torment my already sensitive and responsive clit.

His breath rasped in and out against my ear and the tip of his nose brushed against my cheek as he spread me wide open and took up all the space inside of me. My body welcomed him with grasping inner walls and a rush of liquid pleasure. I throbbed around him and moved on him with every drag and pull of hard flesh across tender nerves and slick surfaces. The further Cy pressed into my welcoming body, the more he wound me up with dirty words in my ear and clever fingers between my legs, the more he redefined what sex should be. This was better. He was better and I was better because I didn't have any choice in the matter. He made me feel everything. He forced me to tell him how good it felt and demanded that I take what I wanted from him while he took what he needed from me.

It started out slow and steady. He moved in and out of my soaked center with a rhythm that barely stirred the water around us. It sent desire threading along each limb, twined it up my spine, and looped it around every sense that he was flooding. Lazy pleasure filled my blood as he rode me gently and with restraint, careful of my injured arm and still throbbing head. It was good, really good, and I told him so, but it wasn't enough, and if I was going to be brave enough to let him in, then I wanted *all* of him.

"Cy." His name wrenched out of me, desperate and frantic.

"Leo." Mine left his lips sounding like a prayer and a plea.

I got my good arm up around his neck and let my fingers drag across the sensitive skin there. It made his big body bow into mine and his sure rhythm falter as he stroked in and out of me.

"I need you to fuck me."

I felt his exhale against the side of my cheek. "That's what I'm doing." The words bit out between clenched teeth.

I shook my head and tossed my head back so that it rested on his shoulder. "No, Cy, I want you to *fuck* me and I want us both to finish." We had made it this far, it was time to go all in and to leave each other with sweaty, sexy, sinful memories that would be impossible to forget.

"Mouthy." His fingers trapped my clit and gave the riotous bundle of nerves a fierce tug. His teeth sank sharply into my earlobe and then he moved me slightly away from him with his heavy arm holding me under my breasts as he bent me over just a little bit. His taunting fingers left the place where we were joined and ended up tunneled in the thick mass of my hair as he listened to what I was asking him for and delivered . . . and then some.

His hips picked up speed and smacked into the water and the swell of my backside. The sound was carnal and raw, so was the way he made me whimper as he pounded into me while I floated, weightless and untethered to anything other than his driving cock. Nothing was holding me to earth or reality other than his fierce erection. His cock was the center of my universe and the way it powered into my body, claiming, marking, and owning every single cell that it touched was the only thing that mattered. I had never felt so wanted, so desired, as important to another person's completion as I did in this moment. It was overwhelming and exhilarating. There was so much power in being the one in charge of a man like Cy's satisfaction.

His fingers pulled on my wet and wildly curling hair, hard enough to have a noise of protest working its way out of my mouth. His teeth nipped at my ear with more force than I was expecting and I was stunned that I like his rough, maybe even more than his sweet.

"Haven't been inside a woman without something between me and her in a long, long time. Never been inside one that burns as hot and feels as good as you. You're a fucking dream with that mouth and those tits, but the icing on the cake is the way you squeeze my cock like you never want to let it go. It feels like you want to fucking keep me and keep fucking me, Leo."

His words vibrated across my skin. I did want to keep him, and there was no way I could go back to whatever existed before fucking him. That was simply a life not worth living, at least according to the way my body was winding up getting ready to let go again.

He was panting a little into my ear and I could feel his broad and heavily muscled chest tighten where I was resting against it. One of his knees nudged mine underwater, forcing me to adjust my stance and lean forward a little more so that my chest was touching the bubbling surface of the pool. He was holding me in place as he pummeled into me, clearly chasing down all the amazing things he had already made me feel. My pleasure was languid and moving sleepily through my body, his was frenetic and feverous, practically bursting off of his skin and out of that

pistoning cock as sensation overtook the control he was struggling to hold onto.

"Put your fingers between your legs. Touch yourself like
you want me to touch you. I can't let go or you'll end up face
first in the water." The touch of humor lacing his harsh command almost did as much for me as the seductive order. "I'm going to fill this sweet spot up until it overflows, and I want you to
feel every drop of it inside of you." Dirty words, but they made
me feel all kinds of shiny and new. I wasn't untouched or untried,
but I was most definitely unexperienced and green when it came
to the kind of sex that made a woman want things she knew she
couldn't have. I was a novice when it came to being possessed
and obsessed by a man who was enough to make a woman want
to give up everything she thought she knew for something that
might be better.

I weaved my hand through the water and trusted him to
hold me and to take me to the edge, dropping me off while he
fell after me. When my fingers lightly skimmed over my clit and
brushed against the stiff shaft moving in and out of the hungry
and hot opening, that was all it took for my eyes to slam closed
and my breath to wheeze out of me. It was too much to take
so I tripped into bliss and dragged Cy right into the delightful
sensation with me. His cock jerked against the back of my fingers. His chest rose and fell as he swore softly in my ear, and his
thighs tightened and locked against the back of mine as the point
where we were joined was suddenly a hundred times hotter than
the water that surrounded us. He burned and I caught the fire. It
raged through me in waves of pleasure.

He filled me up all right but it was with wonder and awe
that I could feel this way, that I could make someone else feel
this way. It made my heart forget to hurt for what it had been
through and what was waiting for it when I had to go back to my

real life, which had no place in it for this man.

I let my head flop back on his shoulder as he pulled me to his chest. His lips hit my temple as he lifted the hand splayed across my ribs to settle over my racing heart. "Destroyed, Sunshine. This is what it feels like to be destroyed."

I hummed a little but didn't say anything. If this was destroyed then I never wanted to be put back together again.

After a few moments so we could get our breathing and blood back into vital organs, he pulled out of me leaving a void that I knew could only be filled by him and his special brand of making memories. I let my body float in the water until I was lying all the way on my back with my eyes locked on the darkening Wyoming sky. It was so vast and infinite. It made the major thing that had just occurred between me and the man who might not be a cowboy but was sure as shit the best lover I'd ever had, seem small and insignificant.

"We need to get it together and go back. I need to let Lane get some sleep so we can alternate keeping an eye on camp throughout the night." His hands grabbed my hips under the water and pulled me down so that I was standing in front of him. My wrist still hurt but the pain was no longer bright and angry under my bruised skin.

"Okay."

We stared at each other for a moment, waiting, watching. Between one blink and the next his rugged expression turned from heart-stoppingly attractive to something that no mere mortal could guard their heart against. No wonder the man didn't smile very often, because when he did, the world stopped spinning. I jolted under the blinding brilliance of the slash of pearly white teeth across that rough and tough façade. He was beautiful and his smile was extraordinary. It made him look like a man who didn't carry the weight of the world and endless responsibilities on his wide shoulders.

I reached up a hand to cup his cheek and shivered when his scruff abraded my palm. "You're smiling, Cy."

"I'm happy, Leo."

Jesus. I blinked hard to hold back amazement and the threat of tears. Talk about the risk being worth the reward. Everything I might lose in the near future was worth suffering through if it meant I got to have this moment with this man smiling at me.

CHAPTER 12

Don't Borrow Trouble

"I HATE YOU AND I think you're a slut."

I almost choked on the way-too-strong coffee Cy had made to keep him awake while he stayed up for the first watch over the camp. I offered to keep him company, but I got a narrow eyed look and was told that he needed to focus. I'd never been anyone's distraction before, so I took it as a compliment and made my way over to the campfire where Evan was sitting watching the two of us with a pinched expression on her face. I poured myself a cup of coffee knowing I wouldn't sleep because I would be worrying about the man keeping an eye on the rest of us, so I figured the caffeine and Cy were my only saviors at this moment. I barely got the first sip in when the teen's words made me choke on the hot liquid.

Lane had turned in for the night since he had to be up before dawn to switch shifts with Cy. Em was playing a game of cards with Evan's mom and brother while her dad did his best to look down her shirt when he didn't think anyone else was looking. The other two men had also turned in early but both offered to help keep an eye on camp if Cy didn't want to stay up all night. There was something about the eager way they both seemed to anticipate running into whomever was responsible for our change in plans . . . that set Cy's jaw in a hard line and made me stare at them questioningly. They had ulterior motives for being out here and were hardly bothering to hide them anymore.

Everyone else was occupied or distracted, which was why Evan thought she was safe in launching her verbal attack. "That's a pretty ugly thing to say to someone you don't know very well." I kept my tone light and low so that we didn't draw attention to ourselves. It was about time someone set her straight.

"Everyone knows why you went into the woods with Cy. You've known him for like a day. That's disgusting and totally slutty. I would be so embarrassed if I were you." Her expression was defiant but there was hurt in her eyes that didn't come from being rejected by a man completely inappropriate for her.

I took another sip of the coffee that I was holding carefully in my good hand. Without Cy's particular style of distraction my wrist was back to throbbing and aching with every beat of my heart. The hot water from the spring and a few Advil had knocked the pain down to where it was bearable.

"The thing is, I don't think you're upset at what's happening between me and Cy, because you're smart and observant so you know there is no way he would ever put himself or his business at risk by messing around with a very young guest. Even if she is very pretty." She looked away at the compliment, and for the umpteenth time I wanted to knock some sense into her parents.

"I think you're tired of being overlooked and ignored by the man in your life who should be paying attention to you. I also think you're bothered by the way he treats your mom. I completely understand why you're crushing on Cy, he's gorgeous and is almost a cowboy, but I think your feelings toward him and toward me are more about what's going on at home than it is about us." I lifted my eyebrows at her as she continued to glare at me, her hands curled into tight fists where they rested on top of her thighs. "You want your mom to tell you to knock it off and your dad to swoop in and defend your honor. You want them to join forces and actually parent you and your brother because that should be their primary job, and they aren't doing it. You want their attention because you spend most of your time separated from them, and when you are all together, it's obvious things aren't working out so great for any of you."

Her bottom lip quivered and she turned away so that her hair covered her face. I lowered myself next to her where she was sitting on Boss's discarded saddle as she whispered out, "You don't know anything."

I laughed a little as my fingers tightened on my tin mug. "You would be surprised how much I know about having a parent who's oblivious to how bad they can hurt you, even if you don't see them every day." I bumped her shoulder lightly with my own and gave her a tiny grin. "My mom didn't want me, still doesn't. She handed me off to my grandparents and they raised me." I shook my head. "When I was growing up I was so oblivious to how good I had it with them because all I could focus on was *why* she didn't want me. It made me miss out on so much. I was terrified of failure and of coming up short so it made me overly careful and cautious. I was no fun. I'm still not most of the time."

Evan cocked her head to the side and considered me thoughtfully for a long minute. "Why are you telling me this? Do you want me to feel sorry for you?"

I shook my head again and reached out to pat the back of her hand. I was silently thrilled when she didn't pull away from the touch. "I'm telling you because you have a mom who can and will fight for you if she has a reason to. She spends so much time fighting for a love that isn't there she's missing the love that still surrounds her. I did the same thing and I regret it so much now.

My granddad passed away before I could tell him how much I appreciated him and everything he did for me. He wasn't here to see me get back on the horse, literally and figuratively."

She wouldn't know what that meant but the way my voice twisted and the way it made moisture cloud my vision communicated how important the gesture was. "If your parents won't focus on you, you focus on them. Remind them of the love they still have even if the love they had for each other is no longer there. Your mom needs someone on her side and you father needs a wakeup call. Be better than they are."

"That's a lot of responsibility." She sounded sad and lost so I put an arm around her and gave her a little squeeze.

"All you can do is try, and if it doesn't do anything for them it will do something for you and for your brother. Be someone you both can rely on. If you do that you're already miles and miles ahead of where I was when I was your age."

She nodded and I let her go as I climbed to my feet. I nudged her foot with the toe of my boot until she looked up at me. "Not very long ago I would never have taken a shot at anything with a guy like Cy, because you're right, I hardly know him and everyone around us knows what's going on. That would have been such a waste." I lifted an eyebrow at her and told her, "The sisterhood needs strong, considerate members, so maybe pull back on the name calling. Women need to hold other women up and not drag them down."

I stared at her until she tilted her chin down in a little nod of acknowledgement. "I'm jealous. I know he's too old for me but he's really hot. I would die if he looked at me the way he looks at you." Her teeth flashed in a saucy grin. I really did like her and felt slightly kindred with her. I hoped she had it in her to help her family find their way to happy. I wish someone with clearer perspective from the outside had knocked some sense into me when

I was busy being a miserable mess. "Maybe I'll switch my attention to Lane. He's closer to my age and he actually seems like he knows how to have fun. Cy seems pretty boring."

He was the opposite of boring but I could see how his stern and no-nonsense demeanor could come across that way.

I told Evan she should stick to boys her own age in her own state, and I stole Emrys away from the card game so she could keep me company while I finished my coffee and tried to quiet my jangling nerves. She apologized some more for making me come on this trip to which I laughingly replied that *coming* on this trip was the best thing that had ever happened to me. And since she was my best friend she wanted a play by play of exactly how the oldest Warner brother had gone about blowing my mind. I didn't mind giving her vague details, but with Cy floating around somewhere beyond the thin walls of the tent I didn't want to get into the nitty gritty. Those were my moments and memories and I was covetous of them.

I must have fallen asleep despite the caffeine, but at some point in the early morning, I was woken up by the sound of the zipper of my sleeping bag sliding open and to cold hands rubbing briskly over the skin under my shirt. I blinked my eyes and tried to get them to adjust to the dim light but all I could see were gray eyes looking back at me and the slash of that heart-stopping smile daring me to take a chance.

"What are you doing? Where's Em?" The tent was too small for three of us, it was barely big enough for him to stretch out all the way, which he did . . . on top of me. His hands found my unrestrained breasts under the soft fabric of my long sleeved T-shirt and I bit down on my lip to keep the strangled sound that lodged in my throat back as he squeezed the plump weight and then brushed his fingers over the rounded sides.

"Sutton showed up a half hour ago. Ran right into camp

because he was following the river the whole way to where he thought we would be. Lane's taking over the watch and Em was helping Sutton get his horse settled. She said she couldn't sleep so she was going to head to the river and try and catch some fish for lunch since our plans have changed and we won't be stopping as many times for the rest of the ride. One of my brothers will go down to the water with her." His nose nuzzled into the side of my neck and it made me shiver. He was cold and blazing hot at the same time. "If they fight over who gets to go with her then we have a problem."

The hand caressing the side of my breast moved so that his palm was rubbing slow, agonizing circles over my nipple. The peak pulled tight and poked enthusiastically into his touch.

"Do they do that? Fight over the same girl?" The words were breathy and broken as his teeth dipped into the collar of my shirt and started to nibble on the side of my neck. I shifted my legs restlessly under the weight of his, which had him grinding his hips into the cradle of mine. There was a bulge behind his zipper that refused to be ignored.

"Not usually, but your girl is a stunner and knows how to handle a rod and a reel. That makes her something worth fighting over around these parts." His teeth dragged down the entire side of my neck as I leaned to the side to give him room. He nipped languidly at the pulse throbbing and ready at the base of my throat and pulled his hand out from underneath my shirt so he could work on getting the barrier off over my head. I put my hands around his wrists to still him.

"Em could be back any minute." And while she had gotten a basic rundown she didn't need to walk in and get an eyeful of everything Cy was working with.

"She's not gonna interrupt. She knew I was headed your way and your girl has your back." He chuckled and I felt it move all the way across my skin. "And my brothers know better. Not much in life I take for myself, so when I find something I want, they don't get in the way of it. It's too early for anyone else to be up yet so be quiet . . . or don't. I don't give a shit either way."

"You want me." It wasn't a question because the answer was clear in his shimmery eyes. I exhaled and curled my fingers into the strong tendon on the back of his neck as he started to tug on the waistband of the soft sleep pants that hardly kept the heat coming off of his erection from scorching my skin. Once I was naked and sprawled underneath him he reared up and began working on his own clothes. He shrugged his black Henley off with an impatient jerk while I tackled his belt and getting his jeans out of the way of that impressive arousal. Somehow, we twisted and ended up with him half-dressed and trapped below me while I ran little kisses all over his chest and across his defined abdominals. It was like sitting on top of a stone statue but his cock felt like velvet and silk where it pressed into the apex of my legs. I moved myself lower down his torso, intent on having all that hard in my mouth.

I practically snarled his name when he diverted me from my very pleasurable task and pulled me back up his body so that he could plant a searing kiss on my pouting lips. He ran his hands up and down my sides while looking up at me from under lowered brows.

"We gotta ride out in just a few hours and I need to get some sleep. There isn't time to play those kinds of games, as much as I'd love nothing more."

I lifted an eyebrow at him and reached down to put my hands on the strong well of his pecs. I loved the way the light dusting of his chest hair felt under my palms.

"Your cock in my mouth is a game?" I was teasing him but I could see that he did look tired and his fleeting smile was gone.

"Sure, because once you get me off then I have to make sure I get you off even better and even longer. Then once I've recovered from having your mouth around my cock, I'll fuck you until neither of us can see straight. I could get off just thinking about your mouth on my dick . . . in fact, I did. You were there for it."

The image of him handling the pulsing cock I was perched over made my insides clench and my mouth water. He was the sexiest thing ever and he was mine for the taking.

"You want me to give you a goodnight kiss and leave you alone?" I figured he had more involved plans since he was the one who stripped me out of my clothes and woke me up with wandering hands and an impatient cock.

That smile that was brighter than the sun on a perfect day moved across his face. It was devastating. "No. I want you to climb on my cock and ride it hard and wild. Fuck me stupid and fuck me fast. I want you to turn us both inside out, and when you're done then you can give me a goodnight kiss." His hands squeezed the flesh at my hips and urged me lift up so that his tapered tip could run through folds that were already warm and wanting. I was slick and ready as his shaft glided through the valley and knocked into my anxious clit. The little tap made me jolt on top of him. He gave me a knowing smirk and repeated the motion until his cock was shiny and covered in the liquid desire rushing to meet him.

I clamped my knees to the side of his hips and reached between us to capture him, rising up enough that I could line him up with my entrance. His eyes watched me with hungry anticipation and I started to lower myself down the ridged shaft. I loved the way my body had to adjust to him. I knew he was there, that he was making a place for himself inside of me. The stretch felt hedonistic and erotic. It was another way he made me burn.

He wanted me to fuck him fast but I had to take my time

getting him where we both wanted him to be. That glide down his erection felt like it took forever. Agonizing minutes while I clenched around him and squeezed him tight. When he was inside of me my body didn't want him to go. I was trying to hold on and the torture of it made him sweat and had his chest rising and falling at a crazy rapid pace as he waited for me make my next move.

Perched on top of him, I leaned forward and put my lips on his as I began to do what he told me to do. I rode him hard and I rode him wild. I rocked my hips back and forth in a frenzied pace and lifted myself up and down in a rhythm that had us both breathing fast. I was leaning on his chest, fingers digging into muscles hard enough to leave marks in his dusky skin. My hair fell around us in curly copper waves that Cy seemed to love.

"So, fucking hot, Leo. I haven't been this warm in years. You really are sunshine."

His words made me move even faster and I tossed my head back as he hit a spot that I didn't even know I had. I was trying to stay quiet so I swallowed a moan and had to bite the tip of my tongue when his hand was back at my breast while his other one moved to where we were joined. His thumb hit my clit with sniper-like precision and began to do a circular dance that had pleasure curling low at the base of my spine and spiraling outward in shivery waves.

"This pussy was made for me." He said the words with confidence and assurance. Maybe he was right. No one filled it or made it feel as important and essential as he did. He made me hyperaware of how female I was next to all his masculinity. He also made me ridiculously aware of how powerful all that femininity was.

I put a hand over the bare nipple that he wasn't tugging on and rubbed the soft point with a much lighter touch than he was using. The opposing stimulation had my head spinning and body spasming in delight. We were melting together, pooling into nothing more than puddles of passion and lust.

It was totally frantic and furious. The entire tent was moving around us and I couldn't keep the soft noises of gratification from squeaking out. It was indulgent and gluttonous the way we took from each other. There wasn't enough time or space for us to get everything we wanted but we made a valiant effort.

His hand left my aching breast and traveled up to my throat. He didn't squeeze it like he did before. He simply put his thumb over my pulse and lightly brushed it. It was a soft touch, one I barely felt but it was a touch that spoke volumes. He was putting his hands on my heart in a very literal sense and getting off on the way he made it react with his body and his words. He pulled me closer so that his lips could feather across mine.

"So close, Sunshine. Give me all you got and break us both." The veins on the side of his neck bulged and his eyes practically glowed silver in the dim morning light.

I didn't want to break us. I wanted to fix us so that maybe there was a way for us to walk away from this fire unscathed instead of scarred.

I pulled away from his challenging tongue and nipping teeth. I arched my back and managed to get into a position where I could keep up my rise and descent and still reach behind me so I could snake a hand between his slightly spread legs. His eyebrows shot up as I worked my hand between the fabric still twined around his hips and got to the cushiony globes between his legs that were drawn tight with pleasure.

It only took a little caress, the slightest scrape of my nails over the sensitive surface to have him lose his mind. He snarled my name, wrapped an arm around my waist and rolled us so that he was over the top of me and pounding into me like he was trying to drive us both into the ground. Skin slapped together, pelvises hit hard enough to bruise, and my body went wet and loose as his kicked rock hard and ready.

His face blurred above me as his head bowed back and his neck tightened. The biceps braced on either side of my head quivered and his nostrils flared. It was primal and so goddamn hot that I orgasmed just from watching him hit his release. Pride chased pleasure and desire from my head to my toes. I made him look that shattered and satisfied. I made him look that soft and replete. I wasn't sure if that was what broken was supposed to look like, but if it was, it looked a lot like love.

I whimpered and shook my way through my own climax with his name on my lips and his body surrounding mine, inside and out. It was brilliant and unforgettable.

He lowered himself so that he was lying over me like a gigantic, muscular blanket and rubbed his bristly cheek against mine. We were still joined in a way that felt unbreakable, and he ran a hand down my thigh and lifted it to rest on his hip. I used my foot to help him get his pants the rest of the way off and caressed his spine as he yawned loudly in my ear.

"I'm ready for that kiss." Sleepy humor colored his tone so I turned my head and met his lips with my own.

"Let me up and I'll let you sleep." His arms tightened around me and his scruff scraped my skin as he shook his head in the negative.

"Not letting you go." His eyes were closed and he was already breathing slower.

I sighed and wrapped my arms across his wide shoulders. "You want me." I still couldn't fully absorb the full impact of how much that meant to me.

He let out a long breath and kissed my temple. "I deserve you. I deserve the way you make me feel even if it's only temporary. Stay with me for a little bit. We don't have a lot of time."

The reminder killed but it also settled me into a more comfortable position in his arms when he turned us on our sides as the sorrow for everything I would leave behind hung over me like a rain cloud. Sex with Cy didn't break me; it made me feel whole and renewed.

I wiggled away from Cy an hour later when his grasp finally loosened and his arms went limp around me. It took some effort to get dressed without bumping into him, especially considering he took up the majority of the space, but I managed even with my weak wrist. I made my way over to where the morning fire was already going with a pot of coffee resting on the coals. Sutton stood on one side and Em sat on the other. They didn't seem to be talking to each other but it was obvious something awkward was going on. Very interesting. It was something I was going to ask her about. When I finally reached them, whatever sexual, tension-filled vortex they were locked in broke.

Em gave me a quick grin and Sutton greeted me with a lifted cup and his typical scowl. Em offered me a cup of coffee and brushed her shoulder against mine as I sat down next to her.

"You look . . . well rested."

I rolled my eyes at her but couldn't hold back a grin, a grin that died when Sutton muttered, "Another vacation fling that's going to crash and burn. I keep waiting for him to find a woman who might actually stick around."

I cocked my head to the side and considered him for a long minute. "Maybe he purposely picks women who can't stay because he doesn't want a repeat of what happened with his wife. When you know the other person has to leave it hurts less watching them go."

The coffee cup in his hand lowered and his brows lowered.

"He told you about Selah?"

I nodded but didn't get into any more detail as he continued to watch me, speculation and curiosity clear in his leafy green eyes, because Em turned to me with wide eyes and told me, "Sutton said that while he was in town picking up his daughter he heard a rumor that the park rangers pulled a body out of the river a few weeks ago."

I looked back at Sutton who shrugged. "I took Daye to the Big Horn, one of the only restaurants in Sheridan, and while we were having dinner, no less than five people stopped by the table to ask if I'd heard about the body. The ranch is far enough out of the city we usually miss all that kind of gossip and talk unless the guests bring it with them. I assumed it was a hiker who got turned around and lost or a kayaker who got into a bad part of the river. Rodie Collins, who just happens to be with the sheriff's office, mentioned that the body had bullet holes in it." He grunted. "Not appropriate dinner conversation for a five-year-old but we don't usually have violent crime like that around here. I think he was excited to actually have a crime to solve. He said they couldn't identify the guy but they've been working on it."

I pushed some of my hair off my face and frowned. "When Boss bolted through the woods we stumbled into a massive pot farm cleared out in the middle of the trees. Cy thinks the people who put it there are the ones doing their best to get us to move on in a different direction. I wouldn't be surprised if that dead body and hidden drug fields go hand in hand."

"Probably, which means whoever wants to keep people away isn't afraid of using violence to keep their grow site safe. We need to get a move on it so you guys are out of the line of fire and we can get you someplace more controlled." Those were almost Cy's exact words, which meant the middle Warner brother also thought this was a situation that could quickly get out of hand.

Shivering, I ran my hands over my arms and inclined my head toward the tent. "Cy was up all night, give him another hour to sleep and then we'll go. We should get everyone else up and fed so that we can hit the trail as soon as he gets up."

Finally, the harsh expression on Sutton's ridiculously handsome face lifted. His lips quirked up in a sideways grin and I heard Em suck in a breath next to me. The Warner men were hard to resist, that was a fact.

Emrys and I finished our coffee and then made our way around the camp shaking tents and getting everyone up and ready to go for the day. The rest of the group grumbled about the ridiculous hour, but by the time Cy finally made his appearance looking rumpled and still tired, the horses were packed and ready to go, minus my tent. Lane shoved a granola bar at his brother while they discussed the best course of action to get us all back to the ranch.

Em and I were working on getting the fire out and properly covered when the first pops sounded. I wasn't really sure what was happening but all of a sudden the horses were freaking out, rearing up on their hind legs, neighing loudly as they pulled at the tethers holding them in place. Evan screamed and wrapped her arms over her head as her mother grabbed her arm and pulled her toward the closest tree away from the wide open riverbank we were camped on. The girl's father took a flying leap to land behind a tent while everyone else scrambled to find safety.

Sutton dove across the fire pit and took Em down to the ground. They rolled when he hit her and he made sure to keep her covered as more loud shots filled the air, sending pieces of earth chunks of bark flying as bullets pinged and popped all around us. Cy grabbed my arm and pulled me with him as he bolted for the tree line, as well. Lane was hot on our heels pushing Evan's little brother in front of him, stopping and pulling the young boy up when he stumbled.

The two men stood in the center of camp while Sutton barked at them to take cover. The older one ignored him while the younger one dashed to his horse. He struggled to dig something out of the pack hanging on the side while the horse tugged and pulled to get free in its panic. The older man seemed to be scanning the dense forest line in search of where the shots were coming from, unconcerned about the bullets zipping past him. The gunshots continued to pepper the open camp but I was more alarmed with the fact that something warm and viscous was sliding down Cy's arm and over my fingers where I held him as he kept me trapped between his body and the trunk of a large pine tree.

"What the fuck is that idiot doing?" The words were growled in my ear as more of his weight pressed into me. I craned my neck as far as I could to see what Cy was swearing about.

Webb and Grady were both standing in the center of the temporary camp, now armed and returning fire at the invisible assailants. The sound of gunfire was deafening as it echoed off of rocks and trees. I squeezed my eyes shut and pressed as close to Cy as I could. I tried not to worry too much about the blood dripping over my fingers since he didn't seem overly bothered by it. I became startlingly aware that although this man seemed impenetrable, he wasn't actually bulletproof.

CHAPTER 13

No Easy Way Out

BOTH THE MEN WERE SCARILY proficient with the weapons in their hands returning fire, so the campsite quickly turned into something that resembled a warzone. The gunshots from the faceless attackers continued to kick up rock and sand while chunks of bark peeled off of the trees all around us. The initial shots were probably meant as a warning, another tactic to scare us. It was clear whoever was doing all of this wanted to get us to move along. My best guess would be that they wanted us as far away from the hidden field of narcotics as they could get us. As soon as both Grady and Webb started shooting back, the threat from those returning fire became more real. A hunk of tree tore off right above where Cy was covering me and I heard him swear as the wooden shrapnel tore across his scalp. A brilliant red drop of blood trickled over the center of his forehead and across the bridge of his nose before he reached up with his injured arm to swipe at it.

I made a noise low in my throat and asked him if he had a pocket knife somewhere on him. Since he was proving to be more of a cowboy than I originally pegged him for, he produced a tiny folded blade from his front pocket. Ducking my head, I wiggled enough space between the two of us so that I could saw off part of the tail of my shirt and wrap the haphazard bandage around his oozing bicep. I knew it must have hurt because he didn't protest the silent fussing or tell me to stop. I tore off another piece to dab at the wound on his head, which didn't look as bad but was sure as hell bleeding a lot.

"What are we going to do?" I hated that my voice shook but I was scared and it didn't sound like anyone was going to stop shooting anytime soon.

Cy grunted and pulled me down lower behind the tree as a branch from a tree next to us took a hit and broke off.

"I wish I had an answer to that question, Sunshine. Right now all we can do is lay low and wait to see what happens when the bullets run out."

"This is bad." I tucked my head under his chin and prayed that Em was okay. I couldn't see much of anything beyond Cy's chest and slivers of forest surrounding us.

He snorted and his hands tightened on my hips where he was holding me to the tree. "It sure as shit isn't good. I knew those two oddballs weren't who they said they were."

I nodded and my hair brushed across the scruff on his face. "Why would they have guns and ammunition with them on a trail ride in the middle of nowhere?"

"That's a good question. One I hope I get the opportunity to ask."

"Son of a bitch!" The scream came from the younger of the two men and had Cy peering carefully around the trunk of the tree into the center of camp. Before I could ask if the man was hurt, all the popping and pinging of bullets stopped.

"You okay, Webb?" That was the older man hollering the question as Cy eased away from me and took a step to the side. I wanted to pull him back behind the tree just in case there was someone still hiding in the woods ready to take aim. I put both my hands on his injured arm and looked at him with pleading eyes.

"Wait." I wasn't sure what I wanted him to wait for but I wasn't up for him being an easy target.

"I have to check on everyone. You stay here until I come back and get you." He put his hands over mine and had to literally pry my fingers loose. I didn't want to let him go.

"They could start shooting again." I whispered the words as he reached up and brushed the back of his fingers over my cheek. He was worrying about everyone else so I decided it was fine that I was so worried about him.

"We have to get everyone together and get out of here. I need to check the horses to make sure they're okay to ride and I need to check on my brothers. Stay low and stay down in case the shooting starts back up."

He slipped past me and I sank all the way to the ground, the bark of the tree scratching my back as my shirt rode up. I peeked around the trunk and watched with concerned eyes as Cy made his way to the center of the camp where Grady was bent over the Webb man. They were speaking in hushed tones and it was obvious that Webb was losing a lot of blood.

Catching sight of Cy, Sutton popped up from the other side of the fire pit after telling Emrys to keep her head down.

"You're hit." Sutton sounded pissed rather than scared as he addressed his brother, but even from this distance I could see worry twist his features.

"It's a flesh wound. It can keep until we get everyone safe. I thought we could ride the river but this was an ambush and I don't want to put any more innocent people at risk if we run across another camp or tour group." He moved toward the two armed men who proved to be full of surprises. "How badly are you hurt?"

Webb, who was clutching his shoulder as red oozed through his fingers and stained his shirt, grimaced. "It went through and through. It's not good but I've had worse."

Cy grunted. "Don't suppose you fellas want to explain why you were armed to the teeth like you were ready for a shootout in the middle of the woods?"

Lane appeared out of the woods in a rush, his words hurried and frantic. "That's a story I want to hear as well but I don't think now is the time. We need to get out of here. I don't know why they stopped shooting but they had enough ammo and enough time to take all of us out. We need to get while the getting's good."

Sutton nodded and ran a hand over his face. "Lane's right. We don't have time for twenty questions. I've got the 12 gauge, Lane has a .357." He pointed to where Grady was still bent over Webb in concern. "And those boys have the semiautomatic pistols they just shot the place up with. Assuming they still have ammunition after that firefight, I think the best course of action is that we split the group up. Each one of us take a few of the clients and head on different trails back to the ranch. We're too big of a target moving all together."

Lane frowned. "If we split up there's no way we can keep in touch with one another if someone gets in trouble. These guys want us off the mountain."

Sutton shrugged and looked to his older brother for validation that his idea was the best option. "We can move faster if we all split up."

Cy looked out toward the trees and down the river like he was trying to see if the threat was still there. After a long minute, he nodded and looked at the two men who were so clearly not who they said they were.

"I have a feeling you two know more about what's going on

here than anyone else. I want the Cliffs Notes version of why you're on this ride, and if I buy that you aren't part of the bad shit going down, you two will ride with me." He motioned to Webb who was now bent over and clearly struggling to breathe steadily. "Plus, we'll be the slowest with my fucked up arm and his jacked shoulder."

Grady looked between his injured friend and the injured trail guide. He was obviously weighing his options and deciding how much he could share. Impatiently, Cy pointed at Webb's shoulder that was leaking more and more blood by the second. "You are on a clock, buddy. Tick-tock."

With a sigh, the former military man rubbed a hand over his face and dragged it across his chin. "The long and the short of it is that we know someone who came up to this part of Wyoming and disappeared. He isn't the type of guy who drops out of communication without a reason. It could put him in a lot of danger if anyone knew that he had people looking for him, so we booked this trip to try and get close but not so close that anyone else looking for him might notice."

Sutton shifted his weight and crossed his arms over his chest. "You the good guys or the bad guys?"

Grady groaned and Webb barked out a brittle laugh that was sharp with pain. "We're both."

Cy grunted and shared a look with his brothers that was clearly them weighing how much trust they were going to put in the two men. Ultimately, their desire to keep everyone under their protection safe won out over any lingering suspicion and doubt. He turned to Sutton and his voice was scary in its intensity when he told his middle brother, "You take the girls. You keep them safe and protect them with your life, you hear me, Sutton?"

There was a sharp nod in reply. "You know I will."

Cy walked over to his youngest brother and clasped him on

the shoulder. "You ride out with the family. Keep on extra close eye on the kids and if the dad slows you down tell him you'll leave his ass in the woods. He's jerked his family around enough, don't let him be the reason they get caught up in something we can't get them out of." Lane nodded in reply, his intensity matching both of his older siblings.

Cy lifted a hand and ran it through his hair. "We have to stick to the trees and the back trails. Try and avoid any paths that are big enough for motorized vehicles, keep an eye on the ground, if there are people out here, avoid heavily traveled areas. Move fast, try and be as inconspicuous as possible. I'll use the satellite phone to call Brynn and make sure she knows what's going on so she can call the rangers and the sheriff and update them on the ambush. If you run across a uniform, point them in the direction of the grow field and let them know they have armed individuals in the area who aren't afraid to shoot at will."

"You might not want to do that." That came from Grady and had Webb barking out his name in protest.

Grady shook his head at his injured friend and shifted his gaze to Cy. "The last official person who was up here looking for that drug field and the growers behind it ended up a missing person. He's our friend we're looking for. The guys who run operations like this aren't innocent farmers or sharecroppers trying to make some extra cash. Most of them are on a cartel's payroll. They won't give a shit if a few tourists end up dead because they got too close."

Sutton grunted and pointed out blandly. "Maybe not a missing person any longer. When I was in town, the sheriff's office was trying to identify a body they pulled out of the river."

An unsteady Webb leapt to his feet and then promptly pitched over as both Cy and Grady reached for him to keep him from biting the dust. "No . . . no . . . no." He folded in on himself as the older man tried to keep him upright.

"Come on, Webb. We don't know that it's Wyatt." I heard a noise and had to squint at the circle of men to realize it was the wounded man choking back sobs.

"Who else would it be, Grady? I told you when we came up with this plan that I know my brother. He would never go this long without checking in with his partner or his family. Motherfuckers!" The dirty word echoed off the surroundings and had all the Warner brothers sharing a look.

"We need to go. We don't have time for this right now. Who knows why they stopped shooting when they did but I don't want to be around if they decide to start up again." Cy's voice was curt and had his younger sibling jumping into action.

Grady gave Cy a hard look. "They stopped shooting because they weren't ordered to kill us. If they had been we would all be dead. They want us off the mountain and away from their crop."

Cy turned and headed toward the horses. "Well, we best be getting out of their way before their orders change. I have a first aid kit in one of my packs we can use to bandage up that shoulder but it isn't going to work miracles. You're in sorry shape, son."

Deciding I couldn't keep my head down or my mouth shut any longer, I moved around the tree on my hands and knees prepared to drop to my stomach if bullets started blazing over my head again. I crept and crawled my way over to where Cy was trying to calm the jittery horses and met his glare with one of my own when he caught sight of me.

"I told you to stay put." He snarled the words at me looking extra fierce as smeared blood from his head wound dotted his forehead.

"I didn't listen." I reached out so I could stroke Boss's neck. He was sweaty and I could feel how nervous the big animal was.

"I don't want to go with Sutton, Cy. I want to go with you."

He sighed and continued to watch me over the top of the line of horses. "Sutton won't let anything happen to you, Leo. My arm is dinged up, the kid has a hole through his shoulder, and has already lost too much blood. You need to be in capable hands and I need to be focused on the task at hand, not on you. This is the best plan. You have to trust me."

I wrinkled my nose at his non-subtle reminder that he thought I was a distraction. "Someone needs to take care of you." The words were quiet but I was sure he heard me loud and clear.

His granite colored gaze lightened and that smile that was becoming less and less elusive touched his lips briefly.

"I better see you again before I head home, Cyrus Warner." And not just because I wanted the chance at a proper goodbye. I didn't feel like I had enough of him to last me the rest of my life just yet.

"I'll see you back at the ranch, Leo. I promise." So far, the man had kept his word so I was inclined to believe him since that meant we would both be back together in one piece, if not a little worse for wear.

Leaving him to his task, I went and found Em who was shaking and looking shell shocked. Knowing it was my time to comfort her, I wrapped my arms around her and pulled her close.

"Hey, it's gonna be all right. Those boys are going to take care of everything." I could hear her teeth rattle together and feel the tremor in her hands as she clutched at me.

"I've never had anyone shoot at me before. I thought we were going to die." She blinked wide eyes at me as her lower lip quivered. "I don't want to die, Leo."

I hugged her even closer and patted her back. "No one is going to die." Well, no one else. It sounded like the body Sutton had told us about may be tied to the two men and their secret agenda.

"You don't know that. I came up here to go fishing and camping. I would never have made you come all the way here if I knew how dangerous it was going to be. This is awful." I pulled back and seized her cheeks in my hands. I could tell she was on the verge of tears and it was slightly alarming how pale she was under her normally tawny complexion.

"Em, this trip was exactly what I needed. I needed the shake-up and the change of scenery. I needed the challenge and the dare to do something out of my comfort zone. Sure, right now things are uncertain and this wasn't part of the plan but we'll get through it, okay?" I sounded so sure that things were going to work out in our favor and I was surprised that the reason for the confidence was because I really believed everything would be okay. I didn't just have faith in Cy and his brothers, I had faith in myself and in her. We would figure it out, and once we were back at the ranch and then eventually back at home, we would have this amazing story to tell.

She moved away slightly and the expression on her face changed from traumatized to wistful. "Did you see the way Sutton jumped over the fire pit so he could cover me? They grow them pretty amazing up here, don't they?"

All I could do was nod in agreement. They did grow them pretty goddamn great out here in the wild, wild west. Not quite cowboys were filling in for the fantasy cowboys just fine.

Sutton and Lane worked on getting the rest of camp broken down and packed up while Cy and Grady took up watch on either side of the camp, each holding a loaded weapon as they watched the trees with unwavering eyes. I did my best to bandage Webb but the injury to his shoulder was far worse than the wound on Cy's arm. The bleeding didn't seem to want to stop, and every time he moved his arm he turned several shades of green and made retching noises like he was going to be sick. He didn't look all that great, and when Sutton ordered us all to mount up so we could go our separate ways, it took both Emrys and I on either side of the man to help him to his feet. The green shade under his skin turned a waxy gray and he pitched forward almost taking both of us to the ground with him.

Cy made his way over to us and reached out to brace Webb on his good shoulder, his expression tight and concerned. "Are you going to be able to ride with that shoulder, kid?"

Webb tried to straighten and shake Emrys and me off either side but as soon as we let go he swayed forward. The only thing keeping him upright was Cy's hand on his chest.

"Once you get me in the saddle I'll be okay." His voice was strained and he kept blinking his eyes like he was having a hard time focusing on the man in front of him.

"Can't put you on one of my horses if you don't think you can keep control of him. That's too dangerous for you and the animal. We'll have to double up." He sounded grim.

Lane instantly objected to the new plan. "You can't ride double and push hard for the ranch. That's too much strain on you and Edgar which also means you'll be moving slowly. You'll be a sitting target if those guys with the guns decide to take you off the mountain permanently."

Grady interjected that he could ride with Webb but he was still a big man and nowhere near as proficient and skilled on a horse as Cy was.

"Not sure we have another option, Lane. It's our job to get everyone back safe and we can't leave him behind just because he can't ride." Lane opened his mouth to protest further but then snapped it shut again when he realized that the options were indeed limited.

I looked at Em and then at Cy. Before I even started speaking, he was shaking his head in the negative and glowering down at me. He knew I was about to go all in when it came to risk taking. There was no time to think how it could all go wrong because there was only one option that made sense. "I can ride with him. I'm not a giant like you, so it'll be easier on the horse and it means you wouldn't have to travel as slowly." I was also handy enough in the saddle that I could control the animal and keep Webb from falling off.

"No." Cy barked out the word the same time Em did, both glaring at me.

I pointed at Webb's nearly white face and his shaking hands. "Look at him. He needs medical attention and we all need to move. There isn't time to discuss all the pros and cons."

"I won't be able to keep you safe." His voice dipped low and the raw agony in his words made my heart tumble and my stomach clench.

I took a step toward him and reached up so I could hold his handsome face between my hands. "You're going to have to trust me to take care of myself and you, Cy. We don't have a choice. Get that man on the horse and then get us the hell out of here." I could sound like a badass when I needed to and my determination to make this happen must have been clear because he didn't argue with me. He gave a jerky nod and pulled away, snapping at Lane to help him get Webb up on his horse.

Em tugged on my elbow and urged me to turn until I was looking at her. She was worried but she was also proud. That was pretty much how I was feeling about it all, so I hugged her and told her, "I'll see you back at the ranch."

She moved away but it was apparent that she didn't want to let me go. "Promise?" We'd been each other's support system for so long that it was unfathomable to think about rushing off into a life-changing race for shelter without having the other to lean on.

"Promise." The word was whispered, slightly shaky, because I'd never broken a promise to her and I hated to think that one this important would be the first one.

Lane and Cy muscled Webb into the saddle then placed me in front of him much more gently. I could feel the tremor in the younger man's arm as he placed it around my waist. Cy gave me one last, hard look and then swung up into his own saddle, hardly looking like he'd taken a bullet himself. We had already wasted what little time we had so there were no drawn out goodbyes as the horses started to move in opposite directions from one another. The Warner brothers all shared a look before heading off their own ways. I gave Em a little wave that she returned with a sad grin. Life was uncertain, and there was no better reminder that things might not work out the way you wanted them to than saying what might be your last goodbye to someone who means everything to you.

It was a silent, intense ride for the first hour. We were moving faster than we would have if Cy and Webb were on the same horse but we weren't moving as fast Cy wanted to. His arm was stiff as he pulled on the reins and worked Edgar through the thick gathering of trees we were foraging through. I couldn't see any kind of actual trail markers but figured that was a good thing since we were supposed to be staying under the radar. When he wasn't maneuvering the lead horse, he was holding his arm close to his side and favoring it like I was doing with my wrist, making me think he was hurting more than he let on.

Webb was also barely hanging in there. More than once his loose hold on my waist had slipped and I'd had to stop to help him readjust in the saddle as he listed precariously off to one side or the other. His skin was getting paler and paler, plus he was sweating like he had the flu. It was uncomfortably close quarters but we kept moving and he never fully let go of me, even if it was very clear he wanted nothing more than to close his eyes and drift away on the pain and discomfort contorting his face.

"So, you want to tell me what you boys are really doing up here and why you're armed to the teeth for a typically uneventful trail ride?" Cy's gravelly voice broke the silence and Grady's heavy sigh followed.

"My real name is Grady Miller and he is Webb Bryant. I'm with . . . the DEA . . . *was* with the DEA." He shook his head and cleared his throat. "My partner, Wyatt Bryant, was assigned a case up here a couple of months ago. He was doing recon on some big growing operations that were rumored to have moved into the Wyoming territory a few months ago. As the senior agent, I was stuck cleaning up a mess at the border, so our boss sent Wyatt in alone thinking it would be an easy observe and report mission." Webb's arm tightened around my waist which made me suck in my breath.

"I called Grady because even when he went undercover, Wyatt always checked in with me to let me know what was going on. We're all each other has. So, when I didn't hear from my brother, I was worried something went wrong. Grady tried to get his boss to cut him loose from his case at the border after getting my call and when the higher-ups wouldn't agree, he quit and flew up here to try and find my brother on his own." Webb's voice was weak but the worry for his sibling was clear in every word he struggled to get out.

"Are you with the DEA as well?" He snorted at my question and it made my hair move.

He bit out a firm, "Hell no," at the same time Grady barked out a sharp laugh full of incredulity.

"Webb and Wyatt Bryant couldn't be any more opposite.

Wyatt was young when he joined the agency, Webb was even younger when he did his first stint in the slammer, but the boys are close and they are like family to me. I couldn't get a bead on Wyatt anywhere up here, too much open space, and too many people who wouldn't give an out of towner the time of day. There was still no word from Wyatt and we were desperate. Webb was the one who came up with the idea to take a trail ride into the mountains and play tourist. We were hoping we would come across something, anything that might point to where Wyatt got off to, or maybe we would run across someone out here who may have seen him." He cleared his throat again and shot a look over his shoulder at the man riding behind me. "We don't know that the body recovered from the river was his, Webb. I won't believe it until I see it with my own two eyes. You brother is a damn good agent."

The man behind me made a noise low in his throat and shifted. He was burning up and shivering at the same time. His voice was thin with pain and weak when he spoke into the back of my head. "I told him a thousand times he needed a different job. He was never home, and every time he got a new assignment, it seemed to be more dangerous than the one before it."

"Some people are just wired to be heroes, I think." I wasn't one of them but I was pretty sure the man leading us through the forest without saying a word about how hurt he was or how worried he had to be about his brothers was one of them.

"Wyatt was always too busy trying to save the rest of the world that he forgot to worry about someone saving him." Webb sounded like he was convinced the body Sutton told us about belonged to his brother.

"So, you're an ex-con?" Cy's voice lashed out angry and pointed. I couldn't see his face but I had no trouble imagining his thunderous expression. He wasn't the kind of man who took being lied to and deceived in stride, especially when those lies had dangerous effects on the people he cared about and the business he had built from the ground up.

I felt Webb nod behind me. "I've done some time, mostly back when I was a kid and couldn't figure out what my purpose was. Wyatt always walked the straight and narrow, was a straight-A student, played football, and was accepted to several top tier colleges. I didn't have any of that going for me so I rebelled, got messed up in some stupid shit, made the wrong kind of friends, and paid the price for it. Now, I'm mostly on the up and up." I didn't want to think about what he did when he wasn't on the up and up.

"You better be on the fucking up and up while you're that close to my girl." I'd never been anyone's girl before, but I kind of loved the idea of being his.

"All I want is to find my brother, and if that is his body sitting in the morgue, then anything that happens afterwards is best kept between me and the mountains." It was my turn to shiver at the deadly intent in his voice. I didn't know who he was before the truth bomb and something told me that whoever he was wasn't someone I wanted to be this close to. He was terrifying in an entirely different way than Cy now that I had hints as to what he was capable of.

"Hot-headed and foolish. That's what gets you in trouble time and time again, Webb. Sometimes it pays to think before you act." Grady said the words wearily, like it was a lecture he had given the younger man many times before.

"If those growers and the cartel killed my brother up here in the middle of goddamn nowhere and tossed his body into the river like he was trash, you really expect me to let that go, Grady? You know me better than that." There was a gasp and then a groan as his arm locked tight around my middle.

I swore too as we both started to slide sideways in the saddle as he lost his balance and struggled to remain seated. The horse underneath us neighed at the shift in weight and tossed his head in aggravation.

"Cy." I called to the man in the lead and gave him a pleading look when he cranked his head around to look at me. "I don't know where we're going but we're going to need to stop sooner than you probably planned. I need to look at Webb's shoulder to and he needs to rest."

His gaze skimmed over me and over the man behind me who was barely managing to stay in the saddle even with my help.

"There's a fire lookout post a few more miles in this direction. It's nothing fancy, just a bare bones cabin the forest service uses to house a ranger when the fire danger is high. There's an observation tower we should be able to see once we get out of the thick of the forest. They might have a better first aid kit than I carry and there should be a bed, so we can let him rest for a couple hours before we push on. You think you'll make it?"

"I'll make it." Webb ground the words out through gritted teeth but I realized Cy was looking at me as he asked the question.

I gave him a lopsided grin and tipped my chin down in a tiny nod of agreement. "I'm holding on for dear life."

And I had no plans of letting go anytime soon.

CHAPTER 14

No Rest for the Weary

A S IF THINGS WEREN'T CHALLENGING enough, another hour into our ride, through the trees and going what seemed like straight uphill, the sky went from sunny blue skies to stormy gray in the span of seconds. The first few drops of rain were huge and splattered noisily when they hit the ground. They were nothing compared to the deluge that followed after the sky opened up and tried to wash all the way down the mountain and back to the river. The water coming from above was relentless and driving. The drops of rain stung exposed skin when they made contact and had the ground underneath the horses' hooves turning into slippery mush. We were already moving at a snail's pace but we had been plodding along steady and sure. The rain almost brought us to a total stop, especially since it made the struggle Webb was having staying on the saddle and holding onto me even more pronounced.

Cy kept insisting the cabin was just beyond the tree line, but the longer we trudged through the forest and the weather, the more I was convinced that the forest never ended. It crossed my mind that Cy might be lost but I quickly dismissed it. Cy wasn't the kind of man who would wander around aimlessly. He always had a destination in mind and he wouldn't put the rest of us at risk by pretending like he knew the way when he really didn't.

He stopped us fifteen minutes into the storm when he found a spot that was partially dry, due to the canopy of the trees above. He dug his rain poncho out of the pack on the side of Edgar. Em and Sutton had ended up with the mules and most of the provisions since there were only two of them and they would move the fastest. He forced me to put it on, even though I protested and told him I was fine. He was bleeding and Webb was on the verge of passing out. I didn't want any special treatment or for him to coddle me. He grunted in response to my argument and pulled the rubbery material over my head, effectively shutting me up.

"Webb is already fighting to stay in the saddle. If he loses his grip on you and ends up in the mud, I doubt we're getting him back on a horse. This will keep you somewhat dry and give him a chance to hold on for the rest of the ride. We need to push hard for just a little bit longer." He'd been saying that for hours. I don't think his idea of a little bit and mine were the same.

Webb wiggled his hands under the drape of the poncho and settled them back on my damp waist. He gave me a little squeeze, as I watched Cyrus walk back toward his horse and pull himself up into the saddle. The motion wasn't as effortless for him as it usually was and there was no missing the wince that followed when he leaned forward and reached for the reins.

"Cy reminds me of Wyatt. My older brother is always looking out for everyone else. They are what good men should be like." The longer we rode the harder it got for Webb to speak. His words were slow and measured, each one an obvious struggle to get out. He was shivering behind me and I could feel the grip he had on my waist slipping.

I turned my head a fraction so that I could catch his eye. "You don't know for sure what happened to him. Everything that's been going on this week proves that things can be unpredictable. Maybe something super important with his case came up and he couldn't contact you. You need to believe in him and have faith that his training and his investment in getting back to the people who love him is enough to keep him safe."

Webb made a noise in his throat and shook his head. "I've been listening to you and your friend all week. You don't exactly have faith in people."

I grimaced a little, not realizing he'd been paying attention to me while I was too busy paying attention to him and trying to figure him out. "I don't have faith in people I don't know well, mostly because I've spent my entire life trying to avoid disappointment. That's impossible, which is a lesson I guess I needed to learn. This trip has taught me that I shouldn't keep trying to build walls between me and the people I do know and trust. It sounds like you and your brother are close and it sounds like he's never given up on you, even though you've made some bad choices along the way." Just like Em had never given up on me, and just like my grandparents had gone out of their way to love me more because my mother couldn't love me at all. "You shouldn't give up on him either."

He made another noise and his fingers flexed at my waist. "I'm not giving up. If something happened to him, I will level this entire forest to make the people who hurt him pay." The certainty in his tone made me shiver because I believed him.

I was trying to think of a proper response when suddenly, the trees started to thin out making the downpour even more difficult to navigate. I saw Edgar slip a little and Cy struggle to keep his balance as the horse danced erratically to the side in the mud. Grady called out to make sure everyone was okay and I almost cried tears of relief when a tiny, nondescript cabin came into view. There was a clearing that was currently nothing more than a mud bog but the cabin was there, just like Cy had promised, looking like a rustic oasis. Behind the cabin was a wood and metal tower that rose high into the sky. I couldn't believe I hadn't noticed before, since it rose like a pillar above the trees. It showed how tired and anxious I was that I had missed it. We all needed out of the rain and the boys needed their injuries tended to.

"Cy, there are tire tracks in the mud. Someone was here not that long ago." Grady pointed out the obvious marks in the loose soil and it had all of us exchanging nervous looks with one another.

"Could be the rangers. Those look like ATV tracks." Cy swung out of the saddle and gave his horse a pat on the side of the neck. "You guys head inside and see if there is anything you can use to fix up Webb's shoulder. I'll take care of the horses. I need to find someplace semi dry to hitch them up."

"I'll help you with the horses just in case we aren't alone. I think making it through one ambush a day is enough for all of us." Grady sounded as weary as I felt and as Webb looked. It was obvious Cy was also running on fumes because he accepted the help with no argument.

Webb limped and shuffled his way to the cabin door with me propped up under his arm as a crutch. I was surprised when the door opened easily under my hand and even more surprised that the interior was far from sparse and utilitarian as the outside had led me to believe it would be. The cabin was decorated with woodsy touches but there were curtains, a braided rug on the floor, a cozy looking comforter on the bed, and a kitchen with cute and rustic tin cookware. The place was fully stocked, looked well lived in, and incredibly comfortable. The only thing missing was a bathroom, which I would have killed for, but knew that beggars couldn't be choosers and a roof over my head during the storm was all I really needed. It was obvious that the rangers who were stationed out here during wildfire season had gone out of their way to make the place as welcoming and as livable as possible. I wanted to kiss each and every one of them in gratitude.

I muscled Webb over to the bed. I pulled off the poncho, which immediately left a soggy puddle on the floor at my feet, and started to scavenge through the cabin for a first aid kit. I opened cabinets and drawers, pulling out anything that seemed useful or necessary as I went. There was plenty of canned food stashed throughout the kitchen, as well as a flare gun and a regular old shotgun along with shells. When I finally found the sturdy aluminum box with the familiar blue and white writing on it I let out a victorious whoop and did a little shimmy as I turned around with the first aid kit held above my head.

I was expecting a similar excitement at the discovery from Webb but when I was met with silence I knew something was seriously wrong. He was pitched over on his side on the bed, clutching his shoulder and shaking all over. Even though the rain had soaked him through, his skin was clammy and fiery to the touch when I grabbed him and rolled him over onto his back.

"It feels like my entire body is burning." There was blood still leaking thick and crimson from between his fingers.

I pawed through the first aid kit and handed him a handful of painkillers. "I wouldn't normally mix Tylenol and Ibuprofen but I think this case calls for extreme measures. Can you sit up? We need to get your shirt off so I can put something on your shoulder to stop the bleeding as much as possible. If you can handle it, I'll pour this peroxide on the wound and then cover it with the antibiotic cream. I think the fever might be from an infection and I don't even want to think about how much blood you've lost. There's nothing in here to close the wound but we can get it as clean as possible and wrap it up as tight as you can stand."

He groaned loud and long as we both struggled to get him

into a seated position so that I could tug his shirt off of him. It was tricky because the material soaked from the rain clung to him. I offered to cut the garment off to make it easier but he shook his head and powered through while I peeled the rest of the shirt down his arms.

The bullet wound was angry, red, and puckered. The skin around it was hot pink. I'd never seen anything like it up close and personal, so it was all I could do to focus and not let the lightheadedness at the sight of the gore and blood overtake me. I found a dishtowel in the kitchen that looked unused and got it wet. As soon as I pressed the material to Webb's shoulder it turned red. I had to switch it out with another before the trickle of blood slowed enough that any kind of bandage would be able to stick to his skin.

I poured the peroxide on one of the bandages and stared at Webb before touching the cotton to his shoulder. "This is going to suck."

His eyes widened and his jaw clenched. "I know, but do it anyway."

We both held our breath as I inched the bandage toward the opening in his flesh. As soon as it touched the injury, a scream that made my ears ring echoed throughout the cabin. One of Webb's hands shot up and wrapped around my good wrist. He squeezed so hard that I knew I was going to have a bruise there, but he didn't pull me away as the liquid stung him and as his blood turned the white cloth red.

I repeated the process on the back side of his shoulder and thought for a second that he had passed out from the pain. His shoulders slumped forward and his head lolled listlessly on his neck as I covered the wound in a greasy layer of antibiotic cream. When I said his name, he muttered, "It's fine. I'm fine." Which both sounded like a big fat lie but there wasn't anything that could be done about it.

I put bandages on either side of the wound and then wrapped his entire shoulder in an Ace bandage so tightly that he could hardly move it. I was just putting the metal clips at the end of the bandage when the door opened and a soggy Cy and Grady dripped their way inside. Before Cy could say anything, I ushered him to one of the folding chairs situated around the card table and treated him to the same amateur nursing Webb had received.

Cy didn't make a sound. I knew the peroxide and the pressure on the gash in his arm had to hurt like hell but still, the man sat like a stone and simply watched me fuss over him like it wasn't necessary. It was totally necessary because even if it didn't make him feel any better, taking care of him and making sure he was as comfortable as possible made me feel better. I was pretty sure he knew that taking care of him soothed something inside of me because he let me hover over him for far longer than was needed. Moments later, when he had enough and pulled me down into his lap with a sigh, he thanked me with a light kiss on the lips. He was wet and chilly but his mouth was warm. I marveled that he was able to burn even when life was throwing everything it could at him to extinguish his fire.

"Let's whip up something to eat and then we can dry out and rest up for a little bit. We can't stay in one place for too long in case those tire tracks don't belong to the rangers. We don't want to be sitting ducks up here and the ranch is only another day's ride, over the top of the mountain and down the other side of it. Hopefully, Sutton has already made his way back home and alerted the authorities." He sounded tired and frustrated.

"If the rangers use this cabin for fire lookouts, wouldn't they have a radio or something to call back to base?" Now that he was outed as a federal agent and fully acting like his real self, Grady's training and intuition was on full display.

Cy nodded at the same time I shook my head no. "I tore this entire place apart looking for the first aid kit. I didn't see anything that looked like a phone or a radio."

"It's mobile so they bring it in with them, and if there was one onsite, it would be up in the tower. If it stops raining for a few minutes, I can climb up there and see if they left one behind. Doesn't matter, though; we still can't stay here even if the rangers are nearby. Webb needs a doctor."

The man on the bed lifted his good hand and let if fall weakly back to his side. "I'll be okay. Leo did a good job wrapping me up and I think the meds are already working on the fever."

"Still not gonna risk it. I want everyone back at the ranch and accounted for. Besides, the sooner I get you back, the sooner you can get to Sheridan and find out if that body is someone you know or not." Cy spoke like a man who was used to having his orders followed.

Cy slid me off his lap and rose to his feet. I helped him pick through the canned goods I put on the center of the table when I'd searched for supplies. I told him to let me fuss with the propane-operated camp stove and getting something warmed up. I had two working hands, even if my wrist was still stiff and sore from my fall and from struggling to control the horse all afternoon. Keeping Webb propped up hadn't done anything to make it feel better. I was playing through the pain in a very literal way and I was proud of myself. It didn't even occur to me to run from something that *actually* hurt. Cy gave in without an argument and I was rewarded with another kiss.

I made beans and canned corn for dinner. It wasn't five-star quality but it tasted better than any fine dining dinner I could remember. By the time I cleaned everything up, Webb was passed out on the bed and Grady had gone outside to keep watch. The downpour had lightened to a drizzle, so Cy went out and climbed the tower only to report back that there was no radio. He also mentioned that he couldn't see the cleared out portion of the forest where the grow field was located from that vantage point. That meant there was a really good chance that the rangers and wildlife officers who patrolled the area had no clue what was going on in the territory. He looked grim when he mentioned that he didn't know if the wildlife officers would be equipped to deal with the growers if they did run across them—especially if they were backed by a cartel that had a lot of financial reason to want their operations uninterrupted.

I silently agreed with him since none of us, including the former federal agent and the hardened ex-con, seemed to know how to deal with the bad guys in this situation either. I went to touch the backs of my fingers to Webb's forehead and was relieved that while he was still warm, he no longer felt like the inside of a furnace. I felt Cy move behind me and reached up to cover the hand that he dropped on my shoulder with my own.

"He's pretty tough for a city kid. Not too many people could have made that ride through those conditions banged up the way he was." There was begrudging admiration in his tome that he usually reserved for his brothers or for when I did something that surprised and pleased him. He squeezed my shoulder as I let out a jaw popping yawn. "As much as I hate the idea, you should climb up next to him and get some rest. You'll sleep easier on the bed than on the floor."

I lifted the shoulder he was holding onto and let it fall. "I'll sleep better wherever you're at. If you're staking claim on the floor, then I am too. But I think I saw a couple of old Army cots stashed in the big cabinet that the first aid kit was in. That might be better than the floor with your arm."

"I'm not going to shut it down, Leo. I don't know how much faith I have in Grady to be the lookout. He's still a stranger and that story of theirs is still crazy even if it's true. Plus, those tire tracks make me nervous. We had to stop because of the weather, and because of Webb, but it isn't a great idea."

I turned around and put my good hand on the center of his chest. His entire frame was coiled tight and vibrating with invisible waves of tension and readiness. If he wound himself up any tighter, he was going to snap and then we would all be screwed. I was adapting to what had to be done out here in the woods, but I was no adventurer, and had no clue how to navigate the unforgiving terrain back to the ranch.

"You stayed up most of the night keeping watch. You rode for hours in the driving rain with a massive gash in your arm. You might look like you're carved from stone but you're made of all the same breakable things all men are made of, Cy. Take an hour and lie down with me. Hold onto me and let me hold onto you, so that I can pretend like things aren't as bad as they actually are." I ran my hands up over his wide shoulders and cuddled into his chest so that my cheek was resting on the steady thump of his heart. "Steal a moment for yourself. You've earned it."

He exhaled against the top of my head and his heavy arms curled around me and held me close. We were both getting really good at holding onto things, which meant when it was time to finally let go, it was going to be brutal. It was going to feel like something imperative and vital to my future happiness was being ripped away.

"I'll give us an hour and then I'll take Grady's place and get us ready to move." It was never enough time. I was greedy and always after more. More time and more of him.

He let me go and muscled out the cots. They had seen better days but they would keep us up off the floor. Cy set them up in the center of the room after he took down the card table. I kept an eye on Webb to make sure all the racket Cy was making didn't wake him up but the man was down for the count. There were a few extra blankets folded up on the end of the bed, so I snagged them and crawled onto one of the cots next to Cy. He shot an arm out and wrapped it around me so that he could tug me to his chest and we were lying face to face, breathing one another in.

I lifted a finger and traced it over the flat line of his lips and shivered when he darted his tongue out to lick the tip of the digit. "I like it better when you smile." He didn't do it very often, so when he did, it was extra special and meant to be savored.

"Haven't had much reason to do that until you came crashing into my life, Sunshine." The words were gruff and low but they were some of the sweetest I'd ever heard.

I nuzzled into him and let my eyes drift closed after I told him, "After all of this is said and done, I hope you have enough happy memories of our time together to keep smiling after I'm gone. You shouldn't keep something that special all to yourself."

One of his hands cupped the back of my skull, his fingers threading through my hair as he held me so close it was almost like he was trying to absorb me. He wanted to take me all in just as badly as I wanted to experience everything he had to offer. It was an exhilarating feeling that dulled the edge of fear and anxiety that was making my nerves tingle.

"This time with you has been unforgettable, Leo. Both the good and the bad. Without a doubt, when I think about you, it will put a big, stupid smile on my face. I've never met anyone like you before. The situation around us keeps getting worse and worse but you keep getting better and better. Letting that go is going to be harder than I want to think about while I still have you in my arms."

The metal bar from the cot dug into my side as I scooted even closer to him so I could throw my leg over his. Everything inside of me was screaming to tell him that he didn't have to let me go, that he could hold on to me as hard as I wanted to hold onto him, but I knew it wasn't realistic. His life was here and it wasn't a life I understood or had a place in, not to mention the mess my own life was in back home. I had to decide if I was going to tell Chris's wife what he was doing behind her back and risk my job and future employment. That was the last string dangling from the frayed fabric of my life before and I needed to cut it off. I needed to straighten things out, get my head out of my heart, and make things right back in San Francisco. It was time for me to do the right thing instead of living in fear of the consequences. Maybe once I did that, I could take an even bigger risk and try and figure out a way that would keep this man and his life changing smile in my world.

"No letting go just yet. Get some sleep, Cy, you need to recharge." We both did, so it was no surprise that when I quit talking to him, his breathing got shallow as his chest rose and fell against mine when he drifted off. It didn't take long for me to follow him into oblivion.

Sadly, the reprieve didn't last very long. It only felt like my eyes were shut for five minutes when I was jerked awake by the sound of raised voices and the whir of an engine. I was going to whisper Cy's name to see if he had heard the noise as well, but he was already wide awake. I watched his brows furrow and his face set in hard lines of concentration. He put a finger over my lips as I nodded that I knew I shouldn't make a sound. He inclined his head toward the now empty bed as the voices from outside rose even louder.

"Hold up! Let me see some identification." The words came from Grady followed by Webb's, "I apologize for the weapons but we've run into a bit of trouble the last few days."

It was a female voice that replied, cautious and careful.

"You're on government land and this is a government outpost, gentleman. I don't care how much trouble you're in or how far out of your element you are, it is never appropriate to greet an armed law enforcement officer with drawn weapons. Now, put down the guns and you show me some goddamn ID."

The woman's voice didn't waver or crack, which I thought was impressive considering she was facing off with two armed men and she had no clue what either was capable of. Cy rolled off the side of the cot and inched his way over to the window by the front door of the cabin, careful to keep his head low and his movements slow and steady. He peered out the window and must have approved of what he saw because he yanked open the door and stepped out front after telling me to stay put until he came and got me.

"Officer McKenna. Sorry to show up here unannounced but these fellas aren't exaggerating about it being a bad few days. Brynn should have called your station to tell you what was going on."

Curious because Cy seemed to know the woman the authoritative voice belonged to, I couldn't stay huddled in fear any longer. I copied Cy's meticulous movements toward the front door until I could peek out of the same window, hopefully without being seen.

The woman was dressed in a khaki uniform and she had a dark baseball hat on top of her head but the drab clothing and the gear covering the top of her icy blonde hair in no way detracted from how gorgeous she was. Taller than Emrys and rocking more curves than a mountain pass, the woman was stunning and clearly not amused at having the barrel of a shotgun pointed directly at her. Her eyes never left Webb, who didn't lower the gun despite her obvious familiarity with Cy.

"I didn't get a call about you being in trouble, Warner. I got a call out because one of the rafting guides called in a report of a couple of mules running loose down by the water. They were loaded down for the trail but no riders or ranchers came up to claim them. The leads had your logo on them, Cy. I was out here looking for your trail group to figure out what the hell is going on."

The news about the mules made Cy stiffen and had Grady swearing under his breath. No longer able to stay hidden or quiet, I poked my head out the door and demanded, "Why wouldn't the mules still be with Emrys and Sutton?"

The beautiful woman shifted her gaze to me and then back to Webb, who finally lowered the barrel of his shotgun. The woman glared at him, and even though he had to be hurting still, a cocky grin pulled at the man's mouth. He clearly appreciated the woman's steely stance and fierce bravado in a different way than I did.

"Like I said, no riders were found anywhere near where the mules were located. We sent a few rangers up and down the river but no one turned up anything. There were reports of dirt bike tracks on one of the more remote trails, but no sign of horses."

"Shit." Cy bit the word out and shoved his hands through his hair. "We were on a ride with eight guests. It's been a shit show. Someone is growing marijuana up off one of the trailheads and the growers are trying to keep the area clear. They rode up on us with dirt bikes and pinned us down in an ambush, way up river. My brothers and I split the group up and we were all racing back to the ranch. Sutton had the mules and one of the girls from the group with him. If you found the mules and not my brother, that's bad, really bad."

The woman blinked slowly and then moved to rest her hands on her hips. "You're telling me you think the people behind the grow field have your brother? Sutton wouldn't go anywhere without a fight, especially if he had a guest with him. You Warners aren't built that way."

Cy grunted his response as the radio clipped to the woman's hip opposite the one with the gun crackled to life.

"McKenna, we got a group of campers on the river who are reporting a speckled appaloosa, minus a rider. The horse is injured and they're reporting that the saddle has blood on it. How far away from the location are you?"

The woman sighed and pulled the radio off her belt so she could speak into it. "We have a problem. Has base reported in with a call from the Warner ranch?" There was a negative reply but the voice on the other end of the radio mentioned several rangers were tied up with another body in the river. The woman swore and replied back, "The brothers were out on the trail and ran into some trouble. Trouble of the gun toting and murdering kind. I think we might have stumbled onto why we suddenly have bodies showing up in our river. I'm at ranger station 15, let me finish up here, and I'll head down to the river and get a statement from the campers."

"Copy that. Be careful out there."

She put the radio back and narrowed her eyes at Cy, who started to pace back and forth in jerky steps.

"Tell me where you think the drug field is and I'll head that way. I have an extra radio on the ATV. I'll give you the spare and call in if I find any signs of your brother."

Cy barked out an ugly laugh and shook his head. "No fucking way, Ten. If they have my brother, then the only way you're getting to the field is if I take you."

"Ten?" The question came from an openly curious Webb and was met with an eye roll.

"Tennyson McKenna. Officer McKenna to you." There was bite in her tone and it had Webb grinning and Grady groaning.

"Well, Officer McKenna, these guys put a bullet in me and

they very well may have killed *my* brother. I'm with Warner. If you want to get to where the bad guys are, then we're going with you."

She huffed out a breath and looked at me questioningly. All I could do was shrug and mutter, "I go where he goes, and if they took Sutton, that means they probably have my best friend, as well. I can't stay here by myself and I can't leave her wherever she is. We're going." There was no time for doubt, no time to consider failure or fault. All I could think about was the fact that Em needed me and I had to be there for her. No matter what kind of dangers might be waiting for me on the way to her.

Cy put his arm around me and gazed steadily at the woman. "You can take Leo back to the ranch and I can call in when I get to the field. The other option is that my little lion is right and we all go in together. They outnumber us but I bet they can't outsmart us."

The woman was silent for a long moment and then she threw up her hands in frustration. "Still as stubborn and as hard headed as always, Cy. You can't ever make things easy. You're impossible. If I didn't know that it'll take me twice as long to find the field without you, I would throw some cuffs on you to keep you all out of my hair. I don't like involving civilians but I don't see how I can stop you from sticking your nose where it doesn't belong."

"I'm not a civilian." That came from Grady at the same time Cy snorted and said, "Show me a man who lives out here you wouldn't want to have at your back, Ten. You know we protect what's ours."

She didn't have a rebuttal.

Because while Cy might not be what I imagined a cowboy to be, he sure as hell was what I'd always imagined what a hero should be.

CHAPTER 15

No Man Left Behind

THE TRIP BACK THE WAY we came went slightly faster with Webb able to hitch a ride on the four-wheeler behind the pretty park ranger. She didn't look like she loved the idea, especially when he refused to give up his weapon, but he was still bleeding pretty steadily and unable to use the arm with the bullet hole through it, so she didn't have much choice in the matter. The rain picked up again, which made the now loaded down horses slip and slide even more in the mud and loose brush. Cy had insisted on taking every single weapon and as much of the canned provisions as he could from the ranger's cabin. Officer McKenna didn't like that plan either, but apparently, she knew Cy well enough to know that arguing with him would be futile and a waste of time we didn't have. Cy was worried about his brother. Webb was worried about his brother. I couldn't let myself think about what may or may not be happening to Emrys if she was in the wrong kinds of hands.

If I let my mind go there, it was going to nosedive right into the worst-case scenario which would render me worthless and useless on this very risky expedition. I was the only one who didn't know how to use a weapon, the only one shaking from more than the cold, and the only one who seemed like they were struggling to keep it together. So instead of thinking about Em and how she was holding up, I was turning over the fact that Cy and the park ranger clearly had history. He had loved and lost, was still missing pieces to his heart, but that didn't mean the man was dead or had lived like a saint in the passing years. I was wondering why the stunning and seemingly perfect for him woman who was part of our rag-tag group hadn't stuck.

Almost as if he could hear my thoughts, he turned to look at me and slowed Edgar down so that he could ride next to me. Rain had made his dark hair even darker and the chill turned his skin a rosy pink that didn't suit him. He was uncomfortable and concerned, two things he made an effort to conceal but the feelings managed to shine through anyway.

"How are you holding up, Sunshine?" Instead of being comforting, the rasp of his voice grated across my skin.

"I've been better." My tone was cool and so was my gaze as I considered him for a long moment. "You and the blonde? What's that all about?" I sort of hated that I felt compelled to ask because I had no claim on him. The fact that I wanted to know made me realize I also wanted to own enough of him that I was entitled to the information. It was foolish but I couldn't stop the sense of propriety where he was concerned. In almost no time at all, I considered him mine, which was insanity considering I had spent a lifetime skipping out of the reach of anyone who wanted to love me enough to call me theirs.

"Ten? We went to high school together. Her folks own the ranch that borders ours. She left about the same time I did with big plans to join the FBI or something like that. I'm not sure what brought her home. She doesn't talk about it much." He lifted his eyebrows up and lifted a hand to wipe the water gathered on his forehead with a flick of his wrist. "She came around after my wife left and we spent some time together, still do if either one of us gets lonely enough and doesn't have any other option available. She never asks for much and she's always gone before morning." He shrugged a shoulder and met my gaze steadily and unashamed. "We never really got along as kids and honestly we don't really mesh well outside of the bedroom. But we both have something the other can use, so it's easy enough." The corner of his mouth curled up in a sardonic grin. "It's not like there is an endless amount of women to choose from out here. Ten is just that . . . a ten . . . and she gets that all I have to offer her is a couple hours in bed. She's good with it because that's all she has to offer as well."

I pursed my lips together and shifted my gaze away from the intensity of his. Those gray orbs could get as sharp and as pointed as the blade of a knife when he was using them to peel layers away from whoever they were trained on.

"You have more to offer than your dick, Cy." He was smart, driven, protective, and he pushed. He pushed and pushed until he shoved you right into wanting to be the kind of person who could match him passion for passion and strength for strength. Not to mention how much he cared about his family and making sure everyone he loved was taken care of. He gave up his own life and his own chance at love in order to preserve a legacy that he never wanted. He sacrificed his own happiness and future to make sure his brothers would have something that would always be theirs. He lost everything so that his father's hard work and memory would never be forgotten. Right now, he was risking his own neck because he didn't know what was going on with one of his siblings.

He was absolutely a good time when he was naked and demanding but he brought about a million more important things to the table than his impressive cock. Any woman willing to settle for a few hours in the dark, without experiencing all the other amazing things that made Cy larger than life, was shortchanging herself and him.

"I know that, Leo, but I don't choose to offer more than what's in my pants to just any woman. I'm selective because there hasn't been a woman who made me forget what I had, and made me dream about what I could have . . . until you." As always, when he said stuff like that, I felt it all the way through my body. His words had power. When he spoke what he meant, it felt like his honesty tore through me and eviscerated everything I thought I knew about caring about another person.

I cleared my throat and lifted a hand to absently rub at my tender shoulder. "We don't make any sense."

It hurt to say, but it was true. I wanted this consuming, burning, engulfing thing that coiled and tangled around us to have reason and rationale but it didn't, which made justifying it and fostering it seem not only impossible but also wasteful. This kind of emotion and uncontrollable reaction should belong to two people who could do something important with it. It deserved to belong to people who could fully appreciate it, instead of the two of us, who were scrambling so hard to exploit it in the little bit of time we had with one another. We weren't savoring, we were rushing through it, trying to absorb it all before it burned us both out. Cy had scorched me through and through, but I was going to torch him as well, and when we were done, the ashes were going to be blown away.

He reached out and grabbed a piece of my hair that was curling out of control due to the weather. The curl he tugged on sprang right back into its tight ringlet making him grin at me. "It's been my experience that the devil you know is the one who brings hell to your doorstep. I don't know why it's you who makes me feel like I'm functioning fully instead of going through the motions. But it is *you*, Leo. You make lonely look ugly and a lot harder than it has been these last few years."

I couldn't think of anything to say to that because I didn't want to tell him that I was terrified of what my lonely would look like now that I realized that's what I'd been all along. With my heart pounding and my skin shivering from the reality of how empty my existence would be once I got home, I changed the subject to the one that was obviously weighing heavily on his mind.

"Do you think the guys who shot at us have Emrys and Sutton?"

His jaw clenched and a muscle ticked in his cheek making him look fierce and ferocious. This was a man who would take care of his own, no matter the personal cost, and there was something about that protective streak that soothed my own abandoned heart. If Cy ever loved me, I knew there was nothing on this Earth that would drive him away. His love was a bond that couldn't and wouldn't be broken, making handing over my heart that had been unwanted in the past seem less dangerous.

"I don't know, but I do know that Sutton will do everything in his power to keep your girl safe if they were taken." That's what I was afraid of. Emrys was the easier target but if the men with the guns tried to take her, the middle Warner brother would have made them go through him first. That didn't bode well, for either of them.

"Why would they take them? If they wanted us off the mountain, why drag them back to the place they're trying to keep everyone away from?" I hated the questions I was asking but I disliked the answers he was giving me even more.

"They may want to make sure that they aren't telling anyone where the clearing is, but more than likely if they took them, it's to use as leverage in case the rangers show up. Or even worse, the DEA." His tone was heavy with dread but I appreciated the fact that he wasn't trying to placate me.

"You think they took them to use as hostages?" My voice broke and my hands curled around the reins so tightly that my knuckles turned white.

"Could be. We don't know anything at this point and it's better not to speculate. If we start doing that, then it's going to make us go off halfcocked without a plan. We can't do that. Right now, we're operating like we're going in there to pull my brother and your girl out of the fire. If we start acting like we're storming the castle for blood and vengeance, all that's going to get us is panic and pain." He flicked his head to the side again as the rain picked up and made his inky lashes spike together.

"I don't know how you can be so calm about everything. Inside, I feel like there are a thousand buzzing bees trying to burst through my skin and every organ and muscle I have feels like it's tied into a knot. It's taking every scrap of self-control I have not to freak out and fall apart. I've never been so scared in my life." I refused to think about what my life would be like without Emrys there to keep me grounded. She was my port in the storm; without her in my life, I would endlessly drift. I had to get her back. That was the only option I was allowing.

"You're here regardless of what's happening on the inside right now, Sunshine. Your girl would be proud of you because you're doing what you need to do, even though you don't know how many ways it could go bad and you're scared. That's brave and ballsy." He sounded proud as well, which made me sit up a little straighter in the saddle.

"Aren't you just a little bit scared, Cy?" I didn't think he would admit to it if he was, but like always, he surprised me.

He turned his head to look at me and the silver shield that masked his gaze slipped away and the foggy color darkened with fear and uncertainty. "I'm scared out of my fucking mind."

The fact that he trusted me enough to show me his vulnerability, his soft underside, made me slip a little closer to feeling like if circumstances were different I could love him forever. There was nothing Cy wanted to hide from me and the fact that he was so open with his strengths and weaknesses, made me feel like I had known him since the beginning of time.

The rumble of the four-wheeler suddenly died out and the ranger's voice echoed to where we were trailing behind her in the trees.

"It's going to be dark soon, so I say we camp here for the night and then head the rest of the way in on foot tomorrow. If we take the four-wheeler they might hear us coming since sound travels so far out here." She hooked a thumb at Webb who was still holding onto her from behind. "City boy here says that it's only about three miles in from where you first encountered the clearing."

Cy shook his head. "More like five. Boss took off on Leo and bolted a few miles into the woods. It'll be a long walk if you're still losing blood."

Webb let go of the pretty blonde after she gave him a look cold enough to leave frostbite and gave a lopsided grin. "I'll be all right but if for some reason I slow everyone down, I'll hang with the horses and the extra radio in case things go to hell and we need to call in the troops."

The ranger rolled her very green eyes and started pulling things out of a big canvas knapsack that matched her drab uniform. "There is no calling in the troops this far out, and half the staff is searching for bodies in the river."

The reminder that people had ended up dead, his brother possibly one of them, because of the goings on deep in these woods, was enough to sober Webb up and wipe the smile off his face. He gingerly climbed off of the four-wheeler and took the sleeping bag she shoved at him with a grunt, as she was a little too rough with his injury. He paled noticeably and the ranger looked like she was on the verge of apologizing but she quickly bit the words back and turned to Cy.

"We should come up with a plan before we trek toward their compound in the morning." Cy nodded as the older man cleared his throat and held up a hand.

"Not to step on anyone's toes here, but up until a few weeks ago I was a highly decorated agent with the Drug Enforcement Agency. I organized search and destroy operations all over the world. If anyone is going to come up with a plan to storm the castle, I think it should be me."

Cy exchanged a look with the ranger and then shrugged. "Fine by me, as long as whatever plan you concoct ends with my brother and Emrys getting out of the compound unharmed, if they are in fact there."

"I was a federal agent, Mr. Warner. It was my job to protect people, not to put them in danger." The older man sounded a little put out and I couldn't blame him. There was a lot of suspicion on Cy's face and in his tone and the pretty forest ranger looked even less impressed by the man's credentials.

"What do you suggest, Grady? I want someone up there to answer my questions about my brother and I doubt we make that happen if we roll in with guns blazing." Webb maneuvered himself to the ground so that his back was resting against the muddy wheel of the four-wheeler—the wet ground and the soggy perch not seeming to bother him at all.

"Guns blazing is your style, not mine, Webb. I think we need to cause a distraction, then we need to get someone into the spot where the growers have to be camped out near the grow field in order to protect the crop. Once we have eyes on the inside we can find out for sure if Sutton and the girl are there. If they don't have our people to use as leverage, then there is no need to risk our necks. If they do have our people, then after the initial distraction we need to create a second one, an even bigger one, so that we can smuggle them out in the chaos. Chances are they'll have people watching Sutton and Emrys if they do have them, but if we make two messes for them to investigate, then they'll have to have all hands on deck. It's not a foolproof plan by any means, but I think it's one that will get us the best results."

Cy crossed his arms over his chest and exchanged a look with the ranger and then shifted his gaze to me. "What kind of distraction are you thinking?" His expression clearly stated that it better not involve my being in any kind of danger. "The crop in the field hasn't come to the surface yet, so burning their drugs isn't an option."

I inclined my head toward Edgar who was packed with a mini arsenal. "There's a flare gun in that stash you took from the cabin. That might work as the initial disruption but I don't know what we have on hand for the second one, especially if it needs to be a bigger bang."

Webb let his head fall forward so that he was looking at the ground between his feet. His voice was still a little weak but the determination in it was evident and unwavering. "You leave the second round of fucking shit up to me." A smile that wasn't nice at all twisted across his features.

"You aren't going to do anything stupid, Webb. I won't let you." Grady scolded the younger man in a no-nonsense tone that Webb ignored.

"We're well past the point where you can control what I do, Grady. I want to know where my brother is and if these dicks had anything to do with his disappearance. If I get to rattle a few cages along the way, well that just sounds like a good time."

Ten shook her head, which sent water flying off the brim

of her ball cap. She pointed a finger at Webb, which made him grin. He apparently liked being bossed around and taken to task by the leggy blonde. "City boy, you sound a little too eager to start trouble, if you ask me. If you're a liability, I'll cuff you to the four-wheeler and come back for you when this disaster is all cleaned up."

Webb held up his hands in front of him in mock surrender. "I'll behave . . . for now. I am serious about handling the second wave of distraction though. That means Cy and Grady can get into the compound once we find it and look for Sutton and Emrys. Leo can handle the first distraction from a safe distance, keeping her cute ass out of the line of fire, and you can keep everyone covered." He wiggled his eyebrows up and down. "Your ass is pretty spectacular, as well. I don't want you to think I didn't notice."

The woman huffed and copied Cy's stance with her arms locked over her chest. "Forget cuffing you, I may just shoot you and leave you for the mountain lions."

Cy made a low noise in his throat that sounded like a growl and narrowed his eyes at the injured man. "Mention Leo's ass again and you won't have to worry about what Ten has in store for you, because I'll rip your fool head off your body with my bare hands."

I put a hand on his arm, which felt like wet stone under my fingertips. "I think everyone needs to go to their separate corners and try and get some sleep. We're going to head out early in the morning and none of us has gotten very much rest over the last few days. We're all wet and on edge but threatening one another isn't doing any good."

If collapsing in a heap on the ground was an option, I would have gladly taken it but I didn't want to end up even wetter and more miserable than I already was.

Cy loosened his rigid stance and moved to put his arm around me. Typically, when he pulled me into his broad chest it was like being engulfed in warmth and comfort. It was a testament as to how crappy the conditions were that he was just as chilled and just as clammy as I was. I didn't snuggle into him like I wanted to, but I did rest my forehead against the hollow of his throat. I couldn't resist the urge to lick at a drop of rain that trickled down the strong column and across my lips. The little touch of tongue to cool skin made him shiver and had his arms tightening around me.

"I need to get a fire started so we don't freeze to death tonight and to keep the predators I'm actually afraid of away." He was trying to normalize the situation for me and I wanted to kiss him from head to toe in gratitude. His caring went bone deep and didn't falter, even when it would be easy and reasonable to brush to the side, considering the circumstances. I let him go and straightened my shoulders because if he could bend but refuse to break, then so could I. And I was going to hold on, and ride out the storm, weather beaten but still standing on the other side. That wasn't something I would have believed myself capable of doing a few days ago, but this trip and all the ways it had not gone as planned was undeniably eye opening.

I left Cy to work on the fire and made my way over to the horses to see if there was anything I could do to make them more comfortable in the drizzle that was still coming from the sky. The poor animals had pushed just as hard as we had and there was no way they weren't exhausted and sick of being wet and cold, just like I was.

In the middle of rubbing Edgar down with a lone dry blanket I found, I heard footsteps behind me that were too light to belong to any of the men in our motley crew. I looked over my shoulder as the ranger approached and tried not to stiffen or launch my automatic defenses when she gave me a considering look that raked from the top of my head to my toes.

"You're pretty good with the horses for a California girl." Her tone was dry and she made no effort to hide the sarcasm in it.

I lifted an eyebrow in her direction. "How do you know I'm from California?'

She lifted a shoulder and let it fall, eyes never moving from what I was doing with the horses. "I asked Cy to give me a run-down of all the guests including where they were from in case we have to launch an official search party."

I nodded at her and calmly told her, "Believe it or not, they have horses in California." I didn't toss her snide tone back at her, I kept mine even and bland. I didn't need her to point out that she was a much better fit for the man hunched over a pile of kindling, trying to make something burn in the nearly impossibly conditions. I knew I wasn't who Cy needed, but there was no hiding the fact that I was who he wanted.

She took her hat off and shook it out. I felt all the air rush out of my lungs when I realized she was something more than beautiful when her entire face was visible. I was starting to think there was something in the water out here that made the men and woman forged from this land outrageously attractive.

"He does this all the time, you know." She put her hands on her hips and gave me a steady look. "I'm not trying to be a bitch but I've known those Warner boys for a long time and the one thing all of them have in common is the habit of wasting time on the wrong women. I admire you stepping up to the plate when you are so clearly out of your element. Most women in your shoes would have demanded someone take them back to the ranch or opted to lay low at the cabin. I don't want you to have some kind of false fantasy built up about Cy, where you think things between the two of you last beyond your time on his turf. Once you're gone . . . you're gone and he'll be onto the next one." The words were callous but I could see that she really thought she was doing me a favor by laying them on me like bricks. She was telling me, like I should have told Chris's wife, the kind of man I was losing more and more of myself to. She wasn't worried about my reaction or the outcome because to her, she was looking out for me in her own blunt and abrasive way.

I straightened up and gathered my hair into my hands so I could wring the kinky mass out. The stands were slippery and chilly to the touch. There was also a knot on the underneath side that I was pretty sure was going to require scissors to remove. Typically, I didn't belong here and this wasn't my place, but right now I did and there wasn't anything that would convince me otherwise . . . even the uncomfortable truth of her not-so-friendly warning.

I raised a shoulder and let it fall. "I'll be gone but not forgotten. I went into this thing with Cy knowing that had to be enough."

She cocked her head to the side a little and a wry grin pulled at her lips. "Again, you're very brave. Most of the women he burns through are so blinded by that face and that body that they ignore the fact that every flame flickers out eventually. You see the burnout right in front of you and you're still playing with fire."

I nodded a little bit and gave her my own grin. "Why wouldn't I? I've never had the opportunity to get my hands on something that hot before. I might as well enjoy the heat while I can."

She slapped her soggy hat back on her head and gave me a smile that was full of perfectly straight white teeth and revealed an adorable dimple in her cheek. The woman was physically something else, she really had to be as perfect as any human could be in order to offset her cool and standoffish demeanor. "I like you, Cali girl, and I like that Cy likes you. It's a shame you can't stick around a little longer because I think you might actually do the man some good. He almost smiled today."

I didn't tell her as she turned and walked away from me that I made him smile all the time when we were together.

CHAPTER 16

Not in the Plan

WE LEFT THE MAKESHIFT CAMP before the first rays of dawn were in the sky. No one slept very well on the wet ground and everyone was on high alert, so the tension and unease made sleep nearly impossible. Officer McKenna called into her headquarters and let them know the general direction we were headed. She also instructed whoever was on the other end of the radio transmission to send someone to where the field was located, just in case we couldn't make it back for the horses. The idea of leaving the animals alone and untended didn't sit well with Cy, but it was the idea of any of us not making it back to take care of them that had me breaking out in a sweat despite the frosty chill in the morning air.

Before we set off on foot through the woods, Cy made sure I knew how to handle, load, and shoot the long barreled shotgun, which ended up slung over my shoulder. My hands shook when I shoved the shells into the weapon, but I was pretty sure I could point and shoot it, if the need arose. I'd never felt so far away from my normal life as I did trudging in a line, barely able to see, chilled to the bone, armed to the teeth, on a rescue mission to save my best friend from men who may or may not be tied to a drug cartel. This all while quickly slipping and falling dangerously close to something that looked like being in love with a man who was never meant to be for me. The whole thing was more than any single, normal person should experience in a lifetime. It was the bombardment of new knowledge and understanding that I was struggling to keep my head above. It felt like if I faltered at all, everything that was going on around me would swallow me up and spit me out, battered and lost on the other side of it. As long as I kept my head up and my eyes firmly focused on what lay ahead, I believed there was a fighting chance to make it through all of this happy and whole, with a wealth of new experiences under my belt. Experiences that would fill up all of the empty spaces when I made my way back to my boring and basic life. Experiences that would keep me company in the dark, while my body longed for Cy's touch and the rough sound of his deep voice vibrating across my skin.

I let out a sigh that I thought was quiet, but it had all three of the men in front of me turning their heads to look at me. The attention made me blush, so I waved a hand and told them, "Don't mind me. This is more exercise than I'm used to. I don't think I was made to hike endless miles through the woods loaded down with gear." I worked in a high rise office, for goodness sakes. The only time I took the stairs was when the elevator was down and even then I complained the entire way.

"Isn't San Francisco all hills?" Webb tossed the question over his injured shoulder and I was annoyed by how even his tone was. He was breathing easy, even though his injured shoulder was drooping obviously lower than his good one. He was still pale and a little bit shaky, but doing a damn good job trying to hide whatever pain he was in. He didn't want to be a liability and neither did I.

"It is, but I don't spend my free time trekking up and down those hills carrying a shotgun and marching into secret drug dens where my best friend may or may not be held captive." There was frost in my tone and the younger man had the sense to look contrite.

"Sorry, Leo. I didn't mean anything by it." His apology had me sighing again.

"I know, I'm just edgy. I'm worried about Emrys and Sutton. I'm worried about what's going to happen when we get to where the clearing is. I don't do well with situations that I can't control and there is nothing about what we're walking into that is controllable or safe." I was drowning in uncertainty and I hated it.

Webb's features contorted into something serious and pensive. His eyebrows lowered into a sharp V over the bridge of his nose, as the corners of his mouth tugged downwards in a deep frown. "Control is an illusion. You think you're pulling the strings in life but you're not. All you're doing is dangling at the end of them and shifting whatever way the wind decides to blow you. The only thing you are responsible for is your own actions, so you might as well make those actions matter. Sutton and Emrys stumbling across these assholes was bad luck and being in the worst place at the right time, nothing more, nothing less. The fact that you're here, that you are willing to do whatever it takes to help your friend, those actions are within your control and speak volumes about the person you are."

There was respect in his voice when he addressed me. For some reason, that praise meant more than any of the throwaway compliments I got from the men in suits who gave me a pat on the back over a job well done in my day-to-day life. This stoic ex-con, with a reckless attitude and revenge on his mind, made me feel better about myself and my choices in a way I had been searching for since Chris shattered my confidence.

I was going to tell him thank you and let him know that his insightful observation was very much needed and appreciated

when an ear-piercing scream split the air. The noise obviously had come from a woman and obviously originated from the
clearing where we were headed. My knees went weak when I
realized the sound had to have come from Emrys. I reached out
a hand and grabbed the closest branch to me so that I could stay
on my feet. I stopped breathing as our little caravan came to a
startled stop and exchanged somber looks.

"We need to move." Cy muttered the words low under
his breath as we wordlessly picked up the pace, maneuvering
through the trees and over the rough terrain with purpose, and
no small amount of panic. There was another scream, this one
louder and longer than the one before it. Abruptly it was cut off.
The shock of the silence made me start crying.

Emrys was out there being hurt and there was nothing
I could do to stop it. Everything that she might be enduring in
order to make her sound like that started running through my
head like the most horrific and graphic movie that ever existed.
The horrifying visions made me stumble and stagger. Luckily, Cy
was there to put a hand on my arm and to catch me before I
pitched forward onto my face. He wiped the tears running down
my cheeks away with his thumbs, but he didn't bother to lie by
trying to tell me that everything was going to be okay.

It took longer than I wanted to think about to get to a place
where the clearing in the trees was visible. Grady made us all
stop far enough away that we were still sheltered in the thicket of the forest and quietly asked where we thought Sutton and
Emrys would most likely be located. When I had fallen and landed on the leveled spot, I didn't notice any kind of buildings or
structures around the perimeter. Cy told the former agent that
he hadn't seen anything either but couldn't imagine that the
growers would want to be very far away from their crops in case
intruders stumbled upon the site.

Tennyson tossed the extra radio to Webb and adjusted the rifle she had on her shoulder. "I'll circle around and get up higher on the hill behind the field so I can keep you guys covered. I'm sure I'll spot wherever they have their base set up once I'm on the ridge."

The men nodded as she shifted her gaze to me. "You up for a little bit of a hike, Cali girl? You come with me so you can set that flare off from up high where no one can miss it. If bullets start flying, I'll need you to be the lookout while I keep the bad guys pinned down."

I gulped, because I didn't want to leave Cy or either of the other men I had been in the trenches with up to this point, but I was smart enough to know this was the ranger's way of putting the civilian, and least experienced member of the group, as far out of the line of fire as she could. This was the way I could help rather than hinder, so I nodded. "I'll follow you."

I took a step toward the ranger only to be yanked back and spun around so I was facing Cy. His gray eyes were stormier than the skies above us had been the last few days and the lines of tension and concern that were carved into his hard face made him appear much older than he was. It was like all of this had finally aged him enough to catch up to the silver threads woven throughout his dark hair and beard.

"Be careful, Sunshine." The rumble in his voice made me shiver and the iron grip he held me in made me tremble.

"I'm not the one heading into a camp full of armed men who have a vested interest in making sure none of us make it home. You be careful. Go get my friend and your brother out of trouble." I put a hand over his heart and startled a little bit when I felt how fast it was racing. He was just as worried about the unknown as I was, but he was letting his actions speak for him.

He exhaled long and slow. When he bent his head to press

his lips to mine, it wasn't a man stealing moments and making memories to hold onto because that's all that would be left. No, this kiss came from a man who wanted to stake his claim. It was a kiss that was meant to imprint and last forever . . . however long that may be. It was a kiss meant to sear and mark the soul, so that pieces of him were eternally fused to pieces of me.

Tongues twisted.

Lips moved ravenously, hungrily against one another.

Teeth nipped and clicked together.

Breath mingled and was stolen and was replaced with soft sighs and murmurs of satisfaction.

Hands held on for dear life because even as the kiss consumed, the fact that we were going to have to let go soon, lingered between us.

I gave him a tight squeeze, felt his heart leap like it wanted to touch me, and then I did what I absolutely didn't want to do. I let go and stepped away from him. We were both breathing hard and looking a little dazed, but there was no time to process what that kiss and all the substantial, important things inside of it meant to us.

"Make sure you get back to me, Leo. I'm not done enjoying my time in the sun." His words were for my ears only, barely a sound, just a breath of noise that hit me like a ton of bricks. No one but Cyrus Warner considered me bright and shiny which was all the more reason my heart seemed so willing to jump wildly and carelessly into his hands.

"We aren't done just yet, Cy. We'll find our way back to each other." My reply was just as soft as I leaned up on my toes so I could give him a quick little peck on the cheek, then I took a deep breath and braced. "I'm ready."

Tennyson nodded, and without a word, started off on a path that was parallel to the scar cut into the earth that was the grow field. She took careful steps, making sure she didn't break branches or kick any rocks that would alert to anyone who might be lurking around to the fact we were sulking through the woods.

"There's a big rock outcropping up on a ridge about twenty minutes this way. The rocks are big enough that they'll offer cover if we get fired at and they're far enough away that no one will be able to find us right away after that first flare goes off. I just hope they set up operations close by, so I can direct the guys to the camp." She was whispering, but even that sound echoed loudly in the vast quiet of the forest surrounding us.

I swatted at a pinecone that fell when I brushed against a branch and made sure to step around it so that the brittle texture didn't crunch under my boots. "They can't be that far. We wouldn't have heard Em screaming if they were too far away from the field."

She looked at me over her shoulder and frowned. She snatched her hat off of her head and tossed it to me. "Put that on. I didn't realize how bright your hair was once the sun was out. It's like a damn beacon and there's no telling how close they are. Sound carries for miles and miles."

I snorted a little bit while trying to shove as much of my hair under her ugly hat as I could, which had her lifting her brows questioningly. "I learned that lesson the hard way. I may have accused Cy and his brothers of not being cowboy enough for this business when we first met. I didn't think anyone could hear me and I was very wrong."

She rolled her eyes with a snort of laughter and turned her head back around as the trees started to thin out, as the terrain got rockier and rougher to traverse. "Cy can cowboy up when he has to, but he's always hated that label and the stigma of what life on a ranch *should* be. I'll deny it if you ever tell him I said it, but I think a lot of his reluctance to own up to being a cowboy comes from the fact his mom never stuck around and stood by his dad. Boyd Warner was cowboy through and through. I always got the impression that Cy believed if he could be all the things his dad wasn't, then maybe he would find a woman who wouldn't leave." She shrugged and looked at me over her shoulder. "He tried to be something else but that man was born with the ranch and the west in his blood. He couldn't outrun his heritage and he found a woman who couldn't deal with how deep his roots ran. She did her best to cut them but they're dug all the way in. He ended up with a woman who couldn't love a cowboy, just like his sorry excuse for a mother. The strong survive out here and the tough flourish. They don't come much stronger and tougher than Cy. He needs a woman who appreciates that."

I couldn't stop my hands from curling into fists at my side. The familiar and intimate way she talked about the man I was going to have to walk away from burned like acid and fire.

"Are you trying to tell me you're the woman who appreciates those qualities in him?" I didn't want to sound snippy and jealous, but I did.

She shook her head and lifted the pale fall of her hair so that she could tuck it into the collar of her shirt. "Those are the qualities that make it impossible for the two of us to spend more than a few hours together without one of us wanting to strangle the other. Cy's a rock, or maybe he's more like a goddamn boulder since he's so big. So am I. I'm just as hard as he is and can be just as immovable. All we do is knock against one another until one of us ends up with a headache. Out of bed, that isn't any fun and wastes both our time."

I hated that she had so much history with Cy, that she didn't have to rush through her time with him.

"If he's a rock what does that make me?" I wasn't easy and malleable enough to be the stream that coursed around the jagged rocks that broke through the surface. I wasn't soft enough to wear the rough edges of stone away after a lifetime of gentle pressure.

She stopped so suddenly, that I almost ran into her back. I stumbled and put out a hand to keep myself from falling as she turned to face me. She let her jade colored eyes rove over me, and when they finally met mine there was a spark of humor in the jeweled depths.

"Well, *Sunshine*," her lips twitched when she tossed out the cutesy pet name Cy had stuck me with. "I'd say you're the only thing on earth that can warm stone up. You're the sun and the shine. You're the warmth that chases out the chill all the way to the middle. If rock gets hot enough it can explode."

I cocked my head to the side and exhaled a long breath. I didn't want to like this woman, mostly because she had the ability to pick Cy's dick out of a lineup and I selfishly wanted to be the only one with that ability. But her honesty and her quirky way of looking at things tugged at me and made me feel like I could trust her. She didn't seem to have any artifice or even like she was in the slightest bit concerned with the impression she made. What you saw was what you got with Officer McKenna and I appreciated that she wasn't interested in having a pissing contest over the man we both had spent naked time with.

"Are you speaking from experience?" Cy said she didn't talk about where she went or what brought her back home, so I wondered if her sunny day had clouded over.

Her teasing expression closed off and the glint went out of her emerald gaze. Her mouth, which was the perfect shade of carnation pink without a drop of lipstick, twitched into a frown that changed her lovely face into something harsh and almost ugly. "Even rock can break if you find the weak point and hit it hard enough. It's even easier to chisel off pieces if you know what you're doing."

She turned back around indicating the conversation was done before I could tell her I had had pieces chiseled off by a skilled manipulator myself. A few days ago I didn't want to show any kind of weakness, refused to be vulnerable and open to anyone witnessing the struggle I was having, pulling my tattered shield back in place. This unexpected adventure had shown me that it wasn't a weakness to hurt or to let other people know you were hurting.

The craggy rock formation was suddenly jutting up out of the earth in front of us, appearing far taller and sheerer than I was anticipating. My instinctive fear of heights made me balk and had sweat breaking out under the brim of the hat on my head. My hands were shaking as we rounded the formation. Ten put her hands on the rough stone and hefted herself up a few feet off the ground.

"Just step where I step, and move slow. It's only fifteen feet or so to the top, but that's far enough off the ground to hurt if you slip and fall back down."

I rotated my stiff shoulder and sent up a silent prayer to whatever god kept an eye on the working men and women of this untamed land and started to follow the blonde up the rocks. She made it look like a piece of cake, even though she had a rifle strapped to her back and was still wearing her knapsack loaded down with supplies.

It wasn't easy.

This was no leisurely afternoon rock climbing trip. There were no harnesses, no helmets and gloves. There was no Cy at the bottom encouraging me and telling me that he had me and wouldn't let anything bad happen to me. The rocks cut into my palms and scraped across my fingertips. I ripped most of my fingernails off, to the point that they were bleeding, and my injured shoulder protested loudly every time I had to swing that arm over my head and dangle by the very tips of my fingers, as I scrambled to find a foothold. My heart was in my throat the entire time and I don't think I took a single breath the entire twenty minutes it took me to inch my way up to the top of the outcropping. When I got to the crest, Ten immediately yanked me down to my stomach which rubbed my knees against the rock surface and ripped holes in my jeans. I was wheezing like an asthmatic which had Ten slapping a hand over my mouth as she jerked her head to the side.

"They built their camp a few hundred yards north of where the clearing is. They kept it in the trees so you can't see the tents from overhead. They must know we use aerial imaging for search and rescue missions and to scout hotspots in fire season. There's no way anyone would see the camp from the air." She breathed the words in my ear so quietly I had to strain to hear them. She asked if I was good and only let go of my mouth when I nodded.

She rolled to her stomach so that we were stretched out side by side and put the radio to her lips.

"We have a visual on the camp. It's approximately two hundred yards north of the clearing, back up in the trees. I can see at least four big military tents and they have a whole bunch of all-terrain vehicles parked around the camp. I don't see anyone and can't tell what tent they might have our people in, but this is no small operation."

I squinted in the direction she was looking and couldn't hold back a gasp as I saw not only the mini tent city hidden away from prying eyes, but also a familiar looking horse tied up near one of the tents. Now, there was no doubt that these people had Emrys and Sutton.

"That horse is the one Em was riding when we split up." I tried to keep my voice quiet but I was shaking so hard it came out choppy and louder than I intended.

Ten gave me a look and then spoke back into the radio. "We have confirmation that the horse the woman who was with Sutton Warner was riding is tied up at the compound. Tell Cy to check that tent where the horses are first when he gets to the camp."

"Roger, ranger." Webb's voice crackled back at us, tense and tight. "Give us fifteen and then set the flares off. We need as many of them as possible out of the tents if we want any chance of getting our people out."

Her face was set in hard line of concentration. "We'll do what we can from up here."

The radio came to life once more and there was no missing the taunting humor in Webb's tone, even through the static that popped and crackled over the top of it. "Just make sure you're aiming at the bad guys and not at me when I go in and fuck shit up."

She swore under her breath and put the radio aside so she could dig the flare gun out of her backpack. She handed it to me and asked, "Was he like this the entire trip?"

I gave an awkward half shrug and tried to find a comfortable spot on the rock to fire the flares from.

"Not really. Neither he nor Grady said much because they were lying about why they were on the trail. Webb thinks the guys in charge of the growing operation might have something to do with his older brother's disappearance. He's been a little off since they ambushed us and put a bullet through him. He's not the kind of guy I would want coming after me with revenge on his mind." And it had little to do with the fact the young man had spent time in jail. There was something about him, something a little unhinged and reckless, that let me know he was the kind of man who didn't give a single thought to consequences or risks.

"He thinks that one of the bodies we pulled out of the river might belong to his brother?" She sounded stunned and a little bit sad when she asked the question.

"He does. We didn't know about the body until right before the ambush. He convinced Grady to come on the trail ride thinking his brother was missing. You can't really blame him for being slightly unpredictable. Not to mention all the blood he's lost over the last twenty-four hours."

She made a quiet noise in her throat, situated her rifle in front of her, and started fiddling with the scope on the top of it. She seemed incredibly capable and steady while I, by contrast, felt like I was going to throw up or pass out as the minutes ticked by. I'd never been so stressed out or afraid in my life. It made all the bad things I was always worried about happening seem trivial and stupid. I understood what a real catastrophe was now, and that there was no way to prevent chaos when outside factors were involved. The only way to live a life that was controlled and secure was to have no life at all . . . exactly what I had been doing before Cyrus Warner and his wild, wild west blew it to smithereens.

Ten's elbow tapped mine and I heard her exhale long and low. "I have a bead on Cy and the older guy. They're on the back side of the forest about twenty feet from the tent where the horse is. I hope the horse doesn't catch a whiff of Cy and throw up a racket. That's a sure fire way to give their location away." She lowered her index finger to the trigger of the long rifle and breathed out again. "I'm going to count to three. On three, light the sky up."

I nodded silently and settled in next to her. I didn't need to aim or brace for recoil. I simply had to pull the trigger several times while the bright discharge shot into the air and exploded in a fall of fire.

We both stopped breathing as she whispered, "One."

I closed my eyes and said every prayer I could remember and a couple I made up as she uttered, "Two."

I peeled my lids back open and focused on the camp where my best friend was suffering through nightmares I could only imagine, as every single muscle in my body tensed waiting for the final number. My nerves felt like they were electric and charged with the tension coursing through me.

Ten's lips twitched, barely, as the number three floated toward me on a puff of air.

I pulled the trigger and set the sky in front of us on fire. Since it was daytime, the explosion and pop as the chemicals ignited weren't as brilliant as they could have been, but the noise echoed and bounced loudly off of every surface of the mountain. It rolled through the valley as a boom shook loud and clear through the trees. It was loud enough it felt like the ground should be moving and vibrating with the noise.

It didn't take long for the racket to have the desired effect. Soon bodies were pouring out of the tents. Men of all shapes and sizes and in various states of dress rushed into the clearing, eyes pointed upward as they tried to locate the unseen threat. All of them were armed and they all looked furious at being rattled away from their typical activities.

"Shit. There's a lot of them." The words slipped out unchecked, but I could tell by the way Ten's shoulder's tensed that she agreed with my assessment.

"Cy's at the back of the tent. It looks like he's trying to cut his way through the fabric."

I watched as the men at the camp started wandering around with their eyes on the sky, waiting for another blast. They were restless and anxious so it was no surprise when several random shots were fired at nothing, and nowhere near where we were hidden.

"Fuck. It's not the right tent. They're moving on to the next one. I hope no one sees them."

I couldn't imagine how anyone could miss someone as big as Cy was, but I kept my fingers crossed that he was moving like smoke and ash through the camp.

"Oh no. They're splitting up to search the area." Ten snatched up the radio and called to Webb. "I don't know what your plan for distraction is, city boy, but it needs to happen right now. The bad guys are on the move."

"Copy that. I'm about to make a whole lot of noise."

"Hurry up. Cy and your agent went into the second tent and haven't come out yet." Her words were rushed and I hated that all I could do was lie there next to her, unable to help the guys on the ground.

Ten went rigid next to me and lifted her head up and then put her eye back to the scope. "Two of the guys are headed to the tent that Cy went into. I'm going to have to start firing if he doesn't get them to stop in the next . . ."

She couldn't finish the rest of the sentence because the world below us combusted. The dirt bikes and four wheelers parked by the tents exploded in a burst of flying metal and soaring shrapnel. The detonation made the noise and the blast from the flares look like a puny sparkler next to a Fourth of July fireworks show. Webb had done exactly what he promised and made a distraction big enough that there was no way the men at the camp could ignore it. Unfortunately, he'd had to get really close to do it, a fact that had Ten cussing up a storm and suddenly popping off shot after shot as the armed men rushed toward the part of the forest where Webb was running.

Hell broke loose and bullets were flying. I held a hand to my mouth as I watched it all unfold like something out of a pulse-pounding action movie in front of me. The sound of the rifle next to my ear was muffling all the sound from down below, but it couldn't stop the screaming coming from my soul and the erratic thud of my heart as I caught sight of Cy scampering through the trees with a limp, dark-haired form over his shoulder. He had Em but there was no sign of Grady or Sutton. That couldn't mean anything good.

"Fuck! Get your head down!" Her hand shot out and slapped the top of my head down and shoved my face into the rock, as tiny bits and pieces suddenly broke off and flew up in our direction. "Get back. Scoot down the other side of the rock. They know I'm shooting from up here and they're firing back."

"What about Sutton? Do you see Sutton or Grady?" I scooted on my ass like she told me, but panicked as soon as I could no longer see what was happening down below.

"Too busy trying to keep that damn city slicker from getting full of holes. They've got eyes on him and are moving in his direction. He's purposely pulling them away from the camp but it puts a target right on his back."

"Not good."

She snorted. "That's an understatement, California."

I was turning back around so I could peek my head over the rise of the rocks to what was going on, but I never got the chance. Before I could get situated, the sound of a man clearing his throat stopped me dead still. Nervously, I looked down and came face to face with a nasty black pistol aimed at my nose and a man dressed head to toe in black, complete with streaks of grease on his face, with his finger on the trigger

This definitely wasn't part of the plan.

CHAPTER 17

No Surrender, No Retreat

I OPENED MY MOUTH TO scream but I stopped myself from letting out the panicked wail that was working up my throat. I was startled and I was scared but I knew if I made a sound, Ten would come back over the ledge of the rocks with her rifle and this guy might shoot first and ask questions later. He smiled at me, which was terrifying considering the war paint obscuring his features. All I could see was a slash of white against the black, making him look like some kind of disturbing Halloween mask come to life.

He lifted the gun up to his lips and made a shushing noise and indicated he wanted me to slide the rest of the way down the rocks, as quietly as possible. Instinctively, I shook my head in the negative, which made him scowl and point the gun at me again. He used a finger to motion toward himself and I sucked in breath knowing that my options were limited. I could go back up the other side of the rocks but I didn't want to distract Ten from keeping the entire marauding camp away from Webb while Cyrus got Em and Sutton out. Besides, the other side of the rocks was a straight drop off into nothing, so if the man followed me up and over, there would be nowhere for Ten and me to escape.

With the memory of Emrys's blood-chilling screams ringing

in my head, I slowly started to inch my way back down the rock face trying to make as little noise as possible. The man below kept the barrel of his gun pointed right at me, which made the descent even more nerve wracking than it already would have been. He watched me, unwaveringly, and that odd grin on his face never faded.

When I was almost halfway down, palms stinging and raw, the back of my jeans shredded from scooting my backside on the rocks, and the insides of my cheeks torn and bloody from chewing on the inside of my cheeks to keep quiet, I made a decision.

I decided that I had to do something . . . anything. I couldn't hand myself over to this unknown threat after everything everyone else had done to get Em and Sutton out of danger. I was not going to be the reason this mission went twenty steps backwards and I didn't care what that meant for me, as long as everyone else made it home safe. I wasn't anywhere close to being a hero, but today, for the people I cared about, I could pretend to be.

Since I was sitting on the rocks and using my hands and feet to slowly inch my way down the rough surface, I was facing outward and happened to be in the perfect position to launch myself forward like a wrestler off the ropes. It meant letting go of my iron grip on every handhold I could find and it meant forgetting how deathly afraid of heights I was. It meant putting the woman who ran from everything that scared her to bed once and for all. It meant fully embracing the woman who could and would put everything on the line, even if it meant losing it all.

There was no guarantee that the man with the gun wouldn't pull the trigger as soon as I pushed myself off the rocks. He could have a bullet in my chest before I made contact with him, but then at least Ten would have some warning as to what was going on down below. I wanted to take the man by surprise. I wanted to catch him unaware and maybe knock him off his stance enough that he would lose his grip on the gun. I wanted to level the playing field just a little bit and honestly, I wanted to put a knee in his balls as hard as I could for scaring me and for pointing a gun right at my face. I was over tip-toeing around the things I found threatening and intimidating.

I gave myself a second to breathe. I sucked in the mountain air, tuned out the sound of bullets ricocheting off of rocks and trees, and told myself that everything about this trip had been about making moments that mattered. This moment was make it or break it. It would either help save the day or end in a tragedy of epic proportions. There was no more playing it safe and keeping harm at arm's length. It was time to jump feet first into the fire and let all the old fear and hesitance burn away. It was time to be the phoenix that rose from the ashes as something fierce and ferocious. It was time to fly because I was done sinking.

Swallowing back the scream that was lodged in my throat, I pushed off the rocks with both my hands and feet. I was immediately airborne with the ground and the startled man in the greasepaint rushing toward me. I heard him call out, "What in the hell! Crazy woman!" but it was too late. I was flying, falling, careening right for him and there wasn't enough time for him to get out of the way or pull the trigger.

"Son of a bitch!" He barked out the words loud enough that I knew there was no way Ten wouldn't hear them. But much to my surprise, as I hurdled toward him, he let the gun fall to the ground at his side and reached his hands up. He acted like he was going to catch me and stop my wild freefall.

I fell fast, so when I hit him it was like running into a brick wall that was reinforced with concrete. The impact was enough to send the hat on my head flying. He was a big man, not as big or as tall as Cy, but wider and stockier. He took the brunt of my quickly moving weight without losing his footing. He wrapped his arms around me as I swung wildly the moment I got my bearings. My tattered and torn nails dug into every sensitive spot I could reach and I tried to kick at him but the effort was wasted as the toes of my boots hit hard leather. The guy was dressed in some kind of tactical gear that might as well have been a suit of armor.

He shifted his hold on me and some of my adrenaline drained away when I realized that fighting against him was futile. One of his beefy arms locked around mine and he used his free hand to wind my thick hair up in his fist, so that I couldn't head-butt him or bite at him. He didn't have to struggle very hard to corral me into a submissive position.

"Listen, fireball, this could be fun if we were both naked and redheads were my jam but we aren't and that Irish in you doesn't do it for me. Calm down and breathe for a hot second and I'll let you go."

I scowled up at him and tried to work my leg into position so I could get my knee between his legs. He blocked the move and growled at me to knock my shit off. "I don't want to hurt you, but I will. I don't know who you are or what kind of fresh hell you brought with you up this mountain, but there's a government-sanctioned raid about to pop off on that compound in less than three minutes and your happy ass has wandered into the perimeter. You need to get gone before the good guys mistake you for a bad guy."

I went limp in his hold, hanging there like a ragdoll. He had to adjust his grip on me to keep me from hitting the ground.

He grunted and gave me a little shake as he asked, "Hey, you okay?" I shook my head slowly and started to push his hands away.

"What do you mean there's a raid happening?" I knew what the words meant but they sounded like an alien language.

"I'd pull out my badge and show it to you, but those fuckers at the camp caught me snooping around a week or so ago. They worked me over, put a bullet in my chest, and dumped me in the river. Idiots didn't check for Kevlar. I was pretty messed up and really fucking lost. It took me a week to find my way to a phone, and a few more days to convince my boss to send a crew in. Usually, these clandestine grow operations aren't a big deal, but this one," he shook his head and rubbed at his camo painted chin. "This one has ties to the big boys in Mexico and they aren't scared to add to an already out of control body count. You need to get out of here before the flashbangs start to go off and chaos takes over the mountain."

Back on my feet, I stumbled away from him and bent over so I could put my hands on my knees. "You wouldn't happen to be Wyatt Bryant, would you?" It seemed like such a long shot but the way he talked, and the fact that his concern seemed to be for me and not the fact I'd tried to take him out with a WWE move, made me wonder.

I saw his eyes widen and his jaw clench at my question. "Why would you ask me that?"

I let my head fall forward and struggled to get my composure back together. "Because I've spent the last week with your brother and your partner searching these woods for any sign of you. They know bodies have been turning up in the river and Webb is convinced one of them is yours. Grady had to quit his job in order to come looking for you. They were worried sick when you didn't check in. Chaos has already ripped this mountain apart and you, sir, are right at the goddamn center of it."

Webb's brother stared at me for a long silent second and then threw his hands up above his head as he started pacing back and forth in front of me. "Fucking Webb. That goddamn kid will never learn. Impulsive as shit, and unstoppable when he gets his mind set to something. I can't believe Grady played into his bullshit."

"His bullshit just saved my best friend's life. Those guys at the camp took her and a local rancher as hostage." I lifted my eyebrows. "Your partner and the rancher's brother went into the camp to get them back. I bet you know what would have happened to all them if they were there when your raid started. You brother is reckless but sometimes someone has to be."

He swore again and continued to pace. "I'm the one who dropped the bodies in the water. The guy in charge of the camp and the grow field sent a couple lackeys to ditch me in the river. I played dead until we got to the shore and then I tried to turn them. Promised them immunity and green cards if they would lead me to the people who set up the operation. It's too well funded to be some fly-by-night dealers. They were either too scared or too loyal to talk. They wouldn't give it up and, unfortunately, they tried to finish the job they started at the camp. It was me or them and I'm always going to pick me."

I snorted. "So does your brother and apparently, your partner . . . they pick you, too."

He opened his mouth to retort but ended up swearing and jumping back a foot as the ground right in front of his feet exploded upward. The ricochet sent dirt kicking up in my direction so I took a step back toward the rocks. Webb's brother dove for the pistol he dropped to catch me and swore long and loud as a bullet dug into the ground inches away from his fingertips.

I looked up at the rock surface and saw Ten standing at the top, her weapon trained on the man who was now lying at my feet. She looked like an ancient warrior queen, ready to defend her territory and punish the intruder.

I called up to her, "He's with the DEA, so you probably want to stop shooting at him." She made a face at me and I shrugged.

"He's Webb's brother. Apparently, he just has a really shitty sense of direction and got himself lost out here, but now the troops are on their way in. I hope they're in time to save your brother, Special Agent Bryant, because he gave up pretty much everything to try and save you, even though he didn't know if you were still breathing or not."

"Webb is clear. He had a few guys hot on his tail when he darted back into the trees, but most of the bad guys turned around to return fire when I started shooting. This spot is compromised so we should move." Wyatt's painted eyebrows lifted at her bossy tone and that distorted smile flashed through the face paint covering his features. Ten looked between the two of us with a sharp frown. "There still was no sign of the older guy and Sutton. That's bad news because there is no way Cy is going to leave his brother in the middle of that shit show. We need to go find your friend and make sure our hero doesn't end up on the wrong end of a DEA strike."

Webb's brother let out a low whistle and moved to collect his weapon. "Now, a ballsy blonde with mile long legs? *That* I can totally get on board with." He gave Ten a wink which made her scowl in response.

I rolled my eyes. "That apparently runs in the family." I huffed out a breath and gave him a hard look. "Don't you want to let your fellow agents know that your partner is at the camp, and that he's armed?"

Ten gave me a look that was bright with agreement but the shine went diamond hard when Wyatt shook his head. "This is a quick strike and there isn't a way to alert them to the fact Grady is on the ground. They'll move in and sweep him up with the rest of the grow crew. The team is going in silent and fast, no radios, so no way to signal a change in plans. We need to move if we want to intercept them before they mistake your friends for enemies and we have deadly friendly fire on our hands." His grin turned rueful and he looked up at the sky like the vast blue held answers to questions he had been asking for a lifetime. "I will never understand how my idiot brother manages to make every bad situation he stumbles into even worse. It's like his superpower."

Ten let out a huff and jerked her head to the side, indicating she wanted us to follow her around the rock formation and back toward the trees. She said we could circle around to the opposite side of the camp where Cy had disappeared with Emrys, but her tone was tense and her words came out tight and sharp. She turned her back on the intimidating special agent but not before she told him, "That idiot just took on a hail of bullets and an entire cartel camp because he was determined to find you, dead or alive. I think brotherly love is probably his superpower and his kryptonite."

Thoroughly chastised, Wyatt snapped his mouth shut, straightened his broad shoulders, and started after her. They were moving fast in front of me, but the serious weight of what was going on around us and the real threat looming ahead of us didn't mean that Wyatt bothered to hide the fact that his gaze was trained on Ten's long legged gait rather than the surrounding area. I might have found it funny, if I wasn't occupied looking for Emrys and praying that Cy hadn't dropped her somewhere he deemed safe so he could run back to the drug compound that was about to be under government siege. Ten was right. There was no way in hell Cy would leave Sutton in that camp, no matter the condition he was in. I didn't want to think about the reasons the men might have had for pulling Emrys out so quickly, while leaving the middle Warner brother behind. It didn't sit right and it had me in knots made up of all kinds of anxiety and concern for Cy.

We hit the tree line, and once again I was dodging branches and twigs that pulled at my clothes and stuck in my hair. It didn't take long to fall behind the two in front of me, both of whom were practically jogging over the uneven terrain. They were trained for this and I was not. Their focus on moving through the woods as quickly and as silently as possible prevented both of them from noticing a barely discernable X carved into the bark of one of the millions of pine trees we were racing past. I stumbled to a stop and put my hand on the rough bark right below the mark so I could catch my breath. Desperately, I looked around for some other indication that Cy or Emrys had been in this part of the woods, but I couldn't see anything obvious.

Ten and Wyatt were quickly getting out of eyesight as they kept moving through the trees, unaware I had halted behind them. I was sucking in lungfuls of air, preparing to sprint to catch back up to them when I heard a soft sound from somewhere above my head. I told myself not to get my hopes up, that it was probably just a squirrel or a pinecone falling but when I looked up I was startled to see a square, metal platform secured high into the tree. It was easily a hundred feet up in the air and there was no mistaking the sound of a woman moaning.

I took a few steps backwards and tilted my head so that I could whisper-yell, "Em, is that you?" I knew I was going to be in trouble if anyone else poked their head over the edge of the tree stand, but deep down in my gut, I had a feeling this was the safest place Cy could find to stash my best friend. When her dark head poked over the edge I had to school my expression into one of relief rather than horror.

Her face was covered in blood and there was a makeshift bandage covering half of it that was stained a furious scarlet. Her black hair was a tangled mess around her head and I could see, even with the distance between us, that her normally golden complexion was shockingly pale and ashen. She didn't look very good, in fact, she couldn't look worse. As grateful as I was that Cy got her out of the camp alive, I was furious that he had left her alone and unreachable in her current condition.

"Em, I'm gonna figure out how to get up there so I can help you, okay?" I circled the tree and couldn't for the life of me figure out how Cy had managed to make his way all the way up there while carrying Em in his arms. There were no steps nailed into the tree, there wasn't a rope or any kind of staggered branches that I could use to shimmy my way up the trunk and Em wasn't helping. She moaned again, and I watched her upper body collapse onto the tiny platform she was perched on.

"Emrys!" I didn't bother to whisper this time when I called her name. Frankly, I didn't care if an army of drug running bad guys came bursting out of the woods with weapons drawn. I was frantic over my friend and determined to get to her. "Em, you have to tell me how to get up there. How did Cy get you up the tree?"

There was no response and I panicked because I thought she might have passed out. I couldn't tell the extent of her injuries but she had been whimpering softly and there was enough blood on her face for me to be justifiably alarmed. I was contemplating if I could hug the tree with my arms and legs and work my way up to the stand like a monkey when there was the rattle of something that sounded like chains overhead.

"Move, Leo." Her voice was raspy and her words sounded broken. I jumped back as a metal ladder with narrow rungs came sailing down from her roost. The thing had barely clattered to the ground in front of my feet before I started to shimmy my way up to the top. Em disappeared from view again on a low groan, and my worry for her made my palms sweat and my knees weak. I had to take a couple deep breaths to get my adrenaline under control so that my quaking body didn't slip off the rungs.

"I'm coming, Em. Just hold on a little bit longer." There was no response and the dead silence made my hand slip. I had visions of falling backwards through the air and cracking my head open on the ground below, but even the gruesome image couldn't halt my hurried progress to the edge of the platform that seemed even higher up in the air from this vantage point. I gulped . . . hard, and wiggled my way on my belly onto the flat surface where Em was lying face down and curled tightly into the fetal position. From this vantage point, I could barely make out the back of Ten's blonde head as it bobbed and dipped deeper into the forest. Wyatt and his scary war paint and tactical gear was much harder to make out as he moved like a big shadow behind her. They hadn't stopped or bothered to wait for me. Both moved with their mission in mind.

As delicately as I could, I pushed Emrys's hair away from her face and sucked in a breath so hard it made my lungs hurt. She was bleeding everywhere, not just from the bandage that was hastily wrapped around the side of her face. Trickles of crimson were leaking out of each nostril and out of her ear. She had ugly, dark bruises all around the eye that was uncovered, and both her top and bottom lip were split open and slowly oozing blood.

"Oh, honey. What did they do to you?" I cradled her head in my lap and futilely tried to clean her face up with the bottom of my shirt.

I knew the guys running the camp were bad news, but looking at Em's face and the way her body lay limp and lifeless across the platform, real terror for what they could and would do to Cy and the rest of the people riding to the rescue choked me up and held me in a stranglehold. It was hard to breathe and even harder to think straight, but I did my best to keep it all pulled together because Emrys needed me and I refused to falter.

Her swollen and distorted eye flicked open and her puffy, torn lips twitched. The tiny movements obviously hurt her a great deal because her entire body spasmed as she struggled to focus on my hovering face. Crystalline liquid started to drip from her lashes mixing with the dried blood on her cheek that I couldn't wipe away.

"They hurt me, Leo, and they shot Sutton." She started to shake uncontrollably and I freaked out thinking she was going into shock. She weakly pushed at my clutching hands because I was holding her tightly enough that it hurt her already damaged skin. She started to cry harder and I couldn't stop my own tears from racing after hers. "The two guys who were supposed to be watching us . . ." she trailed off and started sobbing into my lap. "They . . . they held me down and did things to me." My hands curled into fists against her arms and I shook just as violently as she did. "They were going to rape me, Leo. They had my clothes off and they had their hands all over me." Her tragic face twisted into something even uglier and more damaged. "Sutton stopped them. He went nuts. His hands were tied together but he still stopped them." She hiccupped softly and let her eye drift closed as she burrowed into me. "The guy in charge came in to see what the commotion was all about. He was pissed when he saw my face, and even more pissed when he saw that Sutton had hurt his men." Em curled back into a ball and flinched away from me when I reached out to put a hand on her shoulder.

"He shot Sutton, Leo. Right in the chest. There was so much blood." Her voice cracked and she made a noise that sounded like heartbreak. "He fell to the ground and wouldn't open his eyes. He has a little girl, Leo." She was shaking so hard I could hear her teeth hit each other. "They left him on the ground bleeding. I told Cy to take him first, but he didn't listen."

I shook my head and gently ran my hand over the top of

her head. "Real cowboys save the girl first, Em. No way was Cy going to leave you there looking like this. He went back for his brother, didn't he?"

She nodded jerkily. "He helped me wrap my face up." She pointed a wobbly finger at the blood-soaked bandage. "One of the guys yelled at me that I wouldn't think I was too good for him when he was done with me. I didn't stop fighting him as he was trying to take my pants off. He cut my cheek open with a dirty pocket knife. It hurts and it won't stop bleeding."

I shuddered and pulled her closer to me even though she didn't want to come. "Em, I'm so sorry, but I need you to stay strong and keep fighting. We'll get you help, as soon as I figure out how to get both of us off this stand, without breaking our necks." I didn't have Cy's brute strength to muscle her up and down that precarious, hanging ladder.

"There is no help for what has happened the last few days." She sounded so dejected and defeated that it made my heart sink. She was ready to give up and I needed her to fight. "There is no making this better."

"That's not true and you know it. You never let me give in and wallow, even when that's what I was convinced I wanted. I'm not going to let you surrender either." I leaned over the ledge of the hunting stand and balked at how far away the ground seemed to be. I needed a brilliant idea, and I needed it yesterday.

Just when I thought the only way I was going to get my friend off the ledge was to miraculously grow wings and fly her down, I heard a loud whistle that shrieked through the quiet of the woods surrounding us.

Cautiously, I peeked my head over the edge of the hunting stand and felt my eyes go wide when I saw Webb standing below. He was holding his injured shoulder in one hand, but other than that he looked no the worse for wear. "I circled around and ran into Cy as he was heading back into the camp. He told me where he stashed the girl. I came to help her."

I blinked at him stupidly for a second. I was relieved to see him alive and in one piece. I forgot for a split second that other people I had grown to care a lot about were still in immediate danger and that the DEA was seconds away from laying the hurt down on everyone.

"I saw your brother, Webb. He's alive and he's headed to the camp with Ten." I wanted to smile at him but my mouth wouldn't move upwards. It was locked in a tense frown as I looked between Webb and Emrys. "He said a DEA strike team is on the way to raid the camp. He didn't have any way to tell them that Cy and Grady are on the ground trying to get Sutton out of there." I swallowed hard and shifted my gaze away from Em's fragile form. "Cy's brother was hurt really badly. There is no way he's going to leave him there."

Webb looked at the dangling ladder then back at me with a scowl. He let go of his shoulder and shook out his arm. "A couple of Wyatt's spooks ran across me in the forest when I was leading the shooters away from the camp. They pulled their weapons on me but realized pretty quickly I was running from the bad guys and wasn't one of them. They held me when Ten started returning fire but once the bullets stopped flying, they let me go. I think they just wanted me out of the way. They told me Wyatt had given them the intel on the camp, and that he was the one dropping the bodies in the river. I told them there were civilians in the camp. Fortunately, one of the guys who stopped me worked with Grady in the past, so he knew exactly who I was talking about. We need to figure out a way to get you girls down and back to the camp. The spooks have a copter flying in for extraction." He pointed at his arm. "I think they called it for me but it sounds like your girl and Warner need the evac more than I do."

I blew out a frustrated breath and shifted so that my legs were dangling over the edge of the tree stand. "I don't know how Cy muscled her up here, but I can't figure out a way to get her down. She's pretty banged up and half her face is being held together by nothing more than a makeshift bandage. I'm scared to move her."

He swore and put his hands on his hips looking every bit the forest rogue. I could easily picture him robbing the rich and giving the goods to the poor, while running around with a merry band of misfits.

"I don't think my busted wing is up to hauling both my weight and hers down that ladder, if it even holds up long enough for me to get up there." That was exactly what I was afraid of. We weren't getting down unless Emrys rallied and helped me help her.

I crawled back over to her and reached out to put the backs of my fingers against her uncovered cheek. She cringed at the touch, like my fingers were throwing flames and burned her.

"Em, you've got to get up. I'll help you down the ladder and get you to help, but you've got to move. You can't stay here."

She lifted a hand and let it fall. "Just go without me." She sounded pathetic and forlorn.

"We both know there isn't a chance in hell that I'm doing that. If you stay, I stay. But if you stay and they hold that helicopter when it gets here, you could be delaying Sutton getting medical help." That was a dirty card to play but I was getting desperate and needed something that would break through her despondency.

"There is no help. He's dead, Leo. They put a hole right through the center of him and let him bleed forever. Sutton is dead." She opened her eye and looked right at me. "He died trying to save me."

"Hey, gorgeous!" Webb's deep voice carried up to us and I saw Em's eyebrow twitch in reaction. "When you care about someone, you don't give up on them no matter what. That body in the sheriff's morgue could very well have been my brother . . . but it wasn't. The cowboy put up a fight for you and you need to do the same for him. Let Leo help you down here and let's get this show on the road. I think we've all had enough adventure to last a lifetime."

Her eye welled with tears again and new tracks streaked through the blood on her battered face. "I can't."

I bit back my impatience and tried to be as gentle with her as I could. "Em, you have to. I'm going to make you. I'm going to save you, just like you always save me."

It took longer than I wanted it to, but eventually, she started to move. Each movement was slow and deliberate, the pain etched on her features clear and haunting, as she let me guide her and maneuver her toward the ladder. I went down first. No thought or fear allowed as she crawled at a snail's pace above me rung by rung. Her grip was weak and there were a couple of times I thought she was simply going to let go and take us both to the ground, but step by agonizing step, we made our way to the ground.

Once her feet touched the ground, she collapsed in a heap that Webb wildly lunged for. He kept her from hitting her knees and cuddled her to his chest like she was an injured animal. My heart broke for my best friend and I wanted to storm into the grow camp and lay waste to everything and everyone who had made her hurt like this.

I was getting ready to ask Webb how we were going to get her to the camp and to rescue when the familiar whir of an ATV broke through the trees and had him shifting Em to one side, so he could palm his weapon. He ordered me to get behind him, but I wasn't the girl who hid behind anyone anymore. I stood right next to him and kept an eye on Emrys as the four-wheeler wove its way through the dense forest in front of us.

There were no words to describe how badly I wanted the rider to be Cy.

It wasn't. It was Wyatt in the scary black grease paint looking undeniably similar to the man I was standing next to. "Good thing you didn't blow all the machines, brother. This one came in handy when the big guy calmed down enough to tell us where he stashed the girl. He wasn't a happy camper when our guys pulled him away from his brother." That wild grin died on his face when he caught sight of Emrys's wilted body in his younger brother's arms and he switched to all business mode really quick. "Give me the girl. The chopper is about twenty minutes out and they won't wait once they touch down. The guy with the bullet in his chest doesn't have a single second to spare. They already have an emergency medical team waiting for him in Billings."

He rubbed a hand over his face smearing the messy paint, making him look even fiercer. "The raid went off without a hitch. They rounded up most of the hired guns and a couple of them seemed like they were willing to talk. They cleared the tents and Grady actually had the guy they think is in charge of this particular spot pinned down. A sweep team will spend the next couple of days trying to locate any of the men who escaped the round up and they'll stay behind to make sure the crop is destroyed. Other than the civilians injured, this was a pretty textbook takedown."

Emrys perked up at that news that Sutton was still hanging in there and allowed herself to be transferred over to the care of the special agent. She kept muttering "I can't believe he's alive" over and over again like a mantra. Wyatt told her that he wouldn't be if they didn't get a move on it. I didn't want to let her out of my sight, but I knew they were racing against the clock. Watching her ride away with the older Bryant brother was probably the hardest thing I had ever done in my life.

I looked at Webb and he looked down at me. We sighed in unison and I leaned into his side when he threw his arm around my shoulders. The camaraderie and bonds built in the middle of bloodshed and bullets were something else. I didn't trust anyone . . . ever . . . but given everything that we had survived the last few days, I would give this man, this lying ex-con, the benefit of every doubt from here to the end of eternity.

The experiences I had under my belt now forced me to be the woman I was meant to be all along, and I knew there was no going back. Not that I wanted to. But, I was also scared to move forward because straight ahead was a life without Cy and with a broken best friend.

I knew that I was going to have to figure out a way to fix both of those things if I wanted any kind of shot at finally finding some kind of happy.

CHAPTER 18

Not On My Watch

I T TOOK ALMOST TWO FULL days to get back to collect all the horses and make our way back to the ranch. Once there, we barely had time to get our bearings and get cleaned up before Ten had us on a plane to Billings. The pretty ranger pushed both Webb and myself hard, barely stopping to keep Webb's injured arm wrapped up and clean so it didn't get infected. It was obvious she was as worried about the middle Warner brother, even though she didn't say anything. I also knew she was worried what losing someone else he loved would do to Cyrus.

It was a silent flight into Montana as we all finally had a few restful moments to process everything we'd seen and been through over the last week. It was an adrenaline crash. I'd never experienced anything like it before and I wasn't aware that silent tears were trekking down my cheeks as I stared out at the vast and wild landscape racing by underneath the wings of the tiny plane. I flinched when Webb reached across the minute space between us and swiped his thumb down the tracks of moisture.

"None of that. Everyone made it out alive and that's the best possible outcome. No matter how deep the wound is, it can heal." He settled back in his seat, oblivious to the wide eyed and curious look Ten was throwing his way.

I sniffled a little bit and used the back of my hand to wipe away the rest of the evidence that revealed that my chaotic emotions were no longer being held at bay. "Some wounds are fatal, Webb. You didn't see the look on Em's face when she said those men hurt her. She very well could bleed from those kind of wounds forever and I don't know what I can do to stop it."

He lifted an eyebrow at me, giving me a steady look full of the kind of knowledge that let me knew he firmly believed in what he was saying to me. "You apply pressure, Leo, and you don't let up. You stem the flow for her until the bleeding stops. That's all you can do."

I didn't have a reply to that, since I was already planning on permanently attaching myself to Emrys until the light was back in her eyes. She was vacant and absent, not that I could blame her for retreating. I wouldn't let her disappear. She was my anchor and I had no problem realizing it was time for me to hoist her up and pull her from the depths.

When the plane landed, there was a car waiting to take us to the hospital in Billings. The vehicle moved smoothly through the sleepy streets that couldn't even slightly compare to the hustle of San Francisco. It still held more humans than I had seen in days. The noise and commotion, even as mellow as it was, seemed overwhelming and I wondered how quickly it was going to take my senses to adjust to civilization once again. With a shiver I realized I longed for the quiet. I wanted to be able to hear what was being said and know that the words meant something. I didn't want to go back to a place where life was so full of other things that it was easy to miss the ones that were important. I didn't want the moments that mattered to get lost in the noise.

When we hit the hospital, we were immediately directed to the intensive care unit. I was surprised to find the tiny waiting room full of familiar faces. Lane was propped up on one wall, straw cowboy hat pulled low over his forehead. Brynn's unmistakable red hair fell over his arm as he held the tall woman to his chest. Her shoulders were shaking which indicated she was probably crying, but the shudder was light and barely noticeable. Wyatt was sitting in a chair on one side of Cyrus, Grady sat on the other. Both men were dressed in expensive looking suits sporting sharp creases and there wasn't a sign of either having been adrift in the woods for weeks. They had paperwork in their hands, badges and guns clipped to their belts, and both appeared to be asking Cy questions. Minus the camo face paint, Wyatt's resemblance to his younger brother was startling. They could pass for twins, save for the hardness in Webb, a resilience that had propelled him through the wilderness, wounded and weak with no hesitation. Wyatt grinned up at us as Cy's eyes locked on our little party and flared to life with something that was more powerful and more important than anything anyone had ever looked at me with before.

Irritation.

Relief.

Pride.

Passion.

Possession.

Regret.

It was all there, flashing between the blinks of his inky lashes as he got to his feet and took the few steps required for him to reach me. Our entire short, tragic, and triumphant relationship shone out of his eyes as he pulled me into his arms in a hug that was tight enough to crack ribs. I put my arms around his waist and squeezed him back just as hard. I dropped my head to the center of his chest, listening to the steady beat of his heart, deciding it was the best sound I ever heard. I breathed what felt like the first easy breath I had had in decades. He was just as solid, just as sure and indomitable as he seemed the first minute I laid eyes on him, but now there were cracks in the mortar that held him together and I could feel his emotions leaking out of them. I also felt his lips touch the top of my head in a kiss that was meant to settle us both. It turned my insides liquid and it made my eyes well up again.

I had to clear my throat twice before I was able to ask him which room Emrys was in. She was the only person missing from this somber gathering.

Cy also pushed out a breath and needed to take a minute before he could make his gruff and scratchy sounding voice work. Finally looking at him with clear eyes, I could see that it looked like he hadn't slept in a week. He had dark circles under his eyes and the lines around his eyes and mouth seemed to have dug in even deeper. I knew it was probably just a trick of the bad hospital lighting, but I also swore the silver specks in his hair had doubled and crawled up well into his hairline. He looked worn and worried, older than he had a week ago.

"Em's in the room with Sutton. It's bad, Leo, really bad. Right now machines are basically keeping him alive and the room is sterile. He hasn't opened his eyes or responded to anything since they loaded him onto the helicopter. His blood pressure has crashed twice and the surgeon has opted to put off a second surgery to pull pieces of the bullet out of him because he's so unstable. They're really worried about infection. Only one of us at a time can be in there with him and we can't step into the room until we gown and glove up." He shook his dark head and pulled me close so that he could rest his chin on the top of my head. His sigh sent my hair dancing and pressed his chest into mine. "Em is in a bad way, too. Out of it, not making much sense when the DEA talked to her. She was hysterical and they had to medicate her to calm her down." I felt his fingers tense on my waist as I swallowed the lump in my throat his words raised up. "She went missing in the middle of the night last night. The nurses went in to check on her and couldn't find her. They were getting ready to call the cops and start a floor-by-floor search when someone was smart enough to pop into Sutton's room. Your girl was curled up in the chair next to his bed, talking to him. Who knows if he can hear her, but she just kept talking. Being around my brother got her shit straight."

If that wasn't heartbreaking, I didn't know anything that was. "She was very worried about him. She was convinced he died for her. She's not going to let go of him without a fight."

He snorted. "Clearly. We've all been rotating turns in his room when the nurses pull her out. Sutton's ex even managed to get it together enough to bring Daye up so she could see him. That was fucking hard. How are you supposed to explain to a five-year-old that daddy would say hello and tell you that he loved you if he could, but he can't right now? It was so goddamn heartbreaking. He's the only solid parent that little girl has. She doesn't stand a chance if he doesn't pull through."

"He'll pull through." I whispered the words into his chest.

"You think so?"

I nodded and felt the crown of my head bop into his chin. "I know so." God, I hoped so. If Sutton was the only thing keeping Emrys tied together right now, then I needed him to pull through. He was a good man, and good men deserved more than that kind of ending. "And you won't let anything happen to that little girl. She's your family and you protect your family, Cy. You won't let her go, regardless of what happens with Sutton." I knew that with certainty; that went all the way to my marrow.

He hugged me again, and finally pulled away but didn't let me go all of the way. His long fingers curled around mine and he tucked me tightly into his side like he'd hated every minute it took me to get out of the woods and back to his side. I had never been the type of woman who was strong enough for someone else to lean on. My foundation was weak and the ground I stood on was full of hidden crevices that went deep and dark into my soul. For this man, I could be a pillar. He taught me how. He showed me I could stand and not fall, even with someone else's considerable weight leaning into me for support. I could be just as unmovable and as strong as he was. I could hold him up effortlessly, because I knew he would do the same for me and I knew his need for someone to prop him up was temporary. He bore the weight of responsibility for everyone and everything all the time, with his little brother on the brink of dying, there was no way his ballasts weren't taking on more than they could handle.

"The DEA and the FBI have been all over us the last few days. Endless questions, endless paperwork. I can't get my head around how they make this all seem like it's nothing more than business as usual." He sounded irritated at the fact, and as if to prove his point, Wyatt and Grady both climbed to their feet as we approached.

Both men offered their hands to shake and I let my eyes drop to the older man's shiny badge as I took his hand. "They let you go back to work?"

He chuckled and lifted a hand to rub at the back of his neck. "Yeah. I'm technically on a probation period but this bust is going to lead to bigger fish, and since Wyatt was the lead and refused to work the case without me, they had no choice but to let me take my badge back." He shrugged. "But that badge comes with a job behind it that I have to do. You're going to have to give us a couple hours to go over everything, Ms. Conner."

His use of my formal title startled me and made Cy growl in warning. It was actually Webb who came to the rescue. For a guy who had spent time behind bars, he was actually pretty good at playing hero.

"Grady, chill. We had to wrestle scared horses back to the ranch. None of us even stopped to take a breath before we hustled our asses here. You're lucky we took the time to shower. Leo isn't going anywhere as long as her girl is stuck to the cowboy. You can grill her later."

Cy nodded. "Much later." His gaze shifted down to me and a frown pulled at his now heavily whiskered face. He looked good with a beard, way more like an actual cowboy, but I was pretty sure I was going to forever think he looked good no matter which way he came. "You haven't slept in a real bed in two weeks." It was a statement not a question.

"Nope. Ten's an even tougher trail boss than you are, but she got everyone, human and equestrian, back to the ranch in one piece. And she took care of Webb, well enough that his arm didn't fall off."

Everyone's gaze shifted to the younger man as he involuntarily rotated his busted up shoulder. "I guess, I should get this looked at since I am in a hospital."

Ten snorted and rolled her eyes. "You think, city boy?" There was concern under the sarcasm, and the glint in Webb's eyes let me know he didn't miss it.

I was forcibly turned around by Cy's heavy hands on my shoulders. His slate colored eyes bore into mine and everything inside of me wanted to curl around everything inside of him and latch on.

"We have a bunch of rooms rented out at the hotel next door. Let's get you in to see your girl for a little while, and then I'll run you over and you can get some sleep . . . in an actual bed. Nothing has changed with Sutton for the last few hours, so there's no reason for you to be uncomfortable while you wait with the rest of us." He was trying to be sweet. He must have missed the part where I was here to help him shoulder the entire world that was sitting on his shoulders at the moment.

I pushed some of my hair off of my face and gave him a soft smile. "Cy, I'm not going anywhere until we know for sure your brother is on the mend. I do want to see Em but if you're here, I'm here."

He opened his mouth to argue but I could clearly see the appreciation in his eyes. Cy stood for everyone, he deserved someone to stand for him, and with him . . . even if I could only do it for this moment.

His dark head bent and his lips touched mine so lightly that if it wasn't for the scrape of his beard across my face, I might have missed the kiss all together.

"Never had anyone to lean on before, Sunshine."

I kissed him back, harder, so there was no way he could miss it. "Lean away, Cy." He gave me a little nod and then walked me over to a seat next to the one where Lane was propped up against the wall. Brynn turned her head and gave us a watery grin before burying her face back in the crook of Lane's neck. His arms visibly tightened around the leggy redhead and it was easy to see the need to protect and comfort in him as he held the woman. The waiting room felt a hundred times bigger when Ten and Webb left with Grady and Wyatt to go to the hotel in order to do their interviews with the agents and to catch some real sleep. Webb's shoulder was now wrapped up like a mummy, and he was sporting a fancy sling and a bottle of painkillers that indicated his injury was far from being healed. Pain carved deep lines next to his mouth, which only lightened slightly when his brother promised to take it easy on him over the next few hours. The overwhelming relief the siblings had that the other was alive and well was palpable, but so was the push and pull that existed between the brother in the suit and the one in tattered jeans, sporting a flannel with more than one bullet hole in the fabric. They promised to bring real food back with them and they made us promise to keep them updated on Sutton's condition.

I curled into a ball on the hard, vinyl covered seat and rested my head on Cy's shoulder. I let my fingers play with his while he sat perfectly still and silent, his jaw clenched, and a furious tick moving in his cheek. We sat that way for hours, only moving to get terrible vending machine coffee or to take a bathroom break. I wanted to see Em, but she refused to leave Sutton's bedside and they wouldn't let anyone else in the room as long as she was in there.

Finally, after what felt like an eternity, one of her nurses came out and told us they were taking her back to her own room so they could check her bandages. Cy got to his feet so he could go through the lengthy process of getting himself scrubbed up to go sit with his younger brother.

I wasn't sure what to expect when I walked into the hospital room but Emrys's face sporting more tiny black sutures than I could count, and her chest being wrapped up in what appeared to be miles of white gauze and bandages, was enough to make me take a step back. I hadn't been able to fully see the damage done to her when I was trying to get her out of that tree, but now that the carnage to my beautiful best friend was laid out in front of me, it made my stomach turn and my hands curl into fists.

Her eyes wouldn't focus on me and I couldn't tell if that was from the trauma or the painkillers she was on. According to the nurse who was delicately handling her, Emrys was actually ready to be discharged from the ICU. They were simply keeping an eye on her because of her erratic behavior and her unwillingness to leave Sutton alone for more than a few minutes. The nurse said the doctors all agreed that Em and Sutton were good for one another. There was something to be said about how a smaller hospital handled their patients. If Em had been acting this way back home, they would have drugged her up and put her on the street, regardless if she was ready to be unsupervised or not.

After the nurse left, Em curled up on her side on the bed away from me. She wouldn't talk to me and refused to look in my direction. I asked her how she was feeling and told her I would be happy to go and get her anything she needed, but all I got in return was stony silence. She was shutting me out, surrounding herself in her pain and her suffering. There was no way in hell I was going to let that slide, so after a few minutes of talking to her back I took off my shoes, pushed my hair out of my face, and climbed up onto the narrow bed behind her. She flinched when I wrapped my arms around her in a hug that wouldn't be broken, but she didn't push me away.

Apply pressure.

Webb's words rang clear and true in my ears as I held her tighter as she began to shake in my hold.

"Eventually, you are going to walk me through everything you've been through, Em. We are going to battle the nightmare together."

I whispered the words into her inky hair and was stunned when she responded back with, "You can see my face, Leo, and there are places under these bandages that are even worse. The nightmare is carved into my skin, there are a few places that feel like the cuts go all the way to my bones. I'm going to look at it every single day, so it won't ever go away. No matter who is there to try and help me through it."

"I'm not going anywhere, Em." It was the same thing I told Cyrus, only the time frame with Emrys was infinite. I hated that. I wanted to be the one he leaned on forever as well, but we didn't get that, at least we didn't get that just yet.

She lapsed back into silence but some of the tension in her long, lean body started to uncoil as I ran my fingers through her hair and gave her every gentle word I could think of. It felt like calming a wild horse down that had broken free of its tethers. She was obviously skittish and afraid, but she needed the contact and the reassurance to know she wasn't alone and that someone else was there to keep her safe. I rolled my eyes because Cy now had me comparing women to horses and I was silently amused that he was right about the two creatures having more similarities than not.

I lost track of time lying there with her. The light in the room faded from bright afternoon glow to a dim nighttime shadow. I don't think she ever fell asleep, but she never responded to anything else I said to her as we lay there in the encroaching dark. The nurse came back in and asked Em if she wanted dinner, but all she got was a negative head shake in return. At the mention of food my stomach growled, and finally a normal response escaped Emrys's pursed lips. She let out a strangled little giggle and told me she would be fine while I went and got something to eat. I took it for the dismissal it was and climbed out her bed to my feet. I wasn't surprised at all when she followed suit and told me she was headed back to Sutton's room. She insisted that he shouldn't have to spend the night alone since she was the reason he was laid up in the ICU with a hole in his chest.

I didn't bother trying to tell her it wasn't her fault. I knew she wasn't in a place to listen . . . just like I hadn't been when she dove in to save me from drowning in my own ocean of guilt and regret. Eventually, she would be ready to grab onto something to keep her from going all the way under, but today wasn't that day and I seriously doubted tomorrow would be that day either.

I followed my friend down the hallway, watching her step gingerly and hold onto her side. Em was always the type of person who moved with poise and grace, but now she was barely shuffling along. The damage done to her was more than the marks that were etched into her skin and pieced back together. This experience had altered the way the woman carried herself. That broke my heart and had my brain scrambling for any kind of solution to get her back to her normal, bossy, and ballsy self. While I was contemplating that, suddenly all the medical personnel around us leapt into a flurry of activity. It was like someone had sounded an alarm only the doctors and nurses could hear. They all scrambled out of doorways and from behind desks in a mad rush toward one room on the ICU floor.

Emrys tripped a little bit in front of me, so I reached out a hand to steady her. She brushed me off and gave me a panicked look over her shoulder. "That's Sutton's room they all went into."

Her gait was still awkward and not as fluid as it normally was, but there was definite purpose in her steps as she picked up the pace and moved to the room that was now crawling with what seemed like half of the emergency medical staff. Just as we reached the doorway, only to be told not to come any closer unless we were in the proper gear, Lane came stumbling out of the room, pulling down his paper facemask with obvious tears in his eyes.

His breath was whooshing in and out between his parted lips and his head snapped back as Emrys latched onto the front of his shirt and gave him a shake. "What happened?!" She sounded frantic and hysterical.

Lane reached his hands up and circled her wrists as a single, fat tear started to roll down his handsome face. "He opened his eyes." The words were a whisper, but they shouted things like hope and optimism. He shook himself loose from Em's hold and looked at me over the top of her head. "I have to go tell Cy and Brynn. We are far from out of the woods but everyone in there," he hooked a finger over his shoulder toward the hectic room behind him, "seems to think it's a good sign. If his blood pressure stays stable throughout the night, then they want to roll him into surgery first thing in the morning to get the rest of the bullet fragments out. There's one close to his spine that they're worried about shifting and causing some serious damage."

Lane practically bowled both of us over on the way to his family, but I couldn't blame him and I had my hands full keeping Em from pushing past all the doctors and nurses in her way so she could get to Sutton's side. They didn't want anyone who wasn't necessary in the room as everyone raced around to keep the middle Warner brother awake and well. He had so many tubes and cords running all over him that I could barely make out his form in the center of the bed but Em seemed to know right where to look.

"He's looking right at me." Her words were so soft I wasn't sure that was exactly what she had said. However, she turned to me and repeated them, her heart in her eyes and hope clear on every feature of her face.

I felt a warm hand settle on the base of my spine and didn't have to look to know that it was Cy. Every part of me recognized him, because he was the only one who had ever made me react to something as simple as the brush of fingers along my spine. All of me wanted all of him, so whenever he was close, my nerves fired up and my senses honed in on his nearness.

"Seems like good news." His voice was gruff in my ear but I could hear the hesitant relief in it.

Brynn was bouncing up and down on her toes next to me, clapping her hands together. "Of course, it's good news. He's awake."

Lane put a hand on her shoulder and gave it a squeeze. "One step at a time, darlin'."

The brothers didn't want to get their hopes up to have them dashed if Sutton's condition crashed again. They were bracing for impact.

Abruptly, the body in the middle of the bed started to jerk and twitch. Cy swore over the top of my head and Brynn gasped so loudly that one of the nurses closest to the door where we were lurking turned to look at us with narrowed eyes. Lane rubbed his hand roughly over his face and I jerked forward to grab Em as she lurched toward the door.

"Is he having a seizure?" When no one bothered to answer her, Emrys shrieked the question again at the top of her lungs, which had one of the doctors exiting the room. He took one look at her face, pale and patch-worked together with a million stitches, and put a hand on her arm that she immediately shook off. "Is. He. Having. A. Seizure." She enunciated each word coolly, and crossed her arms over her chest.

I was secretly elated that she was standing her ground. It made me hope against hope that the road back to the old Em wouldn't be super long and twisted.

"Not a seizure. He was reacting to the breathing tube and all the lines we have running into him. He's in a lot of pain, and all that thrashing around isn't good for that bullet still stuck inside of him." The doctor looked at the brothers. "His situation is still critical but this is a big step in the right direction."

Lane looked down at the ground and sighed deeply, while I could feel Cy dip his chin down in acknowledgement. "Let us know how we can help, Doc."

"Don't give up on him yet. They build cowboys tough out here. I have faith your brother will pull through."

We all turned to look at the nurse, who had been scowling at us after Em's outburst, as she poked her head out of the door and interrupted our little party.

"He's trying to say something, but he can't talk around the breathing tube. It's agitating him, do you think we should pull it?"

The doctor shook his head. "No. I don't want to move anything until we get that last shard out of his back. If it hits his spine we could be looking at a whole new problem. Get him something to write with or give him a phone and see if he can type out a message on that. Frankly, I'm stunned he has so much fight in him after the blood loss and the trauma to his body."

Lane snorted. "He's a stubborn bastard."

There was movement around the bed, and without warning, a phone beeped. Cy looked at Lane. "I came from the middle of the forest with him in the helicopter. I haven't seen my cell phone in a month."

Lane pulled a phone out of his pocket and read over what was on the screen. He frowned, looked at me and then at Emrys, before silently handing the cell over. "Keep in mind he's been through hell and has God only knows what kind of drugs pumping through his system right now."

Em gasped and the phone fell from her fingers, as she dropped it like the device was covered in shards of glass. Lucky, Cy had quick reflexes and managed to move forward and grab the device before it hit the tiled floor. Em put her hands to her face and turned her back on all of us as she slowly started to make her way back down the hallway toward her room.

"Em?" I called her name and moved to follow her but stilled when Cy put his hand on my shoulder and handed me the phone.

There in black and white were the words:

-Send her home. I don't want her here.

I couldn't stop the protective growl that escaped me. Sutton had saved her, but just as quickly, I knew he had destroyed her. I knew he was grumpy and sullen, but I had no clue he could be cruel, especially so close to death.

"How could he tell her that?" I mean, he had been unconscious the last few days so there was no way he could know that she hadn't left his side, but he had to know that she was going to want to tell him thank you for taking a bullet for her.

Cy put his arm across my shoulder and pulled me in tight for a hug. "Right now, I'm just happy that he's awake and can communicate at all. I promise to kick his ass later for being an ass to your girl. But for right now, let's be happy he's working toward being okay."

I gritted my teeth together and fought reminding him right now was all we had, and right now, his brother had gone from hero to villain in the span of a second. Em was already sinking and Sutton's dismissal had added extra weight to the load she was already carrying. I wasn't going to let her go down any deeper. That wasn't happening on my watch.

CHAPTER 19

No Such Luck

AFTER SUTTON SENT EMRYS AWAY so callously, and she was no longer visible in the hallway, he settled down and the doctors stopped swarming around him. He drifted in and out of consciousness for the next few hours, but his heart rate stabilized, and they planned to take him in for surgery first thing in the morning. I was going back to check on Em when she surprised me by meeting me outside of her room dressed in street clothes, her hair brushed and pulled back in a braid.

Her eyes still looked empty and listless, but there was a determined tilt to her chin that was familiar and a welcome sight. "I want to go home, Leo."

I nodded at her and gulped as I looked over my shoulder to where Cy and Lane were still huddled together outside of Sutton's room. "Okay, Em. We'll go home." The words wrenched out of me, because as much as I wanted to help her any way I could, going home meant leaving Cy. "You have to give me until tomorrow. There is no way we can fly out of here tonight, but if you give me some time, I promise I will have you in your own bed by tomorrow night."

She gave a little nod and her dark eyebrows twitched upwards. "You're coming with me, right?"

I swallowed again and squeezed my eyes shut. My heart hurt. "Yeah, Em, I'm going with you. I'll be right next to you, for as long as you need me."

"Thanks, Leo."

I didn't really think I had a choice in the matter, even though it felt like my soul was being ripped in two. "Let me talk to the boys. They have rooms at a hotel close by. We can crash tonight and I'll work something out. I still have to talk to the DEA and make a statement as well." It was going to be a long night and that didn't include figuring out a way to say goodbye to Cy. My head ached thinking about all of it, and the inside of my chest burned knowing this might be the last time I laid eyes on the not quite cowboys.

I made my way over to the brothers, and without me having to say a word, Cy stiffened and crossed his arms over his broad chest. "You're leaving, aren't you?"

I bit down on my lip and nodded slowly. "Em wants to go home, Cy. I have to take her."

His heavy eyebrows snapped down over his eyes and the storm rolled deep and dark in the gray depths. "I'll give you the key card to my room." His chest rose and fell, but it was like a black cloud had moved into the hallway with us and was waiting to drop a torrent of freezing rain on all the heat and warmth that moved between us. "You better find a way to come tell me good-bye, Leo."

My teeth dug into my lip so hard that I tasted blood. I hurt everywhere. "I will." The words were broken and ugly because I didn't want to have to tell him goodbye, even though I knew that was what was waiting for us all along. "I have to get Em settled, book flights home, and talk to Wyatt and Grady still. I'll come find you, Cy. I won't disappear on you, I promise."

The assurances didn't make either one of us feel better and

I could feel his eyes bore into me as he watched me walk away from him.

The hotel was literally right next to the hospital, so hustling Em into Cy's room took no time at all. Tracking down a reliable Wi-Fi signal so I could search for flights took a little bit longer, and so did dragging myself out of the room that smelled like Cy and had his things in it. Jeans tossed across the end of the bed, a shirt thrown carelessly next to the sink, and not surprisingly, a plethora of dude stuff for his hair that Lane must have brought in with him when he came from the ranch. It made me smile that the man would worry about his hair but couldn't give two shits about his cell phone. I wanted to linger. I wanted to take in everything that was him and pretend like I would still be able to smell him and feel him in the air around me once I was home. It was a lie that I couldn't even slightly sell myself, so I grabbed his discarded T-shirt, the Jack Daniel's one from our first meeting, and buried my nose in it. I hoped it wasn't his favorite because I was taking it with me when I left in the morning, and nothing was going to stop me from stealing a tangible memory of the man who had forced me to be the woman I was always supposed to be.

Em was resting, or at least she had her eyes closed and was lying still as stone after I told her our first flight out was at ten in the morning. We had to fly from Billings to Denver and then sit at DIA for a couple of hours before our connection left from there. She nodded at me, but I wasn't sure the words were sinking in. She looked bad before Sutton sent her away, now she looked hollowed out and drained. It was hard to find any kind of life in her, even if her defiance and hurt was right at the forefront of the emotional wall she was building to protect herself. Once I was sure she was settled, well when I was sure she was still breathing and not drowning in her own tears and suffocating on silent sobs,

I found the room number that Cy mentioned the DEA guys were in and knocked on the door.

Wyatt answered, dressed down in just his button up shirt, minus his blazer, and he'd switched his slacks for a pair of jeans with a hole in the knee. He looked so much like Webb, I did a double take until I saw Grady sitting at the little desk in the room swearing at his laptop. The Wi-Fi really did suck.

Wyatt ushered me in the room, turned on a tiny little device that he said would record the interview, and then launched into a million questions. I didn't realize how tired and how stretched thin my nerves were until I had to recount every single crazy experience I'd been through since landing in Wyoming. I wanted to cry. I wanted to fall onto one of the beds, bury my face into a comforter, and scream until my lungs burst. I wanted to throw the remote against the wall and watch it shatter. I wanted to grab Wyatt by his shoulders and shake him while telling him there weren't enough words in the dictionary to properly describe everything I had lost, and even more, what I had gained over the last week or so.

All I did was curl my hands into fists so tight that my fingernails cut into my palms deep enough to draw blood and carefully, thoughtfully go over every single minute of the last week. I spoke slowly and precise, making sure I hit every detail, captured every moment of fear and panic that had overtaken me once I realized we were under attack. Both men listened with a sympathetic ear and watched me with eyes that were kind, but still sharp and trained to pick up on anything I may have exaggerated or left out. It was intense and when I was done, my legs felt like Jell-O as I climbed to my feet to head back to Cy's room. Wyatt offered to walk with me but I brushed him off, needing the short commute to pull my defenses back up so that I could be strong for Em. Telling them how I found her up in the tree, cut up and torn, telling them how all she said was that they hurt her, it caused a lump in my throat I couldn't swallow around. Wyatt mentioned they still needed to talk to her and that she was probably going to get pulled into the case as a witness, but he assured me that both he and Grady understood she wasn't ready for the pressure any of that would put on her. Frankly, I wasn't sure when she would be able to stand back on her own two feet and fight, but I didn't share that with him.

I paused at the door to collect myself and to pull my features into a mask that I hoped was one conveying confidence and assurance, just in case Em was up. Even if she wasn't, I felt like I needed to fool someone into believing I had my shit together.

The lights were out, but with the door open behind me I could clearly see that the bed was empty and missing the lump that was my best friend. I had a moment of panic before remembering she might simply be in the bathroom. The light was shining through the crack at the bottom of the door and I could hear someone moving around inside the small space. I rubbed a hand over the back of my neck and walked toward the door.

"Em, the nurse said you shouldn't get those dressings on your stitches wet. I told you I would help you clean up if you wanted to take a shower." The process wasn't easy considering the amount of skin on her that was currently being held together by staples and string.

I didn't get a response, so I lifted my hand and knocked on the door while calling her name louder. The wood swung open under my hand and I blinked stupidly at the sight that greeted me. My brain shut down and my heart took over as Cy turned around from where he was wrapping a towel around his lean waist, water cascading enticingly over the muscles that cut across his upper back. His hair was blacker than black with water as he flicked it out of his eyes and looked me up and down. He ran a hand over his obviously tired face, but his lips kicked up in one of his rare grins and I felt it like a punch right in the center of my chest.

Tired and scared for his brother, worn out and battered from our week through hell and back . . . and yet . . . he still smiled for me and at me. It was the single most precious gift I had ever been given and I would treasure it forever.

"Sutton is down for the night. They gave him a sedative to keep him still, so he doesn't inadvertently shift that bullet fragment. He's not moving, so the doc kicked me and Lane out and told us to rest up. Waiting seems like it should be easy but he assured us it's not, and even though he's awake, Sutton's still on borrowed time." He took a step closer to me and I reached out a hand so that it was resting on the center of his wide chest. He felt so warm, so vital and alive. I had no idea how I was supposed to walk away from it and be okay.

"Where's Em?" I gasped as he put a hand over mine and slowly started to move toward me. His actions made me step out of the bathroom. His bare feet pushed mine all the way across the room until the backs of my knees hit the edge of the mattress in the center of the room.

"I showed up and told her I just needed to grab my shit, so I could move rooms. She had a little fit I wasn't still at the hospital with Sutton and asked me who was going to sit with him tonight while we wait for his surgery. I told her the staff banned us from the room for the night, and before I could stop her she was out the door and on her way next door. I caught up with her and walked her to the ICU." He shook his head and moved his hands so that he was holding onto either side of my face. He tilted my head back and lowered his head until our lips barely touched. "The nurses didn't even try and talk her out of going in the room. She settled herself in the chair next to his bed and told me she would be back here in the morning before he woke up. I figured I would come back here, clean up and wait for you to show, so we could have a proper goodbye." His words kissed my lips and wrapped around me. "I don't know what Sutton was thinking, sending a girl like that away, but something tells me when he gets better he's going to regret it more than he regrets any of the other shit choices he's made about women."

I sighed and it made him shiver. I let my hands dance over the rock hard expanse of his chest, collecting hidden water droplets along the way. I was headed for that ineffective knot holding the too thin towel closed at his waist and he knew it. His abs tightened under the tips of my fingers and his thighs flexed against mine. Not to mention, the material of the towel did nothing to hide the way that heavy erection between his legs jumped and rose more fully to attention the lower my touch traveled.

"Your brother is a hero, you all are. She's not going to let the fact he saved her life go, no matter how hard he pushes. Right now she's bleeding from too many places to realize he is too." I hooked a finger around the knot and gave it a little tug. That was all it took for the fabric to fall and for all that glorious, straining manhood to be on display. The sight made me suck a breath in and it made my mouth water. Even in the dim light, he was the most beautiful man I had ever seen. It made me feel powerful, special by being the one he was standing before, stripped and sure. The man was hard to read on a good day, but in the dark with our end hovering over both of us, there was no missing the importance of this moment.

I lifted up enough to give him a real kiss and worked my eager fingers around the hardened flesh that was pulsing against my stomach. His cock throbbed in my grasp and his hips involuntarily kicked toward mine as our tongues tangled and our teeth tried to devour. We were going at each other like the other person was our last meal and our time on death row was coming to an end. It was messy. It was voracious. It was wet and wild. It was going to bruise and hurt when it was over, but that meant it was a kiss I got to take with me when I got on the plane tomorrow. It was a kiss I got to keep and I wanted him to have one that left him with the same. My lips tingled and fire seared up my spine as his hands pulled me closer and dug into my skin. His knee shoved between my legs and pushed his hips and his thick erection into the cradle of my hips. I circled the slick tip with my thumb and felt him growl in response against my aching lips. My mouth was under attack but it felt like love, not war. It was a battle that wouldn't have a victor because we both won as we took everything the other offered, and I knew we were both going to lose as soon as the sun came up in the morning and we had to officially say goodbye.

"Always so hot and so bright, Sunshine. You burn in the best ways." I gulped a little and pushed him back a step, so I could sit on the edge of the bed in front of him. His cock jumped in anticipation and pearly liquid beaded up at the tip. I used the pad of my thumb to swirl it around and squeezed the shaft as I rolled my thumb to trace the sensitive lines running underneath the plump head.

I thought he was the one who blazed and burned. I thought he was the one who ignited everything that had long been dormant inside of me. He was the spark, but I was the flame. I was the one who tore all the longing and feelings of inadequacy down and built something better up in their place. I was the one who realized that just because the wrong people didn't love you, didn't mean you had to be afraid of the right ones loving you, and then some.

I bent forward, lowered my head, and dropped a kiss in the center of his chest. It made his hands flex on my skin and his breath hitch. I circled a hand around his hip and let my fingers sink into the granite-like globes of his backside. The muscle there twitched against my fingers as I traced each defined ab along the front of his abdomen with the tip of my tongue. His stomach didn't have an ounce of give to it and the light dusting of dark hair that darted under his belly button toward the base of his erection tickled the tip of my nose as I worked my way steadily lower. I dipped my tongue into the concave circle of his belly button and was rewarded for the teasing taste with my name barked out harshly through clenched teeth.

I started to slide my hand slowly up and down the shaft that was pulsing impatiently against my palm and swooped my head down, so that I could engulf the engorged head in the wet heat of my waiting mouth. I whimpered at the way his heat immediately flooded into me. He filled my senses up and left an imprint on every part of me that was touching him. I swore my tongue would never forget that first taste, that first swipe that had him swearing and bucking into me.

One of his hands landed on the top of my head and slowly started to thread through my hair. He pulled me closer and I had to breathe out slow and steady as he pushed himself deeper into my sucking and swirling mouth. Cy wasn't the type to take things slow and steady, so he burned across my lips and pulsed in my mouth as he started to thrust lightly against my face all while telling me, "Just a little bit more" and "Leo, you fucking own me."

There was something about the coiled desire in his voice and the taut tension that had his muscles locked from head to toe that made me desperate to give him what he wanted. I sucked him in deeper. I squeezed him harder. I felt him grunt and groan as his leaking tip touched the back of my throat. I had to close my eyes and concentrate on keeping a steady rhythm and on moving my fist up and down in time with my rapidly moving lips and tongue. The sight of his neck muscles bulging and his veins popping as he wrapped himself in the pleasure that I offered was enough to make my heart race and my blood boil. I could feel moisture pooling between my legs, and every time I moved my head over him and my nipples brushed against the fabric of my bra, I wanted to moan loudly and wantonly. Getting him off was the biggest turn on I'd ever experienced because it made me feel like I did indeed own him.

I was the one putting that look on his face.

I was the one making him say dirty, dirty things, as he struggled for control.

I was the one lapping up the desire and want that dripped out of him, tangy and salty on my tongue.

I was the one he was both harsh and gentle for.

I was the one who got all his soft and all of his hard.

I was the one who was going to swallow him whole and then go back for seconds, because this was going to be our best goodbye and I wanted the memories we were making on the way to being over, to be some of the best ones either of us could have.

I was working him with everything I had. Hands, lips, teeth, tongue. I was breathing just as hard as he was, and could tell by the way his spine stiffened, and the way his thrusts turned erratic and wild, that he was close. It was more than I ever took from any man I was intimate with, but for him I wanted it all and then I wanted him to give me more.

I could feel him pulsing heavy and hard in my mouth. I was ready to explode watching the way the corded muscles in his stomach contracted and released. I wanted to touch myself while I watched his eyes cloud over as foggy gray rolled in and made everything dark and dangerous looking. His jaw clenched and the hold he had on the top of my head shifted so that his hands were around the base of my skull. I was skirting my fingers across the flexing surface of his ass, aiming for those soft little sacs that were drawn up tight and anxious for release, but he didn't let me reach my destination.

I wanted him to finish, he wanted me sprawled out on the bed underneath him.

He was bigger, so he got his way and before I could utter a protest through swollen and shiny lips. He had the button on my jeans undone, a wide hand spanning the space between my hips and a rough, calloused finger on the center of my desire. That little point pulsed so hard against his touch that it made my back bow up off the bed and my eyes cross as I moaned his name. My underwear was shoved to the side, the buttons on my shirt flew in a million directions under impatient hands, and my aching nipples rose up in victory as they were set free as he shoved the cups of my bra up and out of his way.

It was my turn to thread shaking fingers through thick hair, as his dark head lowered to my chest, so that his strong teeth could scrape across begging flesh. It made me whimper and it made my entire body quiver under the weight of his. He urged me to lift my hips up so he could pull denim and cotton out of his way, but he muttered the words around my puckering nipple that he refused to let go of. The pressure from his mouth and the bite of his teeth felt like some kind of glorious torture. I never wanted it to end, and I was excruciatingly sad that I knew what it felt like, because I was going to miss it when it was gone.

I whispered his name as he finally rose up over me enough to get the rest of my clothes out of the way. My legs shifted restlessly against the side of the bed, as that heated spot between them throbbed heavily for his touch. He watched the motion with hooded eyes and I couldn't stop myself from letting my limbs fall open under his intent stare. I put a hand low on my belly and the other on the breast he had left wet and ready. I touched where I needed his hands and he watched me like I was his favorite movie.

He shook his head slowly and ran his tongue over the curve of his bottom lip. It was puffy and slick from my ravenous mouth. "There are so many things I want to do for you, and do to you. The list is endless and I feel like I'm working against the clock here, Leo." He leaned forward and pressed his mouth against mine. This kiss light, precious. I was surprised that it felt like it would last just as long as the one that had hurt. "I want you on my tongue. I want you to come all over my fingers and I want to come all over those perfect fucking tits." His head shook again and the corner of his lips quirked up and a slash of white broke through the darkness in the room as he grinned at me. "I want to let you finish sucking me off. I want to bend you over and take your ass. I want you to sit on my face and let me leave razor burns all over the inside of those pretty white thighs. I want all of it and there isn't time for any of it."

I gulped and moved the hand that was playing with my nipple to my throat. I'd never done most of those things, but hearing him list out all the ways in which he wanted me, it made me furious with fate that I wasn't going to experience them with him and if not with him, then never. I trusted him. That was the thing that had been missing from the men in my life all along. I could never open myself up to them the way I did with Cy, because I didn't trust them and I didn't trust myself.

I reached up to grab him and sighed when he let me pull him back down on top of me. He braced his weight above me with an arm crooked over my head and we both let out a sigh of contentment when I wrapped both my legs high around his waist. His hardness found my wetness with little work and I panted a choppy little breath as he dragged the tip of that hard erection through silken and damp folds. I felt myself pulse and blood pound in anticipation but my hands held him tenderly, reverently.

"There's no clock right now, Cy. There's just me and you. We would hear it ticking because there's no place for the sound to hide. All I can hear is your heartbeat and mine, racing to keep up with it. All I see is you and all I feel is the way you make me feel special and important. There wasn't a lot of time for you to do that, but you did. So, right now we focus on the ways we can have each other and not on the ways we can't." Because if I started thinking about everything I would be missing once day came, and I focused on the experiences with him that I would never have, then I would fall apart and this sexy goodbye would turn into a tearful goodbye and I didn't want that for either of us.

His hips pressed forward at the same time he lowered himself so that our chests were touching as our tongues tangled and our hearts marched forward together, my beat matching his perfectly. I was nothing but liquid want and warm passion, so he sank in deep and rocked his pelvis into mine in the most delicious way. I thrashed a little as my body adjusted to take all of him in. Muscles quivered around rock hard flesh and sensitive nerves danced happily along the veiny length. I loved the way he filled me up, took up every single bit of space, like he was right to do so. I liked the way his weight pinned me down and made his movements and mine more deliberate. I liked the way he fucked me, and the way he encouraged me to fuck him back. I liked the way our bodies grew slick and slipped against one another. I liked the way he made love to my mouth, his kiss mimicking the sexy, raw way his cock pushed in and out of my body. His tongue teased mine the same way he teased my greedy, aching center by sliding almost all the way out so that I was begging, pleading for him to pound back into me, only to have him inch back in, so slowly that I thought I was going to lose my mind. I almost died when he gentled the hammering, thrashing thrusts by cupping my jaw and running his thumb lightly over the curve.

He was taking what he needed from my body, giving me what I needed with his, but he was also taking the time to remember this, to remember us. His eyes never left my face and I could tell he was watching, waiting for that moment he gave me so much pleasure I couldn't take anymore. He wanted to keep what I looked like when he broke me, split me open with desire and longing, someplace safe so he would never forget it. He wanted to know that he was the only one who could make me look that way and I didn't need to tell him, because my entire body attested to the fact.

My head tossed from side to side. My toes curled. My thighs clamped around his sides like a vice. My fingers scratched furious lines of passion into his back. My lips screamed his name over and over again. My center went molten and flooded with satisfaction. My nipples drew into points so hard, they had to be poking into his chest. My cheeks heated and filled with a sex flush that I knew would take hours to fade. All of it he could see, he could feel. All of it was proof that together, we made moments that were meant to last. The only secret I had, the only thing his unwavering eyes couldn't see was the way my soul shattered and my heart fractured. I didn't want just this moment . . . I wanted all the moments and I wanted them with him.

As soon as my pussy pulsed and clamped down around him, as soon as he watched me fall over the cliff of pleasure he had been pushing me toward, I felt him let loose. His thrusts lost their calculated rhythm. He was pounding into me, chasing his own moment, his own release and he didn't have very far to run. His legs tensed, his back locked hard under the clasp of my legs, and his pretty eyes went coal dark. He grunted my name in a thick tone and then let his head fall forward so that his nose was buried in the curve of my neck while his teeth clamped down sharply on the ridge of my collar bone.

He filled me up in a different way and I took it all in. The furious rush of desire made my head spin and the still way he lay on top of me after he was spent and burned through, made everything inside of me feel like it was churning and whipping around, furious underneath my skin. I didn't want to go but I also knew I couldn't stay.

"Best goodbye ever." I whispered the words into his ear and felt him sigh into the side of my throat.

He lifted his head, eyes infinitely dark and unreadable. "The goodbye doesn't matter. It's everything that came before the goodbye that is important. I'll forget about the goodbye in time . . . everything else . . ." he trailed away and I wanted to tell him I would remember all as well, but I couldn't get the words out. I was greedy. I wanted more than memories.

I ran a hand over the side of his face, let his whiskers tickle my fingers, and traced the silver specks that made him look so distinguished and rugged at the same time. I felt my lips quirk up in a grin that was similar to the one he usually gave me and lifted my eyebrows up even though I wasn't sure he could see my expression in the dark. "So, about that thing you said where I get to sit on your face . . ." I let out a yelp as he rolled us over with a laugh that quickly turned into a growl.

Say what you mean . . . I wanted to tell him that I was pretty sure I could love him . . . and maybe more importantly, I could let him love me. But I kept the words to myself because he would hear that I meant them, and I had a feeling he would say something similar back and that would make leaving even harder than it was already going to be.

CHAPTER 20

No Time to Waste

I THOUGHT ONCE I WAS back in the Bay Area, my life would settle into the familiar grind and rhythm that I had been sleepwalking through for years. It was what I knew. It was habit and routine. I thought I would be able to bury the longing that engulfed me the minute I stepped on the plane and went back to day-to-day business. That everything inside me calling to the wild and calling to Cyrus Warner would be drowned out by the sounds of the city and commotion I used to distract myself with.

I was wrong. So very wrong.

Chaos came crashing down around me as soon as it became clear there was no way Em was fit to be left on her own. She was listless, skittish, and acting like a shadow of her former self. She wouldn't talk to her family. She refused to go back to work, even after the bandages came off of her face and the stitches came out. She isolated herself from the rest of her social circle and holed herself up in my guest room. She only came out when I made her or when I got a message from Cy updating me on Sutton's condition.

She seemed to live for those moments. Every time news came through email or a brief text message, her face lost some of the sallow, haughtiness that had overrun it. It was the only time I could see a glimmer of life spark in her dull gaze.

Sutton was improving. The progress was slow, agonizingly so, as there had been complications during the surgery to remove the fragmented bullet. Cy didn't elaborate, but the gist was that his middle brother was having some mobility issues and was far from being released from the hospital. There was no telling how permanent any of the damage was at this stage, so everyone was trying to keep Sutton's attitude on the positive side of things. It wasn't surprising the grumpy cowboy was fighting them every step of the way. Cy's messages were never long, always to the point and lacking any kind of personal touch. As happy as they made Em, they had the opposite effect on me.

I knew there was no point in making promises we couldn't keep, to draw out the moments that weren't meant to last. That didn't mean it didn't feel like a knife in the heart every time I clicked a message open. I knew he wouldn't say he missed me, and knew all I could do was reply back just as formally. It was painful to not tell him that I had no idea how he had survived after losing half his heart when his ex left him, because I felt like I was dying without him. I may have been living an incomplete life before my eyes were forced open, but that paled in comparison to living as half of a person. I swore the majority of my soul, and everything that it was made up of, was left high in the backcountry of Wyoming. I left it in the hands of a man who was still undefined, and yet had my heart identifying him as belonging to us. There was no logic to it all, which made me think it had to be love or something scarily close to it.

If dealing with Emrys's emotional state wasn't enough of a full-time job, I had to go back to my actual job a few days after I got back home. I was out of vacation time and had to use the last couple of sick days I had to get Em settled into my place and to bully her into going to see the doctor. I wanted her to talk to a specialist about the scar on her face and the ones that were left on her chest, but she flatly refused. I would catch her staring at herself in the mirror in the bathroom, tears running over her now less than perfect face. She never said anything about it, and I didn't push. I was afraid she was fragile enough to break and I wasn't sure I had the skills needed to put her back together. I knew she was going to need a professional so between work, dodging worried calls from Em's parents, and the emotional vortex at home, I spent my time researching victims' advocates in both the Bay Area and in Wyoming. I didn't delve too deeply into why I felt compelled to look in both places, but in either case I was armed with the names of the top qualified professionals when she was ready to take that step.

I wasn't sure what it was going to be like having to face my ex's wife again. Before I had been so worried about how the truth would affect my career and my reputation. Now carrying it around was affecting my conscience and my integrity. I still had a few months left on the contract with her company, and things were going so well I knew she was going to make an offer to extend the work my team did for her. Every time I walked into her office and sat across from her, that picture of her happy family smiling stared right at me, taunting me. The ball of regret, and remorse grew in my gut. I knew, without a doubt, that getting fired was far from the worst thing that could happen to me in this life. One only had to the look at the shattered woman using my home as a refuge to know that. I also knew whatever the outcome of me coming clean with Chris's wife was, it couldn't hurt as bad or leave me as aching and raw as walking away from my not quite a cowboy had.

I waited for a day we were both working late. I knew the conversation was going to be unpleasant and that it could very well end with me getting handed my walking papers, so I didn't want witnesses or a scene. I practiced what I was going to say all day long. I went over it a thousand times in my head and even prepared myself for things to get violent and ugly. I would let her get a swing in if she needed it. That was only fair, but she was only going to get one. The rest she would have to take home to her philandering husband.

When I asked her if she had a minute, she smiled at me and it made me feel like slime. She was smart. She was successful. She was pretty and she was nice. The cosmetic contract had been one of my favorites to date and it made everything inside me clench and squeeze to know that I had had a part, no matter how unwittingly, in deceiving her.

"I've been meaning to talk to you, Leora." My full name made me jolt. I was so used to being Leo, the little lion, I forgot that another me even existed.

I didn't want to sit down, this felt like a conversation we should be having while standing up, but I took a seat and crossed my legs. I folded my hands together so tightly that my nails pricked my skin hard enough to hurt.

"About the contract?" I didn't want her to offer up an amazing opportunity right before I brought her entire world crashing down around her. That didn't seem fair or right.

She nodded at me and put her hands together so that her manicured fingers were steepled and hovered over her meticulously painted lips. "Yes, I want to speak about the contract and I want to make sure you know that if we do extend it, I want you to head up the team. You've done a marvelous job here and I want to keep you on board." I opened my mouth to interject that I had something important to say when she held up a hand and lifted a perfectly sculpted eyebrow at me. "I need to know that when I bring the new contract forward to your bosses, that your personal relationship with my husband won't be an issue. I need you to work closely with me as we expand the brand and look at the global market. I can't have your personal life interfering with your professional one. I let your hesitancy slide these last few months because it's clear you're brilliant at your job, but moving forward I need you to sweep that under the rug and put your game face on."

I felt my jaw unhinge like a snake trying to swallow a rabbit whole. I heard my breath wheeze out of my lungs, and I was pretty sure I blacked out for a second because when my eyes refocused on her, she looked impatient and aggravated, not shattered or heartbroken.

"I . . . we . . . you . . ." the words wheezed out as I lifted a hand to my throat and told myself to focus and calm down. "How long have you known that I had an affair with your husband?"

She waved a hand in front of her and rolled her eyes at me like it was a silly question to ask. "Chris is nice enough to look at, gets the job done in bed and he's a passable father. He's neither a rocket scientist nor is he a challenge. He doesn't flaunt his affairs but he doesn't hide them either." Her other eyebrow lifted to match the first. "I've always been the breadwinner and the one with drive and ambition and he's supported me in everything I've done. I wanted an empire, he wanted to get his dick sucked. When I wasn't around to do it, he found someone, anyone who was willing. As long as he doesn't bring his girlfriends around my kids or parade them in front of the people I do business with, I let him have his fun, and honestly, I have mine." She leaned forward in her chair a little bit and her gaze locked on mine. "You were the first one I actually worried about. I knew I needed your particular skill set but if you were willing to fall for Chris's particular brand of bullshit, it made me question how bright and dedicated you really were." She grinned at me and while I thought she was going to be malicious and nasty it actually seemed like her typical, friendly smile. I was so confused that I felt a little nauseous. I wondered if she'd be as nice about me throwing up on her floor as she was about me fucking the man she was married to. "You kicked Chris to the curb as soon as you saw the picture on my desk. I still question your taste in men, but not your integrity. I think your guilt made you work even harder."

I leaned forward in the chair and rested my forehead on the point my crossed knees made. "I felt like acid was eating me alive inside every single time I saw you. I wanted to tell you what happened, but I was so scared. You knew all along and you never said a word."

I heard her scoff a little. "I'm not the one who had the affair. I was under no obligation to make your life easier or your deception easier to live with."

She was right. She didn't owe me anything, but I didn't like the way she had leveraged my guilty conscience into making me a pawn she could use how she saw fit.

"He made it so easy." I choked on the words as every single way Cy made it so difficult flashed through my mind. He wasn't going to fit unless I made him fit and right now there was a hole so big in the center of me that I needed him to fill it up in order to make sense of anything. Half a life before him, no life without him, at least not one that had anything I wanted inside of it.

She gave me a sympathetic look and that bile rose even harder up in my throat. She felt sorry for me; that I had been foolish enough to fall for someone as simple as her husband. I didn't want her pity and I knew deep down into my bones that I didn't want to work for or with someone who was okay using another person's emotions against them like a weapon. "He does that. That's why we've stayed together as long as we have. He makes it easy for me to live my life around him. Now about that extended contract . . ."

Say what you mean and mean what you say. I pushed to my feet and shook my head at her. "I can't sign on for an extended contract. I'm happy to finish out the one I'm already committed to, but I don't want to do this anymore."

She frowned at me, seeming to be genuinely confused. "Is this about working for me now that you know that I know about you and my husband?"

I shook my head again and felt one of Cy's not quite smiles tug at my mouth. "No. This is about me being sick of the noise. I don't want to manipulate people into spending money on stuff they don't need with clever words and glossy images. I don't want to be seduced by easy and uncomplicated." I took a step toward the door and gave her a steady look. "I want to know what I'm dealing with up front, because you can hear the truth ringing in every syllable spoken. I want complicated and problematic. I want to get on the horse every time it throws me and not be afraid of being hurt because . . ." I took another step toward the door, my heart kicking against my ribs and determination like a fire in my blood. Everything that happened before goodbye was what lingered, but I could make what happened after goodbye be the most important choices I ever made. "I want to be happy for once in my life, and I want to mean it when I say that I am. I'm not just done with your company after the contract is finished, I'm done with this half-life." It was my turn to lift my eyebrows at her as I put a hand on the door and pulled it open. "What good is having an empire if you're the only one around to appreciate everything you've worked so hard for?"

She scoffed again, but I could tell she had moved past irritated and was now actually angry. I wanted to tell her that she would have a much better life if she got worked up that way about the state of her marriage, rather than her business, but it wasn't my job to save her relationship, not when she was the one who let it wither in the first place.

"Bad taste in men and bad business sense. Don't think I won't be going to your bosses about your unprofessional behavior and your refusal to work with my company further. They won't be happy."

I shrugged, already trying to figure out what I should do about Em and the lease on my apartment rather than worry about the state of my former career. "The only happiness I'm worried about is my own." And a certain unsmiling not quite a cowboy's happiness, too, but she didn't need to know that. She wouldn't appreciate the challenge and didn't deserve to know that my taste in men had vastly improved.

I shut the door even though she was still speaking to me and I couldn't stop the face-splitting grin that stretched my mouth wide as I made my way back to the apartment. I threw open the door with more gusto than it required and called Em's name at the top of my lungs. She didn't respond, which was nothing new, so I went to the guest room to tell her I was quitting my job and chasing after the biggest risk ever. I thought she would be happy for me. I thought she would support my decision. I thought maybe she would even hug me and let her pretty smile back onto her newly scarred face. I thought she would be curled up in a ball under the covers on the bed like she had been since we got home.

I thought wrong.

The room was empty. The bathroom was empty and there were no signs of her anywhere in my house. I panicked at first, calling her cell no less than twenty times in a row. Every call went to voicemail and when I called her parents, they were just as lost and confused as I was. I tore through the room, looking for anything that might give me a sign as to where she went, when my phone rang. I didn't want to answer it in my frantic state, but it was my grandmother's number and there was no way I could ignore her after being out of touch for so long.

"Hey, Gram. Now's not a good time, can I call you back in a little bit?" I was going to call the police and fill out a missing person's report. I was going to call Grady and Wyatt and see if they could use some kind of super government tracking system and locate her. Okay, maybe that was a little bit irrational, but I was desperate to find my friend.

"Leo, I need you to listen to me for a minute." She only used that tone with me when I was in trouble or when something bad had happened. Usually those two things involved one person and I was beyond done with her and the way she tossed me away. I had more love than I knew what to do with. I was no longer missing hers.

I groaned and shoved a hand through my hair. "Gram if this has something to do with Mom, I don't care."

"It's not about your mother, dear, it's about Emrys."

I stopped digging through the drawers in the room that were now empty and looked up at the mirror my best friend had spent hours crying in front of. I don't know what she saw when she looked at herself in the reflection, but all I could see was the same gorgeous, warm, wonderful friend who had kept me afloat when all I wanted to do was drift. Her outsides had changed and maybe her insides had too, but she was still made of the same stuff that always made her my favorite person in the entire world.

"What about Em?" I whispered the words and whipped my head around as I heard knocking on my apartment door. Thinking it might be the woman we were talking about I took a flying leap over the bed, and not so gracefully scrambled back to my feet as I raced toward the living room.

"She called me today and told me you met a man. She said this one is very different from the last. She told me you wouldn't go to him as long as you felt like you had to stay and take care of her, so she asked me if it would be okay if she came and stayed with me for a little while." My grandmother sighed. "I asked why she couldn't stay with her parents and she told me I would understand once I saw her." Another sigh, this one deep and sad. The pounding on the front door grew louder and more impatient and I wondered if Chris's wife had changed her tune and wanted to take a swing after all. "Her poor face. The girl needs to rest and she needs someone to talk to."

I skirted around the couch and pulled the chain on the door and flipped the deadbolt without looking through the peephole. This was the city, not the wild, wild west so I knew it was stupid but I was distracted and worried. "Gram, did she tell you what happened?"

"No, not all of it, but I gather she met a man too. Her eyes are so sad, Leo. She needs time."

I sniffled a little bit and pushed back tears as they threatened. "I was taking care of her. I want to help her." I felt like that was my job, my real job, one I wouldn't walk away from until it was done.

"I know, sweetie, but she's worried you'll focus on her and forget about you. I love Emrys like she's family. I'll take care of your girl while you take care of you, and then you can come and get her and you can take care of each other. She needs space right now, Leo. She's hurting and she doesn't know what to do with that hurt. I'm sure you can relate." There was dry humor in her tone that made my lips curl. "Whatever happened, I'm sure you were there for. You're tied to that memory right now and as much as you want to help, you might be making things worse." I hated that, but my grandmother was never one to beat around the bush. If Em needed time, I had plenty of it to give.

"I'll take care of me, Gram." I pulled open the door ready to demand an explanation for all the racket, and felt everything inside of me that had been cold and sluggish fire back to life.

On my doorstep was the cowboy I'd been waiting for all along.

Tight faded blue jeans held up with a buckle the size of my head at the center of that trim and toned waist. A broad chest covered in a well-fitted, plaid shirt with pearl snaps on the front and black piping along the seams. The cowboy boots on his feet looked as new as the ones I wore last time I saw him, but the black Stetson on his dark head was well loved and looked unbelievable on him. There still weren't any leather chaps or a Sam Elliott mustache, but he had left his facial hair so that it was now trimmed into a perfectly groomed goatee. He was a western dream come true, and he looked so good, and I missed him so much, I couldn't make words come out of my mouth. We stared at each other in rapt silence for a long minute until I heard my grandma's voice squawk over the phone asking me if I was still there.

Robotically, I put my phone to my ear and told my gram I would call her back. I didn't look where it landed as I tossed the thing over my shoulder and reached out to grab the big, brooding man in front of me by the shirt.

It had only been a couple of weeks, but it felt like an eternity. Time had no meaning where this man and the way I felt about him were concerned. I thought it was impossible to fall in love within a few short days, but I was wrong. I figured falling in love with someone who was hard, who was a challenge, who forced me to live my life with them instead of around them was impossible. I was wrong about that as well. I liked the work Cy took and I liked the work he had to put into me. I was certain it had only taken hours to hand my heart over to him and it had taken minutes to realize that leaving him wasn't going to be an option. There were no easy answers how any of this was going to work out between the two of us, so I didn't bother asking the questions.

Instead, I fused my mouth to his as his hands landed at my waist once the door was slammed shut behind him. I didn't need words to tell him how much he was missed when my kiss and clutching hands conveyed my feelings for me. I also didn't need to hear him tell me why he was here or that he was missing something out of his life with me gone. Not when he backed me into the door with a thump and held onto my face like I was something precious and prized. This wasn't a kiss hello, this was kiss that sealed our fate. This was a kiss that filled in the missing pieces and made promises that we were bound to keep. This was a kiss that made my blood blaze and had my heart shooting sparks of happiness and relief.

His teeth sank into my bottom lip and the bite made me whimper. He growled against my lips and lowered his hands to my thighs, his rough fingers easily finding their way under the hem of my boring work skirt. I looked better in the tight denim he was used to seeing me in, but the unremarkable taupe skirt sure was a lot easier for him to maneuver around with his grabby hands and hard flesh. His pelvis leaned into mine and he lifted my legs up around his waist so that we were pressed together as intimately as we could be without actually having sex.

I lifted an eyebrow at him, because the show of strength it required to keep me elevated as he caressed soft skin between my legs was impressive, but unnecessary. I was already enthralled by him, wanted him in a way that hurt and healed at the same time, and had no trouble giving him access to any part of me that he wanted to put his hands on. The fog that perpetually colored his gaze had cleared, the clouds lifted to reveal the pretty, pearly dove gray underneath. That clarity, that light in the dark that was shining through, told me more than any words ever would about why he was on my doorstep. He only had half of a heart left to give and he wanted me to have it.

I made him smile.

I made him happy.

I was his Sunshine in the storm.

His forehead fell forward and landed against mine as his rapid breaths touched my wet and swollen lips. Eye to eye, heart to heart, heat to heat, all of us lined up and fit together like we were supposed to. There were no missing pieces anymore because together we were complete.

I lowered the arms I had wrapped around his shoulders to grab the front of his shirt. I pulled it open with both hands, disappointed the snaps popped easily instead of it having buttons to send flying. His skin scorched under my palms and his heart raced as it rushed to tell me all the things his lips were too busy to say.

The tip of his nose traced the edge of my jaw and then skated underneath my ear as he dropped tiny, sweet kisses everywhere my pulse pounded for him. The brim of his Stetson obscured his face and his features when he lowered his head, and as much as I liked the way he looked in it, I liked the way he looked at me when he had me under him and over him even more. I used the back of my hand to send the hat sailing to the floor and had no regrets when I saw his eyes flare and his jaw clench as I squeezed my legs around his waist to urge him to go faster.

The fingers of one of his hands dug hard into my hip as the other slipped and slid under stretchy lace to get at the very center of my desire for him. My vagina was just as happy as the rest of me to see him and there was no hiding it. The fabric between my legs was soaked and clingy as his fingers trailed through moisture and taunted very needy skin. I finally whispered his name on a strangled huff when the edge of his knuckle purposely rubbed against my clit. My entire body vibrated at the brief touch and every ounce of longing that had been pent up over the last few weeks screamed through me in a rush. I put my thumb under his chin and forced his head back up so that I could seal my lips back over his.

I missed the way he tasted.

I missed the way he teased.

I missed the way he felt pressed against me and I missed the way I felt like I could conquer the entire world when I made him sigh and shake with just the flick of my tongue and the nip of my teeth.

He tugged the silk shirt I had worn under my blazer to work out of the top of my skirt. Since I actually liked this shirt and wanted to be able to wear it again at some point in the future, I leaned back so that my shoulders were pressing into the door and wiggled the expensive fabric off over my head. The cups of my lacy bra were immediately shoved up over the crest of my breasts, making the plump flesh bounce a little. Cy grinned, looking like a wolf with its prey in sight. I didn't mind being dinner, as long as I got to eat, too.

I curled a hand around the side of his neck so that the raised vein there throbbed under my fingers. I used the other hand to wrestle with that massive belt buckle, which I quickly became annoyed by. It looked cool, but it weighed a ton, and when I finally got it loose, it banged against my leg hard enough to hurt. I scowled at him but his eyes were locked on the way my nipples pulled tight and beaded up for him. They were begging for his mouth. They were pleading for his tongue. He wasted no time in hefting me up a little and lowering his head just a fraction so he could pull one needy peak into his mouth. The heat engulfed it and flames licked at my blood. A rush of wetness hit his playing fingers and he must have decided it wasn't time to play anymore.

His teeth scraped across my aroused and drawn nipple. His facial hair lightly abraded my skin where it dragged across my chest as he moved from one breast to the other, raising little bumps of pleasure and anticipation in its wake.

Since I was struggling with the weight and stiff leather of his belt, he pulled the thing out of the loops and efficiently popped open the button at the top. The press of his erection and the heat from his hand had little flutters of desire working through my damp folds and had my core clenching and unclenching in readiness and need. He had to lower me long enough to pull my underwear down my legs, but he didn't give me enough time to strip off the skirt before he had it shoved back up around my waist and my legs spread wide and open to him. As soon as the heavy fabric of his jeans was out of the way, the center of where we touched was filled with a hard, unbending erection. The instant that rigid shaft hit my soft, wet, center we both groaned, ragged and rough.

I moved my fingers to his hair while he continued to eat at the aching, distended tips of my breasts. I tossed my head back until it connected with the door and bit my lower lip as he tilted his hips forward, driving the length of his cock through my folds and moisture that coated them. I swore at him impatiently as he rubbed himself back and forth but ignored my wiggling and squirming to get him where I needed him. I wanted him inside of me. I wanted him filling me up and spilling out of me. I wanted him looking directly at me while we moved on and with one another, so that he could see that he was it for me and that I intended to be it for him. I wanted him to rule and ruin me too.

I wove an arm across his massive shoulders. They were strong enough to hold me and the entire world up. I put a hand on his cheek and leaned forward so I could touch my lips light to his and then twisted my head so that my lips touched his ear.

I traced the outside curve with the tip of my tongue and felt his entire, big body quake.

"I missed you, Cy." The words came from a place that was beyond any doubt or reservations I may have had. They were words that had survived being scared and unwanted. They were words that painted a future and overcame my past. They were words that made me stronger and weaker than I had ever been before in my life because I missed him, and I missed who I was when I was with him.

His midnight eyebrows slashed down over his stormy eyes, and without warning, I was pierced, spread open, and pinned to the door as he thrust his rigid cock into my waiting body. The pressure from his invasion made my eyes pop wide and had my breath hitching. I could feel every burning inch of him as hard flesh dragged across sensitive nerves. He hooked the bend of my knees over his arms and pressed even more fully into me. This was as open as I had ever been, both figuratively and literally, for anyone. He was seeing all of me, he was taking all of me, and it felt like a tornado made up of flames as it pulsed and beat inside of me.

His hips canted, angled hard and fast against mine. This wasn't seduction or persuasion. This was primal, uninhibited slacking of a need. This was working out the sting of being apart and leaving something unforgettable in its place. This was imprinting on one another, so when the other moved, there was no way to forget that we had been joined. I felt Cy in every line and curve of my body. And as he pounded, drove, and hammered his way deeper and deeper inside of me, I could tell by the tense lines in his face and the furious clench of his jaw as he struggled to remain in control that he felt me in all his tendons and fibers as well. We were weaving ourselves together through passion and promise, so tightly that nothing would ever be able to unravel us.

"Leo . . . two weeks is two too many. I'm not going to make it much longer." That rare smile that was mine moved over his mouth. I felt my inner muscles clench around him, making him grunt in surprise, at the sight. The goatee made the grin wicked and dangerous. It was hot. He was hot. We were hot together. "I want you to always open the door when I knock and I'm about to blow . . . so help a desperate man out before he embarrasses himself, Sunshine."

He was going to come before me, and for a guy like Cy, that wasn't okay. He wanted to get his, but not until I got mine . . . which kind of made him perfect. I skimmed a hand over his collarbone and over the bulging, hard planes of his chest. There was no give, only corded, unyielding strength. He could hold onto me forever and never let me down. I let my finger tickle over his delineated abs, the muscles clenching and tightening under my touch. My fingers slipped easily between us, taunting, teasing both of us at the same time. I knew exactly where he wanted me to put them, that he needed a finger on the trigger so we both could go off, but I missed him, and I missed the way he felt slippery and slick as he moved in and out of my body.

The backs of my fingers danced over his straining erection as he slowed his rapid fire pace, breathing hard and looking at me with a whole new kind of storm brewing in his eyes. I smiled at him, and when he smiled back there was no more denying what we both needed. I brushed my fingers over my clit, the little nub stiff and eager for attention. The gentle caress was enough to make my eyes cross and it had everything inside me locking down around Cy and coating his cock with endless rivers of desire. He grunted as my body held onto his and it only took a couple of careful circles with my fingertip and some purposeful pressure from my thumb to push me over the edge. I wasn't the only one falling, because as soon as I broke, I heard Cy mutter,

"Thank fuck," as he followed after me.

Knees shook, pelvises rubbed together hard enough to leave marks, muscles quivered as lungs struggled for air. Lips twisted into smiles that stretched infinitely and hearts tripped over each other as they reached out to let the other one know they were still there.

I was going to have the imprint of his jeans branded to the inside of my thighs for days and beard burn on my chest for twice as long. I wouldn't forget him and I didn't want to.

"I missed you, too, Leo." He pressed me into the door, holding me captive, not that I was going to run anywhere. "I loved one woman enough with a normal kind of love that I was able to let her go, but you, Leo, I'm pretty sure I can love you with more than that, so I won't ever be able to tell you goodbye and mean it. I'm not asking you to be with me where I am, but I am asking you to let me be with you wherever you are, when I can make that happen." He sighed, his eyes serious and telling me more than his words were. "I've always managed to keep my feet under me. No matter what hit me, I stood standing. You left and I fell to my knees, Sunshine."

My throat closed and eyes welled up with tears. I'd never taken anyone to their knees before, and the fact that it was this man, this bastion of strength and fortitude, made me feel like the most powerful woman in the world . . . and the most loved. He was willing to live his life around his history and his obligations for me. He was willing to take on the challenge.

I put my hands on his face and moved forward so that my head touched the place in his chest where his heart was thunder and his soul was lightning.

"It's too noisy here, Cy. I can't see or hear anything that matters. I don't want to be lost in this chaos anymore. I want to be someone who is heard because she says what she means, like I mean it when I tell you I could love you with a love that is more than love too." I lifted my eyes to his and watched as our moments stretched from stolen fragments to a lifetime. "I don't know how it's going to work for a while. You come to me, I come to you, and when we see each other we'll come together." He smirked at me as I wiggled my eyebrows at him. "I'm up to the challenge." I really was. The easy road hadn't gotten me anywhere, while the mountains I'd always been terrified to climb had given me everything.

He nodded and I kissed him. I told him he looked sexy in the cowboy gear, but I liked him better out of it. The buckle was annoying, his boots made him taller than he already was, the hat hid his amazing hair and even more amazing eyes.

He was always going to be not quite a cowboy, and that was just fine by me because he was going to be *my* not quite a cowboy. I didn't care about the things he wasn't because it was all the things he was that made me want better, made me be better, and made me appreciate what I had instead of miss the things I didn't.

He was everything to everyone, but I was the only one who made him smile.

CHAPTER 21

No Time Like the Present

"ARE YOU A REAL COWGIRL?"

The question came from a little girl who was only nine or ten years old. It made me smile and it had Lane snorting from where he stood next to me as we welcomed the family he was taking on the ride the next day. She was a cute kid but her skepticism at my authenticity was extra adorable. I mean, I had the look down, faded denim that was frayed at the hem and torn at the knee. A much smaller version of Cy's black Stetson perched on top of my head that was a must to keep my pale skin from turning cherry red and also happened to look awesome when I pulled my curly hair into twin ponytails on either side of my head. I was fond of fitted plaid shirts. The Justin Ropers I bought the first time I took a step on this dusty soil were now finally broken in and battered the way they were meant to be. I was still mad at the giant belt buckle and how difficult they made getting into Cy's pants, so I refused to wear one, but even without it I thought my cowgirl gear was pretty on point. Leave it to a precocious little girl to see right through it.

I winked at her and gave Lane a nudge with my elbow to stop his laughing. "I'm not quite a cowgirl, but I'm something close to it." I hooked a thumb toward the grinning man next to me and gave her a smile. "But this one here is the real deal. You couldn't ask for a better cowboy to spend your vacation with and to show you around Wyoming."

That seemed to appease her and she bounced off with the rest of her family as Lane led them toward one of the bunk houses to get settled for the night.

I wasn't ever going to be a cowgirl, there was too much of the city in my blood. However the longer I was able to spend my days under the open sky, and the more fresh air I breathed in, the more I felt this untamed land take root inside of me. I had no problem playing dress up to meet new clients. I liked it. The fact that what I wore to work was often covered in dust and torn by the end of the day, was a thousand times more rewarding than a day spent keeping linen skirts unwrinkled and stilettos unscuffed. I loved it here. I loved the people here. I loved who I was here. And I appreciated all of it even more because it had taken much longer than I wanted for me to come back.

For two months, Cy and I logged an ungodly amount of frequent flyer miles back and forth to see each other. We never said goodbye again, because it was never good and it was never bye for very long. I had to finish out my contract for Chris's wife. A task that became more and more unbearable each day that went by. The woman didn't want to let me go and she didn't want to let the fact that she felt like I owed her more than I did drop. She tried to cajole me into staying. She tried to threaten me. She tried to bribe me and when all of that persuasion failed, she actually had the nerve to send Chris in to try and convince me to stay.

Unfortunately for my ex, he picked a weekend to make his move when Cy was visiting. As soon as he was greeted by the towering pillar of fury that was Cyrus Warner, he tucked tail and hightailed it back to his wife. He must have mentioned that I was making far better choices in the men department to her because she finally shut up and let me finish out the contract in peace. As soon as my last day was done, I wanted to throw everything I owned into a suitcase and catch the first flight I could to Wyoming, but it wasn't possible.

Sutton's injuries were far worse than anyone was ready to deal with. He wasn't able to walk the entire first month he was out of the hospital and it was only after intensive physical therapy that he could maneuver around with a walker. The middle Warner brother was not taking the changes well, and as a result had lashed out at his family. Cy was worried about his brother and his worrying made him scarily overprotective, which only served to further infuriate Sutton. The grumpy cowboy had turned sullen and withdrawn. He hardly had anything to do with the day-to-day operations of the ranch and the tour company anymore, and Cy said he was barely making any effort to see Daye. Lane let it slip during one of my too short visits that the moody Warner was also hitting the bottle pretty hard, as well as popping pain pills when he didn't seem to need them. All of it accumulated into a tense and hostile vibe at the house and prompted Cy to hire several employees from the surrounding area to pick up the slack.

I wasn't about to insert myself into the middle of the Warner family drama even though late night phone calls, sexy sessions over Skype, and definitely X-rated FaceTime chats were getting old. I always loved to hear Cy's gravelly voice and there was something undeniably erotic about watching my rough and rugged man get off to nothing more than the sound of my voice, but none of it matched the real thing. I needed to have my hands on him, my lips tasting him, and my heart near his. The distance wasn't making it grow fonder but it was making it desperate and needy.

Plus, while Cy was dealing with Sutton, I still had to make

sure Emrys was going to be okay. If I wasn't flying to Wyoming for the weekend, then I was off to the sunny shores of Florida to check on my best friend. She wasn't making much progress mentally, but apparently, my grandmother's neighbor at the condo was a retired plastic surgeon, and also Gram's sometimes boyfriend, I was stunned to find out. Somehow, he managed to talk Em into letting someone he recommended look at the scar on her face. She agreed to getting it treated, so the mark was less visible and her face was back to being beautiful, but she was still sullen, withdrawn, and lost inside herself. She refused to talk to a professional and only agreed to see her family when they showed up unannounced on my Gram's doorstep, demanding some face to face time with her. It didn't help anything when both her parents broke into uncontrollable tears when they caught sight of her. The scar on her face was barely there, but the one on her chest was still visible and glaring. There was no missing the fact that Em had been right on death's doorstep and was lucky there was no answer when it knocked.

My grandma did a wonderful job giving her a shoulder to cry on and a safe place to hide away from the world. Em was really good at beating all the other retirees at bridge and bingo, but eventually her time seeking shelter was up. Gram wanted to go on a cruise with the plastic surgeon so there was no way Em could stay at her place while she was gone since it was strictly a community for older folks. I was getting ready to make my move to the ranch, so it was time for some tough love.

I sat Em down and told her I would be there for her no matter what it took. I told her that I understood she was healing at her own pace but that pace seemed to be stuck in neutral. I begged her to come with me to talk to a therapist and then I pulled out the big guns and told her that Sutton was having just as hard of a time getting back on his feet as she was. I didn't want her to blame herself for the cowboy's condition but she had to know she wasn't the only one walking away from the confrontation in the woods with wounds that ran deeper than the bone. I was hoping the shock of hearing how hard a time such a strong man was having bouncing back would guide her to the realization she wasn't alone.

My plan backfired.

The day I was supposed to leave, and was planning on taking Em back to California to her parents, I woke up to an empty apartment. Gram had left for her cruise and Em had packed up her meager belongings and disappeared once again. This time there was no place to run to. This time there was no welcoming sand for her to dunk her head underneath. I had no clue where she was running to, but wherever it was I doubted she was running fast enough to leave all the demons and doubt that were chasing her behind.

I called my new friends who worked for the government and asked Grady to keep an eye out for her. They still needed her in the case they were building against the cartel, so I knew they wouldn't let her get too far before having to pull her back in. Grady gave his word that I would get a phone call if anything suspicious popped up in relation to Em's name. I did the hardest thing I had ever done . . . I let her go.

There was no expiration date on my willingness to help her, but there was on my tolerance for letting her abuse herself and take the blame for something that was beyond her control. I couldn't cram help down her throat, she would choke on it.

All in all, it took about four months to get myself back where I felt I belonged. At first, I told Cy I would stay in one of the bunkhouses on the property or look at living in Sheridan while we adjusted to each other. I didn't want time we spent together filled with words and worries. I did want the time we spent together to be a whirlwind of hands, mouths, and naked bodies trying to get as much from the other as we could. We still didn't know each other that well and I didn't want to rush something that was so important.

Cy gave me that look, the one that told me I was being overly cautious and careful. The one that said he knew I was still running. I was used to keeping everyone at arm's length and he refused to let me do that with him. He told me if I was moving into a bunkhouse, then so was he. If I rented a place in Sheridan, then he was moving there with me until I was ready to call the ranch home, which he pointed out was a ridiculous plan. He relented some when I balked at his pushy and demanding attitude and agreed that I could have my own room in the main house, as there were plenty of empty ones for me to claim. I figured that was a fair tradeoff and agreed. It had been months, and I'd yet to spend a night in the room where my stuff was. The room pretty much acted as nothing more than a closet, because just like I told Cy at the hospital, where he was, I was. I didn't want to go to bed without him.

Letting me into his life and into his bed had been easy enough. Letting me into his business hadn't gone as smoothly. The man was a control freak and it was like beating my head against a very sexy brick wall every time I tried to get him to let me help him with the marketing and the branding of the ranch. He was a savvy businessman, but he was out of touch with the human element. I reminded him, over and over again, that I made my living convincing people to spend money, but got nowhere until a competitor located in Jackson Hole reached out and asked if I would be interested in working on a new campaign for them.

I told Cy he could either let me in the gates at home or watch me lead the enemy into battle and eventually, after a few days of brooding and a few nights of no sex, he came around. Making up was fun, but digging my hands into something that would be around forever and would be passed down to generation after generation of Warners, was even better. There was reward in convincing people that Cy's ranch and the backcountry tours Lane led were better than everyone else's because I really believed that. This place was a part of me now and I wanted everyone who visited to love it and be transformed by it like I had. I meant every single word I said when I went to work convincing the world they needed to leave their cares behind and visit here to shut out the noise.

Cy had been on conference calls all day, so I hadn't seen much of him. He still wasn't overly friendly with the guests, but he was getting better. His permanent glower had been replaced with a grin and the storm in his eyes only raged now when we were alone, and when that happened, I couldn't wait for it to crash into the shore.

I was navigating the massive, rustic house when my phone beeped with an incoming email. Every time that happened I hoped against hope it was Em . . . but it never was.

This time when I saw who the sender was my disappointment was shoved to the side and a smile tugged at my lips. The contents of the brief email made me chuckle as I pushed into Cy's office, eyes immediately going to the big desk and the even bigger man behind it. He was still on the phone and the scowl on his face indicated that he wasn't liking whatever he was hearing on the other end of the conversation. I made my way over to him, climbed over one of his legs, and propped myself up in the center of his desk right in front of him while I tapped out a response to the email. His other leg pressed into the outside of my knee so I was caged in. I liked that his scowl had switched to a seductive smirk as he watched me watch him.

He still favored soft tees and beaten denim. His hair still looked better than mine at any given minute of any given day. He still wore motorcycle boots instead of cowboy boots and the only time he wore his Stetson was when I begged him to bring it to bed. It never stayed on for very long but I liked the way it looked on his dark head. I may have let him get away with all the dirty things he wanted to do with me when he wore the hat. It was a weakness and I never could deny him a thing when he had it on.

Not that I wanted to.

Climbing the proverbial sexual mountains with Cy wasn't something I would change for the world. The view from the top was unbeatable . . . the view from the bottom wasn't all that bad either.

He cut the conversation short and rolled the leather chair closer to me, his hands on either side of my hips.

"What has you grinning like you're up to no good, Sunshine?"

I pushed the brim of my hat back with a finger and set my phone down on his desk. "I got an email from Evan. She's trying to talk her mom into bringing her and Ethan back to the ranch for winter break. Her parents are getting divorced and it sounds like Meghan is taking Marcus to the cleaners. I guess getting caught in a shootout in the middle of the woods was an eye opener for her." It was also the reason she wasn't too keen on bringing her kids back to the ranch, even though they begged endlessly. Everything that had happened gave Evan and Ethan the best stories to tell back at school. They were the most popular kids in their class once their faces had hit the news.

He chuckled and used his grip on my waist to pull me closer. I put my hands on his shoulders and bent my knees so I could climb on top of him in the chair, perched over his thighs.

"She also mentioned she has a new soccer coach and that he's really cute." Cy grunted and moved his hands around my back so he had a firm hold on either side of my ass. I obliged him with a sigh as he lifted me up a little bit and let me fall so that the seam of my jeans where I was soft and warm pressed against the line in his that was growing hard and stiff underneath me.

"She needs to learn to chase after boys her own age." He grunted as I wiggled on top of him in search of more friction. He squeezed my backside in response and lifted me up and let me fall again.

"She says he's only twenty. Not great, but better than where she was." I pressed forward so I could touch my lips to his. He always tasted like coffee and life. I grinned as the salt and pepper brush above his lip tickled me. "How's business?"

He sighed and gave me a kiss that was harder, wetter, and lasted a lot longer than the one I gave him.

"Business is good, in no small part because of you." I wanted to preen under the compliment. Instead, I kissed him again.

"You can hire someone to push paper and talk on the phone if you don't want to be trapped in here all day." He was making enough money between both the functions of the property. He didn't have to be chained to this desk unless he wanted to be.

He rubbed his bristly cheek against mine and it made me shiver all over. So did his questing fingers as they worked their way under the hem of my shirt. He pulled it out of my jeans.

"I don't mind it. It's all a game and I'm better at playing it than most." He still liked to be in the saddle but he was better at outmaneuvering the money men than he was at tending fences and birthing calves. He didn't mind getting his hands dirty when he had to, but preferred matching wits with the other movers and shakers in the industry. He was rebuilding his father's legacy in all the ways his old man hadn't been able to. There was modern thinking and practice put into play on this ancient land and it was beautiful to see the past and the future collide in such an important way.

My shirt was over my head and sailing to the floor between one breath and the next. My bra soon followed. I took my turn stripping him, the cotton of his T-shirt softer than the scrape of his chest hair against the hard tips of my bared breasts. The slight abrasion always made me catch my breath, so did that seductive sound of a zipper sliding down. There was all kinds of business that went down in this masculine office, but the kind where I ended up filled with hard cock and whimpering against hot skin was my favorite kind.

I liked the way he looked behind his big desk, he liked the way I looked bent over it, ass in the air.

Pants dropped, hands hit wood as he moved over me. His palms were full of my breasts and I was full of him. I rested my forehead on the cool surface and panted as he drove into me from behind. It never got old. It never stopped feeling more important than any sex that had come before it. It never failed to make me feel like I was exactly where I was supposed to be,

His teeth nipped at the back of my neck. His chest pressed me farther into the desk as he pulled my hips up into his thrust. We moved together like we were made to be connected from head to toe.

As far as afternoon quickies, this one ranked right up at the top. I managed to make it through my orgasm and his without losing my hat. The realization made me laugh as he flipped me over and ran the end of his nose along the sensitive inside of my thigh. I threaded my fingers through his hair and reached for my phone as it pinged with a text message next to my head. I sighed in heavy satisfaction as the wet tip of his tongue ran along the back of my knee and as his index finger lazily chased after all the sex and satisfaction that was smeared all over the inside of my legs. There was a smug smile on his face that quickly shifted when I bolted upright and almost fell off the edge of the desk when I saw the message that I had been waiting for since Emrys disappeared.

I put a shaky hand on Cy's shoulder to steady myself as he rose to stand between my spread legs. He put his hands on either side of my neck and used his thumbs to tilt my head back so I was looking up at him.

"What just happened, Sunshine?" His deep, rough voice never failed to settle me.

"It's Em." I held up my phone with one hand and wrapped my fingers around his wrist so I could feel his pulse with the other. "She said she's coming to see me."

His raven dark eyebrows both shot up so high they almost touched his hairline. "She's coming here?"

I looked at the message again and nodded dumbly. "Yeah. She's coming here."

"Does she know that Sutton is in a bad way?" The middle Warner had moved out of the main house and was drinking himself into an oblivion while he drowned in his sorrow. Cy hated it. Lane hated it. Brynn was heartbroken over his behavior and I wasn't sure what role I was supposed to play around him.

I was still pissed he sent Em away, which sent her spiraling, but I felt bad that his heroism had resulted in nothing but heartache. I tended to avoid him when his brothers forced him to join the land of the living. I had no idea what Em's appearance was going to mean to the wounded warrior.

"She knows. She wasn't in much better shape the last time I saw her, to be honest." I squeezed his wrist and looked at him under my lashes. "Do you want me to tell her she can't come?" It would kill me to tell her then, but I would do it, and then I would go to her. Wherever she was.

He stared at me for a long, pensive moment and then that smile that owned me and made my entire world spin slashed across his perfectly rugged face. "It might do some good for Sutton to get shook up by your girl. If it turns bad, we'll ride it out, like we always do."

I exhaled in relief and told him with every ounce of sincerity I had within me, "I more than love you, Cy."

His broad chest rose and fell with his own heavy breath as he replied, "I more than love you back, Leo."

We meant every word.

The End

Shelter

Emrys and Sutton's story coming soonish . . .

I will love you forever if you made it this far and you take the time to leave a review on whichever retail site you purchased Retreat on!

Read on for a sneak peek of Riveted the next Saints of Denver book coming February 14th. It's the perfect Valentine's Day treat!

SNEAK PEEK of RIVETED

PROLOGUE

M Y MOM MET HER PRINCE Charming when she was a
freshman in college and my dad leaned over and asked to
borrow a pen so he could take notes. Rumpled, obviously
hungover, but flashing a smile that promised a good time and
with a twinkle in his eyes, he was impossible to resist. She always
told me and my sister that it happened that fast. In a split second
she knew he was the one for her.

It was a sweet story. One that my parents shared with us often, both still sharing private smiles and eyes still twinkling, but
neither one of us gave it much thought until my younger sister
met her very own prince before she was old enough to drive.
It was during a hard time for my family, hard for all of us, but
especially for her. She'd always been the baby, been spoiled and
treated like a princess. When the attention was yanked off of her
in a really ugly way, she was lost and let the family tragedy consume her. Lost in grief and confusion, she somehow managed to
sign herself up for auto shop instead of an extracurricular that
actually made sense for my very girly, very feminine younger sibling. She spent five minutes in that noisy, greasy garage, but she
spent years and years leaning on and loving the quiet, enigmatic,

auburn-haired boy she met in those five minutes. He saved her and even though she was way too young to know anything about anything, she had the same story that my mother did . . . she just knew he was the one for her.

It happened fast in my family. We fell hard and we didn't get up once we fell. We stayed down and we loved hard and deep. I also learned as I watched all my friends, the men I worked with, the women who I considered sisters of the heart, that when it was right for anyone, it happened fast and that they did indeed *just know.* They knew when it was right. They knew when it was going to last. They knew when it was worth fighting for. They knew when they had found the person who might not necessarily be perfect, but who was, without a doubt, perfect for them. *They just knew.*

So I waited, admittedly impatiently and anxiously, for my shot, for my turn to fall. I waited through my family healing, for them to come back with a love that was even stronger. I waited through my sister screwing up and desperately trying to repair her perfect. I waited through weddings and babies. I waited through danger and drama. I waited through one bad date and one failed relationship after another. I waited through nights alone and nights spent with the occasional someone I knew wasn't *the* one for me. I waited and waited as good men fell for even better women, all the while wondering when it would be my turn. I waited and watched love that was easy and love that was hard, telling myself I was far more prepared for my fall than anyone else around me was. I wanted it so bad I could taste it . . . but the more I waited, the more certain I became that I was never going to fall.

I would be lying if I said that I didn't think Dash Churchill was something special the second he walked into the bar where I worked—all coiled tension, sexy swagger, and with a black cloud of attitude hanging over him that would dim even the brightest summer days. I had eyes and I had a vagina, so all the things that I thought were special were the things those parts of my anatomy couldn't miss. Long limbed, with a body that looked like it was ripped from the cover of *Men's Health* magazine, bronze skin, unforgettable eyes, and a mouth that, even though was constantly frowning, brought to mind every single dirty, sexy thing a pair of lips like that was capable of doing. I liked the way he looked . . . a lot . . . but I couldn't say I much liked him. He was sullen, distant, uncommunicative, and there was an air about him that marked in no uncertain terms that he was dangerous. But more than that he came across as a very unhappy individual, and no amount of rest, relaxation, and good friends seemed to shake that dark cloud of discontent that hung over him. It was a warning that I was smart enough to heed. I liked my days spent basking in the sun, not dancing in the rain.

I was friendly to Church because I was friendly to everyone. The first month or so we had an uneasy working relationship that involved me dancing around him while every other single and not-so-single woman who came into the bar where we worked did their best to catch his eye. It worked out well for me and seemingly for him, so I went back to waiting for my perfect, my fairy tale, my heroic knight, my unmatched hero. He had to be out there somewhere and I was starting to think if he wasn't looking for me I needed to start looking for him. My patience was wearing thin and my typically affable attitude was starting to get just as gloomy and gray as the one that hung over Church.

But then it happened and *I just knew.* I knew like I had never known anything as clearly and as unquestionably in my whole life. I knew with a rightness that shot through my soul and made my heart flip over in my chest.

I was trying to cash out a group of overly intoxicated and

obviously difficult young men. It wasn't anything new. I'd been a cocktail waitress for a long time and knew how to handle myself and the customers. This drunken group was no better or worse than any other one I'd had to deal with in all my years slinging drinks and working the floor, but they were loud and the things they were saying were easily heard throughout the bar. Some of it wasn't so bad. They liked my hair (curly and strawberry blonde—who didn't like my damn hair?) and they liked the way my shirt fit tight and snug across my chest. I was a solid D cup, so again, who didn't like my tits? But they also had a lot to say about my ass. Apparently, it was too big for my small frame, and they didn't love my freckles. That red hair was authentic and as real as it could be, so there wasn't much I could do about the colored specks that dotted the bridge of my nose and brushed the curve of my cheeks.

I had pretty thick skin, you had to when you worked in a bar and liquor loosened tongues, so I was ready to brush the entire conversation off and snatch the credit card off the table when I felt a hand on my lower back and a storm not just brewing off in the distance but collecting and gathering, ready to unleash hell at my back.

"You good, Dixie?" The question made me freeze and it wasn't just because it was asked into my ear with an unmistakable slow and very Southern drawl. It wasn't because he was so close I could feel every line of muscle in his massive body and both the heat of his skin and the chill of his icy anger pressing into my back.

No, I froze, riveted to the spot and stunned stupid, because in twenty-six years no one had ever bothered to ask me if I was good. They always assumed I was.

I was the girl who could handle myself and everyone else around me.

I was the girl who never asked for help.

I was the girl who always smiled even when that smile hurt my face.

I was the girl who always had time for a friend even when I really didn't have that time.

I was the girl who everyone ran to with a problem because I would drop everything to help fix it even if it was unfixable.

I was the girl who never let anything or anyone drag her down and fought to keep everyone else up with her.

I was the girl who everyone always assumed was good . . . so they never asked . . . but he had and the world stopped. At least the world as it was before I fell headfirst into the kind of love that was bound to hurt with Dash Churchill.

I gripped my pen and struggled to clear my throat. "I'm good, Church." My voice was barely a breath of sound and I felt his touch press even deeper into my lower back.

"You sure?" No, I wasn't sure. I was as far from good as I had ever been and I had no clue what to do about it.

I gave a jerky nod and blew out a breath, which had him taking a step away from me. I looked at him over my shoulder and he returned the look. There was no warmth in his fantastic eyes. There was no change in the harsh expression on his face. There was no knowledge that he had fundamentally changed my life in the span of a few terse words.

He was simply doing his job, making sure everything in the bar was okay and that the staff was safe. Meanwhile, I was shoved unwillingly into the kind of love that had my arms flailing, my legs kicking, while a-scream-ripped-from-my-lungs in love with him. Of course I did that all silently and in my head as he walked away from me, because I might have now *known* he was it for me, but it was evident Church didn't have a clue.

No one had ever given me any idea how to handle it when

the right one came along, but you weren't the right one for him.

Dixie

"Um . . . I had a lovely evening." No, I hadn't. It was awful. It would go down as the worst first date in the history of first dates, which was something, considering my recent run as the awful-first-date queen. But it wasn't in my nature to say so. I just wanted to say goodnight and hide in my bedroom with a glass of wine and my dog for the rest of the evening.

"Aren't you going to invite us in for a drink?"

I fought to hold back a cringe and looked over the shoulder of the very cute but painfully shy young man I had accepted the date with after several weeks of online chatting. I'd met him through one of the dating apps I had signed up for when I decided I was done waiting for my perfect to realize that I was perfect for him.

My terrible luck in love had held true and this date, with this cute boy . . . and his mother, the person who had asked about coming in for a drink since my actual date seemed incapable of speech. Yep, it solidified the fact that I was bound to end up alone. That beautiful, blinding thing that everyone important in my life I loved seemed to find with such ease was clearly not in the cards for me. I wanted a fantasy but every day was faced with the fact that all I was getting was a cold, hard, and very lonely reality.

I sighed and reached up to push some of my wayward, strawberry-colored curls out of my face. I was annoyed that not only had I clearly been cat-fished—there was no way the son was the one running his dating profile, not if he couldn't string two words together, and not if he couldn't look at me without blushing and trembling nervously—but by the fact that I had wasted a perfectly cute outfit, killer hair, and a face full of flawless make-up on this sham of a date. I was typically a very low-maintenance kind of girl, so pulling myself together like this took time and effort that I would never have expended if I had known it was all for a woman with crazy eyes and a psychotic interest in finding her grown child a suitable mate. Honestly, I was surprised the woman hadn't asked for blood and urine samples before the appetizers arrived. She'd grilled me like I was a POW for the entire date, and when my answers didn't meet her expectations I could feel her disappointment wafting from across the table.

Anyone else would have gotten up the instant their date showed up with parental supervision. They would have chalked it up as a loss and deleted the guy off the app. I, unfortunately, wasn't wired that way. Nope, I was predisposed to believe every situation, no matter how bad, had a silver lining. I thought maybe my date would loosen up and tried to reason that it was actually kind of sweet he was so close to his mom. I figured after dinner and the interrogation I would be vetted enough that maybe he would want to do something without our eagle-eyed chaperone. I thought his shy demeanor made him seem vulnerable and that he was even more adorable in person than he was in his profile picture.

It didn't get better.

It got worse, and I quickly realized the lining was never going to be silver because it was made out of lead, and I was sinking with it to the bottom of the bad-date ocean. I tried to think of a polite way to get out of the rest of the evening but the woman wouldn't give me a minute to breathe. She even went so far as to follow me to the bathroom so I couldn't send out an SOS call to one of my friends for a convenient escape. It was brutal, but I powered through, thinking once they followed me home and saw me to the door in an old-fashioned but still over-the-top gesture that it would be over. I had a boatload of nosy neighbors and a big dog in my apartment, so I didn't fret too much about him knowing where I lived (the mom was a different story).

I was wrong.

I shifted my weight on my feet and bit back a sigh. I should have known she was going to be persistent, but I was done playing nice for her when it was clear her son was so beaten down that he was too scared to make a move or even speak for himself. She was a tyrant and I wasn't going to subject myself to her vile company anymore. As soon as I slipped inside my apartment I was going to delete all the dating apps I had on my phone.

"I have a dog and she's leery around strangers." That was partly true. I did have a dog, a massive blue pit bull that I rescued from a shelter just days before she was supposed to be put down. Dolly looked like a brute, but she was a sweetheart and had never met a human she didn't want tummy scratches and love from. We were kind of kindred spirits in that way. I mean, I didn't need my ears scratched or my belly rubbed, but I was afflicted with the pressing need to be liked and accepted by pretty much everyone I came in contact with. It was ingrained in me to at least try to make everyone a friend, and if they didn't reciprocate my kindness it only forced me to try harder. Sometimes I hated that about myself, and sometimes it was my favorite personality trait because the men and women in my life weren't the easiest nuts to crack. They all loved me and let me in because I'd refused to let them shut me out.

Well, all except for one man.

I couldn't hold back my flinch when he crossed my mind because he had warned me about online dating from the get-go, and I hated that he was right about it. I also hated that he was the reason I was desperate to find a man . . . a man who wasn't him . . . in the first place.

Mommie Dearest shook her head and clicked her tongue at me. "Joseph is allergic to dogs. Your pet will have to go as things progress between the two of you."

I felt my eyes pop wide, and the forced smile I had plastered on my face for the entire evening finally slipped away. I already knew she had a few screws loose, but she was taking her crazy to another level if she thought she could tell me to get rid of my dog or what to do with anything in my life.

I straightened my shoulders and tilted my chin up. It was a look that worked on the drunks and unruly college kids that I hustled out of the bar where I worked every night.

"That's not going to be a problem because things are not progressing beyond my front door. Thank you both for dinner, but if you'll excuse me I'm going to go inside and cuddle my dog and erase every online dating app there is."

The woman narrowed her eyes and stepped around her son. The young man made a noise low in his throat and his eyes widened. I thought he was scared of his mom, but the closer I looked at him the more obvious it became that he was scared for me as the woman advanced. He reached out a hand to grab his mother's elbow, but it fell away before making contact, like he knew the repercussions for intervening would be severe and drastic.

"Listen here, you little . . ." I lifted my hand before she could throw at me whatever insulting word she was going to label me with. I don't think the woman was used to anyone standing their ground with her because she gasped and fell back a step.

"Stop. I thought I was talking to Joseph. I thought he was a nice guy, maybe a little sheltered and awkward . . . but a nice guy. Obviously it wasn't him running his dating profile and there was some other agenda here from the start. I'm well past the age where I need a mother's approval or permission to date her son, so I'm going to go into my apartment and end this date before either side gets nasty." I looked at the shell-shocked young man hovering behind his mother and mouthed *good luck* before turning my back on both of them and inserting my key into the door. Dolly barked loud and deep from the other side, which was both comforting and reassuring.

I turned the knob on the door and pushed into the apartment without looking back. Once the door was shut and my dog was happily rubbing against my legs, I tossed my head back and let out a sigh that felt like it was tied to my soul. I was tired, so tired.

I loved my life. I had a job that I enjoyed going to every day, and I worked with people I adored and admired. I was never going to be a millionaire doing what I did, but I was good at it and most of the time it felt more like spending time with friends than actual work. I loved and was deeply loved back by my family, even if my younger sister was an idiot. I had a cute apartment, an active social life, and great freaking hair. There wasn't a lot I could complain about on a day-to-day basis and things that did get under my skin were things I had a hard time explaining to anyone who didn't grow up knowing love at first sight was real, and that when you found the other half of your heart, life was infinitely better.

I was only twenty-six, still plenty of time to live life and settle down, but I felt ancient and overlooked when I compared myself to my younger sister. She'd found the fairy tale our parents had laid out for us when she was still in high school and I got nothing but lonely nights and a string of dates so bad no one believed me when I tried to tell them just how bad.

I jolted when there was a knock at the door behind me, making my ears ring since my head was still resting against the wood. Dolly growled low in her throat when she felt me tense up, so I put my hand on the top of her broad head and used the peephole to see who was interrupting my pity party.

My new neighbor, the girl who moved like a ghost and

spoke so softly I often had to struggle to hear what she was saying, stood on the other side. Poppy Cruz, quiet, withdrawn, but so sweet and smitten with my dog. I'd totally leveraged that love she had for my pet into a budding friendship that Poppy was obviously reluctant to have.

I knew some of her history through stories from her friends and family who were all regulars at my bar, so I was careful not to push too hard, even though all I wanted to do was cuddle her and tell her the clouds have to part on even the darkest of days. She was comfortable enough with me now to knock on my door well past the acceptable visiting hours, so there was no way I was going to leave her standing in the hall, even if that meant my wine and sob-fest were further delayed.

I pulled the door open and Dolly immediately lunged for the visitor on the other side. Poppy was willowy but she had no trouble bracing for the impact from the dog, and she seemed just as excited to receive the slobbery kisses as Dolly was to give them.

"I heard you talking out in the hallway and I just wanted to see how your date went. It didn't sound like it ended on the best note." Her quiet voice drifted to me as I shook my head and snorted.

"It didn't start on a great note either. He showed up with his mom. Can you believe that? I need a glass of wine, do you want one?"

She wrinkled her delicate nose and wrestled the big dog into the apartment so she could shut the door behind her. "I don't drink, but thank you."

She didn't do much of anything. The product of a very strict and religious upbringing, Poppy was as straight and narrow as one could get. She'd suffered severely at the hands of a man her father had handpicked for her and it was clear that every single day was one more step in the process of healing from that.

"I forgot. I'm in the bar so often I forget that there are humans in this world who can cope without alcohol." I lifted an eyebrow at her and made my way into the kitchen. "I'm not one of them."

She laughed lightly like I'd meant her to, and followed me into the tiny galley-style kitchen.

"So, his mom?" Her eyes were the color of hot cider and they gleamed with gentle humor. She was impossible not to like, and as much as I wanted a different life for myself, I also wanted one for her. I hated that her history was so ugly, but I loved that she'd survived it and was pushing herself to live beyond her experiences. That was beautiful and hinted at an inner strength her delicate appearance kept hidden.

I snorted again and rolled my eyes. "I thought the guy who took off halfway through the date with my wallet was as bad as it could get. I was wrong. Really wrong."

"I can't believe it gets worse, Dixie." She shook her hair at me and I wanted to reach out and touch the bronze strands. They glimmered like they were lit from within. Everything about her was meant to shimmer and shine through the shadows that surrounded her. Eventually that inner glow was going to break free and I hoped I was around to see it. "I didn't think it could get worse than the guy who wanted you to be the third person in a ménage à trois with his wife."

I sucked back a mouthful of wine at that and shuddered. "Yeah, when he told me it was fine because their kids were with his parents for the weekend I almost threw my water at him. That was bad, but this mother was still the worst. It was a shame because her son was actually really cute and I think if he wasn't so browbeaten he might actually be a good guy." I lifted a shoulder and let it fall. "Oh well, you live and you learn."

Something crossed her beautiful face, something tragic and

painful that hurt to look at, but it was only there for a second and then her typical serene and unaffected expression was firmly back in place. "If you're lucky you get to live. So no more online dating?"

I nodded and finished off the rest of my wine. "No more. There seems to be an infinite amount of crazy out there in the world and I'm a magnet for it."

They can be whoever they want to be on the Internet, Dixie. You'll never know whom you're dealing with, and that's dangerous. Church's warning drifted through my mind and it made me want to hit something. He was right. He always seemed to be looking out for me, which would be thrilling, exciting, and exactly what I wanted if he did it out of something other than some misguided need to watch out for me because we worked together. If he cared about what happened to me because he cared about *me* in some way, shape, or form, I would be over the moon. But really it all boiled down to the fact that I was important to the people who were important to him, so he didn't want to see anything bad happen to me.

I was turning to pour another glass of wine when Poppy and I both jumped as someone started pounding on the apartment door. I gasped a little as Poppy jumped to her feet in a panic with a startled yelp pealing out of her throat. Alarmed by the human's distress, Dolly started to growl and stalked to the door like the born protector that she was. She let out a sharp bark that had me practically sprinting across the room to see who was causing the commotion so that her gruff growling and sharp yapping didn't wake up the neighbors.

I glanced at Poppy and frowned when I saw that she was as white as my countertop and looked like she was going to pass out. Her hand was to her throat and her fingers were shaking so badly I could see the tremors all the way across the room. She was terrified. I wanted to fix that for her but I didn't know how.

"Dixie, open the door. I left Kallie and I need a place to crash for a few days." The voice on the other side of the door was as familiar as my own. His words made me swear out loud as I pulled the door open without another thought given the fact that Poppy might end up face-down on the carpet.

"You left Kallie?" I barely got the words out before my little sister's obviously furious and clearly frustrated fiancé barreled into the tiny living space. I shut the door behind him. Dolly went about her typically happy greeting once she realized she knew the tall, lanky, auburn-haired man now frantically pacing through my living room, raking his heavily tattooed hands through his messy hair.

"She's been cheating on me . . . again. I was such an idiot to believe her when she told me it would never happen again after the last time. How could she do this to me after all we've been through together?" His heated blue eyes locked on me and I could see he was struggling to keep both his emotions and the moisture trapped in his eyes in check. "We're supposed to be getting married in a few months." His voice cracked and I couldn't stop myself from walking over and wrapping my arms around his trim waist.

"Oh, Wheeler. I'm so sorry." My sister was an idiot, but in all honesty, so was he. My sister didn't know how to be an adult without him and he didn't know how to be a family without her. They were scarily dependent on each other and had been since they were kids. Now Kallie was barely twenty-two and had everything I wanted in the palm of her hand—the brand-new house Wheeler bought for them to start their lives together and an engagement ring that made my heart squeeze with envy. I would treasure the love and promises she had been given and part of me died every single time I watched my sister be careless and reckless with what Wheeler had handed her. "You can stay here for as long as you need to. Do you want me to call her?" If I did I was going to rip her a new one. I loved my sister dearly, but at the moment I would gladly strangle her with my bare hands.

I felt his broad chest rise and fall where I was squeezing him. He heaved another deep sigh and pulled back so he could shake his head in the negative. "Not tonight." He growled from low in his chest and roughly dragged his hands over his face. "I need a minute . . . or ten."

There was a delicate clearing of a throat and we both shifted our gazes to where Poppy was pressed against the front door like Wheeler could grow razor-sharp claws and mile-long fangs to eviscerate her at any moment. Her eyes were twice their normal size and her teeth were buried so deeply into her bottom lip I was surprised she wasn't drawing blood.

"I'm going to go." Her voice quivered and her hands were still shaking.

I felt Wheeler tense where I was still holding on to him, and I watched his eyes narrow as they locked on Poppy. His gaze was normally a mellow light blue that looked amazing with his reddish hair and the dimples that dug into his cheeks. Tonight it flared like the blue at the base of a flame and those adorable indents in his cheeks were nowhere to be found.

"Sorry. I didn't mean to interrupt anything. It's been a shitty night on top of an even shittier week and I'm not thinking too clearly at the moment. I didn't mean to barge in and make an ass out of myself." And that was why I loved Hudson Wheeler with every single bit of my heart and soul. His world was crashing down around him. He was drowning in an ocean of his own bad choices (and I would call Kallie a bad choice to her face for this bullshit) and misery, but he still had the wherewithal to gentle his tone and rein in his temper so that he didn't further terrify the young woman plastered against the only exit. He was a good guy . . . no, a great guy . . . and Kallie was a world-class moron for screwing around on him . . . again.

"It's fine. You're . . . um, fine. Dixie, I'll see you later." She leaned down to pet Dolly one last time and then slipped out the door, shutting it silently behind her. She moved like smoke and vanished just as fast.

I pulled away from the man who was set to be my brother-in-law and tunneled my fingers through my wild hair and squeezed my head. "That's my new neighbor."

He grunted and threw himself down on my well-worn couch. The springs protested under his weight and then groaned again when Dolly climbed up next to him and put her head on his denim-clad thigh.

"I know her. She's Salem's sister and Rowdy grew up with her back in Texas. He brought her by when she needed a new car. I tried to sell her a '64 Bonneville that needed a little work. She would've made that car look gorgeous. She ended up with a Toyota Camry. It was a goddamn travesty. A girl who looks like that should have a car that stands out, not something safe and predictable." I forgot that Wheeler knew a bunch of the boys who frequented my bar because they were family—some by blood and some by something more—with my boss, Rome Archer. Rowdy St. James also worked at the tattoo shop that was responsible for the majority of the ink that covered Wheeler from head to toe. I should have realized he would have run across Poppy at least once or twice since she'd come to Denver, even if Kallie tended to keep him on a tight leash.

I lowered myself onto the only available seating left in my small living room and kicked my feet up so that they were resting on my coffee table. "Poppy isn't really the standing-out type and she can do with a little safe."

His gaze shifted to mine and his mouth pulled into a frown. "That's a damn shame, too."

I agreed with him, so I didn't say anything else.

After a solid hour of sulking, I finally got up and took Dolly out for her nightly ritual. I dug up some sheets and blankets to make a temporary bed for Wheeler on the couch, a temporary bed that was going to be as uncomfortable as hell considering his long legs . . . and eventually found my way to my own bed.

I wanted to cry for all of it. For Wheeler's broken heart, for my sister's stupidity and blindness to what she had thrown away, for Poppy's obvious emotional scarring and her fear of other people, for Joseph and his creepy relationship with his insane mother, and for me. Unrequited love sucked. I hated it.

No tears fell as I climbed under the covers. Like I always did, I told myself there was bound to be a light at the end of the tunnel . . . there had to be, because I refused to live the rest of my life in the dark.

ACKNOWLEDGEMENTS

As always, a huge, sloppy thank you to anyone who picked up this book and gave it a shot. I love my readers so hard. I honestly wouldn't know what it was like to have a dream come true without you. YOU ARE EVERYTHING.

Same to all the bloggers and book pimps out there. Thank you for doing what you do. Thank you for sharing your love of reading and romance with the world. Thank you for giving me a shot to share my stories with you.

There were a whole bunch of people who told me HELL NO when I told them about *Retreat*. A whole bunch. It was hard to hear, and frankly, did quite a number on my confidence. It's hard to hear that you shouldn't try something new, that what you think is a fun, romantic adventure isn't good enough. It gets so boring hearing over and over that I should write *this* or *that* because it will sell better. I just want to write the stories I want to read. The ones that are in my head demanding to get out. It takes a lot to ignore all those no's and go in search of the people who will say yes.

So, I really need to thank those people who told me yes.

My agent Stacey never tells me no. She never questions me when I tell her "I'm writing a story about this." She embraces every crazy idea and believes in every book as much as the one that came before it. It's cool when my confidence crashes because she has enough in me for the both of us.

When I told my mom I wanted to write about not-quite-cowboys she told me to "Fucking go for it." She said people will read it or they won't, but I would never know until I write the book and publish it. Sometimes it's easy to forget my writing and publishing journey started with nothing more than chance and luck, and Mom's good at reminding me anything can happen. It's worth the risk.

Obviously, Mel has known about these wild boys for a while. She never told me I was crazy for wanting to go so far away from what I typically write. She encouraged me to write whatever it was that made me happy, and honestly, that's something authors don't hear often enough. When passion and business collide somewhere along the way, the actual work part of writing can take over the desire to create from the heart. Mel always . . . and mean always . . . tells me to write what I want.

I have to thank my friends, Ali and Denise, Stacey, and my bestie, Heather. They all agreed this book didn't suck and immediately asked for *Shelter* when they finished, which made me feeling like I did something right along the way. Sure, they're all biased because they love me, but still, hearing that they didn't hate these words (even though Ali hated Leo) meant the world to me.

I had a dream team who helped me wrangle this book into professional shape in a ridiculously short time frame. The fact that they said "yes" when I sent out frantic emails begging for help so I could self-publish for the first time in four years, guerilla-style at that, was humbling and so very appreciated.

Elaine York manhandled this story into something that was far better than I ever imagined. I learned so much working with her, and I don't think I've ever been so wonderfully challenged to make my story better and brighter. Edits and revisions are always tough, but this time around, the struggle was very rewarding.

I've always had a creative crush on Hang Le. I think she's

brilliant and her covers are stunning. I haven't had the opportunity to work with her up until now and I was positive, since I decided last minute to get this book out this year, that she wouldn't be able to help me out. I'm so stoked that she wiggled me in after the proper amount of begging and pleading. I couldn't ask for a better cover or a better Cy. (That was all Wander Aguiar. The man knows his stuff and can take one hell of a photo!)

My friend C.J. Pinard has long been someone I turn to for making sure all my I's are dotted and my T's are crossed. She is meticulous and miraculous. I hated asking a friend to squeeze me in at the very last minute, but because she's awesome, of course she said yes. You can thank her for making sure there aren't ten million run-on sentences in this book.

I also need to thank my sweet, sassy friend CA Borgford. We've been book friends since the start and she has always encouraged me to do things my own way with my own slant. It was such a treat to get to work with someone I adore in a professional capacity! She made all my words so pretty.

I owe a huge debt of gratitude to my publicist, KP Simmon. When I dropped this project on her with no warning, she didn't strangle me, not that I would have blamed her for wanting to. She jumped in with both feet and put a battle plan together like a boss with the limited information she had. It's hard to keep a book a secret but still get people excited that something cool is coming. She always does a great job, but she really stepped up to the plate with these wild boys. It's nice to have someone unwavering and rocksteady in your corner.

Last but never least, I need to thank my boy bestie, Mike Maley. This year was a shit show for me in a lot of ways and I think Mike was the one who held me together through all of it. He's a good man and an amazing friend. I'm so thankful he is one of my people.

If you made it this far and read *RETREAT* I would be so stoked if you would take a minute to leave a review for the book on a retail site. Good or bad, telling other readers your thoughts on a book makes a huge difference.

ABOUT THE AUTHOR

JAY CROWNOVER IS THE INTERNATIONAL and multiple *New York Times* and *USA Today* bestselling author of the Marked Men Series, The Saints of Denver Series, and The Point and Breaking Point Series. Her books can be found translated in many different languages all around the world. She is a tattooed, crazy haired Colorado native who lives at the base of the Rockies with her awesome dogs. This is where she can frequently be found enjoying a cold beer and Taco Tuesdays. Jay is a self-declared music snob and outspoken book lover who is always looking for her next adventure, between the pages and on the road.

GUYS!!! I finally have a newsletter, so if you want to sign up for exclusive content and monthly giveaways you can do that right here: www.jaycrownover.com/#!subscribe

You can email me at: JayCrownover@gmail.com
My website: www.jaycrownover.com
www.facebook.com/jay.crownover
www.facebook.com/AuthorJayCrownover
Follow me @jaycrownover on Twitter
Follow me @jay.crownover on Instagram
www.goodreads.com/Crownover
www.donaghyliterary.com/jay-crownover.html
www.avonromance.com/author/jay-crownover

Made in the USA
San Bernardino, CA
29 January 2018